W9-BRF-708

Once Upon a K-Prom

HYPERION
Los Angeles   New York

First Edition, May 2022
10 9 8 7 6 5 4 3 2 1
FAC-020093-22091
Printed in the United States of America

This book is set in Caslon/Monotype
Designed by Marci Senders

Library of Congress Cataloging-in-Publication Data

Names: Cho, Kat, author.
Title: Once upon a K-prom / Kat Cho.
Description: First edition. • Los Angeles ; New York : Hyperion, 2022. •
Audience: Ages 12-18. • Audience: Grades 7-12. • Summary: Instead of
going to prom, seventeen-year-old Elena Soo wants to spend her time
saving the local community center, and she is determined to keep her
priorities straight even when her childhood best friend—who is now a
K-pop superstar—returns to make good on their old pact to go to prom together.
Identifiers: LCCN 2022000479 • ISBN 9781368064644 (hardcover) •
ISBN 9781368066983 (paperback) • ISBN 9781368066754 (ebook)
Subjects: CYAC: K-pop (Subculture)—Fiction. • Community centers—Fiction.
• Fame—Fiction. • Dating (Social customs)—Fiction. • Korean
Americans—Fiction. • LCGFT: Novels.
Classification: LCC PZ7.1.C5312 On 2022 • DDC [Fic]—dc23
LC record available at https://lccn.loc.gov/2022000479
Reinforced binding

Visit www.hyperionteens.com

For Axie, who fed my love of K-pop and
gave me the courage to write and publish my stories

ONE

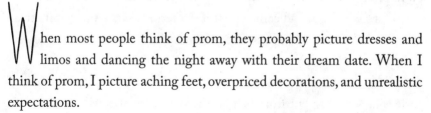

When most people think of prom, they probably picture dresses and limos and dancing the night away with their dream date. When I think of prom, I picture aching feet, overpriced decorations, and unrealistic expectations.

Obviously, I was in the minority, though. As was proven by the long line of upperclassmen willing to spend their entire lunch period standing in line to buy prom tickets.

It was day three of ticket sales, which meant it was also day three of the Awareness Club's alterna-prom initiative.

It was . . . not going great.

Okay, fine, it was a big fat failure.

We'd set up a station where students could donate their change to West Pinebrook's Community Center after buying tickets.

"Any more donations?" I asked, leaning over the table.

Max Cohen shook his head. "Sorry, Elena."

I glared at the jar. It was almost empty. The dollar bill I'd placed in there was still the only donation. I'd thought maybe having money already would make us look less pathetic, but it just looked sadder somehow.

I glanced at my carefully written spreadsheet. I'd made it to predict potential donations. We were way behind what I'd projected. But I guess I hadn't factored in teenage apathy.

"Has anyone taken a pamphlet?" I looked at the suspiciously full pile.

"To do that they'd have to stop avoiding our table like we all had the plague." My best friend, Josie Flores, rolled her eyes.

I'd spent days writing those pamphlets up, included photos of the kids from the community center at last year's holiday party and the fundraiser website to donate online. It explained that we weren't telling people *not* to go to prom, but to rethink how they spent their money on the dance.

That's why Josie had come up with the term "alterna-prom initiative." It hadn't helped, though. Everyone just thought we were flat-out protesting prom.

"Come on, El, if they won't take a pamphlet, let's just hand them out," Josie said, stepping out from behind the table. She was willow thin with smooth brown skin, a pretty, narrow face, and dark hair that framed it in curls. It was everything I used to wish for when I was little instead of my round Korean face, short legs, and flat stick-straight black hair.

"I'll help!" Max jumped up.

"No, you guard the table and the . . . dollar," Josie said, eyeing the sad jar.

I gave him an "I'm sorry" shrug. But he dutifully sat back down. He'd do anything for Josie.

Since sophomore year, he always mooned at her behind his

wire-rimmed glasses. They weirdly worked on him, like nerdy-white-boy chic. His curly hair used to be cropped short in middle school, but he'd grown it out now and it flopped into his eyes. It was cute in a Shawn Mendes kind of way.

Josie started down the line, handing pamphlets out, making sure each person at least opened it before she moved on. She didn't seem to mind the annoyed looks she got or the rude comments. I wished I could be that confident, to not care what everyone thought of me.

"They're in danger of losing funding," I said to a group of juniors I'd just handed pamphlets to. None had opened them. So I took one and opened it myself to a bullet-point list of ways to save on prom. "Instead of spending hundreds on limos and dresses and tuxedos, you could just wear an old suit or a dress from Rent the Runway and drive yourself. Then donate what you saved to the center."

"Hey, you're Ethan Soo's sister, right?" One of them squinted at me as if trying to see the family resemblance.

I sighed. It was common for kids to remember my brother before they remembered something as pesky as my actual name. He was the popular twin, after all. And he never did anything as annoying as asking kids to donate their prom money.

"I'm Elena," I mumbled. "So, back to the community center—if you don't have any extra cash right now, there's an online donation site you can use too."

They all just blinked at me before returning to their conversation about some new movie that had just released. Were these people heartless? Did they not see the adorable children smiling out at them from the pamphlet?

"I'm sorry." I tried to get their attention again, but they kept ignoring me.

"El, you gotta stop apologizing all the time," Josie said, walking over.

She was down to her last few pamphlets, and I felt guilty that I still had a full pile.

"I can't help it." I frowned because she was right. It was just such a knee-jerk reaction for me to apologize every time I had even an inkling that someone felt uncomfortable around me.

"I don't think this is working," Josie said, scowling at the line of students doing their best to ignore us. "I think we'll have to use more radical methods."

"Well, unless you want to go full Robin Hood, I think pamphlets and peaceful protest are all we've got right now." I sighed.

"I have something to help our cause," Josie said, taking off toward the exit.

"As long as it doesn't make a mess!" I called after her, but I wasn't sure if she heard me as she pushed out of the cafeteria.

As I waited for Josie to return, the line moved up and a girl swung her bag into me as she turned to talk to her friend.

"Can you find somewhere else to stand?" she asked, huffing in annoyance.

"Sorry," I mumbled before I could stop myself.

"Did you see her weird-ass pamphlets?" the girl's friend said, not caring that I was standing right there. "Imagine spending all your time trying to ruin prom."

I sighed and stepped back, turning away from the line and the annoyed glares. I wasn't trying to ruin prom. I just thought this was a chance to support a good cause. And I guess I also didn't think prom was as special as everyone else thought. I'd watched every one of my three older sisters get excited about the dance only to come home let down in some way or another at the end of the night. It gives perspective to a kid, even if I was only ten.

I leaned against a lunch table as I waited for Josie to get back. It was filled with a group of freshman girls sighing over a music video playing on one of their phones. I could barely hear it over the loud volume of voices crashing through the cafeteria, but I recognized the group: WDB.

WDB had achieved something no other K-pop group had done for over a decade: entered the hearts of teens across the whole globe. And somehow became the first Korean group to win an MTV Video Music Award and American Music Award, which got them invited to other award shows, and they'd even performed on *SNL*. It was all so impressive, but there was an extra layer of surrealness for me as the face of the main rapper, Robbie Choi, graced the screen. It was a face I knew well, even though it had lost all the baby fat that had puffed up his cheeks when we were ten. We'd been best friends. I knew things about him that weren't written in his official profile.

I knew how he got that little scar through his eyebrow. (He'd fallen out of a wardrobe during an epic game of manhunter and into the edge of a coffee table.)

I knew that even though he was famous now for his luscious locks, which had been dyed the whole rainbow during his career, he'd once let me shave a stripe through them because we'd wanted to see if we could write his name in his hair. (Spoiler: We could not. And yes, we did get into epic trouble with our parents after that stunt.)

Now there were girls swooning over him and giggling whenever his face popped up on-screen.

But Robbie was another reason I knew prom would be a disappointment for me. I'd once been just like everyone else, looking forward to a magical prom night filled with slow dancing and perfectly posed photos. But I'd always imagined it with a specific person. And since he was no longer in this country, let alone this town . . . why bother with the effort?

When you knew something wouldn't work out, it was best to just move on.

"Robbie is my bias!" one girl declared, and I almost wanted to tell her about that time Robbie had fallen into mud during our third-grade trip. I'd had to walk behind him the rest of the day so no one thought he'd pooped his pants.

Or maybe I'd explain how he'd forgotten all his old friends when he got famous. . . .

"JD is my bias. He's just so . . . mysterious."

I watched as another member of WDB gave a sly wink on the screen. I'd never met JD, even though he was Robbie's older cousin. I had to admit the song the girls were playing was pretty catchy. And perhaps I'd found myself downloading a few of WDB's singles. But it was still so weird for me to think of my childhood bestie as a heartthrob.

I remembered the last day I'd seen Robbie. We'd been ten, and we stood in front of his empty house. All of his stuff had already been shipped over to Seoul ahead of his family. I'd had friends move before. Becca Kuss had moved to Ohio in first grade. And Emily B. had moved to the next town over last year. But Robbie was my best friend and he wasn't moving twenty miles away. He was moving to the other side of the world. We'd clutched each other, tears streaming down our faces. Robbie's nose had been as red as a cherry. I told him so, and he said mine made me look like Rudolph. And then we'd hugged again.

"I'll email you every day," I'd promised.

"I'll message you every day," Robbie had said. "You downloaded KakaoTalk, right?"

I'd nodded. I'd never used the Korean messaging app before, but Robbie had said it worked all over the world, so no matter where we went, we'd be able to talk.

"And I'll come back when we're in high school and we'll go to prom together," he'd said with a wide grin. "And we'll take pictures just like Sarah's with those silly flower bracelets."

"They're called corsages," I told him. "And only girls get them."

"Says who?" Robbie pouted.

I laughed. "I don't know. Fine, we'll get matching corsages."

"But I want mine to be made out of Legos," Robbie said.

"Then I want mine to be made out of butterflies!" I said.

"Ew! Like dead bugs?!"

"What?" I squeaked, horrified. "No! Like fake ones!"

"Nope. You want to wear dead bugs. You're a dead-bug wearer!" Robbie taunted, and despite our tears and our impending parting, he made me laugh. And I took off after him, chasing him around the yard until his mother called him to get in the car.

"See you at prom," Robbie said before climbing in.

I'd watched him drive away until I couldn't see him anymore.

And in the seven years since, he'd become a part of the biggest K-pop boy group of all time and I wouldn't be caught dead at prom.

"Here it is!" Josie crowed as she returned, snapping me out of my memories. She held up a megaphone.

"What am I supposed to do with this?" I asked. "And why did you have this in your locker?"

"It was from our save-the-whales rally," Josie said. And I suddenly had horrible flashbacks of watching Josie dressed as a whale, marching through the courtyard with her megaphone. "Use it to rile up the crowd." Josie held it out. "Give a speech. Get people excited."

"I'm not really a public speaker." I folded my hands behind my back. In fact, I'd had to quit debate club because I couldn't stand in front of the twelve other kids and argue my point without turning bright red.

"El, I keep telling you that you can't be a good activist unless you get over your fear of speaking in public," Josie said. I didn't have the heart to tell her that I didn't think activism was really in my future. At this point I was only still in the club for her.

"Come on," Josie said, dragging me back to the prom ticket table.

Caroline Anderson and Felicity Fitzgerald sat behind the table, accepting cash for the fancy embossed tickets. They were both pretty white cheerleaders, with the kind of perfect looks that graced CW shows and teen movies. Currently, they both wore their cheerleading uniforms even though it wasn't a game day. I guess they thought the school spirit would flow through them and into the ticket buyers who were plopping down a whopping sixty dollars per ticket.

"Elena, tell the truth," Caroline said, resting her chin on her fists. "You hate the prom because you know no one will ask you."

I froze, my mouth falling open. "What? No, I don't care about that stuff."

"Oh, come on, Elena. You were super jealous when I got my first boyfriend in seventh grade," Felicity piped up.

"Really?" Caroline asked, her sharp eyes sparkling with glee.

"Yeah, she pouted for a whole week and didn't even come to my birthday party in protest." Felicity let out a laugh.

I'd been sick that weekend, and my mom wouldn't let me go to her party. But I knew if I said that now it would sound like an empty excuse and just throw more fuel on Felicity and Caroline's fire.

Felicity and I had been close once. After Robbie had left, I'd had no one to hang out with, and in middle school, I'd somehow glommed onto Felicity and her small girl gang until my decision not to go out for cheerleading in ninth grade made me outcast-worthy. I still remember the day after cheerleader tryouts in the lunchroom, when Felicity went full-on Gretchen Wieners, shouting, "You can't sit with us!" Except less pink.

Josie nudged my shoulder. "Come on, El. Don't let them get to you."

She pulled up a chair and stood on it, shouting into the megaphone. "Attention, everyone! We have an announcement to make."

She stepped down and pushed the megaphone at me.

"I can't get up there," I whispered, trying to push it back.

"Just think of the community center. Speak from your heart."

"Is the announcement that you finally realize how pathetic your silly protest is?" Caroline called out, and Felicity laughed.

It made me remember that freshman lunch where she friend-dumped me in front of the whole cafeteria. Which incensed me enough to climb onto the chair and lift the megaphone.

But as I looked at all the staring faces, my mouth quickly became so dry I couldn't even get out a squeak. I felt like I was sweating, but when I rubbed my hand over my forehead, it came away dry. I looked at Josie, who gave me a thumbs-up, and I pressed the button. I cleared my throat, and a high-pitched feedback sound made me wince. But at least it got the attention of the cafeteria. All eyes were on me now. Oh goody. I took a deep breath and remembered Josie's advice: *Speak from your heart.*

"Um, hi," I muttered, and the megaphone squeaked again. "Sorry."

Josie pinched my leg and mouthed, *Don't apologize.*

I nodded and I cleared my throat again.

Remember the community center, I reminded myself.

"Um, so I'm here to talk about a place that means a lot to me." I glanced nervously at Josie, and she mouthed again, *From your heart.* "And . . . and it also means a lot to this whole community." Some of the freshmen at the tables closest to me were watching and they weren't laughing or sneering, so there was that, at least. Pulse hopping, I kept going. "I don't know if anyone remembers what the West Side was like when we were kids. But less than ten years ago, there wasn't a lot there. Just the old, closed factory and not even any parks."

A few kids nodded. Pinebrook High served this whole area, which included kids from the middle school in the West Side. It bolstered me to see that recognition of my words, so my next words came out smoother. "West Pinebrook Community Center repurposed the factory to create a safe space for kids from the West Side elementary and middle schools to go after school. Miss Cora, who runs it, says that a building can become more than bricks and windows if it's filled with passion and love. Isn't a place like that worth fighting for? Aren't you tired of adults saying we're wasting away with our noses stuck in our phones?"

I saw Josie shake her head and noticed some of the kids frown and turn away. Oh crap, I was losing them. The freshman girls who'd been watching the WDB video looked supremely pissed off. I started fumbling my words as I tried to finish so I could go hide. "S-so, if you want to show how passionate our generation can be, you can just donate what you'd spend on dresses or limos to keep an important neighborhood institution open!" I tried my best to channel Josie's spirit and lifted my hand in the air. "Together we can make a difference!"

There was a thick silence until Max tried to start a slow clap, which sounded sad and pathetic when no one joined in. Josie let out an enthusiastic whoop, which echoed throughout the cafeteria. But, disappointingly, most of the students went back to their lunches.

Caroline stormed out from behind the ticket table, her blond ponytail swinging furiously. "This has to be illegal," she complained. "You can't just sit here shouting in our ears all of lunch."

Josie stepped forward. The two were the same height, so they were a pretty even match. Except, if I were a betting girl, I'd put my money on

Josie. "Sorry to tell you this, but the school charter says that students can hold rallies as long as they are not disrupting class periods or using vulgar language," Josie said with a shrug.

Felicity joined her friend and rolled her hazel eyes up at me. "Elena, if I get my dad to donate a thousand dollars to your dumb community center, will that shut you up?"

I stepped down from the chair. "Sure," I said, and Felicity folded her arms, a smile of triumph spreading on her teen-drama-level-pretty face. "For now, at least. Every little bit helps, Felicity. But that won't be enough. If you donate what you'd have spent on your nails, your hair, your dress, limo, tickets, and dinner, then think about how far that would go. Think about if you got your friends to do it, too. Don't you want to do something good with your popularity?"

Felicity stared down her nose at me, and for a fleeting second, I thought she might be considering it. Then a sneer lifted her lips. "You're delusional, Soo. How do you expect to change anyone's mind about prom when your own *twin* isn't listening to you?" She nodded past my shoulder.

I turned and spotted Ethan standing in line.

"Ethan," I groaned. This *did* look bad—betrayed by my own flesh and blood.

Ethan and I were proof that any theories about twins having an innate connection were total baloney. The two of us were polar opposites. Ethan was charismatic and the kind of cute that was annoying because my classmates always tried to get information about him from me. While I was awkward and completely forgettable. He'd been on the varsity lacrosse team since freshman year and sat with the "popular kids" in the courtyard for lunch. I usually ate lunch with Josie in the journalism room. And now, it seemed, Ethan and I were on opposite sides of this prom debate.

Ethan gave me a shrug and a wry smile. "Sorry, Twin, it's just that you know prom tickets are discounted the first week on sale."

Usually, hearing him call me "Twin" made me smile even as I wanted to roll my eyes. But this time I was just annoyed.

"You know how important the community center is to me, Ethan."

"I do, but I just . . . I want to get discount prom tickets."

Ethan didn't get it. He never really cared about anything I did. As I started to turn back, Caroline pulled the megaphone from my hand.

"Hey!" I tried to grab it, but she danced away.

She lifted it. "Announcement! I've decided to host a pre-prom party at my place. Why limit the fun to just one night? But you have to have a prom ticket to get an invite!"

A cheer went up, and the kids in line surged forward, as if suddenly the prom tickets were a limited commodity.

It was like that scene in *The Lion King* when Simba is staring wide-eyed at the stampeding wildebeests. Except there was no Mufasa to save me as I tried to back out of the path of the crowd.

Of course, with my awful luck, I forgot about the chair behind me. And instead of scrambling to safety, I felt my feet tangle with the metal legs. I heard Josie shout my name as I tried to keep my balance, but the chair won the battle and I fell backward, my arms pinwheeling like a cartoon character as I tried to catch my balance. I ended up sprawled on the sticky ground.

My hands, which I'd thrown out to catch myself, were covered in some kind of gooey substance, and my hip was throbbing from meeting the edge of a table on my way down. I watched the kids trample my pamphlets, crumpling them as they crowded around a triumphant Caroline.

TWO

On Wednesdays I went to the community center after school. Usually I'd be excited to go and see the kids. But today, the weight of failure was heavy on my shoulders.

As I walked to the junior parking lot, I saw Ethan and his friends loitering in the courtyard before their lacrosse practice. They were laughing, ripping up pieces of paper and throwing them in the air like confetti. If Josie were here, she'd lecture them about littering. The last time she'd tried to talk to this group about the recycling program, they'd looked at her like she was speaking French and then Tim Breslow had purposefully lobbed his Coke bottle into a nearby trash can.

The thing was, even though I definitely believed in what the Awareness Club fought for (pretty much any environmental or social justice cause), it was more Josie's thing. I was not brave or bold enough to convince anyone to fight for change without my best friend. I just didn't have what it took to confront anyone on my own, even about something as small as littering. So I started to make a detour around the group, keeping my distance.

A light breeze picked some of the bits of paper up and swirled them in my general direction. I could practically hear Josie's voice lecturing me. So I bent to pick one of the pieces up. And I froze when I saw a familiar smile, the edges of his face ripped in jagged lines. One of the kids from the community center. The one I'd printed on my pamphlets.

They were ripping them up! I couldn't just let this go, right? I had to say something—my pride demanded it. But when I started toward them, I heard Ethan's laughter ring out. He was laughing at my pamphlets? He wasn't even telling his friends to stop defacing them. He was just sitting there joking around with them while they did it.

Seething, I stormed past. The laughter quieted as they caught sight of me. I didn't even look back. I didn't want to see the smug look on Ethan's face as he mocked something I loved.

I shouldn't be surprised. Ethan never chose me over his friends. I'd stopped expecting him to.

By the time I arrived in the west side of town, my anger had dulled to a low-grade headache. Being mad at Ethan was a futile effort. It wasn't like he'd change, and my parents would never take my side if I complained. So I just took ten deep breaths like I always did and told myself it was easier to let it go.

The community center's side entrance led to individual rooms where it sometimes hosted classes. But right now they were just filled with kids goofing off while pretending to do homework. Each room had a theme, like the ladybug room, currently filled with five fifth-grade boys arguing over who was going to be DM in their game of *D&D*. I recognized the giant binder I'd personally written up for the game.

One of the boys looked up and spotted me. "Hey! Elena's here. She can be Dungeon Master."

I won't lie, I basked in the warm greeting. Every kid at the center knew me by name. It wasn't "Ethan's sister" or "Soo Kid Number Five" here. "Sure," I started to say, but remembered I had a task to finish first. "Pick your characters and then I'll be back. I gotta talk to Miss Cora."

They all nodded, happily settling down together. I was pretty proud of the *D&D* club I'd created at the community center. At first, I'd been worried the kids would dismiss it as a nerd thing for losers. But a group of them had really latched on. It reminded me of when Robbie and I would act out adventure games of our own when we were kids.

I remembered coming to the community center freshman year thinking I'd just do my volunteer hours and then go home. But every time I came, I found myself staying longer and longer. Thinking of new programs that I would have wanted when I was younger. And when I'd first drummed up the courage to suggest one, I remember the huge surge of pride I'd felt when Cora had said it was genius. I fell in love with the kids, and I admired Cora Nelson, the woman who single-handedly ran the community center.

I came to the big open playroom we used for babysitting the younger kids. The TV was on in the corner, though no one was actually watching it. But I did spot two of my community center faves, Tia and Jackson, in the far corner by a small bookshelf.

"Elena!" Jackson called when he saw me. The four-year-old waved his arm so widely that I was afraid he'd fall off Tia's lap. His brown hair flopped into his bright blue eyes that he'd inherited from his mother. "Elena Elena ElenaElenaElena! Guess what!"

Tia's blond hair was falling out of its ponytail, and she reached up absentmindedly to tuck it behind her ear as she smiled at me. She was tall and thin (the kind of thin my mom would react to with a click of her tongue and a bowl of food) and looked young enough to be on a college campus.

"Thank god you're here, I've had to pee since we arrived," Tia said, transferring Jackson to my lap as soon as I sat down.

"What's up, Jack-Jack?" I asked.

"I can read!" he exclaimed.

"Oh, really?" I said, meeting Tia's eyes as she stood up.

She just laughed and shrugged. "What can I say? I'm raising a genius."

"Watch!" Jackson said, pulling open the book.

I leaned close, and he started telling the story and turning the page. And it was a word-for-word recitation. I would have been tricked, except he'd accidentally started "reading" at the copyright page and was a whole page off the entire time. Still, the kid was clever for having memorized the whole book, and I clapped when he'd finished to give him his due.

Jackson laughed and looked up; then his eyes widened and he jumped up. "Mama?" he called. "Mama!" he shouted, whirling around.

"Hey, Jack-Jack, it's okay. She just went to the bathroom," I said, trying to take his hand. But he spun away, tears pooling in his eyes.

Tia came rushing back in, pulling Jackson into her arms. "Oh, baby, it's okay. Mama's here."

Jackson gave little sad hiccups as Tia gave me a shrug. "He's been having separation anxiety ever since I took the evening shifts last month. His preschool teachers say that can happen when schedules change."

I nodded, my heart squeezing at the sight of Jackson's tearstained face. "Hey," I said, making my voice bright to distract him. "I heard it's someone's birthday soon."

Jackson's face lit up with a smile. "Yeah!"

"I wonder who it could be," I said, stroking my chin in thought.

"Me," Jackson shouted, raising his hand. "It's me."

"Oh, really?" I smiled at his infectious enthusiasm. "What do you want for your birthday? Tickles?" I poked at his ribs, and he fell into fits of laughter, wriggling until he fell onto the ground.

"Not that?" I asked, pretending to think it over. And then I had an idea. "You know, when I was a little girl, my best friend and I used to give each other wishes. Would you want that?"

Jackson's eyes got big. "Yeah," he breathed out. "What can I use it on?"

"Anything." I shrugged. "Just think about it."

"Okay." He smiled. "I want a book!"

"Really?" I felt a proud glow. This was a kid after my own nerd heart.

"Yeah! A *big* book." He held his hands out to encompass his whole wingspan.

"Done. Why don't you try to find another book right now to read me, bud?" I said.

Jackson scrambled up and went to the shelf, very seriously perusing his selections.

"You're so good with him." Tia smiled. "I'm lucky to have you looking after him. These late shifts would be hell if I didn't have a safe place to drop him off."

Any pleasure the compliment would've given me died away as I imagined what would happen if the community center closed. The afternoon and evening babysitting services were for more than just the kids. They were services for parents like Tia who couldn't afford sitters when they had to work late shifts. So many families here didn't function by the normal nine-to-five that others took for granted.

"Any luck getting an earlier day shift again?" I asked.

Tia shrugged. "I applied for a floor manager promotion and I got an interview, but we'll just have to wait and see."

"I'll cross my fingers." I did so now, holding them close to my heart.

Tia smiled. "Speaking of crossed fingers, how goes the crusade?"

"Well, if my new projections are right, we'll make enough to help the center in about twenty-six years," I said with a heavy sigh, and Tia gave me a sympathetic smile. "I don't think I'm that good at this whole activism thing."

"Well, it might just take time," Tia said. "And the Awareness Club is the first one you haven't quit after a semester."

"That's because Josie would find me, no matter where I hid." I laughed. But Tia was right. I just never meshed with any other extracurriculars I'd tried. And I'd tried a lot of them.

Tia asked, "Did you ever end up trying out for the girls' weightlifting team this semester?"

I winced. I'd thought it would look good to have a sport on my college applications, and the weightlifting team took anyone who tried out, except . . . "I dropped the bar during my tryout and almost broke the coach's toe. I'll go down in Pinebrook High history as the only person who couldn't make the team."

Tia laughed and said, "I wasn't going to crush your dreams, but I didn't think that was for you anyway."

I shrugged. "I had to learn the hard way. For now, I'll stick to being ostracized for 'ruining prom.'"

"I didn't go to my prom, you know," Tia said.

"Really? Why not?" I asked, seriously curious. It seemed that everyone around me thought I was ridiculous for not wanting to go to prom.

"I was in my third trimester." She shrugged. "I wasn't really in the mood to dance in high heels when I was as big as a house."

I bit my lip and nodded. I kept forgetting that Tia was younger than my sisters. But I knew that she'd still been in high school when she'd gotten pregnant and her parents had disowned her for it.

"Hey, what happened here?" Tia asked, picking up my arm and pointing to a Band-Aid on my wrist. I'd scraped myself on something during the stampede in the cafeteria. It didn't hurt as much as my pride did, though. "Was it that Felicity girl you told me about?"

"Why? Are you going to go tell her off?" I asked, holding back my smile.

Tia sighed and let my hand drop. "Like it would do anything. Kids who push others down are either insecure or nasty sociopaths. And it's not worth our time to figure out which it is."

I nodded. Tia's advice was always to rise above it. She said that way once you're out of high school you'll still have your pride. Josie's strategy was to fight back, which, I guess, worked for her. I'd rather just avoid them at all costs. And I'm pretty good at being invisible. At least it's good for something.

"Where's Cora?" I asked, glancing around the common room.

"Last I saw she was still making calls in her office. Trying to get some more people on our side before the city budget meeting this June."

"Any luck?" I asked, dreading the answer.

Tia shook her head. "They had to let Mrs. Lewis go this week."

"What? Mrs. Lewis has worked here since it opened!" I said. She was a semi-retired teacher who taught all the healthy eating and cooking classes. "We can't let this keep happening."

The TV across the room started blaring with a commercial break. I didn't really watch regular cable anymore, but it seemed as if the commercials always played at a much louder volume than the shows. I'm sure it was some kind of evil consumerist trickery. And this commercial was even louder because it was advertising the musical guest on tonight's late-night show: WDB.

"Hey, didn't you tell me you knew one of those kids once?" Tia asked.

"Yeah, like a lifetime ago," I said just as Robbie's picture flashed past before the whole group shot was shown.

Tune in at eleven p.m. to feel completely inadequate when compared to your famous childhood bestie!

Okay, fine, the television didn't say that, but it might as well have.

"We don't even talk anymore," I said. We hadn't since we were thirteen and he became too famous to remember my number. I gathered my bag. "I'm going to run in and talk to Cora."

"But book!" Jackson protested as he ran back with not one but five books precariously balanced in his little four-year-old arms.

"I promise I'll come right back and read all of these with you."

"Promise!" He held out his pinkie, and I laughed. I'd taught him how to do the pinkie swear last month, and it was all he wanted to do now.

"Promise." I looped my finger through his. "Now seal it," I said, and, pinkies still looped, we pressed our thumbs together. "And stamp it." We slid our palms together. "And post it!" We let go and pressed our hands to our foreheads.

"Again!" Jackson said with a laugh.

I so wanted to stay and just play a thousand games with him. The kid's laugh was so irresistible. But I needed to talk to Cora.

To get to Cora's office, I had to walk through the big rec space. It was the heart of the community center. Where the majority of the kids liked to hang out and play, using the basketball court or playing handball in the corner. There was even a small indoor track. It took advantage of the soaring space that used to be a factory floor. This was what made the center so useful. That, plus the fact that the center was across the street from the elementary school and walking distance from the middle school.

When I knocked on Cora's door, it swung slightly open. The space was no bigger than a janitor's closet (and I secretly suspected it used to be one), but she had insisted on using this space instead of one of the bigger rooms. She said those should be utilized for activity rooms or study spaces.

Cora sat behind her desk. She was a tall, slim Black woman who'd worked in the city for over a decade as a social worker before taking the role of director of the West Pinebrook Community Center. I realized what I originally thought might be the worst music playlist of all time was actually awful hold music playing through her phone speaker.

"Oh, I didn't mean to interrupt—" I started to say, but she waved me in as she typed furiously on her computer.

"You're not interrupting. You're saving me from slamming my phone into the wall. I've been listening to this music for twenty minutes. It's going to haunt my nightmares."

"Calls not going well today either?" I asked, flopping down in the only other chair in the room, which was wedged between the desk and an overflowing filing cabinet.

"Nope," Cora said just as someone picked up the line. She snatched the phone out of its cradle. "Hello? Councilman?" She sighed. "No, I was told I would be connected directly with the councilman. Well, I was told this was when he'd have a moment to talk. . . . I *have* called back. This *is* me calling back." Cora pinched the bridge of her nose. "Yes, I can call back again. When will he have time in his schedule?" She typed quickly into her computer, adding the time to her schedule. "Okay, tell the councilman I look forward to discussing this with him Friday at four p.m."

She hung up and then let her head fall onto the desk with a thud.

Part of me wondered if I should just go, but Cora breathed out a heavy sigh. One so weighted that I couldn't leave her alone.

"I'm sorry, Cora," I said.

"It's fine. It just means I'll have another date with my phone Friday." She started typing on her computer, then winced. "Oh, I forgot."

"What is it?" I asked, leaning forward to look at her screen.

"I have the shift for the Friday-evening babysitting. Maybe I can call Dee to come in."

"I can do it," I volunteered.

"Really? You sure? Don't high school kids like to go out on Friday nights?"

"Are you saying I'm boring because I don't want to go party on a Friday night?"

"No, I'm saying you're a saint and I'd never malign you or take you for granted."

I laughed, but inside I was preening. I always felt such a glow whenever Cora complimented me.

"Speaking of," I said, pulling up the community center's fundraiser page that I'd started with Cora two months ago. "It's not much from this week. Just a hundred and fifty dollars. I'm sure we'll get more donations soon." I showed her the new total: $371.

It felt so pathetic just saying it. Like a kid offering her piggy bank to help pay the mortgage. But it was all I had.

"Elena, this is amazing! Thank you for all your hard work," Cora said. And the thing was she genuinely meant it. Cora never just said things to placate people; it was why I always trusted her opinion.

"Every little bit helps. And we just need to raise enough money to keep the community center running until you can get more funding from the city or new sponsors, right?"

"Sure," Cora said. "And if we have to close for a couple of months, we'll still fight to reopen."

"Close?" I blurted out. "No, that can't happen. Where will the kids go?"

"I'm not sure, but even if they vote to give us more funding in June, we won't make it until then. We'll run out of funds next month."

"No, there has to be more we can do," I insisted.

May was prom. If we could get enough kids to budget and donate some of their money to the community center, then it was possible. Some kids spent almost $1,000 on all the trappings. I'm sure Felicity was one of them. We'd just have to come up with another strategy for getting the kids to listen!

"Don't give up hope. I'm not going to," I said. "I can figure this out, I promise." I pulled out my phone, typing furiously into my Notes app with random thoughts I wanted to bring up with Josie at the next Awareness Club meeting.

Cora gave me a slow smile. "You're right. It's not over until it's over. We owe it to our kids."

That's what I loved about Cora. She didn't just think of this place as a job. She thought of it as a family.

The community center was more than just a place to me.

I'd seen Jackson and the other kids grow up. I'd helped Deena Romero braid her hair for her first recital. At the community center, I was an important part of running the place. Three of my project ideas had been made into events for the kids, with *D&D* night the most successful.

There was no way I was going to let this place close down, not for two months, not ever. It seemed like it was time to change up our strategy. I would overcome my social phobias and hand pamphlets to every kid in the hallway if I had to. People would understand why the community center was so important. I'd make them.

THREE

parked in the driveway beside Ethan's shiny Infiniti. He'd gotten a new car for his sixteenth birthday. I'd gotten a new cell phone. How is that fair? But he *is* the only son of the family. I'm just the extra baggage that came out with him.

My mom and dad let me drive my sisters' old 2008 Nissan Sentra. It had been used when they originally bought it for Esther. Now it had almost 150,000 miles and was always breaking down.

I'd gotten home a bit later than normal, and it was almost dinnertime. Which meant Mom would probably comment on how late I was. In the Soo household, dinnertime was family time. Even though we were now just four instead of the full Soo seven.

I decided to go in the front door to throw my mom off the scent. I opened it as quietly as possible, toeing off my shoes immediately. I was

24

greeted with the shiny wooden Korean chest in the foyer that prominently displayed family photos. There were at least half a dozen pictures of Ethan doing various activities: lacrosse, basketball, a random photo of him at the aquarium. And the college graduation photos for my sisters. But all I got was a janky class photograph from third grade. It was the worst photo of me too. Robbie had made me spill juice on my pristine outfit and I had to wear one of his old sweatshirts instead. It was too big on me, and I'd been pissed. It was reflected in my strained smile. Why Mom chose to display that photo of all my class pictures was beyond me. But it seemed weirdly fitting. Why put any effort into displaying your add-on kid?

I reached the staircase and was almost home free. But I swear, Mom has those supersensitive mom ears that are probably gifted at the hospital along with the first child. Because just as I was climbing the bottom step, Mom called out, "Allie, is that you? Come in here a sec."

I sighed. There was no use correcting my mom when she called me one of my sisters' names. So I slumped into the kitchen, where Mom was chopping a zucchini into thin slices. Marinated tofu was already frying on the stove, and the room was filled with the glutinous scent that could only mean fresh-made rice.

"Why are you late?" Mom asked without turning.

Right on cue. "I go to the community center on Wednesdays, remember?" I said, even though I knew she didn't.

"Oh yes. And how was the rest of your day?" She used a tone that made it sound less like a question and more like a test. Her black hair, meticulously dyed and permed every other month, was now pulled back from her face with a scrunchie so old it was frayed. Some of it was falling loose, and I could see gray in the roots, which meant she would visit the Korean salon again soon.

"Fine," I said with a shrug that was unnecessary, since she couldn't even see me.

"A little birdie told me lunch was pretty eventful."

"Does that little birdie's name rhyme with Bethan-better-mind-his-own-business?" I muttered, glancing toward the stairs. If I got my hands on my twin . . .

"It's not his fault. I pulled it out of him."

"Of course." Nothing was ever Ethan's fault.

"I don't get why you hate prom. You love dancing. You were so good at jazz dance classes."

"That was Esther," I reminded Mom. She did this all the time, interchanging me with my sisters. A part of me couldn't actually blame her. Ethan and I had not been planned for, and Mom had to get a job to make ends meet when I was a kid. I was raised more by my sisters than by my parents in the first seven years of my life.

"But still, you shouldn't hate prom," Mom said, finally turning to me. She held up the knife, which I would have taken as a threat, except she was trying to use one of her wheedling mom smiles on me.

I shrugged. "Prom is one night out of three hundred and sixty-five. I don't need a night like that when I know my money could help keep the community center open."

"I'm glad that you have something you're so passionate about." Except she said this like she was frustrated that I wouldn't let it go. "But isn't the community center like one of your dozens of other hobbies? When you get bored of it, won't you regret giving up prom like this?"

I could feel frustration rising in me like mercury in a thermometer. Mom always did this, brushing off any of my interests as a hobby. She'd never do this to Ethan. But I knew it would be useless to complain.

And I knew I couldn't just say thinking about prom reminded me too much of my old best friend. Robbie had promised he'd never forget me and he'd come back one day to go to prom together. But he'd already broken one of those promises, and I wasn't foolish enough to hope he'd keep the other. The idea of prom just reminded me that I was yet again not important enough for someone to remember.

If I told Mom all that, she'd just assume I was bitter because of a boy and completely misunderstand. It was better to keep this reason to myself.

"This isn't about prom," I insisted. "It's about saving the community center."

"But why can't you just wear one of your sisters' dresses and go?"

"Why does everyone act like prom is some kind of magical night?" I asked. "Don't you remember Sarah coming home with punch spilled down the back of her dress? Or how mad you got at Esther because she stayed out past her curfew? And Allie came home upset because the heel of her shoe broke and she sprained her ankle and spent the rest of the night watching her date dance with someone else."

"Oh, honey, even Allie said that was a freak accident, and she said she still had fun hanging out with her friends."

Yeah, she'd said that to Mom—but I'd heard her crying to Sarah in her room later.

"I'd just hang out with Josie and Max at the dance anyway. Why not do it in the comfort of our own house for free?"

Mom sighed, and I could tell she wasn't convinced. "Is it because no one has asked you?"

I hated that Mom said this, such an echo of Caroline's words. The funny thing was that I *had* gotten asked to prom. Seven years ago. Not that it mattered now. "No, Mom, not everything is about dating!"

"If you don't date, then how else will you find love?"

"Mom, I'm only seventeen."

"I was seventeen when I met your father," Mom reminded me.

Yeah, like a thousand years ago.

But I didn't have a chance to give an actual reply because the door-bell rang.

"Can you get that?" Mom said, dipping a zucchini in flour and egg to fry.

"Of course," I mumbled mostly to myself. It's not like Mom expected me to do anything else but comply.

I assumed it was the UPS guy. He was the only one who rang the doorbell. Josie and Ethan's friends always just texted when they were here.

Wondering what was being delivered, I unlocked the door, and just as I was about to open it, I got a strange feeling that made the hair on the back of my neck stand up. Something that told me that it wasn't the UPS guy. My maternal halmeoni used to have prophetic dreams, and she always told us it ran in the family. Esther told me she was talking nonsense, but sometimes I get these feelings that remind me of her words. And this was one of those moments.

As I opened the door, that strange feeling bloomed like heat in my chest. And my mouth fell open as I stared at Robbie Choi standing on my doorstep.

It was like opening the door to the past, except this Robbie Choi was no longer the pudgy kid who was the same height as me. It's not that I was short; I guess I was pretty average height at five foot four, but this Robbie towered over me, almost six feet tall. For some reason, I noticed his clothes first. They were so much cooler than the faded T-shirts and ill-fitting pants he wore in elementary school. His jeans were a little tighter than I'd have chosen for him, but they still looked good. And his hair. The same hair that I'd once shaved off when we were nine now brushed the collar of his shirt, and it was pastel pink. Somehow it worked really well with his pale complexion. Instead of making him look clownish, it made him look glamorous.

"Robbie?" I said. "What are you doing here?"

He gave a roguish smile that flashed deep dimples, and despite myself, my pulse sped up. It was the smile that made thousands of girls fall in love in an instant. He held out his hand, and in it was a single rose. "I'm here to take you to prom."

FOUR

This couldn't be real. Robbie Choi could *not* be standing on my doorstep, let alone asking me to prom.

This was way too coincidental. I had just been thinking about Robbie and prom today, and now he was on my doorstep. Maybe my maternal halmeoni was right, and we were more than just psychic. Maybe we were witches.

More likely, I was hallucinating from all the stress over the community center. But even when I squeezed my eyes shut so hard that I could see those little light explosions behind my lids and opened them again, Robbie still stood in front of me.

"Lani?" he said, and the sound of that nickname—one only Robbie had ever called me—shocked me back into reality.

"Robbie?" I could only squeak out his name.

"Are you going to answer my question?" he asked with a smile that brightened his already too-handsome face. But when I still didn't answer, it fell a bit, uncertainty taking over his expression. Oh no, why couldn't I say anything?

"Or . . . can I at least come in?" he asked.

Instinctively, I started to open the door wider, but as he shifted, I noticed someone behind him. A man in dark clothing. I would have thought he was a bodyguard except he held up a camera.

Why would they be filming this? Suddenly all I could think about was my messy hair and I almost lifted my hands to smooth it down but thought it would be too obvious. So I kept them clamped to my side, gripping the edge of my shirt.

Was this some kind of hidden-camera prank? Like those anxiety-inducing reality shows Ethan watched. But if it were, weren't the cameras supposed to be, well, *hidden*?

"What's going on here?" I finally said, pulling the door tight to me to block the foyer. I did *not* want my awkward class photo from third grade on camera.

"Oh." Robbie aimed another thousand-watt smile at me. He rubbed his hand through his hair, which somehow made it look fashionably mussed. He was way too perfect-looking. Not the Robbie I remembered with dirt always staining his pants and the latest bad haircut his mom had given to him in the bathroom.

I realized I couldn't recognize anything in the Robbie standing in front of me. Not his clothes, not his hair, not his perfectly crooked (like so perfect it had to be practiced) smile.

"Don't worry about the camera," Robbie said. "It's kind of a thing we do. *WDB TV* for our fans. I thought it might be fun for them to see the old neighborhood where I used to live."

"Why does it have to be *here*, though?" I asked, shifting uncomfortably on my feet. I hated being filmed in general. But knowing this could be on such a famous channel was making me even more nervous.

"It's fine. You'll get used to it."

Get used to it? How long did he expect to be here? The old Robbie would never have asked me to do something that made me feel uncomfortable. He knew that I hated having my picture taken, let alone being part of some internet show that thousands would probably watch.

"Okay, but why are you here?" I asked. I couldn't seem to keep my eyes from darting back to the camera every five seconds. "We haven't even talked in, like, four years."

Robbie laughed, a soft and genteel chuckle. Nothing like the braying laugh I remembered. Honestly, it had been like a donkey. And I'd loved it. I didn't know what to do with this calm and gentle chortle that came out of him now.

"I know I've been really busy lately. It's been kind of nonstop with all the tours and trying to meet as many of my fans as possible." He lowered his head slightly like he was embarrassed about how many adoring fans he had. But he smiled at the perfect angle for the camera to capture. It all looked so rehearsed. I fought the urge to roll my eyes. "And I told you, I'm asking you to prom," Robbie continued. "Remember our promise? I always keep my promises." He hit me with another one of those dazzling smiles and added a wink.

No, you don't, I wanted to say. *What about the promise that we'd stay best friends forever? That you'd keep in touch and always text me back? What about that promise?*

"Come on, Elena. You *do* remember, don't you?" he asked, and there was something about the smoothness in his voice that grated on my nerves.

Like he was a suave guy in a corny movie using a pickup line. Or more like he was a celebrity used to girls falling down at his feet.

"I do," I said slowly.

"Great!" he said, and shoved the rose into my hand. "Should we meet at your school to buy the tickets?"

"What? No, I'm not going to buy tickets."

"What do you mean?" Robbie frowned, and even that looked perfect.

"You don't have to take me to prom," I tried to explain. "That promise was years ago. You don't have to keep it."

Now it was Robbie's turn to blink in confusion. He let out a cutoff huff, like he wanted to laugh but thought better of it. He leaned in close and whispered so low the camera probably wouldn't pick up his question. "Is it because you're nervous going with someone like me?"

Wow, he seriously thought I was starstruck by him.

"To be honest, I don't really follow your music," I said, pursing my lips the way I used to see Allie do when someone annoyed her. "But I hear you're doing well, so congratulations, I guess."

"What?" Robbie scowled and finally forgot to be handsome while doing it.

"And for your information, I'm not going to prom. At all. With anyone."

He lifted a single brow in surprise. I hated when people did that, mostly because I couldn't. "But isn't it your junior year? Why wouldn't you go to prom?"

His judgmental tone was the final straw. I lifted my chin and set my shoulders back. "Because I don't want to. So, have a great stay in the US."

And I closed the door quickly. I had to get away from the disappointed look in Robbie's eyes and the bright red light of the camera behind him.

FIVE

Robbie didn't know what to do. He just stared at the closed door for three minutes before he fully processed what happened. He considered ringing the doorbell again but was acutely aware of the camera on him. This was mortifying, but all his media training flooded his brain. Do not be too aggressive. As the maknae, his image was quiet and chic, not pushy or demanding.

So, he just turned to his manager, Hanbin, who still held the camera. "Can you turn it off, Hyeong?"

Hanbin nodded and let the camera fall to his side. "Don't worry, Robbie."

Robbie just shrugged, pulling up the hood of his sweatshirt and walking back to the van waiting on the curb. It was one of those sleek black vehicles that Koreans lovingly called idol vans.

As he approached the car, Hanbin rushed forward to open the door for him. He was a round and jolly-looking guy whose hair was already thinning at the age of twenty-eight. Robbie sometimes worried it was the stress of the job. Being one of the managers of a K-pop group is not really a glamorous job, but Hanbin had been with them since the beginning.

Robbie climbed into the van and immediately pulled out his own headphones, hoping it would discourage any conversation. He did not look forward to the barrage of questions he knew would eventually come his way.

Before Robbie could turn on his music, Hanbin climbed into the driver's seat and said, "You can try again, Robbie."

"Sure," Robbie said automatically. Even though he was still mortified from the rejection.

Elena had looked so happy when she'd first opened the door, and then she'd looked horrified, like he'd been holding a knife instead of a rose. He'd fully expected her to give him the biggest hug as soon as she recognized him. The hard-squeeze hug that stole his breath that only Elena had ever given him. But instead, she looked like she'd rather die than touch him.

Maybe that's why he'd thrown up the idol shield. Because suddenly his nerves had taken over. And the only time he could fight back nerves was when he was onstage, presenting the side of himself that loved to perform so much that he forgot to be nervous. And even as he'd poured on the charm, he could see he was losing her.

She'd looked good, though, despite glaring at him the whole time. She'd really grown up in the last seven years. Her cute face had become pretty, like sweet girl-next-door pretty. When she'd opened the door, his pulse had picked up just seeing her again.

Jongdae leaned over from his seat and plucked Robbie's earbud out of his left ear. "Museun iliya?"

"English!" Hanbin cut in. "We're in America for your North American tour. Speak English while you're here. Especially with Robbie, so you can practice."

Jongdae sighed, but he didn't argue. Robbie wanted to tell Jongdae they could practice later in private, but he was afraid his hyeong wouldn't like Robbie implying he needed special treatment.

"What's the matter?" Jongdae asked again, this time in English.

"Nothing," Robbie said. Another automatic response. Then he turned in his seat to face his older cousin. "Have you ever frozen up in front of a girl? Where you couldn't seem to think of the right thing to say?"

Jongdae's voice rose in surprise. "She said no?"

Robbie shook his head. "She didn't say the word 'no' exactly. She just said she wasn't planning to go to prom."

Jongdae laughed and patted Robbie's shoulder consolingly. He was five years older, but he was also the person who knew Robbie the best. Being an idol had a way of breaking down the age hierarchy in Korea. In any other profession, Jongdae wouldn't be so chummy with his younger cousin. But they were idols and they'd come up together, debuted together, risen to fame together. It was a bond you couldn't easily break.

"It sounds like you got rejected. I guess our maknae isn't as charming as the fans think," Jongdae teased, mussing Robbie's hair.

"Ya!" Robbie protested, pushing Jongdae's hand away. He should have known his hyeong wouldn't understand as the visual of the group. Girls practically threw themselves at Jongdae's feet.

"It's okay," Jongdae said, still teasing. "You're young. It's not surprising you have no idea how to talk to girls yet."

"I know how to talk to girls. I talk to them all the time at our fan meets."

Jongdae laughed. "That's completely different. Those are fans. You can't talk to a girl you like the way you talk to fans."

Robbie frowned. That wasn't what he was taught when he was a trainee. They said to treat every girl who comes up like she's your girlfriend already. To be nice and loving, but not too loving because that would be creepy. He thought he'd been doing a good job. After all, every fan he met seemed excited to see him. But maybe Jongdae was right. He'd never come up against a girl who wasn't already happy to see him. And since he'd been in training to be an idol since he was eleven, he hadn't really had a lot of time to just hang out with kids his age outside of practices and lessons. Still, he hadn't expected it to be hard to talk to Elena. She was from his before life, when he'd just been Robbie, not "WDB's Robbie." Shouldn't she know the real him? Or did that person not even exist anymore after all these years?

"I don't know, Hyeong," Robbie said. "I did everything right. I smiled. I brought her a flower. And she still didn't say yes. And Hanbin caught it all on camera."

"Don't worry. We'll fix this," Jongdae said. "We're in Chicago for a few weeks before KFest. You can try again."

"How many ways can you ask a girl to prom?"

"What did you say to her?" Jongdae asked.

"I just said I was here to take her to prom."

"And what did she say?" Jongdae asked.

"She said she's not going to prom. And that we haven't talked in four years."

"That's your problem!" Hanbin piped up from the driver's seat. "I could tell she was annoyed that you ghosted her."

"Ghosted?"

It's true he hadn't talked to Elena in a while. Would she really be this pissed about that?

"You have to make it up to her," Hanbin said with a knowing nod.

"How?" Robbie's mind cycled through the possibilities. More flowers?

Gifts? He was starting to realize he had no idea what a girl his age actually wanted. "Maybe . . . I should try to explain things to her?"

"It's too late. You have to make a grand gesture! Prove that you really care about her," Hanbin said.

"I don't know. Elena was never into those big flashy things."

"Oh, Robbie, Robbie, Robbie," Hanbin said, shaking his head sadly like Robbie was a lost cause. "You don't get it. It's fine because you're so young and you don't know the ways of the American teen anymore."

Robbie grimaced. Even though Hanbin was in his twenties, he sounded like an old ajusshi.

"And how would *you* know what an American teen wants?" Jongdae asked with a laugh. Robbie smiled. Jongdae was good at giving Hanbin a hard time. Probably because he'd had to share a room with their manager when they'd all lived in their first cramped dorm during debut.

"I watch videos online. I read articles. I have to stay up-to-date on your fan base."

Robbie held in a laugh. Hanbin sounded even older now, like his harabeoji.

"Fine, then what do you think I should do?"

"You have to make it a big event! Like we do in Korea when we want to declare our love to the world. But because it's prom, they call this type of thing a promposal." Hanbin said the last word like it was a magical phrase.

"Promposal? That sounds . . . ridiculous," Robbie said. They didn't have proms in Korea and he hadn't been well versed in the culture around them at ten, so this was all new territory to him.

Hanbin sighed. "Fine, if you don't want my help, then don't take it."

Robbie hesitated. Even the word "promposal" sounded embarrassing. But he'd been made to do more embarrassing things when he first debuted. Like when the whole band had to act out popular scenes from K-dramas for the end-of-the-year concerts. Or when he'd had to dress in ajumma clothes like an old lady and go stomping around a rice paddy for a variety show. He could do this promposal thing if it meant getting Elena to say yes. Robbie didn't want to give up on this chance to spend time with his old best friend. Not when he'd jumped through so many hoops just to see her again.

"Fine, tell me more about promposals," he said.

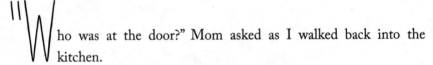

"W ho was at the door?" Mom asked as I walked back into the kitchen.

"No one," I said quickly. I didn't want the questions that would come if I told her what just happened. I actually wasn't completely sure what just happened. I tried to take a slice of fried zucchini that sat on a paper-towel-lined plate and got my hand slapped away.

Ethan came running down the stairs, stomping like a herd of elephants.

"When's dinner? I'm starving!" he said, snatching up the piece of fried zucchini I'd tried to take and popping it in his mouth.

"Soon!" Mom said. "Sar—Elena, can you finish setting the table?"

Mom never asked Ethan to do chores.

"Who gave you that?" Ethan suddenly asked.

"What?" I said, blinking at him. He was staring at my hand, and I realized that I still held the rose. "Oh, no one," I said, hiding it behind my back like a kid caught stealing candy.

"Elena!" Ethan said with an exaggerated gasp. "Do you have a secret boyfriend?"

I could tell he was mocking me, as if I were so grotesque that no one could possibly want to date me. I was about to hit him with a killer comeback when my mom spun around.

"A boyfriend?" she squeaked, like I had finally done something good. Like, oh joy, your daughter now has worth because a big strong boy-shaped thing has given her some kind of attention. "Elena, you didn't tell me you were dating someone. Is that why you don't want to go to prom? Because he hasn't asked you yet?"

"What? No!" I said. "I am *not* dating someone. And someone did ask me and I said no."

"Who asked you? How come I didn't hear about this?" Ethan asked.

Wait, did he actually care about knowing what was happening in my life?

"Was it someone from your Nerd Awareness Club?" he said.

And there's the punch line. "It's just the Awareness Club, Ethan. Which you definitely know."

"Yeah, but I think nerd awareness is important too. Nerds deserve representation." He grinned like he'd said the funniest joke.

"Sure," I said, clenching my teeth.

"No, really, who was it?" Ethan asked.

"No one," I insisted, glancing at Mom, almost hoping she'd nag me to do another chore so I could escape this torture. But she just watched me expectantly too.

It looked like there was no getting around this. I considered lying but knew that Mom would see right through it. I was a horrible liar. "Robbie," I muttered under my breath.

"Who?" Ethan asked, leaning in.

"Robbie," I said again. I threw the rose on the counter, not wanting to even look at it anymore.

"Robbie Choi?" Mom's voice rose.

"No way," Ethan said with a laugh. "Why would Robbie Choi be here?"

"He's here for that KFest thing," Mom said, and Ethan and I stared at her in surprise.

"How do you know about that when we don't?" Ethan asked.

"All the ladies at the Korean salon were talking about it a couple weeks ago. It's the first KFest in Chicago, and WDB is one of the main acts. It's already completely sold out. We're all so proud of Robbie. Local boy who's accomplished so much at such a young age. His mother must be so proud." Korean parent talk for *Why haven't my children done anything worth bragging about?*

There's a phrase in Korean: eom-chin-ah. It means your mom's friend's kid, but it really means "perfect kid." The one who makes everyone else look bad. And our eom-chin-ah went and became a worldwide mega star. How can a kid top that?

"Well, I don't care what he's in town for," I said, pulling open the utensil drawer to grab spoons and chopsticks. "He hasn't even called or texted me in four years, and all of a sudden he shows up and expects me to keep a seven-year-old promise. Yeah, right." I slammed the drawer shut, and my mom tsked. She hated it when I slammed things.

"I'm sure he's been very busy. With all of his touring-and-singing stuff," Mom said.

I almost laughed because sometimes it felt like my mom went to acrobatic lengths to never take my side.

"How would he even have time to go to prom?" I asked, pulling out plates and setting them by the rice cooker so Mom could scoop a serving onto each.

"*Why* would he want to go to a high school prom at all?" Ethan asked.

"Exactly!" I said, pointing my handful of utensils at him. Finally, someone was on my side.

"And more importantly, why would he want to go with *Elena*?"

Okay, so not so much on my side . . . but I'd still take it if it helped get Mom off my case.

Before we could continue, the front door opened and Dad's voice rang out. "Yeobo, when's dinner? I'm starving!"

"It's ready now," Mom called back.

Dad walked into the kitchen and laid his work bag on the small desk built into the wall. It was cluttered with Post-it notes all over a desk calendar that Mom still wrote our appointments on even though we'd shown her how to use the calendar app on her phone. Dad took off his suit jacket and hung it over the chair and kissed Mom on the cheek. He looked like any average middle-aged Asian man, with graying hair and wire-rimmed glasses. We only ever saw him during dinnertime, to the point that I immediately felt hungrier whenever I saw him. Like a Pavlovian response.

I picked up the plates to carry to the table, piles of rice steaming from them. When I walked back to grab cups, I stared at the rose. I picked it up, opening the trash can to shove it inside. Then I paused. No one had ever given me a flower before. No one except Robbie, I remembered, when we were eight and he'd picked a half-dead daisy for me. It was weird to remember that now, when I still felt the residual awkwardness from his prom invite. Still, I set the rose back on the counter. It's not like the flower had done anything wrong.

"So, what did you do today?" Dad asked as we all sat at the table.

"I got an A on my Algebra test," Ethan announced.

"Good job," Mom exclaimed like he'd just announced he'd discovered the secret to cold fusion.

"Keep it up," Dad said, "and you'll follow your noonas to Northwestern."

Ah yes, the inevitable and very regular reminder that our older siblings had gone to a Korean-parent-approved college. It would be a shame for me and Ethan to disappoint.

"I've been looking at Duke," Ethan started.

"Duke?" my mother said. "That's so far away."

I held back the urge to sigh. My sisters were all pressured into going to Northwestern because it was a great college right next door. But as soon as they graduated, they'd fled. I guess I couldn't fully blame them, except in fleeing Mom's stifling grasp, they'd left me behind too.

"Coach says there's a chance I can get into Duke through lacrosse," Ethan said, looking at Dad hopefully. Like he was waiting for the praise. I don't know why he kept doing this. Mom was the more emotional parent, even though most of the emotions she aimed at me were wrapped in disappointment.

"That would be nice," Dad said like Ethan told him it would be partly sunny tomorrow. It was actually a lot coming from him. "But it would be best if you could also get in academically." And there was the other shoe, dropping just on cue.

"Oh yeah," Ethan said. "I just want to cover all bases. That would be the smartest way, right?" I almost felt bad for him. Asking Dad for approval was like asking for your work to be dissected and nitpicked.

But Dad just gave an absent nod and asked Mom to pass the kongnamul.

"Elena, did you also have a math test?" Mom asked.

"Precalc doesn't have the same test schedule," I said. And then felt like a jerk when I saw Ethan frown. I didn't say it to make him feel bad. But it wasn't my fault that he was in standard math and I was in honors. Why did Mom and Dad assume we were always doing the same things at school?

"Ah, okay. Well, study hard," Mom said.

"Okay," I said, and spooned a mouthful of moo gook into my mouth. The broth was too hot and burned going down.

"Yeobo, Elena got asked to prom today," Mom said like it was an announcement.

I slouched lower in my seat.

"Really?" Dad asked.

"It was Robbie Choi!" Mom chirped.

"Robbie?" Dad frowned over the name. "You mean that boy who used to live down the street? The one who's in a rock band?"

"A K-pop group," I said.

"Yeah, and he has strange-colored hair now, right?" Dad asked.

I almost laughed. Of course that's what Dad would notice.

"Anyway," Mom continued. "He's back in town for a big concert, and he asked our Elena out to prom."

I slouched even lower in my chair. I was only "our Elena" when I'd done something good. And I really didn't count getting asked to prom as an accomplishment.

"Well, if you want to go dress shopping, you can get whatever you want as long as it's not more than two hundred dollars," Dad said.

My eyes almost bulged out of my head. Two hundred dollars! That was a ridiculous amount to pay for a dress.

"Well, actually," I said, straightening in my seat. I saw Ethan straighten too, shaking his head at me in warning, but I powered on. "I think that kids just spend too much money on prom and it would be better used for something charitable. So, if I could just have the money you would have let me use for prom for the community center—"

"You still volunteer there? I thought your assignment was over," Dad said, reaching for the steaming serving plate of spicy dwejigogi.

"Yes, my assignment is over. But I still work there in my own time, remember?" I'd told my dad this at least a dozen times, but he always seemed to forget.

"Your father is busy at the office. He doesn't always have time to remember things you tell him," Mom reminded me. Like it was my fault Dad was so busy.

"I know," I said. "I just meant could we please donate something to help the community center? They really need it."

"Isn't it supposed to be funded by the city?" Dad asked. "Why do they need our money?"

I thought about explaining it, but Ethan caught my eye again, his brows lifted in a "You know he's not actually listening" expression. So I sighed and said, "Never mind."

"Honey," Mom said. "Your father works very hard to provide for us all. We shouldn't just be giving away his money."

And buying a prom dress for two hundred dollars isn't like throwing our cash at a department store? I thought. But I kept my mouth shut.

"Mom, Dad, you're coming to my game this week, right? I'm starting," Ethan said. I slouched again in my chair, for once grateful for Ethan taking the attention.

"Of course," Mom said.

"I'll try," Dad said. "There's an issue with one of our projects, so we might need to stay late this week and get on the phone with China." He said it in that noncommittal voice that told us that "I'll try" meant "I won't."

I looked over at Ethan, who just silently nodded. We all knew that we were lucky that Dad had such a great job.

"It's okay if you don't make it," Ethan said. "It's just a regular-season game. I'll definitely be starting again in another one."

"Well, Elena and I will be there," Mom said reassuringly. She must have noticed how disappointed Ethan was, because she never made me go to his games.

"Actually," I said slowly, already anticipating her disapproval. "I have plans on Friday. I promised Cora I'd go to the community center and help babysit."

"Oh, Elena, why would you promise that when you know Ethan has games on Friday?" Mom said, the annoyance so thick in her voice that I felt like melting into my chair.

Because I never go to Ethan's games, I wanted to say. But I didn't. Instead, I tried to explain: "It's when they needed me. Lots of parents depend on these babysitting services so they can make their evening shifts."

Mom sighed, obviously not very moved by my explanation. "You know your brother's games are important to him. You could make more of an effort."

And what about what was important to me? I wondered. They were acting like the community center meant nothing.

"It's fine," Ethan said. "Elena can go to her community center thingy."

"See?" I said, still stinging from Mom chastising me. "Ethan doesn't care."

Mom pursed her lips. "Fine, go to the community center."

And even though I'd technically won this argument, I felt like I had totally lost. That was the power of mom disappointment.

tend to get left behind a lot. I'm not saying that to get sympathy; it's just a fact. Not in any kind of tragic way—it's not like I'll be writing a college essay about it or anything. But in an almost boringly normal way. My sisters all just outgrew this place and moved away after college. Esther to the East Coast for med school, Allie traveling the world for her fancy international consultant job, and Sarah to California to work in tech. Robbie left because of his dad's job. Even losing my friendship with Felicity was mostly just normal teenage growing pains. But it did sting, the way it always felt like I was the one getting left and never the leaver.

After dinner, I stared at my laptop blankly. I was supposed to get started on a history report, but I couldn't focus. Opening my desk drawer, I shuffled past sheet music from when I'd joined the school band in middle school and tried to learn the clarinet, the flute, the trumpet, even the drums, until Mom said the noise of my practicing was giving her chronic migraines. Old scripts from when I'd joined the theater department freshman year. A fifth-place ribbon from when I ran track and sprained my ankle at that first (and only) meet I attended.

My coping mechanism for the loneliness after my sisters left was to constantly reinvent myself. I tried chorus, soccer, math competitions. I practically took that song "Stick to the Status Quo" in *High School Musical* and tried to fit into every group they described.

I guess I thought that the issue was that I didn't have a "thing" that made me interesting enough to stick around for. Everyone around me seemed to have one. Ethan had lacrosse. Josie had her activism. Max was totally into photography; he took all the photos for Josie's rally posters. But Elena Soo was a nobody who dabbled in a lot of things but wasn't passionate about any *one* thing. Almost like the universe forgot to give me a purpose when it made me. Like I was forgettable even before I was born.

Even Robbie had turned a childhood interest in music into a thing. And it was a pretty huge freaking thing.

I finally found what I was looking for. A shoebox where I'd put all my old Robbie keepsakes. Ticket stubs to the first movie our parents let us go to alone. A seashell he'd brought me after his summer vacation to the Outer Banks. And the rules to one of our endless adventure role-play games. It all seemed like a thousand years ago.

And now he was back. Except the Robbie who had made this box of memories with me was nothing like the chic, suave idol who'd knocked on my door. I shoved the box back into the drawer and closed it with a definitive click. I shouldn't dwell on this. I had to finish this history report or I'd fall behind on my schoolwork.

Yet I ended up clicking on my music playlists instead, scrolling until

I came to a small section of K-pop songs. And there, among Twice, BlackPink, and NCT was WDB.

There was a period of time when I was really into K-pop in middle school.

I might have kept loving it, but the second semester of my seventh-grade year a brand-new entertainment agency called Bright Star released trainee bios of their flagship group. And the third boy to be revealed was Robbie. At first, I became really popular among the girls who lived and breathed K-pop. They wanted to know all about Robbie. But then I realized it was just like when people only talked to me because I was Ethan's sister. I wasn't Elena Soo anymore; I was the girl who had once been friends with Robbie Choi.

And it all came to a head when they demanded I call him. At that point, we hadn't texted in months. I wasn't even sure if he'd pick up. But I'd done it. And it had immediately informed me that the account no longer existed. The girls had laughed at me, saying they knew I'd been making it up, that I wasn't really friends with Robbie anymore.

And it wouldn't have hurt except I suspected they were right. He'd changed his number and hadn't told me. He'd been too busy pursuing his dreams and leaving me behind.

So I stopped hanging out with those girls and I stopped loving K-pop.

I opened my YouTube playlists. There was one that I hovered over. It was named "..." because I was too chicken to call it anything.

Dozens of unwatched videos about WDB popped up. I'd saved them in this playlist because I didn't have the courage to watch them but I didn't want to lose them, just in case.

It had been so long that some of the saved videos had gray error graphics, probably taken down because of copyright. But there were still dozens of videos where Robbie smiled out from the thumbnail.

I clicked on the first one. When Robbie had debuted. He'd just turned fourteen. He looked so young but, at the same time, so old to me. Because my eyes were so used to seeing his ten-year-old face.

He spoke in Korean when the interviewer asked him questions. I recognized every other word. My Korean was only good enough to understand my grandparents' slow and measured speech patterns. But most of these videos came with subtitles. And they said he was talking about how WDB stood for 원더별, which meant "Wonder Star" but it was pronounced "Wondeo Byul." He said the Bright Star CEO had formed the group and named it himself. He wanted their name to be that mix of English and Korean so it sounded like "Wonderful." And he hoped they filled their fans with wonder.

But usually they just called the band WDB. As if the meaning of the initials wasn't important. Just the boys themselves. And it was true. The world loved them. They'd broken barriers, broken records.

So many of the comments in the videos were about how dreamy the "oppas" were. Which was also so weird to me. Technically Ethan was my oppa. He'd been born fifteen minutes earlier than me.

But "oppa" was also used as an affectionate term for an older boy you were close to.

I watched a video where the boys announced that their fandom name was officially "Constellation." I remembered a girl walking up to me in the hallways of school. She'd wanted to know if I'd really known Robbie Choi when we were young.

"Yeah," I'd admitted, hunching my shoulders. By then I was really annoyed about being asked this so much.

"So, are you a Constellation?" she'd asked.

"What?" I'd scrunched my face. I'd had no idea what she was talking about.

"A fan of WDB?" she said, like something was wrong with me for not knowing.

"No, I don't really listen to them."

"Oh," she'd said, her voice dropping in disappointment. Then she'd returned to her friends, and I heard her say, "I guess she wasn't that close to Robbie. Maybe she's lying about knowing him."

"What a weirdo," her friend had replied.

But now Robbie was here. Not only was he here, but he'd asked me to prom. On camera. Was that mean girl from school going to see that video? Oh no, was the wave of people asking me about Robbie going to start up again? I sighed and closed my laptop, letting my head fall onto my desk. Maybe I could just lie here for the rest of high school. It seemed like a preferable solution.

WDB (원더별) MEMBER PROFILE
STAGE NAME: Robbie
NAME: Choi Jiseok (최지석)
GROUP POSITION: main rapper, subvocal, maknae
BIRTHDAY: June 19 • **SIGN:** Gemini
HEIGHT: 178 cm (5'10") • **WEIGHT:** 66 kg (145 lb)
BLOOD TYPE: O • **BIRTHPLACE:** Incheon, South Korea
FAMILY: Mom • **HOBBIES:** Gaming
NICKNAMES: Roro, Ro-Star, Robiya, Kangajiseok
EDUCATION: Seoul School of Performing Arts
LIGHTSTICK COLOR: Purple

ROBBIE FACTS:

• He was born in Incheon, South Korea.

• He moved to a suburb of Chicago, Illinois, when he was six.

• He moved back to Seoul, South Korea, when he was ten.

• His father passed away when he was eleven.

• He joined his uncle's new entertainment company, Bright Star, when he was eleven.

• He was in a G-Dragon MV when he was 13 (14 Korean age).

• His favorite number is 8.

• He first became well known when samples of him rapping his own original songs were leaked when he was 13 (14 Korean age).

• He was announced as the third member of WDB (원더별).

• Debuted when he was 14 (15 Korean age).

• His best friend is his groupmate Jaehyung.

• WDB's leader, Jongdae, is his cousin.

• He is fluent in English and Korean and can speak some French that he learned from WDB member Moonster.

• His role models are Big Bang's G-Dragon, Epik High's Tablo, iKON'S Bobby, and Bruno Mars.

• His favorite colors are blue, pink, and black.

• He once said he doesn't have an ideal type.

EIGHT

"Flowers? Check. Guitar? Check. Hair? Check." Hanbin ran his pen down the list on his notebook as they sat in the van.

Robbie waited patiently. This was Hanbin's obsessive habit. He always checked his lists three times. The boys joked that this made him more thorough than Santa Harabeoji.

"Are you sure this isn't too much?" Robbie asked, already antsy about what he was about to do. "I don't want to embarrass her."

The Elena he remembered didn't really like being the center of attention. But no matter how often he told Jongdae and Hanbin that, they'd just ignored him. Claimed this was different. Everyone wanted a promposal like this. And then Hanbin had made Robbie watch a dozen videos online to prove his point. He claimed the girls loved it, but Robbie thought that the girls looked shocked and embarrassed half the time.

"You just don't understand girls. They love being wooed," Hanbin claimed.

"Hyeong, I don't think anyone talks like that anymore," Robbie said. "And if you know what girls like, then why are you still single?"

"Ya!" Jongdae smacked Robbie on the back of the head.

Hanbin looked pleased that Jongdae was defending him.

"Focus," Jongdae said. "Hanbin's lack of game isn't the point."

"Hey!" Hanbin protested.

"Just stick to the plan," Jongdae said, holding out the guitar. "Pretend like it's another concert. You're great onstage. And girls love it when a guy performs just for them."

Robbie nodded. Jongdae was right. And he definitely knew how to win over girls better than Robbie. Even when they were trainees, Jongdae had a long line of female admirers. And thinking of this like a performance helped. If Robbie knew one thing, it was how to drown out the world and just focus on the music. He was confident when it came to music. When he was singing, he was no longer Robbie Choi; he was WDB's Robbie, International K-Pop Star. He took three deep breaths, his before-concert ritual.

"I know you'll be great, Robbie. Remember why you're doing this," Jongdae said with an encouraging smile.

Robbie finally nodded. "You're right. I can do this."

"Go get the girl," Hanbin said, hitting the button to open the automatic sliding door.

NINE

Of course, the next morning my car wouldn't start. So I'd had to call Josie for a ride, since Ethan had already left for morning lacrosse practice. As soon as I told her what happened with Robbie, she started plying me with a million questions.

"This honestly sounds like a freaking K-drama, right? Are you sure you didn't just fall asleep watching one and have, like, a lucid dream?" Josie asked as she parked her hand-me-down Jetta in the junior lot.

"It wasn't a dream," I said, climbing out of the car.

"So, what's he like?" Josie asked, leaning on her hood to stare at me.

"Handsome. Cocky." *Different.* I shrugged. "I don't know. I didn't really talk to him." I grabbed my bag, and started toward campus, hoping that Josie was done with her questions now that we were at school.

Josie hurried after me and dashed my hopes by saying, "My cousin is the president of the Mexico City Constellations. Can I tell her about this? She'd die."

"Fine," I acquiesced as we entered the courtyard. It wasn't like it mattered. I'd never see Robbie again.

I usually loved school early in the morning. The quiet kind of felt like the calm before the storm. A chance to prepare myself for the day. Every morning, the upperclassmen scattered in small groups around the stone benches placed against the walls surrounding the courtyard. Lounging and gossiping until the first warning bell rang. But today, they were all clumped together to the side.

"What's going on over there?" Josie wondered, mirroring my own thoughts.

"I don't know." Had they moved the prom ticket table out of the cafeteria?

"Oh my god, it's a promposal!" Josie said, pointing at a clump of latex balloons visible above the heads of the crowd. In fact, they formed a giant arch. It was so big that it had to have taken dozens of red and pink balloons to make it.

"Who is it for?" Josie said, craning her neck. We joined the back of the crowd. I might have had no interest in going to prom, but I was only human—I was curious who had gone so all out for this spectacle. I hoped the poor sap wasn't rejected in front of half the upper class.

"Hey," Josie said to the boy standing in front of us, a senior I barely recognized. "Who is it?"

"I dunno, but a bunch of girls were freaking out earlier," he said with a shrug.

"Maybe it's one of the football guys. But they never do this much to ask their girlfriends to dances," I said. At most, they might bring a single rose to school. Noah Jordan did that for homecoming this year, and his girlfriend had carried it like a trophy all day. If one of them was doing a huge promposal, then I could see some of the juniors totally swooning over it.

"Hey." Josie moved on to her next potential informant. "Do you know what's going on?"

I recognized the girl from our homeroom, Diana Walker. She turned to Josie, started to speak, then saw me, and it was like a falcon zeroing in on her prey.

"Hey! She's here!" she called, reaching out and pushing me forward. Everyone turned at Diana's announcement, making a small path for me to stumble through.

More people started pushing me. And more people started moving out of my way. It was like being pulled out to sea by the undertow. You don't think it should be that strong, but once it's got you, you can't fight it.

I lost Josie in the crowd and just heard her annoyed voice say, "What the heck, Diana? Why'd you do that?"

Some people were craning their necks to see me, and I could feel my cheeks burning at the attention. I was still trying to piece together what was happening when I spotted Ethan near the front. He had on a wide-eyed "Oh crap" expression.

What? I mouthed at him.

But he just grimaced and gave me a sad, weak thumbs-up.

I had no idea what that was supposed to mean. Not even a small inkling of a clue. Seriously, we're the worst twins ever.

Finally, the crowd parted enough for me to see the promposal in its full glory. The balloon arch was just the beginning. On the ground was a literal garden of flowers. Mostly roses, but some lilies thrown in. They were organized into a giant heart with a ring of those fake LED tea-light candles.

And, oh god, there was a banner. And the banner had all the letters that were supposed to spell out my name, but they couldn't. That was impossible. Except in the middle of the heart stood Robbie Choi.

He was wearing a black button-down shirt that must have had some kind of metallic thread woven in because when he shifted it shimmered.

I felt someone push on my back, urging me forward. I'd stopped at the mouth of the crowd, and people were gathered around me in a half circle, keeping their distance but also straining to see what happened next.

Robbie leaned forward, and I finally noticed the microphone. *Why* was there a microphone? We were at school, not Madison Square Garden.

In my peripheral vision, I could see a dozen phones. Most of them aimed at Robbie, but some, I realized with horror, were aimed right at *me*. Oh my god, I'd just thrown on the same wrinkled jeans I'd worn yesterday. And my sweater had been lying on the armchair in my room. I didn't even know if it was clean! But it was navy blue, and I figured if it was dirty no one could ever tell. But what if these photos got out and people could somehow tell I was wearing dirty, day-old clothes?

"Elena," Robbie said, and I jerked to attention. "I have a question I wanted to ask you."

And then he started to play the guitar. He'd gotten so much better than I remembered. He played a sweet melody that was vaguely familiar. It itched at my brain for the first few notes before I recognized the tune.

The song was called "Gobaek Hamnida." "Gobaek" literally translated to "confession" but really meant "love confession." Like when you told a girl you liked her. I remembered swooning over this song, and once even admitted to Robbie that I thought it was the most romantic song a guy could sing for a girl. It would be sweet to think he remembered that moment if I wasn't absolutely mortified by all the eyes and cameras focused on me. The thing no one tells you when you're a silly ten-year-old daydreaming about your first big movie-worthy romantic moment is that movie romance doesn't fit into the real world. It just feels too extreme and corny.

I was sure my face was bright red. Great, now a dozen cameras were filming me turning into a tomato.

Then Robbie started singing. He always did have the sweetest voice. Lower than you might expect because he had such a cute face. And when he sang, his dimples flashed. Even through my anxiety, I couldn't help but wonder how this oddly beautiful boy grew out of the awkward, bumbling best friend I used to have.

And then the song was over, and the kids around me broke out into applause.

"I've missed you the last seven years," Robbie said. He picked up a bouquet of flowers from the edge of the flower heart and walked over to me. "Will you go to prom with me?"

He held out the bouquet, and I had no choice but to take it. The flowers were so large I couldn't hold them with just one hand, so I had to cradle the bouquet in the crook of my arm.

I could see a phone camera lens directly in my line of vision. Diana Walker was holding it, her eyes wide with anticipation. What was she going to do with this video? Why was everyone just staring at us? Why couldn't I say anything? I heard my blood rush through my eardrums, loud as white-water rapids. "Lani?" Robbie said, and I looked up at him only to see that his smile had fallen. Oh crap, he could feel how awkward I was being. This was going south fast.

Say something! my brain screamed at me. *For the love of anything that is holy, say something or you'll have to stand here forever and you'll just die here holding a bunch of dead flowers!*

"What's going on?" someone asked from beyond the crowd. And it was like the question unfroze everyone, and they all started murmuring.

I distinctly heard someone ask, "What's wrong with her?"

Suddenly, I could move my limbs again, and I whipped around. There were too many faces staring at me. Too many cameras aimed at me. I raced toward the edge of the crowd just as Felicity was making her way over, her neck craned to see better. A second too late, I realized I couldn't stop in time. I tried to sputter out her name in a last-ditch effort at a warning, but it came out a high-pitched "Fiii!" before my forward motion crashed me right into her. The flowers in my arms practically exploded, petals flying everywhere. By some miracle of balance, I caught myself before I went careening into the crowd of bodies. I let the mangled flower stems fall from my arms.

I heard people calling out Felicity's name and used the resulting chaos as cover to run.

And run. And run.

TEN

didn't stop running until I was out of breath and halfway across campus in a hallway beside the locker rooms.

I'd seen enough teen dramas to know that locker rooms are a great place to hide in humiliation. So I ducked inside and went to find a good toilet stall to die in. I'd just become a Korean toilet ghost. (Oh yeah, that's a thing. . . .)

I'd only been hiding for five minutes before I heard footsteps. I pulled my feet up, so I was crouching on the toilet lid like Gollum when Josie said, "El, I know you're in here. There are flower petals all over the floor."

Darn it! I didn't realize that there were still flower guts all over me, proof of my embarrassment.

With a sigh, I unlocked the stall door and stepped out.

"How bad is it?" I asked.

"Well, Robbie's gone."

I didn't know if that made me feel better or worse.

"Were you planning to hide in here all day?" Josie wrinkled her nose at the locker room. It wasn't the nicest place in the school. And was mostly used by sports teams after school to change for practice.

"It felt like a better choice than being out there with people."

"It's not that bad," Josie said, but she drew out her syllables too much, the way she did when she was lying and trying really hard to hide it.

"I can't believe that happened," I said.

"What actually happened?" Josie asked. "Why didn't you say anything?"

"I just kind of froze." It was hard to explain the special mix of anxiety and self-consciousness.

"Was it because part of you wanted to say yes?"

"What? No!" I said so forcefully that it echoed in the locker room. "I'd never give up on the alterna-prom initiative like that." Did Josie really doubt my commitment to the cause?

"The point of the initiative isn't to boycott the dance. It's to stop unnecessary consumerism and use the excess funds to help the community center," Josie said, so matter-of-factly, like of course we could go to prom if we wanted to.

"I don't want to go to prom, and definitely not with Robbie Choi," I said, trying to make my voice hard and definitive. I wished people would stop thinking I would suddenly do a one-eighty because Robbie Choi deigned to come back to town.

"Is it online?" I finally asked the question that had been gnawing at me.

"I mean . . ." Josie trailed off, obviously aware that I'd never believe her if she said no.

"Just tell me." I could feel my stomach twisting with anxiety nausea at the thought of all the people who might see my humiliation.

"It's being shared by all the kids. But most of them are just focused on Robbie," Josie piped up, like this was great news. "There's one, though . . . it's kind of epic."

"Epic?" I asked, not sure what she meant by that.

"Here. You should just watch it." Josie clicked through her phone and handed it to me. With dread weighing heavy in my chest, I watched as the video began.

"Lani?" Video-Robbie said after he had finished playing his song.

"What's going on?" Video-Felicity's voice rang out. And then I watched in horror as Video-Elena spun around wildly like a frightened chicken. And I went barreling right into Felicity.

The roses seemed to explode between us. Petals bursting from our collision and raining down. As I sprinted away, the video turned to slow motion, a horrifying post-production addition that emphasized Felicity's wide-eyed shock. Her arms wheeling as she tried to catch her balance. She fell into the crowd behind her. Some of the kids tried to catch her, but her momentum was too strong and instead she took three of them down with her like human dominoes. She let out a sad wail that sounded thick and low with the slo-mo effect. Roses were scattered around her. A stem stuck out of her hair straight into the air. Her mouth opened again in distress, and then the video faded to black.

"Oh. My. God," I said slowly as the video started to autoplay again. "Oh my god. Ohmygod." This was all too much. This was horrifying. For the first time in years, I felt actual pity for Felicity Fitzgerald.

"Right? It's epic," Josie said, a grin wide on her face. "I already saved it to my phone so I can watch Felicity fall on her ass over and over."

"I can't go out there," I said, grabbing Josie's arm. "Felicity will kill me."

"Oh no, she already went home. She claimed she got hurt and had to take a day off."

"I *injured* someone?" I cried.

Josie let out a laugh. "She's not hurt. I saw her walking to her car. She's fine. She's just embarrassed and used it as an excuse to leave."

"She's smart," I said quietly. "I wish I could leave."

"You want to?" Josie asked. "We can go if you want."

I sighed. Josie was a great friend. I mean, she was definitely very comfortable with taking a day off. She called them her mental health days. And honestly, I didn't know anyone as go-with-the-flow as Josie, so it seemed she was onto something. But I couldn't do it. I'd feel guilty about skipping school. And if my mom found out, I'd never hear the end of it.

"No, I should stay. Come on. Let's get today over with," I said as the warning bell rang. And I gathered my things and followed Josie out to my doom.

ELEVEN

t wasn't as bad as I thought it would be.

It was worse.

Even though the warning bell had rung, kids still loitered in the hallways. So I had to walk past dozens of staring eyes. Groups of kids would start to stare and whisper once one of them recognized me. I'd never had so much attention in my life. I tried (and failed) to recede into my sweater, like a turtle going into its shell.

Our homeroom became completely silent when Josie and I stepped in.

Then Jacob Schmidt started a slow clap and the other kids joined. Soon, there was a thunder of applause as all the kids clapped. But there was a mockery to it. I could see sharp eyes and wide grins. They weren't clapping for me. They were clapping for what a joke I was.

Today was going to be a long day.

★☆★

I never knew so many people could have opinions about my life, but lots of them were more than happy to tell me.

"Hey, Ethan's sister," Tim Breslow called as I passed by him in the hall toward Precalc. "Didn't know you were so picky. What's a guy gotta do to get you to say yes? Own a country?"

I lowered my head and hurried down the hall as laughter chased me.

Then, at lunch, when I was setting up our alterna-prom table, kids kept coming by to show me a dozen different versions of the promposal that had been posted online. It had been captured at every single angle possible. Some of the videos had been edited with music or special effects. It was humiliating. But the worst was when Diana Walker gleefully came up to the table. I started to hand her a pamphlet, but she waved it off.

"Guess this whole anti-prom thing is just for show, huh?" she said, eyeing me.

"What?" I scowled, sick of all the rumors I'd already heard floating around. The worst was that I'd somehow paid Robbie to do the promposal as a way to get attention.

"Yeah, I mean, why would you have Robbie do such a big show if you're protesting prom?"

"That's not what we're doing," I muttered.

"Don't worry, though," Diana said, ignoring my reply. "Looks like Robbie's already over it." She held up her phone where she'd cued up an instastory on JD's account. The boys were obviously getting ready for some kind of photo shoot or event. JD was talking nonsense, saying what he had for lunch and stuff. But then he turned the camera to Robbie, who was sitting sullenly in the corner. JD's laugh rang out. "Oh, is our maknae sad after his epic rejection?"

Robbie shrugged, a jerking motion of his shoulders. "Whatever, it's not that big of a deal."

Not that big of a deal? Is that really what he thought of the most mortifying moment in my life?

One of the other members popped into the frame and flung a friendly arm around Robbie's shoulder. "Look at the bright side. Now you can be a tortured artist."

Robbie laughed and shoved his other groupmate away. "Sure, I'll write an epic song about it."

"That's the spirit, Robiya," JD said. His hand came out to punch Robbie on the shoulder.

Robbie gave the camera a sly grin. "You win some, you lose some, right?"

"At least it's good that he's not upset about it, don't you think, Elena?" Diana's voice was sharp, like she was waiting for me to crack so she could report the gossip back to her friends.

So I plastered on my biggest fake smile and said, "Yeah! It's such a relief. Thanks for showing me."

Diana pouted in disappointment. She looked like she was going to say something else, but I turned back to the table, focusing all my attention on organizing the pamphlets until she finally walked away. Then I let my shoulders slump. *You win some, you lose some?*

I'm not a trophy, I fumed.

Chemistry was the last class of the day and I couldn't wait for it to be over. I kept glancing at the clock as I worked on the day's lab.

I was teamed up with Karla Hernandez and her phone was buzzing incessantly the whole time. She kept glancing at the screen and then stealing looks at me. This happened maybe five times before I huffed out, "Can I help you?"

"Oh, no, I'm sorry," she muttered. When her phone dinged again, she turned it over, but not before I saw what she'd been staring at. A WDB chat room.

Annoyed, I said, "If you want to ask me something, just do it."

She shrank back, and I immediately felt bad. I knew I shouldn't be taking my frustration with the day out on her. "Oh, I don't . . . I mean, why didn't you say yes?"

"What?" I was surprised. It was the first time someone had asked me that. So far, everyone was just so interested in pointing and laughing at my expense. No one had even wanted to know how I was feeling.

"I just, I can't believe you didn't say yes. I'd die if someone from WDB asked me out."

"It's not like that," I murmured.

Karla leaned in, her eyes wide and curious. "What's it like?"

"Robbie wasn't asking me out like on a date. It was just a silly promise we'd made once when we were kids."

"That's so cool." Karla sighed. "So, you're going to go with him?"

"No," I said.

Karla looked genuinely confused. "Why not?"

"Because I'm standing for a cause with the alterna-prom initiative," I started to say.

"Oh yeah, I forgot," Karla said with an awkward frown. The kind of look I so often got whenever I started talking about the community center. Karla's phone dinged again, but this time Mr. Taylor was walking by.

"You know the class rules," he said, picking up the phone. "You can get it back after class."

Karla sighed and slumped low in her chair.

"What are they saying?" I asked, unable to help myself.

"You don't wanna know," she said in a distracted voice as she watched Mr. Taylor place her phone in his desk drawer.

When school finally let out, I practically ran across the parking lot to Josie's car. Josie wasn't there, so I leaned against it to wait.

A few other juniors walked by, whispering and giggling when they spotted me.

I wasn't in the mood for any other jokes or teasing at my expense, so I pretended that I'd dropped something as an excuse to crouch out of sight beside Josie's passenger door.

I pulled out my phone to text her, then opened the browser app.

Don't do it, Elena, I told myself. *Nothing good can come from reading any articles or comments. You're smarter than this.*

But Karla's comment in Chemistry had been stuck in my brain. She obviously meant that WDB's fans had found the promposal. How could they not? Robbie and WDB were tagged in half of the videos. Were they mad at me for rejecting Robbie? Maybe they understood that it had been absolutely mortifying. I really shouldn't look at all. But I couldn't stop myself and searched: *"Robbie Choi promposal."*

A dozen posts came up. And I scrolled through. Holy crap. There was a hashtag.

And memes. A still of me crashing into Felicity and flowers exploding around us. And then a second shot of Felicity on the ground with petals falling around her and captions like "Gives new meaning to 'flower power'" or "That feeling when your future barrels into you full force."

And Karla had been right. Because there were also a bunch of comments by Constellations. The comments were written in so many languages that I couldn't understand half of them, but of the English ones, I could see that most of them were not happy with me:

Who tf is this girl?

OMG, did she reject Robbie-oppa!

Where does this b*tch live?!

No! Robbie is mine!

I swiped to close the window. I wished the motion could delete the comments too. Could you get internet in a cave? Because that's where I'd have to move to get away from all this. It would be a simple life, but I'd learn how to forage for my own food and how to fish.

"Elena?"

I practically jumped, but because I was crouched so low, I just lost my balance and tipped into Josie's car.

"What are you doing?" Ethan asked, stepping closer. He was so tall that someone was sure to see him talking to an empty car.

"Shhh!" I said, pulling at his jeans so he was forced to crouch down too. "What does it look like I'm doing?"

"Did you drop something?" he asked, glancing around.

"No, I'm hiding," I said. "Because my embarrassment has been plastered all over the internet for the whole world to see."

Ethan laughed, and the sound grated on my nerves. "It's not that bad. It's just a promposal. People will forget it as soon as the next one happens."

"Yeah, if the next one is done by Tom Holland."

"I'm actually really impressed," Ethan said. "Robbie went all out. You gotta give him credit for that, right?"

I gave Ethan my hardest, most unamused glare, and the smile fell from his face.

"Come on. Lighten up. Promposals are supposed to be fun."

"Yeah, it's fun when you *want* one."

"Why couldn't you just have said yes to the guy and told him later you didn't want to go?" Ethan asked.

"Because I am the *head* of the alterna-prom initiative! Think about what that would have done for our credibility!"

"I really don't get why you're anti-prom."

I'm not *anti-prom.* I felt like pulling out my hair in frustration.

"You wouldn't get it," I said, finally standing up. My legs had started to tingle from being crouched so long, and I hit my fists against my thighs to get rid of the pinpricks running through them.

"I guess not," Ethan said. "But I'm sure everything will be fine. Tomorrow's Friday, and then it's the weekend. Everything will blow over."

I could tell Ethan was trying to comfort me, which I would normally love. But he was just doing such a bad job at it, and I knew that anything I said would just make *him* feel bad. And if Mom found out I upset Ethan, there'd be hell to pay. So I just stood there and stared at him.

"Sorry I'm late!" Josie called, running up to us.

"It's fine. Let's just go," I said, waiting impatiently for Josie to unlock the car.

"I guess I'll see you later," Ethan said, his face tight, and I knew I'd upset him anyway.

Great, dinner was going to be an awful passive-aggressive cherry on top of the disaster sundae that was my day.

"Yeah, see you," I said, shutting the door between us.

I really needed today to be over.

TWELVE

By the next day, I wished people could go back to just thinking of me as Ethan's loser twin. I was tired of kids asking me about Robbie. Asking me about prom stuff. Asking me anything.

I'd successfully avoided anything internet or social media related, though Josie had now taken to sending me GIFs of Felicity falling on her butt. Speaking of Felicity, she'd come to school today. Caroline had loudly praised her in the middle of the courtyard, saying she was "brave" for coming back to school so quickly. As if she'd been attacked by a rabid animal. But I knew why she'd come. If she didn't attend classes during the day, she wouldn't be allowed to cheer at tonight's game. It was a rule.

After school, I wanted nothing more than to go home, but I couldn't. I'd promised Jackson a new book for his birthday, and I wanted to bring it with me tonight when I went to the community center. So I sucked it up and went to the mall.

I'd just parked when I got a text from Mom. She never texted me unless she wanted me to pick something up for her or she wanted to yell at me.

> **MOM:** Where are you?
> **ELENA:** The mall.
> **MOM:** Will you be there awhile?
> **ELENA:** I'm just buying a book. Do you need me to pick up something?

I waited for her to reply, but she didn't. I told myself maybe she wanted to make sure I was being safe. It meant she cared, right?

I was not a leisurely shopper on a normal day. I know there are some people who like to wander the stores or aisles. To see what's new and might pique their interest. Not me. I just got what was on my list and got out of there. Which was why the mall was not my idea of a good time.

But what made this all so much worse was it was a month before prom, which meant lots of kids from my school were there shopping for dresses or makeup or shoes. If I ran into them, they might bring up the awful promposal.

I was stressed out just thinking about it.

I made a beeline for the bookstore. It was pretty much the only reason I ever came to the mall, since it was the sole bookstore in town. I'd just entered the store when a group of three girls blocked my path. I started to go around them, but one of them shifted to block me again.

"Do you need something?" I asked. *Like a lesson in manners?*

"You're that girl, aren't you?" one of them asked.

"You'll have to be more specific," I said, a sinking feeling in the pit of my stomach. I didn't recognize her from any of my classes, but that didn't mean she wasn't a freshman or sophomore.

"You're the one who turned down Robbie-oppa."

Oh crap. I was not in the mood for this right now. "Listen." I thought I could just explain things reasonably. But the girl shoved me. It wasn't a light push; it was a hard, rude shove.

"You don't *deserve* Robbie-oppa!" she said.

"I don't *want* him," I finally said.

"Why?" the girl's friend asked, stepping forward. "You think you're too good for him?"

This was ridiculous. First they *didn't* want me to be with Robbie and now they did? Could they make up their minds?

"Hey!" Karla jogged up, and I stared at her. Was she a part of this? "You guys, come on. I know her. She's okay."

Finally, someone who made sense.

"But she embarrassed Robbie in front of the whole world!" the first girl insisted, glaring at me. I couldn't decide if I wanted to avoid her gaze or glare back.

"It's not worth it," Karla said. I wasn't sure if she was putting on an act or really thought I was worthless, but I honestly didn't care at this point. She could call me a pile of mud if it would get these people off my back.

"Fine, whatever," the first girl said. "Let's go to the stationery store."

I escaped into the tall bookshelves and went straight to the children's section. I was pretty sure I wouldn't run into any wayward Robbie fans back here, unless he reached demographics younger than seven. Actually, I couldn't really be certain he didn't.

Instead of perusing the books, I just flopped onto the floor and let my face fall into my shaky hands. I'd never been in a situation like that. Was this a case of "Be careful what you wish for"? I'd spent half my life wishing

I wasn't always in the shadow of others. But now people knew me for all the wrong reasons. I hadn't known what to do or say to those girls. Thinking back, I wished I'd told them that my personal life was none of their business. But I'd just seized up, wanting to avoid any kind of confrontation.

I had to snap out of it. I couldn't let a few horrible people ruin the rest of my day. I'd given way too much of my week to this situation. It was time to put it behind me.

I was waiting in line with Jackson's book when I noticed a person loitering by the registers. He stood out because he had on a baseball cap worn low. The hood of his sweatshirt was pulled over it. And he wore sunglasses even though we were inside.

I glanced around, searching for mall security, but no one seemed that worried about a weirdo obviously trying to hide his face. And Josie always did say I overthought things too much. The last thing I needed was someone to record me freaking out to a security guard and post it on the internet. I told myself to stop being paranoid. I was just on edge after that confrontation with those girls. I would pay for my book and mind my own business. I lowered my head, refusing to look at the person who obviously wasn't here to buy books.

After paying, I heard steps behind me. Not the normal mall-traffic kind of steps. These were weirdly matching mine. Like the exact pace I was walking. And when I sped up, so did they. I chanced a look behind me, and Hoodie Guy was definitely speed-walking after me.

Holy crap, I should have trusted my instincts! Was this another WDB superfan? Were they following me because they were going to try to do something to me?

A part of me thought maybe I should just scream. Or would that make him angry? If he had a weapon, would he just lash out? I had taken that kickboxing class once when Mom dragged me to the gym with her for a month. No, that wouldn't work. All we'd done was punch and kick sand-bags, and I missed the bag half the time.

I decided it was best to make a run for it and headed toward the elevators. But before the doors could ding open, someone grabbed my arm.

"I know kickboxing!" I screeched, lifting my fists in front of my face.

"What?" The voice sounded eerily familiar. "No, Elena, it's me." He pulled off his sunglasses and hat to reveal the face of Robbie Choi.

"What the hell were you thinking?" I said, punching his arm to release some of the adrenaline still coursing through me. "You don't chase some-one through the mall dressed like you're about to hold up a bank!"

"What? No, I didn't mean to do that. I tried to signal you, but you wouldn't look at me."

"Yeah, because you look like a total weirdo."

He bit his bottom lip in a gesture I recognized. Robbie used to do that all the time when he was nervous. "I didn't want anyone to recognize me."

"Well, goal accomplished," I said, making my voice harder as I pushed away the tingle of nostalgia. "You look absolutely ridiculous."

"Yeah, I feel ridiculous every time I wear this getup," he said, and I couldn't help but feel kind of bad for him. He sounded so frustrated.

"How did you know where I was?"

"I went by your house, and your mom told me you were at the mall."

"She just told you?" That must have been what the weird text was about. I guess it was wishful thinking to hope my mom randomly cared where I was.

A group of kids walked by as the elevator arrived, and Robbie hunched his shoulders, lowering his chin. He pulled me into the elevator quickly, jabbing the CLOSE DOOR button.

"What are you doing? Where are we going?" I asked, noticing he hadn't pressed a floor.

"Nowhere."

"What?"

"Maybe I just wanted to 'elevate' the conversation." He gave me a sly grin.

I groaned. "You don't still do those awful puns, do you?"

"Are you trying to say you never liked them?" Robbie frowned in such an exaggerated fashion that it made his lip stick out in a pout.

I almost cracked a smile back, when I remembered I was angry at him.

"You didn't answer my question." I pointed to the elevator buttons.

His face fell, and he sighed. "I just wanted to avoid the crowds. I can't risk being recognized."

I pursed my lips. "If you want to avoid crowds, then why did you come to a mall?"

"Because you're here." Did it look like he was blushing? Or was it just the shadows from the fluorescent mall lights? "I wanted to talk to you about yesterday."

My heart lodged uncomfortably in my throat. I didn't want to talk about yesterday. I didn't want to think about yesterday. If I could find a machine that would completely erase yesterday from the timeline, I would. And then Robbie had to go and make it all worse by asking, "What was your deal?"

"My deal?" I repeated incredulously. Was he really blaming it on me? "*You* showed up at *my* school and made a spectacle in front of half my classmates. I don't know what kind of publicity stunt this is all for, but can you just find another girl to be your unsuspecting leading lady?"

The muscle in his jaw ticced. "You think this is about publicity?"

He sounded so upset, I almost automatically blurted out an apology, but Josie's voice echoed in my head: *Stop apologizing all the time.* I thought of the viral video and how all the negative comments were about me, while everyone sympathized with Robbie as the "poor victim" of my evil, conniving ways. I crossed my arms and asked, "If it's not for publicity, then why did you come to my house with a camera?"

"Well—" Robbie began, then stopped with a frown.

"Exactly." I nodded at his lack of comeback. "The last two days you put me in two really nerve-racking situations for no reason."

"Nerve-racking?" Robbie's brow lifted, as if intrigued. "Like you're nervous around me?"

Was he being serious? "Nervous around *you*?"

"Yeah." Robbie looked like he was musing over this theory and found it pleasing. "I mean, I get it. When I first debuted, I was around so many big stars that I never knew what to say. But you don't have to be weird around me. I'm still the same old Robbie."

"No, you're not," I said before I could stop myself.

His mouth dropped open. "What?"

I shook my head. "The old Robbie wouldn't put on this ridiculous celebrity persona in front of me because he'd know I don't like when people put on an act."

"Fine," Robbie said. "Maybe I have changed, but so have you with this whole prom thing."

"Changed because I don't want to go to a ridiculous dance?" I wanted to laugh in disbelief.

"No, because when you were younger, you were all about keeping promises. I once wanted to break a pinkie promise I'd made to a *stuffed animal*, and you spent twenty minutes lecturing me about honesty and loyalty."

I was frozen in shock.

And I hated that he'd succeeded in making me feel guilty. Like I was breaking some kind of sacred pact and not a silly promise I'd made when I was ten. But he wasn't wrong—promises had been a big deal to me when

I was younger. Esther had always said that if you made one you kept it. Period. And I'd taken that to heart.

But what about when the person you were when you made the promise wasn't the same as the person you were now?

"Look, it's not like I set out to embarrass you yesterday," Robbie said.

I just shrugged, and maybe it was me being defensive, or maybe I just wanted to be petty, but I said, "Well, you win some, you lose some, right?"

At least he had the good judgment to wince. "You saw that?"

"Half my school saw it," I muttered.

"I'm sorry," Robbie said. "JD caught me in a bad moment."

"Whatever, it's just an Instastory. It's gone by now." I jerked my shoulders.

"Lani—" Robbie began, and hearing the nickname made my chest tighten. It was too confusing hearing him say that name right now. It had once meant so much between us, but I didn't recognize the guy using it anymore.

"I said it's fine. I don't want to talk about it anymore," I said quickly. This topic was making my stomach ache.

"Come on, I can tell you're mad at me."

I wanted to roll my eyes; *now* he could suddenly read me so well? What about when he embarrassed me on camera two times in as many days?

"Tell me how to make it up to you," Robbie said, tilting his head with a shy smile. It was a patented look to make hearts melt. So I purposely steeled mine against him. I wouldn't be another girl who fell at his idol feet. "I'll do anything." His smile widened, as if trying to coax a matching one from me.

I forced my lips into a scowl. "You can leave me alone."

"Anything but that." Then his eyes lit up, his grin turning sly, like it used to when he had a brainstorm. "What about a wish?"

"What?"

"Come on, you haven't forgotten, have you? I'll give you a wish, whatever you want. But you have to forgive me when I grant it." He lifted his brow in a silent question, as if daring me to accept.

Why did he insist on bringing up all these things from our childhood? Things that I'd rather keep stored away where he couldn't mar them with his slick idol hands. "You really think a random wish will help?"

He nodded thoughtfully. "Fine, two wishes."

I couldn't help but be intrigued. But I forced myself to scoff and try to push the DOOR OPEN button to escape.

He shifted to block my way. "Three! Final offer! Three wishes, whatever you want."

Three wishes? It could take time to finish three wishes, especially since it would take me some time to think of them. Did that mean Robbie was planning to stay in the area for a while? "Whatever I want?" I asked.

His brow furrowed as if he was realizing how much power he was granting me. "Within reason." He held out a hand. "Call?"

I cracked a smile at the Korean term for making a deal. "Call." I accepted the shake.

He smiled, and it was sweet and sort of self-deprecating. My pulse jumped. It's not like I hadn't seen him smile before. But this smile wasn't one of those photo-shoot perfect grins, but soft and wry and almost like the Robbie I remembered from seven years ago.

He put a hand on my shoulder. And I went still as a strange tingling sensation raced along my arms. Why was I reacting like this? "I really am sorry," he said. "If I had it to do again, I'd do it differently."

"What?" I breathed. I couldn't stop focusing on his hand on my shoulder. It was making my skin feel too hot.

"I wouldn't have come to your house with a camera or put on a show at your school. I'd have asked you to meet me on your mom's old swing bench. Does she still have it?"

"Yes," I said. I couldn't think of anything more to say.

Robbie lowered his eyes; he was definitely blushing now. "I'd have really asked you instead of assuming anything. And I'd have apologized for not calling you by singing that song we wrote together when we were nine. Remember?"

"What?" I said again, because apparently I could only speak in single-syllable answers.

Then Robbie started to hum. And I did remember. We'd written it on his old piano and even recorded it on his mom's phone as an MP3 to gift to our parents. It didn't have any lyrics because we kept fighting about whether it was a love song or a dance track. It was neither, but we were only nine.

"You can't *sing* a song that has no lyrics," I pointed out.

"Then I'd write some," he said. "I am a musician, after all."

"Do you still write songs?" I asked, latching on to any topic, trying to veer the conversation somewhere neutral.

"I dabble," he said.

It was a strangely noncommittal answer, and there was an odd look in his eyes for a second before it disappeared. Curiosity filled me, and I wanted to prod for more information, but I never got the chance, as the elevator doors opened again. I recognized Karla Hernandez's voice before I saw her face.

I know it sounds clichéd to say everything slowed down, but I swear it did.

I could see Robbie start to turn, like he wondered who had just gotten onto the elevator. If he kept turning, Karla would see his completely undisguised face. I only had a second to react. I pulled him forward so he'd be hidden in the corner, lifting his hoodie in the process to cover his hair. That's all I was thinking about, hiding his face so Karla couldn't recognize him and start a mob. But of course, I didn't think about how pulling him into the corner meant pulling him into *me*.

Before either of us could move, someone rolled in a giant dolly with wide boxes and caused everyone to squeeze to the sides.

Someone bumped into Robbie, and he fell forward, reaching out to stop himself before he crushed me. I was plastered into the corner, his cheek now practically against mine, my hands still wrapped around his neck. I wanted to pull them away, but doing so would elbow him in the chest. So I just stood there, my fingers gripping the fabric of his hoodie. He smelled like my mom's fresh-linen-scented candles with a hint of something earthy, like these green tea-fields I'd visited with my family in Korea.

I felt him say, "Ummm," as he started to pull back, but I tightened my arms around his neck.

"Be careful," I whispered in his ear. "They're fans." I hoped he'd understand what I meant. And it seemed he did when I felt his small nod as he kept his face pressed into my shoulder.

His arms caged me in, the cap he held pressing against me. I decided to just concentrate on that, the feel of the hat, its brim jabbing into my arm. That way I wouldn't think about how Robbie was pressed against me. About how soft his skin was against mine. How I could feel his breath on my neck.

"Ugh, some people are so gross," I heard Karla's friend say, and it took me a second to realize she was talking about us. Because it looked like we were . . . No, I couldn't think like that. I was just trying to protect Robbie. Like I used to when we were ten. This was nothing. We'd been closer when we used to hug each other goodbye. Or that one time I tackled Robbie because he wouldn't give me back my iPad. Except my heart didn't beat this fast when nine-year-old Elena had jumped on nine-year-old Robbie. My brain didn't get this fuzzy when I held him to the ground. And I didn't feel strange tingles all over when I wrestled the iPad from his hands.

The elevator finally stopped, and everyone else filed off.

Robbie pulled back just a couple inches so his face wasn't pressed against mine anymore. This was somehow worse, being able to look him in the eyes. They were the same ones I remembered, except there was an odd glint in them that I'd never seen before. Questioning and intense. It made shivers race down my arms until goose bumps rose.

Then the elevator jerked as it began to move again, and the spell was broken.

Robbie took a step back, and I was left pressed into the corner of the elevator.

"I know them," I explained quickly, a flush rising up my cheeks. "They're huge fans. So I was sure they'd recognize you, and you said you didn't want that."

"Oh yeah, I mean, that makes sense." Robbie's voice sounded thick, and he coughed into his sleeve.

"I just . . . I wasn't sure if you thought I was actually trying to—"

"Oh, no!" Robbie said, shaking his head so hard that he looked like a human bobblehead. "I would never think you'd do that. Not that you can't. I mean, I assume you have with other . . . I mean . . . I don't know what I mean."

I nodded, trying to think of a way to brush off the awkwardness that made my skin feel too tight. "It's no big deal, right? It's not like we haven't done that before." *Oh my god, why did I just say that?*

"What?" Robbie asked, his eyes widening.

"Nothing," I said quickly, silently cursing myself. "You probably don't remember. I hardly do. I mean, I obviously remember, or I wouldn't have brought it up. I don't even know why I brought it up." I was rambling. And the more I said, the worse I was making it. I couldn't look at him. I knew that if I did he'd be staring at me like I was a total weirdo.

"I remember," Robbie said, and I finally looked up.

He *was* staring at me, but not with disgust or annoyance. He was looking at me so seriously it made me self-conscious. What was he thinking? It was killing me not knowing.

The elevator stopped again with a ding, and I practically jumped out, scaring two middle-aged women waiting to get on. I muttered an apology, but I had to get out of the elevator. It felt too small all of a sudden.

Robbie had put on his hat and sunglasses again. Back to being the aloof idol. "I should call my manager."

My stomach dropped. Was he really in a rush to leave?

No, that shouldn't matter to me. Every time I saw Robbie, things got so confusing and complicated and I ended up in a situation tailor-made to make me look ridiculous. It would be better if he just left.

As he moved off to make his call, I wasn't sure what to do. It felt rude to just leave while he was on the phone. I should at least wait until I could say a proper goodbye, I told myself.

But as I hesitated, I spied Caroline and Felicity walking toward the exit holding iced coffees topped with whipped cream. I prayed they'd just walk by. I reasoned with the universe that I had dealt with enough crap the last couple of days. But the universe apparently didn't care, because Caroline zeroed in on me.

"Here to stop wasteful prom-goers from spending any money at the evil mall?" Caroline asked with a laugh.

I gritted my teeth and considered pretending I couldn't even hear her.

"Really? You're just going to ignore me?" Caroline scoffed.

"Caro, I'm bored," Felicity said dismissively, taking a sip from her drink. "Can we go? We're going to be late to warm-ups."

She didn't even look at me, and more than Caroline's rude remarks, Felicity acting like she could see right through me pricked at my pride. That's probably why I said, "If I'm such a nobody, why do you care so much what I do? Why can't you just leave me alone?"

Caroline took a step forward, and it took all of my courage not to retreat as she shoved her pretty face into mine. "You're right, why do I care about a loser like you? As least there's one good thing about your little anti-prom protest. You won't ruin my night by actually coming to prom yourself."

I clenched my fists, my cheeks heating with embarrassment. My eyes flicked to Felicity, who was staring at her phone, tapping her foot impatiently.

Caroline stood there, her eyes shooting daggers into mine for three breathless seconds before she turned so sharply her ponytail whipped my cheek. It was more insulting than if she'd slapped me. I blinked furiously as I felt hot tears threaten. And without a backward glance, Felicity and Caroline pushed out of the exit.

I turned to swipe at my damp eyes and saw Robbie watching from only a few feet away. I couldn't see his eyes behind his sunglasses, but he was too close not to have heard what Caroline had said.

I avoided his gaze and dug my nails into my palms, focusing on that pain instead of the mortification I felt at knowing he'd witnessed that.

It was bad enough that I was faced with an ex–best friend who'd accomplished as much as Robbie had. Now he knew that once he'd left me, I'd become less than a nobody. It was so embarrassing I could die.

"Elena."

"Don't," I said before he could continue. I could already hear the pity in his voice. "It doesn't matter."

"Of course it matters," he said, his voice low like he was trying to soothe a wounded animal. "They shouldn't have—"

"I said don't," I bit out, and he finally stopped. "I should get going."

"Wait." He reached out as if to grab me, and I gave him a glare that made him drop his hand. "You shouldn't drive when you're like this. It's probably unsafe or something."

I scowled in confusion as part of me felt pleased at his concern even as I still couldn't meet his eyes. "I'm fine," I muttered, though my voice sounded too tight.

"Is she why you don't want to go to prom?" Robbie asked.

Some of the pressure in my chest lessened as I barked out a laugh. "Caroline? No. She's a jerk, but she's not the reason."

"Then what is?" he asked.

Before I could reply, his phone lit up and I recognized the Korean characters for "manager." He started to answer it and I grabbed his wrist. I realized that I didn't want him to leave with this awful image of me as a prom-hating social pariah. I said slowly, "Do you really want to know?"

"Yeah." He nodded as his phone stopped ringing.

"Do you think your manager will let you go somewhere with me?" I asked.

"Right now?" He frowned.

"Yeah, right now. It'll be one of my wishes," I said, watching him expectantly.

He smiled, a soft, kind smile, and this time I let myself smile back.

THIRTEEN

The night I got my first kiss was also one of my top five saddest nights.

I was ten, and it was summer break. I was helping Sarah wash the dishes after dinner. She scrubbed and rinsed, and I dried. Mom never used the dishwasher unless it was after a dinner party or Christmas.

Robbie called just as I was finishing. He asked me if I could meet him at the swing bench, and Sarah said she'd cover for me. I ran outside; it was warm and humid, and felt like rain was coming.

There was a strange electricity in the air, and it made me giddy as I ran toward Robbie.

He was already waiting for me on the bench, pushing off with his feet so it swung gently.

"What's up?" I asked, plopping next to him and pushing off harder. He grabbed the chain to keep from falling, and I laughed at his surprise.

"I have something to tell you," he said. For some reason, he wouldn't look at me. And I felt a strange pit in my stomach, like when Mom and Dad sat us down to tell us Harabeoji was sick.

"Are your parents okay?" I asked.

"Yeah, they're fine."

"Then what's up?" If everyone was okay, we could figure things out.

"We're going to Seoul," he said.

I pushed off the ground again, wondering how high we could go. "Okay, well, I'll see you when you get back."

He dragged his feet against the ground to stop the swing and finally looked at me and there were tears in his eyes. "That's the thing. We're not coming back."

I didn't process it at first. It just didn't make sense.

"But what about school?" I asked, even as it started to dawn on me. Robbie wasn't going on summer vacation. He was moving. To Seoul. Halfway across the world. My best friend was leaving like Esther and Allie had left.

"Is it for sure?" I asked, my voice breaking on the question.

"Yeah, Appa said that he only came here to help Samchon with his business, and now that it's all set, he has a job offer back in Seoul. It's too good to pass up."

"Well, how come you and your mom have to go too?" I remembered the story about how Harabeoji had come to the US to work for a few years without Halmeoni and my dad and his sisters before sending for them.

"We're all going. And I don't know when I'll see you again." He sniffled and wiped his nose with his sleeve.

"But why?" I whispered.

He shook his head and made a sad choked sound, and I realized none of my questions were helping. I reached out to pull him close. His arms came around me, squeezing me so tight it was almost hard to breathe. But I didn't want him to let go.

"We'll text all the time," I said into his shoulder. "And call each other. And FaceTime."

"Sure," he said.

"We'll talk so much that it'll be like you never left."

"Yeah," he said, breaking the hug to pull back. I almost protested, but my arms were starting to ache from holding him so tight.

"I'm going to miss you so much, Lani," he whispered.

"I'm going to miss you too, Robbie. You're my best friend." My throat felt really tight, like it didn't want me to say the words.

Then Robbie leaned forward and pressed his lips to mine. It was quick. A peck, actually. And it tasted salty from our tears. But it was a real, true kiss.

My first kiss.

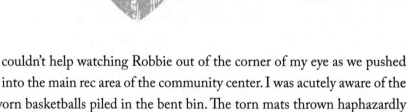

couldn't help watching Robbie out of the corner of my eye as we pushed into the main rec area of the community center. I was acutely aware of the worn basketballs piled in the bent bin. The torn mats thrown haphazardly in the corner. The walls that had scuff marks against the yellowed concrete blocks because the center couldn't even afford a fresh coat of paint. The scent of sweat and must that perpetually hung in the air. I'd never really noticed how worn down the space looked before, but now, with Robbie beside me, it was all I could focus on.

I led him past a group of kids playing four square. They paused and stared curiously at him. Robbie lowered his head a little as if worried about being recognized. Or was it because he was judging the space?

"What is this place?" he asked.

"It's my favorite place in the world," I said simply.

In the large playroom, there were kids playing loudly in the corner and the TV was blaring. A couple of them were arguing over a board game spread out on a secondhand rug designed to look like a roadway.

Jackson spotted us and raced over from the couch.

"Who are you?" he asked, staring up at Robbie.

"Oh, um, I'm Robbie." He looked a bit out of his element, and I almost smiled at his surprise.

"You have weird-colored hair," Jackson said.

I started to tell Jackson that it was rude to say things like that when Robbie laughed and ran his fingers through the aforementioned hair. "Yeah, I guess that's true."

Jackson smiled widely. "Come on! You're missing *Dragon Ball Z*!" He took Robbie's hand before grabbing mine. He pulled with all his four-year-old might. Robbie gave me a look that was half-confused, half-amused.

I shrugged. "You heard him. We're going to miss *Dragon Ball Z*."

The show was already playing on the giant secondhand plasma TV. It was one of those older models that was heavy as a brick and sometimes got the picture burned into it if you kept it paused too long.

Ethan and I used to watch *DBZ* episodes religiously when we were kids. Esther had gifted us her old DVDs, and we watched them over and over until Mom threatened to break them all if we didn't watch something else. And now I'd gifted them to Jackson and the community center.

"Oh, hey! You're here," Tia said, standing up from her place at the edge of the couch. She checked her watch, and I felt guilty about being late. I usually wasn't, but Robbie's manager had gotten lost twice on the way here. (That was a condition of Robbie coming here; he had to be escorted.)

"But, Mama, the best part!" Jackson shouted, jumping up and down and pointing a small finger at the screen.

"Baby, I know, but I have to go to work." She gave him a quick kiss on his pouting lips.

"Sorry I'm late," I said quickly.

"It's okay. I just want to try to get to work early this week since this promotion is on the line," Tia said, pulling her hair up in a tight ponytail, the rubber band clenched between her teeth.

"Don't worry," I said. "If you leave now you'll still be early."

"Yeah, probably." Then Tia's eyes traveled to Robbie, and she stopped fidgeting. "Um, Elena. Do you want to introduce me to your friend?"

I felt a flush climb up my neck. "This is Robbie. He was my . . ." How did I describe our relationship? "Neighbor when we were in elementary school."

Robbie lifted a brow at me, making me question my word choice. But he turned to Tia. "Nice to meet you."

"Same." Tia smiled, taking Robbie's offered hand. I waited, counting slowly to ten in my head as Tia's eyes widened as recognition lit in them. "Robbie," she said slowly. "Choi?"

I was shocked to see Robbie blush. "Guilty."

Tia's surprised eyes moved between me and Robbie, back and forth, like she had a thousand questions and she wasn't sure how to ask them.

"I thought you were going to be late," I reminded her.

"Oh yeah," Tia said, still staring at Robbie.

"Tia, you still want a ride?" Maria, another one of the West Pinebrook moms, stood in the doorway, keys swinging from her finger.

"Yeah, I'm coming," Tia said.

"Mama! *Dragon Ball Z*!" Jackson shouted again, tears pooling in his eyes.

"I'm sorry, baby, we talked about this. I have to go to work, but I'll be back right after." She gave him another kiss, this time on the forehead, but her eyes kept sliding back to Robbie. She gave me a hard stare, and I could practically read her thoughts: *We are going to talk later.*

"Tia, I don't want to be late!" Maria shouted.

"Coming," Tia said, giving me one final, pointed look.

"Mama!" Jackson called after her.

"It's okay, Jack-Jack," I said. "I'll watch *Dragon Ball Z* with you."

"But it's Mama's thing!" Jackson wailed.

I was scrambling for a way to distract him from his separation anxiety when Robbie spoke up. "Wow, your mom knows all about *Dragon Ball Z*?"

Jackson paused mid-sob. He blinked with tear-filled eyes at Robbie.

"You're so lucky," Robbie said with a smile that made his dimple flash. "My mom doesn't know anything about cool TV shows, so I didn't really get to watch. Can you tell me who this pink guy is?"

Jackson rubbed a hand over his tearstained cheeks. "Majin Buu," he sniffled.

"He looks like a big pink marshmallow man. Is he nice?" Robbie was looking only at Jackson. It was like he was creating a little safety bubble just for him and Jackson, and I couldn't help it—my heart softened. I tried to tell myself this was just his media training, but it didn't look like he was putting on an act as he waited patiently for Jackson to reply.

"No, he's evil. We don't like him," Jackson explained, turning toward the TV again, finally forgetting to be sad about missing his mom. "But that guy is Goku. He's the best and the bravest, and right now his hair is black, but when he gets more power it becomes yellow."

"Wow, cool. You know, I had yellow hair once," Robbie said.

Jackson let out a giggle and reached up to run his little fingers through the ends. Robbie bent down to give him easier access. "It's funny-looking," Jackson said in the unaffected way kids have. I started to interject, but Robbie replied with a smile.

"You don't like it?" Robbie lifted his hand to his hair. There was still a pink tinge to it, but it was almost completely faded now.

"It's okay," Jackson said with a mischievous grin.

"Really?" Robbie frowned in a comically exaggerated way, and I couldn't stop myself from smiling. "Well, what color do *you* think it should be?"

"Blue!" Jackson said.

"Blue's Jack-Jack's favorite color," I informed Robbie, who smiled. My breath caught. I'd known he was cute—of course he was—but there was a look in his eyes now. Like the warm caramel that my sisters used to make when it was fall so we could dip apples into it. And my insides turned into soft goo just like that caramel.

"Or you could do rainbow! Or polka dots!" Jackson declared, breaking the moment. And Robbie laughed as he focused on Jackson again.

"That's an interesting suggestion," Robbie declared.

"Hey! If you make the suggestion, then you have to be willing to do it yourself too!" I said, tickling Jackson until he wiggled out of my lap.

"You're good with him," I said to Robbie as Jackson ran across the room.

"He's fun," Robbie said. "I can see why you like this place."

"Really?" I asked, relieved. I hadn't admitted it to myself, but I'd been scared Robbie would be bored here.

"Yeah, I don't get to do stuff like this often. Just sit on the couch and talk about anime. Maybe we can go out later and try to scrounge up a game of pickup basketball?" He looked hopeful, like a kid asking to go outside and play.

I was a little surprised he was so excited to do such an everyday activity. I'd assumed being a celebrity meant being glamorous and jetting off on vacations and owning houses with private movie theaters. Wouldn't babysitting and basketball with elementary school kids sound boring to someone like that?

"So what does this place have to do with prom?" Robbie asked, looking around.

"The recession hit our main sponsor hard and they can't afford to support the center anymore. So, until we can convince the city to allocate more funds, we're trying to convince kids to donate money instead of spending it all on prom."

Robbie nodded. "That's great, Lani. Really."

I smiled, bolstered by his compliment. "Yeah, and—"

I was cut off when Jackson ran up to us again, trailing the rest of the younger kids.

"Come on! You're it!" Jackson shouted, pressing a hand to Robbie's arm and taking off again, the other kids squealing and darting in different directions.

Robbie looked at me with a lifted brow, and I shrugged, trying to hold in a laugh. "I guess you're it."

"Really?" His eyes tilted slyly.

"Wait!" I jumped out of his reach as he lunged, surprise causing my heart to race. Or at least that's the reason I told myself. "You have to give us a head start!"

"Nope! It's no-rules tag! And I'm going to get you!" Robbie said, leaping up from the couch. And with a laugh I darted away toward the hallway, where I could hear Jackson scream-laughing.

★☆★

I hadn't expected Robbie to fit in so easily with the chaos at the center. He played tag with the younger kids. And taught some of the older ones different games in the rec space. He didn't care about getting sweaty or when Jackson smeared peanut butter on his designer jeans. And the kids loved him.

At the end of the night, when Cora announced it was cleanup time, Jackson dragged Robbie with him to put away the Legos they'd taken out. But ten minutes later, I found them sitting among the still-scattered toys as Robbie read Jackson a book. I had to smile. That kid was a master at getting people to read to him. It was like his adorable superpower. Jackson was enthralled by the story, and Robbie was leaning down slightly so he could point out the different animals on each page.

I realized this was the first time I was watching Robbie when he didn't know he had an audience. Was this the real Robbie? A guy who laughed as he tried to help Jackson pronounce "hippopotamus"? This guy with a soft, patient smile and kind eyes was the one that I'd dreamed of going to prom with. Wait . . . I wasn't still thinking about prom. That was an open-and-shut case. There was no way I would be convinced to go. Except . . . hadn't I said the main reason I didn't want to go was because the only person I wanted to go with wasn't here? And now, it seemed, he was.

I started to step forward, when Jackson looked up at Robbie and asked, "Will you come back and play with me again?"

Robbie hesitated, and it stopped me in my tracks. Of course he'd say no. He had more important things to do than babysitting. And eventually those important things would take him away again. The door to my heart that had started to creak open slammed shut again. I should have remembered that this wasn't where Robbie belonged. And if I let myself open up to him again, go to prom with him, feel . . . whatever it was that I was starting to feel, then it would hurt all the more when he left.

"Please!" Jackson said, blinking up at Robbie like the cat in *Shrek*.

I stepped forward again, this time to intercede. "Jackson—"

But before I could continue, Robbie said, "I'll definitely try."

I could feel my chest tighten. Like Robbie had been talking to me instead of Jackson. Why was this somehow worse than hearing him say no? Like how it felt whenever my dad said "We'll see." The pain of still wanting to hope when you knew it was useless.

"Promise!" Jackson said. "Pinkie promise you'll try."

I started to shake my head. A pinkie promise was sacred to a four-year-old. But Robbie reached out with his pinkie. And Jackson linked it with his.

Then Robbie said, "Seal it!" And pressed his thumb to Jackson's.

"Stamp it." They slid palms.

"And post it!" They both slapped their hands to their foreheads.

"Hey, how did you know that?" Jackson asked. "That's Elena's thing!"

"Who do you think taught her?" Robbie asked with a wide smile as he looked up at me and winked. And my already confused and strained heart thudded against my ribs. I made myself smile back. "Okay, time to actually clean up now."

Jackson gave a resigned sigh that belonged to someone ten times his age. But he dutifully threw Legos back into the bin. With the three of us working, it didn't take long, and soon I heard Tia's voice calling down the hallway.

"Mama!" Jackson flew up into his mom's arms.

She let out a laugh, burying her face in his neck as she scooped him up. "Did you have fun?" she asked.

"Elena and Robbie taught me how to play H-O-R-S-E!"

"Did they?" Tia's eyes tracked over to us, looking pointedly at me and Robbie.

"Robbie, didn't you say you had to go?" I said, pulling at his arm so he stood with me.

"What?" He looked between me and Tia in confusion, obviously picking up on our silent signals.

"Yeah, you were saying your manager was getting impatient." I practically pushed him past Tia's hawklike stare, avoiding eye contact and any accompanying questions. I knew it was the coward's way out, and that she would bombard me with questions next week, but I just couldn't handle them right now. Maybe because I had no idea what any of the answers would be with how twisted my thoughts were tonight.

I pulled Robbie down the hall toward the side exit, hoping to also avoid Cora. For the first time, I wasn't in the mood to linger in the community center.

"Hey, everything okay?" Robbie asked as I pulled open the door.

"Yeah, I just don't want you to get in trouble with your manager," I said, ushering him out into the community center's garden. It was surrounded by a large picket fence for security and privacy, and was a bit neglected, especially after Mrs. Lewis's departure. I made a mental note to bring some kids out here next week to do the weeding.

"If I gave you the impression I had to leave, I didn't mean to," Robbie said, hesitating by the door.

"Oh?" I said, wondering why he'd say that. Did he want to stay longer? With me? "Then do you want a tour of the garden?"

"Sure."

It wasn't really big enough to require a tour. But maybe he was using it as an excuse not to end the night. The thought of it sent a small thrill racing up my spine. I knew it was silly, like when Sarah and her boyfriends would linger on the phone, even though no one was saying anything. But was it so bad that I just wanted ten more minutes with this version of him? I guess I was scared that tomorrow he'd go back to being cocky celebrity Robbie.

"This is where the kids plant vegetables. We don't get much of anything out of it, but they get really excited when they see a tomato sprout or a pepper." I pointed out each plant as I spoke. "And then Tia and Anna, one of the other moms, planted some flowers in the corner. The roses look really beautiful when they bloom." I walked along the path of large flat stones to that section, pointing at dormant, thorny bushes.

"So, how'd you start volunteering here?"

"All freshmen have to do a volunteer project for Civics class," I explained.

"And you chose the center because it would look good on college applications," Robbie finished for me.

I frowned; when he said it that way, it sounded so calculated. "Why would you say that?"

"Because it's how you always were, even when we were kids. Planning ten steps ahead."

I sighed. "Yeah, because when you plan, you can—"

"Anticipate any problems," Robbie finished for me again. And I glared at him. Had he been this annoying when we were younger?

"Oh, come on, I always liked how you planned everything. It meant I didn't have to worry," Robbie said, bumping me with his shoulder.

"Well, it's not like I could anticipate everything. You still moved away," I muttered.

Robbie's brow furrowed. "I really did miss you, Lani."

My throat suddenly felt blocked and I coughed a bit to clear it. "Anyway, yeah, this is where I spend a lot of my time. And it's why my friend and I started the alterna-prom initiative."

"It's a great place. And you're doing something great trying to support it. Even if the other kids can't see it. . . ." He trailed off, and I knew he was thinking about what happened at the mall.

"The other kids are just really attached to the idea of prom," I said.

Robbie shook his head. "You don't have to explain anything."

"I just don't want you to think that I'm an anti-prom loser," I explained. "I know I haven't accomplished as much as you, but I'm working on it."

Robbie frowned. "Elena, this isn't a competition about who's done more since we were kids."

I scowled. That was easy for him to say, since he was winning.

"Anyway," I said quickly before he could try to placate me more. "Thanks for coming here with me. You were pretty good with the kids. Do they teach you how to entertain kids as a trainee?"

Robbie nodded, seeming to take the hint that I was changing the subject. "We're taught how to talk to fans of all ages," he said. "But I've always liked kids. I have a couple of younger cousins in Seoul. Today reminded me how much I miss them. I don't really see them that much these days, though."

"Really? Not even on, like, weekends?"

Robbie laughed. "Idols don't get weekends off. Especially not in the beginning. Maybe it was different for us because Bright Star was such a new company. But we did a lot of our own guerrilla marketing. Doing pop-up shows in Hongdae or Myeongdong. Or doing small appearances on radio shows. And Bright Star sent us abroad a lot, so with all the travel, it was just hard to find free time in the schedule for the first year. And then, when we thought maybe things would slow down a bit, we were invited to the MTV Video Music Awards and things just kind of . . . exploded."

I remembered that. It was in the beginning of sophomore year. The Korean-salon ladies were very excited about the idea of Robbie showing up on American television. Once you're a part of our community, you're always a part of our community. So the Korean ladies in our town always talked about Robbie like they'd all raised him together. It was a Korean solidarity thing that Ethan and I always laughed about. But secretly, it felt nice whenever they talked about something good we did. It was like validation from the unofficial Korean lady council. And whenever we impressed them, Mom was always in a good mood.

"Is that why—" I broke off, already too embarrassed to finish the question.

"What?" Robbie watched me curiously.

"Is that why you stopped calling me?" I asked, telling myself not to hope for an easy answer even as I held on to the possibility. "When you changed your number I thought . . . that maybe you thought once you debuted you were too good—"

"Oh, no," he said, reaching out to take my hands, squeezing them. "That's not it at all! I swear! When you're about to debut, you have to give up your old personal phone. We're not allowed to have phones as rookies. So my mom just stopped paying for mine, and the number was disconnected."

"Yeah, I guess that makes sense," I said. "I mean, I knew you were busy. It's not like I didn't hear about all the cool things you've been doing. *Late Night. SNL.* And you met Randall Park and Steven Yeun!" Another very Korean thing, latching on to the few Korean American celebrities. My mom even cried when Sandra Oh spoke Korean during her Emmy acceptance speech.

We both realized at the same time that Robbie still loosely held my hands, and he let go of them awkwardly, letting his swing back to his sides. I shoved mine into my pockets, like out of sight out of mind.

"Yeah, it's cool." Robbie smiled sheepishly and rubbed a hand over the back of his neck. God, why did he have to look like the sweet hero straight out of a K-drama? It made it hard for me to concentrate. "I honestly couldn't say two words when we met Beyoncé at the AMAs. But it also gets kind of . . . exhausting." He frowned. "I know I shouldn't say that. It sounds so ungrateful. But sometimes I wish I could just have one week where I didn't have to do anything."

One week? That's all he wanted? It sounded so sad to me.

"If you're so busy—" I started to ask, then stopped myself.

"What?"

I tried to shake my head. To say that it wasn't important. But Robbie leaned in. "Go ahead, you can ask me anything."

This close, I could see gold flecks in his eyes. I remembered thinking it was so unfair that he had such beautiful eyes when mine were such an ugly mud-brown color. Had they always been this mesmerizing, though? I couldn't seem to look away from them.

And he smelled so good. Fresh and earthy. It was oddly alluring.

But that's the thing. Robbie was supposed to be alluring. He was supposed to attract you. It was his brand. He was a person with a brand. I was just a person who had no idea what she was doing half the time.

"Elena?" Robbie said, and I realized I'd been staring at his throat, like some kind of starving vampire.

"Oh, I was just—" I stuttered. What was I just doing? Other than being horrifyingly embarrassing. I stepped toward a batch of blooming flowers in the corner. I stopped like I was studying a purple tulip so I wouldn't have to look at Robbie when I said, "I guess I was just wondering, if you're so busy that you can't even see your family, how would you even go to prom?"

Robbie rubbed the petals of a pink tulip between his fingers. "Hanbin-hyeong owes me. He said he could pull some strings, since we're already in the Chicago area for KFest."

"Why would you waste a favor on something as silly as prom?"

"Because we promised each other we'd go. Because it's what we wanted when we were ten and . . ." Robbie trailed off, and I felt like maybe I was wrong for pressing. "I don't know, I guess when we were ten was the last time things felt good and simple. Things got so complicated when I moved to Seoul, when my appa—" His voice broke on the word, and he fell silent. He didn't finish the sentence, but I knew how it ended. When his appa died. A car crash.

Now I felt awful. Not only had I pushed things, but I'd pushed them in a direction that made Robbie think of his dad. "I'm sorry," I said. "I didn't mean to make you talk about these things."

"It's okay," Robbie said.

I wanted to wrap him in a hug. But I wasn't sure if he'd be okay with that. I never used to second-guess how to act in front of Robbie. No matter how ridiculous or absurd I was, he always stood by my side. And I did the same for him. But now this beautiful, polished Robbie had lived through things I couldn't understand. It hurt a little to realize that, in a lot of ways, we didn't know each other completely anymore. It felt like I'd lost hold of something important to me. Like I had to finally recognize that a part of my childhood was gone and wasn't coming back.

"I don't mind talking about it," Robbie said.

"Really?" I asked, trying to study his face to see if he was just being polite. I hated being so unsure of what he was thinking.

"Yeah, I hated when people tried to ignore the subject. Like not talking about him makes the pain go away." Robbie shrugged. "It's why my mom let me become a trainee. I think she wanted to do anything to distract me."

His phone buzzed, and I could tell from his expression that it was his manager. Probably asking him what was taking so long.

"We can go out this way to reach the front," I said, unlatching the gate.

I led Robbie around the front of the building, when there was sudden shouting. Cameras flashed, blinding me before I could squeeze my eyes shut.

Robbie pushed me behind him, holding his arm out as if shielding me from an attack.

"Robbie! How are you connected to this community center?"

"Are you volunteering here?"

"Is this why you came to the Chicago area so early?"

"Robbie! Who's your friend?"

Robbie pulled me to the front door of the center, slamming it closed behind us and blocking out the shouting voices.

Cora was just turning off the lights when she paused at our rushed entrance.

"Elena, what's going on? Are you okay?"

"What?" I said, still blinking to get rid of the bright lights in my vision.

"We're fine." Robbie pulled out his cell. "Hyeong? The press is here. Yes, okay, we'll wait for you."

"Oh crap, they're here because I brought you here without thinking about how public this place is," I said, holding my face in my hands as guilt lit a fire in my chest.

"Elena?" Cora's brow wrinkled in confusion.

"Cora, I'm so sorry," I said. "I didn't mean to cause such a scene."

"No, Elena, this isn't your fault. It's mine," Robbie said. "I did this."

"What do you mean?" I asked.

At that moment, Robbie's manager Hanbin pushed through the door, letting in the shouting voices of the paparazzi.

"Whoo," Hanbin said, shaking his head like he'd just come out of the rain. "Thank goodness this is a community center, right? The stories they'll write about this will probably help WDB's image." He let out a laugh.

Robbie shrugged. "Yeah, it's better than the costume malfunction in San Francisco."

They were talking about the center like it was a PR opportunity.

"Wait, did you call them here?" I asked. "Is this some kind of publicity stunt?"

"What?" Robbie scowled, and I watched him, willing him to deny it. But he didn't. And the longer the silence dragged on, the more my stomach clenched.

"Robbie, just tell me you didn't call them," I tried to prompt him.

"No—" he began before Hanbin broke in.

"Come on." He ushered Robbie toward the door. "We should go before more of them show up and it turns into a mob."

Had Robbie been saying no, he didn't call them? Or no, he wouldn't deny it?

As Hanbin reached for the door, Robbie looked back toward me. "Elena, we'll take you home."

"I'm staying."

"But how will you get home?" Robbie glared at the cameras outside, ready and waiting to take his picture.

"They're here for you, not me," I said.

"But—" Robbie started to argue.

"She's right," Hanbin said. "Come on, we've got to go. I've had you out late enough."

Robbie finally let Hanbin usher him out, jogging him through the cameras and toward the van idling by the curb.

"Elena," Cora said quietly, and I jumped at her voice; I'd forgotten she was there. Great, yet another embarrassment with an audience. At least I knew Cora wouldn't tell anyone. "I'm sure he didn't mean for this to happen."

"Then why didn't he deny it?" I asked, trying to fight back tears that would only embarrass me more.

"Elena," Cora said again.

But I shook my head at her platitudes. There was nothing anyone could say to fix the burning disappointment that filled my stomach.

FIFTEEN

Robbie's head was spinning as he hurried into the waiting van, his shoulders hunched against the flashing cameras and shouted questions.

This wasn't right. Robbie thought that he could feel a change with Elena tonight. Like maybe she was opening up to him. Like maybe she didn't completely hate the person he'd become. But if that was the case, how could she so easily believe that he'd use the community center for publicity?

Okay, maybe he'd refused to outright deny it. But who could blame him for being offended by even being asked such a question?

Oh crap, he should have denied it. Knowing Elena, she would spiral over this until she'd created a worst-case scenario out of it. Robbie pulled out his phone, thinking to text her, when he remembered he'd forgotten to get her number. Double crap.

"You okay?" Hanbin asked from the front seat once they'd successfully escaped.

"Hyeong! How did the press find us?" Robbie asked, letting his frustration spill out onto his manager.

"They must have gotten a heads-up. Maybe from someone inside?"

"No, they wouldn't do that. They're just kids. Why didn't you get rid of them?"

"It was just a few of them. And a little bit of good press doesn't hurt. I would never have let them go into the center. I know how to do my job," Hanbin said dismissively, like it wasn't a big deal.

"Yeah, well, maybe good press isn't worth disappointing people over," Robbie said, crossing his arms and slumping down in his seat.

"I had it under control."

Robbie fumed. Sometimes he felt like his manager was too focused on the image of WDB instead of the people in WDB.

"Whatever," Robbie said. "Elena hates me, by the way. She'll never go to prom now."

"Oh, you'll figure out how to make it up to her. You're Robbie Choi! One of the top twenty under twenty in Korea!"

Usually a statement like that would make Robbie laugh, but he wasn't in the mood. At times like this, he hated being WDB's Robbie Choi. A person the company had built out of the pieces of who he actually was. There were so many things that took practice and careful cultivation.

Like when they'd first started going on interviews, Robbie had been frozen and silent, too nervous to speak up unless it was something prescripted. It had earned him the reputation of being a chadonam, the cold and silent type. And the fans had loved it. So the company went with it.

But now Robbie felt burdened by keeping up the chic, aloof, and stylish facade. Sometimes it made him feel so fake. He wasn't cool, just shy.

When Robbie had first joined the company, he'd thought it would be as a songwriter. His uncle had promised as much, saying that attending trainee dance and singing lessons was just standard and that Robbie should go so it didn't look like he'd get special treatment just because he was the CEO's nephew.

It had made sense at the time. Even Jongdae went to all the required trainee sessions, despite the fact that his dad owned the company. But Jongdae-hyeong loved being a trainee; it was like he was born to be a celebrity. Robbie felt awkward and wooden whenever he tried to dance.

Then his uncle had taken Robbie's sample tracks where he'd recorded guide vocals and "leaked" them. Robbie had been horrified. They weren't done! And he had never meant anyone to hear this version. But the songs went viral. People loved that it was a thirteen-year-old ingenue rapping with such skill. He'd even been asked to be in a big idol's music video. And it had sealed Robbie's fate. He'd been added to the WDB lineup.

He remembered being hesitant about joining a K-pop group. It wasn't what he'd been expecting. He wasn't a great dancer, and WDB's choreography, even as debuts, was intense. But his uncle had insisted it would jump-start his career, and once he was well known, he could write and produce any song he desired for any singer in all of Korea.

At first, he'd felt like a fish out of water.

He practiced his dancing over and over so that he wouldn't be a burden on his hyeongs. And because of that, he'd had almost no time left to spend on his actual passion, songwriting. The company had let him co-write some of WDB's songs but always at their direction, with concepts they'd pre-chosen. It had still felt so . . . manufactured. They'd explained that it took a lot of effort to build a brand, to gain a loyal following. They said there were too many moving pieces for him to fully understand it all. That he should just trust them.

But now that WDB had become more well known, Robbie was hoping he could get back to writing music his way.

It was what Hanbin had promised. A deal that had seemed too good to be true. All he had to do was be his "charming self." Except he was starting to wonder if he'd made another hasty decision and let smooth talkers convince him that this was the only path to getting what he wanted.

No, he wouldn't worry about that tonight. He had more pressing things to figure out. Like how to get Elena to forgive him. He was constantly messing up with her. And it was so frustrating.

There had been a time when he felt like they could practically read each other's minds. He had known what every expression on her face meant. He'd known the deeper message of every one-syllable statement she made. But now he had no idea what she was thinking or why. It was like the seven years that sat between them was actually seven hundred. And he had no idea how to cross this new divide.

SIXTEEN

As soon as I opened the passenger door to Josie's car, she leaned over and said, "Last I checked, it's not 'bring your idol to work' day."

I tried to play it cool. "What are you talking about?"

She handed over her phone.

I didn't want to look. I was seriously considering moving out into the countryside and disavowing all technology. But I knew Josie would just bug me until I looked, so I glanced down at an article on a celebrity sighting blog: *WDB's Robbie Choi visits a local community center with mystery girl.*

"Already?" I complained, slouching in my seat. "How are they so fast with this stuff? I need to change my name, get plastic surgery, and disappear forever."

"Or," Josie said, "you could take advantage of this."

I stared at her in shock. "What do I have to gain from any of this but hate mail from Robbie's fans?"

"Look at the comments," Josie urged.

"I just said I *don't* want to read hate messages."

"Just look," Josie said. She reached out as if she would scroll down for me, but I held the phone out of her reach.

"Concentrate on the road," I said. "The only thing worse than the week I just had would be if I ended it by dying in a fiery crash."

"Fine, but just read the comments. I promise you'll be surprised."

I sighed and scrolled down. Josie was right; it was not what I was expecting. Instead of the mean comments calling me horrible names, there were dozens of WDB fans wondering where the community center was and how to support it.

If Robbie-oppa volunteers there, then we should help too! one fan wrote.

How can I volunteer there? another asked.

There were only a handful of comments wondering who I was. And, surprisingly, there was one that mentioned that I was probably the girl from the promposal, but it was weirdly neutral.

"Did you see?" Josie asked, glancing over.

"Yeah, I'm reading them," I said, scanning more comments about how kind and generous Robbie was. Maybe this wasn't a purposeful PR move, but they were definitely getting that good press they wanted.

"They're all so supportive of the center!" Josie exclaimed.

"They do seem nice," I admitted. "But I don't think we need a hundred WDB fans descending on the center."

"But we could do with a few hundred WDB fans *donating* to the community center."

"And how are we going to do that? Release a press statement

saying 'Hey, Robbie Choi was here once, so could you please donate to our fundraiser?'"

"I mean, maybe," Josie said, pouting at my lack of enthusiasm. "Or!" she exclaimed. "A pop-up concert."

"What? How would you even organize something like that?"

"Maybe Robbie's company will see the good press and want to capitalize on it," Josie said.

I bristled at the mention of "good press." Still, if they could use us, why couldn't we use them? I could already see how it would work out. If we could get just 10 percent of the people who'd commented on this post to donate, then maybe we wouldn't need the alterna-prom initiative anymore. And I was finally able to admit the initiative wasn't going anywhere.

But for this new plan to work, I'd have to ask Robbie for a favor. And I wasn't sure if I wanted to do that right now.

"I don't know. Robbie and I didn't really end tonight on good terms."

"You have to ask," Josie said as she parked her car beside mine in the mall parking lot. She gave me a sad smile. "You told us the other day that the center is running out of emergency funds. They need to last until the new budget meeting in June. Shouldn't we do everything we can to help them? Even if it's a long shot?"

I sighed. I hated when Josie gave me one of her sincere pep talks. Because they always worked on me.

"Fine," I said. "I'll ask Robbie if he'll do something for the center. But we can't depend on this. We'll have to brainstorm new fundraising ideas as a backup."

"Agreed. Oh my god, I might get to meet Jaehyung!" Josie said with a dreamy smile.

My mouth fell open, like a surprised cartoon character. "Josie! Do you . . . Do you like WDB?"

"I *told* you, my cousin is the president of the Mexico City branch of Constellations. I listened to her talk about them enough that I finally watched their music videos, and that Jaehyung is really cute," she said with an unaffected grin.

"Wow, you're just *using* me to meet your crush!"

"I would never!" Josie slapped her hand over her chest. "I truly think this is best for the community center. And if Jaehyung and I just happened to meet and fall in love and get married, then that's just a positive side benefit."

I laughed and punched her in the arm before climbing out of the car.

"Are you going to message him?" Josie asked, leaning over the center console so she could still see me through the passenger-door frame.

"I'll see what I can do. Now go home and dream about your crush or something."

"Yes, boss!" Josie said with a salute.

I laughed and swung the door closed.

SEVENTEEN

avoided the task of contacting Robbie all of Saturday. I think a part of me was hoping he'd somehow reach out first. After all, he'd shown up in front of me three days in a row, was it so weird to wonder if he'd do it a fourth? But there was no knock on the door, no call from an unknown number, no slide into my DMs.

I knew I needed advice, so I clicked into the group chat with my sisters. The last five messages had been from me. It stung a bit to be reminded that my sisters were all off living their lives without me. But I told myself that the last few things I'd sent didn't warrant replies. A message for Sarah's birthday, a couple of memes I thought were funny, and the last message saying, *Kill me now*. Sent the day of the promposal.

That one kind of hurt. Wouldn't you reply if your sister sent you that text? We'd started this group chat as a way to keep in touch after Esther complained that she couldn't always jump on FaceTime while she was studying for the boards.

But sometimes it just felt like I was texting myself.

I shook my head to stop from becoming a complete sad sack. *My sisters might be busy,* I told myself, but when I asked them a direct question, they usually answered.

Hey, can I get some advice? I typed.

When the app informed me *Allie is typing,* I felt relieved. I knew one of them would reply.

Hey, just boarded a flight, but go ahead and send your question. I'll answer it when I land!

I stared at the message and tried to tell myself that this was fine. It's not like she'd ignored me. And it wasn't like I could get mad at Allie for being on an airplane. I just missed my sisters. I felt like I was always making the wrong decisions without them around to give me advice.

I wished I could forget about talking to Robbie at all, but I knew Josie would nag me on Monday, and if I admitted I hadn't even tried she'd never let me hear the end of it. But there was the small issue that I didn't have his number.

I'd just message him on social and hope that he didn't have those ridiculous celebrity filters. Or . . . maybe I was hoping he did. That way it wouldn't be my fault if he didn't reply, right?

I found his account pretty quickly. He was the top "Robbie Choi" account, though there seemed to be a bunch of fan-run ones too. I was surprised to realize he'd only made the account last year. Then I remembered reading an interview at the height of my own K-pop obsession where one of my favorite idols said they weren't allowed to have social media as a rookie.

I clicked to join the seven million other fans who followed his account.

Should I open it with a casual "Hey"? Should I start by apologizing for yelling at him at the community center?

I remembered the anxious look on his face as he'd tried to block me from the cameras. As he'd tried to protect me. It really did seem like he'd been surprised to see the paparazzi there. Then why didn't he just tell me that?

I couldn't dwell on that. I finally decided on a simple *Hey,* and pressed SEND. My heart did a backflip as the little balloon appeared with my message. I stared at the screen, willing the little "read" icon to appear. But it didn't. Five minutes passed. And then fifteen.

This was ridiculous. I wasn't some lovesick girl waiting for her crush to message her back. I was just trying to see if a friend would participate in a community service. I should not be this nervous.

So I decided the best thing to do was forget about it for the night and go to bed.

The next morning, I checked my phone as soon as I woke up. Still nothing.

I was about to call Josie to complain and try to beg off our agreement when Mom called from downstairs. "Ethan! Al—Sar—Elena!"

Wow, only three tries, today was a good day, I thought.

"What?" Ethan called back from his room. I walked out of mine to look down the banister at Mom in the foyer.

"Get ready, we're going to family lunch at Halmeoni and Harabeoji's."

"But we went last week," I said.

Family lunch at our grandparents' was a monthly thing because Dad was too busy at work to go every week.

"Youngmi-como is in town. It's the respectful thing to go and greet her," Mom said, a telling glint in her eye.

I looked at Ethan, who'd come to his open doorway, hair still mussed as proof that he'd just woken up. We shared a knowing look. Mom had a weird competitive thing going with Youngmi-como. Which meant she'd want us to be on our best behavior at lunch.

Sighing, I went into my room to change. Maybe this was a good thing. Maybe it would distract me from the unread message on my phone.

After going through two outfit changes, Mom was finally happy, and we all piled into Dad's SUV. He was grumbling about not having time for this. But when Mom was in one of her moods, even Dad couldn't say no.

Once a month, we drove to our old neighborhood, where my halmeoni and harabeoji still lived. It was far more Korean than our new one. It had a giant Korean spa, the Korean market, and the Korean church we used to go to.

Youngmi-como opened the door before we even reached it. She was tall and thin with her hair pulled up in a twist. She often reminded me of the rich mothers in K-dramas, always stylish and perfectly done up.

"Little brother." She hugged Dad before stiffly embracing Mom.

"Are these two young teens you picked up somewhere?" Como said, turning to us. "Because they can't be my niece and nephew. They're too old."

I laughed. I couldn't help it. I didn't know much about Mom's weird rivalry with Como, but she'd always been nice to me. And she brought me Korean face masks and cute stationery whenever she visited.

"Eomeoni! Abeoji!" Como shouted. "Sangchul and Hyunjoo are here!"

Halmeoni shuffled out of the kitchen, super-long cooking chopsticks still in her hand. She rushed up to Dad and wrapped him in a hug, then gripped Ethan's shoulders. The long chopsticks almost poked me in the face, so I took a wide step back.

"So tall and handsome," she said. "Just like your abeoji."

"Kamsahamnida," Ethan said, pulling out the rare Korean we used mostly with our grandparents.

"Elena, get the extra stool from the garage," Halmeoni instructed me immediately.

I nodded, knowing it wouldn't do to resist. I was always the chore mule in this family. I went to the garage and found the short stool beside the large kimchi fridge. It was a little wobbly and should've been thrown into the trash a long time ago, but it's the only extra seat for the table whenever Como visited. I just knew I'd be the one forced to sit on it. A cast-off stool for the cast-off kid.

As soon as I'd set it by the table, Halmeoni's voice rang out from the kitchen. "Elena, come cook the bindaetteok."

The kitchen was filled with the most delicious smells, and it was actually my favorite space in the house. Two thin mung-bean pancakes were already frying on the stove next to a boiling stew that was as red as a fire truck. I was placed in front of the oil-filled skillet with a spatula and giant set of chopsticks in my hand. The oil spat at me, and I winced, jerking back a bit to avoid the splash. When the bindaetteok looked golden brown, I deposited it on a paper-towel-covered plate. Then I repeated the process. Pretty monotonous, but not that bad when you considered I got to eat the messed-up pieces.

"Let me help too, Eomonim," Mom said, coming in and pulling an apron out of the pantry.

Halmeoni just grunted. Even though Mom was a great cook, Halmeoni never acknowledged her skills. In a strange way, it was the only time I felt like Mom and I had anything in common. But I was sure she'd never see the parallel.

"Eomonim, Ethan is one of the best players on his varsity lacrosse team. They even gave him an award for his playing last season," Mom said.

Here we go, I thought. Mom listing off all of Ethan's amazing accomplishments as a way to show off.

"Good. He takes after his strong abeoji," Halmeoni said. Then, like a periscope searching out the next target, she turned to me. "So, Elena, you have namja chingoo?"

Before I could give the usual awkward answers, Mom spoke up. "She was asked to prom."

Halmeoni narrowed her eyes at me, probably watching my face get gradually redder and redder. "Your boyfriend?"

"No, not boyfriend," I clarified, and watched Mom sigh out of the corner of my eye. "Just a friend."

"Who's just a friend?" Youngmi asked, coming into the kitchen. It was a little small for the four of us, but Halmeoni held out a paper-towel-wrapped bindaetteok for Como to try.

I glanced into the living room and saw Harabeoji, Dad, and Ethan watching golf on the couch. Ethan looked back at me with a pained expression. I just shrugged. Golf might be boring, but to my mind, he had the easier task. Lazing around as Dad and Harabeoji grunt-communicated to each other.

"Elena?" Youngmi prompted me when I didn't answer her question.

"Oh, we were just talking about Elena's good friend Robbie Choi. He's in WDB," Mom said as if she were explaining I'd been nominated for a Nobel Peace Prize.

I wrinkled my nose at her using my childhood friendship to one-up Como.

"WDB?" Youngmi-como's brows rose, clearly recognizing the group. "You're friends with them?"

"Well, I used to know one of them. Like seven years ago," I mumbled when Mom sent me a sharp stare.

"He came all the way to our house to ask Elena to prom. So sweet," Mom said. "I always liked him."

"That's wonderful, Elena," Youngmi said, taking a taste of the stew.

She picked up a bottle of fish sauce, and Halmeoni immediately plucked it out of her hands.

"Too jja," Halmeoni said in Konglish.

"It's not, Eomma."

"Your abeoji can't have anything too salty," Halmeoni insisted.

"You don't need fish sauce for kimchi jjigae, Unnie," Mom said a little too sweetly to Como.

Youngmi-como, unfazed, turned to me. "So, Elena, if you have a friend in Seoul, you should come work at my hagwon this summer."

"What?" I asked at the same time my mom did.

Como ran an academy that catered to middle school and high school students looking to get better grades. Like Kumon on crack.

"Yeah, it's getting more popular. Our classes are so filled, we had to add more, especially English classes. You should come help out and then maybe you can spend more time with your Robbie."

I felt uncomfortable hearing him referred to as *my* Robbie. Especially when I wasn't sure if Robbie and I were even talking anymore.

Before I could even think of a reply, Mom said, "No, she's too young."

"What?" I asked. "Allie and Sarah both taught there."

"When they were in *college*."

"Yeah, but—"

"But nothing, Elena. You'll wait until college just like your sisters," Mom said.

I wanted to argue that I wasn't just like my sisters if only on principle. That not everything we did had to be exactly the same. But I knew it wouldn't matter to Mom.

Youngmi-como leaned in and whispered, "Don't worry. Invitation's always open if you get her to change her mind."

She gave me a wink, and I smiled back. But I was thinking maybe this was how it was supposed to be. Going to Seoul to spend time with Robbie was silly. Why would I follow someone halfway across the world when I wasn't sure if we were even on speaking terms?

★☆★

After lunch, as expected, I was assigned dish duty. Ethan was allowed to sit with the adults and eat slices of Korean pear that Halmeoni had skewered with tiny forks.

I was trying to unstick the fingers of an ancient pair of dishwashing gloves when Ethan wandered in with his empty glass. He opened the fridge and stared at the contents. His choices were orange juice, prune juice, or podicha, a chilled barley tea that I knew he despised.

He chose orange juice but didn't leave immediately after pouring it. Instead, he gulped half of it down and watched me struggle to pull the gloves on. "Why don't you just load them all in the dishwasher?"

I almost laughed at his naïveté. The kind of question asked by someone who had never been told to wash a dish in his life. "You mean the Asian household drying rack?"

Ethan let out a huff that sounded like a half laugh. "So, did you and Robbie have a fight?"

"Why would you ask that?"

Ethan shrugged. "I saw some story about you bringing him to that community center you love, but you've been in a shitty mood all weekend."

"Yeah, so?" I said, wondering why Ethan even cared.

"I just didn't realize you were that close again," Ethan said. "You don't even ask me to go there with you."

Yeah, because Ethan would laugh in my face if I did.

"Well, we didn't get into a fight. We just aren't really talking right now. Or at least *he's* not replying to my messages."

I started scrubbing the dishes furiously. Maybe the physical labor would help me work out my frustration.

"He's ghosting you?"

I glared at him out of the corner of my eye. Did he sound somehow happy about that?

"He's not ghosting me. I just DM'd him and he hasn't replied yet. In sixteen hours. Not that anyone's counting."

"What did you say?"

I faced Ethan now, still suspicious but also curious enough to ask, "Are you trying to offer me boy advice?"

Ethan's eyes widened in part surprise, part horror. "No, definitely not. Just asking a normal question."

I almost returned to the dishes and ignored him. But without Josie or my sisters, I was kind of getting desperate for advice. Finally I replied, "I said 'Hey.'"

Ethan snorted a laugh but stopped when I narrowed my eyes at him.

"Maybe he's just busy. Or can't check his messages."

"Yeah, maybe," I mused. The way Ethan said that so casually made me think that maybe Robbie wasn't ignoring me completely. Maybe he really just hadn't had time to reply.

I was probably just overthinking it because Robbie made me nervous and defensive. Like a long, continuous prank was being played on me. I hated being in any situation where I couldn't predict the possible outcomes. "So, you think I should find him and apologize?"

"Sure? Go the extra mile or whatever Dad says."

"Yeah, if I can find him," I said.

Ethan laughed and patted me on the shoulder as he started out the door. "I'm sure you'll figure it out. You always do, Twin."

Huh, who'd have thought that Ethan was the one who'd give me the advice I needed for this. I guess weirder things had happened. Like an international superstar showing up on my doorstep.

But where do you find an idol's location? Well, Robbie said the paparazzi follow him everywhere, right? So maybe I should start there.

I pulled out my phone and googled *WDB schedule.* All I got was a bunch of stuff about their upcoming performance at a morning show in NYC and KFest Chicago. I wondered if I could find one of those fan forums that Karla was looking at. I googled *Constellation forum.* And quickly found out I had to register and be approved.

I was about to give up and clicked on Instagram again, thinking maybe I could just message Robbie my apology, when I noticed his latest post. The caption read, *Preparing a gift for our Constellations.* It looked like a nondescript dance studio, but I could make out half of the logo reflected in the mirror behind them. I recognized it because for a hot second in middle school I thought I wanted to be a dancer and begged my mom for ballet lessons. That's before I found out most of the dancers had been in ballet since they were, like, four years old and I was way behind the curve. It was the nicest studio in the area. And it was where WDB was right now.

EIGHTEEN

A s I drove into the dance studio parking lot, I spotted the now-
recognizable black van. But I hadn't been expecting the fans. There
were a couple dozen. They were sitting in little circles, signs beside them
with messaging like *I love you Jaehyung-oppa!* or *Jun! Fighting!* or *Robbie
사랑해요!!!*

Some of them looked up at the sound of my car coughing down the
street. I seriously needed to take it in to have the muffler looked at. If it
even had a muffler anymore.

I wondered if any of them would recognize me from the viral promposal video. Just in case, I lowered my head as I drove past and parked at
the far end of the lot. I knew a side door that would lead to the back rooms.
But as I made my way there, a man in all black stepped out and blocked
my path.

"You can't go here. It's closed," he said.

"Oh, I'm just here to see a friend," I said vaguely.

He crossed his arms, muscles bulging from under his black T-shirt. "You can go sit with your friends and wait until they're done with practice." He pointed to the fans still sitting on the sidewalk.

"Oh, no, I'm not with them. I'm not even a Constellation, I just need to talk to my friend." I realized now that I probably sounded like a desperate fan trying to get in to see WDB. But I was hoping the guard would be able to see the truth in my words.

"Wait with your friends," he said again.

Whoever said honesty is the best policy had never come across a suspicious celebrity security guard. "Fine," I said, slowly turning. Then, in a last-ditch effort, I spun around and tried to sprint past. The guy didn't even blink as he lifted me in the air so my legs were kicking at nothing.

"I just came to see a friend! I'm not a fan. I don't even listen to their music."

"Really? Not even one song?" said an amused voice.

The security guard paused, and I wiggled out of his arms, landing hard on my feet. Robbie stood in the side doorway, his arms crossed, his lips quirked in an amused smile.

"I wish I had my phone. That would have been a hilarious video," he said. "Might even have kicked the promposal off the top trending spot."

I winced at his mention of the promposal video.

"You know her? She's really your friend?" the guard asked, still eyeing me like I might make a break for it and tackle Robbie.

"Yeah, I know her," Robbie said. But I noted that he didn't say that I was a friend.

"Come on," he said. "Let's go in before we're spotted."

Inside, the fluorescent lights were bright, and the building looked strangely empty. I'd never been here when there weren't half a dozen classes going on. But WDB's company must have rented out the whole space for the boys to practice.

"How did you know I'd be here?" Robbie asked.

I almost winced at his cool tone. "Instagram."

"Stalker," Robbie said, but his lip twitched like he was trying not to smile.

"Why are you practicing here instead of somewhere in the city?" I asked.

"We're staying in the area for a few days before we're the city for KFest."

"Oh," I said, then figured I might as well get the apology over with. "So, about Friday," I started, but paused, not sure exactly what to say.

"I'm sorry," Robbie said, beating me to the punch.

"What?"

"Isn't that why you came?" Robbie asked. "Because you wanted me to apologize?"

"No," I said, realizing that he didn't look mad so much as confused. "I'm here so *I* can apologize."

"Oh" was all he said.

"Anyway, I'm sorry about accusing you last night," I said quickly.

Robbie nodded. "I understand. It's hard to get used to the press. They're really intense. And, Elena, I had nothing to do with them being there."

And as soon as he said the words, it was like the band of anxiety around my chest finally released and gave me permission to take a full breath again. "Why didn't you tell me that on Friday?"

Robbie shrugged. "I guess it hurt that you thought I could do something like that."

I was surprised at the idea that I could hurt Robbie. He was literally adored by millions all over the world. I didn't realize my opinions could still matter to him.

"I overreacted," I admitted. "It's just that the community center means a lot to me. It's hard to explain."

"Because you're all a team," Robbie said.

"What?"

"It's like me and my group. I'd be really defensive of them too. I can see how you all have built up a routine and trust. Those kids really love you."

After all this time, how could Robbie reach right into my core like this? Even my own family didn't really get why I loved the community center so much. But Robbie had always been different. He'd always been able to understand me better than anyone else. And Robbie was the only person who had always chosen me first. I didn't know how much I'd been missing that.

"Robbie! Everyone's ready to film!" Hanbin shouted from the practice room.

"Oh, I'm sorry. I didn't realize you were in the middle of something," I said, blinking hard to pull myself together. "I thought you were just practicing. I can wait out here."

"Why don't you watch?" Hanbin said.

Robbie gave his manager a strange look, and I wondered if he didn't want me to. I thought we'd been getting along after both apologizing, but now I suddenly felt a strange tension in the air. Why was it so hard to get in sync with Robbie again?

"I don't want to get in the way," I said, thinking to give Robbie an out.

"You can," Robbie said with a jerking shrug. "If you want."

"Oh, okay," I said slowly, trying to figure out if he meant it or he was just being polite. "Are you sure?"

"Yeah," Robbie said, this time with a nod. "Come on." He took my hand, his fingers so long they easily looped around mine as he led me inside. I stared at the back of his head, wondering if he realized what he'd just done. It had seemed so natural. Like he did it all the time. Oh my god, did he do this all the time? Of course he did; he was an idol. I bet girls threw themselves at him. Wait, no, why did I care about that? Robbie could do whatever he wanted.

I thought it would just be the members of WDB inside, but there were half a dozen staff, some leaning in corners and talking with each other. One was carrying a camera. Another was setting up a tripod.

As we walked in, everyone stopped what they were doing, and a dozen eyes turned to us.

NINETEEN

A boy stepped in front of us, and my mouth fell open as he smiled at me. "Hello, random girl." His voice was playful and curious, and I immediately found myself shifting to hide behind Robbie.

"Minseok-hyeong, don't scare her," Robbie said, poking the other boy in the forehead to push him away.

Minseok was slightly shorter than Robbie and wore a sleeveless tank top that showed off his well-toned arms. He had eyes that tilted slightly upward, giving him a perpetual mischievous look. His hair looked brown, but when he moved, I saw it was tinted magenta.

I tried to remember the bios I'd read online.

"Minseok," I said slowly. "Moonster. Lead rapper?" And the only other member of WDB that spoke fluent English.

He dropped into a deep bow, less formal Korean-style and more performer accepting applause. "Moonster is my stage name. Pretty friends of Robbie can call me Minseok. Or Oppa, if you'd like," he said with a wink.

I was thrown off by being called "pretty," so I didn't notice as two of the other band members came up to stand beside Robbie.

"Noogoosaeyo?" one of them asked. I turned toward the voice asking who I was and almost squeaked at how close he stood. He had leaned down so we were eye to eye, and all I saw was smooth skin, dark eyes, and a straight nose. Did all celebrities have perfect complexions?

Robbie elbowed the other boy hard enough to have him move back.

"Cheoneun Elena-iyayo," I said in stilted Korean.

"Oh, you can just speak English," Robbie said. "They're supposed to practice anyway.

"This is Jun." He gestured to the one who'd been staring at me. Now that he was standing straight I saw that he was tall, taller than Robbie. His hair was cut into what could only be called a mullet, but it looked good on him. Almost like he'd stepped through time from 1980s punk New York. "This is Jaehyung," Robbie continued. The other boy waved shyly.

"Jun is main dancer. Jaehyung is main vocal," I recited from my research.

"Lead vocal," Jaehyung said, his voice low and shy. He was the shortest of the group, and had a sweet baby face. I knew he was still a year older than Robbie, who was the maknae.

"There's a lead *and* a main?" I asked.

Robbie laughed. "Jongdae-hyeong is main vocal." He gestured to the only boy who hadn't come over to greet me. Robbie's cousin. The heart-throb. He was standing by the speakers, chugging a bottle of water. He looked so perfect he could have been filming an ad.

"You guys ready yet?" he asked, coming over and barely sparing me a look.

This close, Jongdae was stunning. I could see why he was called the visual of the group. It was like staring directly into a blazing star. Tall, strong jaw, great cheekbones that my mom would kill for. And sharp eyes that looked like they could gaze into your soul. Or right through you as if you didn't exist, like they were doing to me right now.

"Sure. Let's get started," Minseok said affably, throwing his arm around Jongdae. "Elena, take a seat and prepare to be dazzled."

"Not in the front, though," Jongdae said without even looking at me. "You can sit by our manager."

I nodded, feeling suddenly like I was intruding on something.

"Okay, music!" Jongdae said as the boys positioned themselves closely together.

I'd watched a few of WDB's dance practice videos, and I'd been in awe then. That was nothing compared to seeing them live. It was impressive how they worked together, their movements completely in sync. Something that truly only came from hours and hours of practice. What had Robbie said before? A team had a routine and trust? I saw that now as the five guys moved together in perfect synchronization.

Robbie's rap section started, and he broke free from the rest of the guys. A gorgeous dancer girl stepped forward, and Robbie trailed beside her as he rapped. She acted aloof and unfazed as she stepped gracefully across the floor. How did some people make something as simple as walking look beautiful? Robbie was playacting like he was heartbroken that the girl wouldn't give him the time of day. And at the end of his verse, he was finally rewarded as she let him spin her into his arms before she sauntered off, and Robbie was joined by the rest of the boys to dance to the chorus again.

"That was great!" Minseok said with a whoop as the boys landed in their final pose, breathing hard. "We should have recorded that one."

"We'll record this one," Hanbin said, moving the tripod in front of the mirror. "Do it exactly the same."

Minseok laughed. "Sure, no problem," he said like a robot. The other boys laughed too, even Jongdae. Maybe he was only cold with newcomers.

The music started up again. And even though Minseok had been joking, the boys began dancing exactly like before with perfect precise movements. Except this time when Robbie's rap began, the girl let out a cry and stumbled. Her ankle twisted beneath her, and she went down hard. The room let out a collective gasp as the boys crowded around her. Voices tumbled over each other in hurried Korean.

Hanbin called for the music to be turned off and knelt down beside the dancer. When she tried to stand, she let out another cry and collapsed, gripping her ankle.

A staff member lifted the dancer like she was light as a feather, carrying her quickly out.

"I guess that means we can't record the dance practice video," Minseok said.

"We have to," Hanbin said, opening a notebook and flipping through it. "The one we filmed in Seoul was lost and we promised the fans that if they got your MV views to fifty million in one week, then they'd get a dance practice video. It got that many views in one day."

"Wow," I breathed, impressed. I didn't realize I'd said it out loud until the boys turned to me.

"Wait a minute," Minseok said, a sly glint in his eyes. It reminded me of the look a character in a sitcom might wear when coming up with an idea that will definitely end badly. "We just need someone to walk across the floor, right?"

"Wait, what are you thinking, Hyeong?" Robbie asked, worry in his eyes as they met mine.

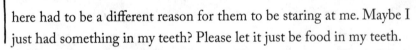

TWENTY

here had to be a different reason for them to be staring at me. Maybe I just had something in my teeth? Please let it just be food in my teeth.

"Oooh," Jun said, then spoke in Korean so hurried I couldn't follow.

"No," Robbie said. "We can't ask her to do this without any prep."

I felt the blood drain out of my face as I started to catch on. No, this was a horrible idea. I had to shut this down.

"She just needs to walk past you, smile, and then let you spin her. Anyone can do that," Minseok said.

"Great, then you do it," I finally got out. "I'm a horrible dancer."

"It's not dancing, really," Minseok explained, taking my hand. He gave me a smile so charming and dazzling I started to smile back before I remembered that I was supposed to be standing strong. This was ridiculous; I could *not* dance with Robbie. "Plus!" Minseok chirped excitedly. "It can help after that disaster promposal video."

My spine stiffened; why did people keep bringing up that video?

"This is silly," I said. "How could this help with that?"

"You gotta think about public image," Minseok said, lifting his finger in the air in an almost comic exaggeration of someone making a point. "The fans don't know what to think of the mystery girl that Robbie failed so spectacularly in front of. Really, it was very entertaining for me. I love you for that alone," Minseok said, gripping both my hands. "But the fans don't know what I know. That's why they're so confused. If we put Elena in the video to show there are no hard feelings and explain on WDB TV that she's Robbie's old childhood friend, then I'm sure they'll warm to her."

It sounded ridiculous, but the more I thought about it, the more it made a weird kind of sense. The fans already seemed less mad at me in the comments about the community center photos. Maybe if they associated me with more positive things, then they might forgive me for not saying yes to the promposal.

Robbie shook his head. "Minseok-hyeong, if she doesn't want to, we can just ask one of the manager noonas."

"They're not the right age," Minseok insisted.

A part of me wanted to claim ageism, anything that would get him to let go of this wild idea. But Minseok insisted. "This will be great. Don't you think, Jongdae-hyeong?"

I waited for JD to back me up. There was no way he could agree to this.

But he just nodded and said, "It could work."

"Great!" Minseok said, clapping his hands as the other boys started talking too.

Robbie leaned closer to murmur to me, "You don't have to do this. We can ask one of the hairstylists."

"No, Minseok actually had a good point about the netizens," I said.

Robbie winced. "I was hoping you hadn't read any of that."

"I'm a naturally curious person, Robbie. You really don't remember that about me?" I asked with a wobbly smile.

He grinned back. "Well, for what it's worth, I think he's right. If they see that you and I have been friends forever, I bet they'll love you."

Hanbin turned to us. "Elena, come here. Robbie, you'll need to work harder to guide her so she falls in line."

I almost winced at the words, like Hanbin already expected me to mess up.

"We'll keep it simple," he said. "I'll stand next to you, and when I give you the cue, just walk across the floor. Each step is one beat, okay?"

I nodded, trying to keep this all in my head.

"Robbie is going to come up on your left side." Hanbin gestured to Robbie, and he did as instructed. "And you just need to let him spin you."

Robbie pulled on my hand, but I wasn't prepared and I overshot him. I let out a scream as I lost my balance. I windmilled my arms, hoping to steady myself and not mess this all up royally. But I could feel gravity taking me, and in a panicky last-ditch effort to catch myself, I wrapped my arms around Robbie's neck and brought him down with me. The air was pushed out of my lungs as I hit the ground with a thud and Robbie fell on top of me.

"I don't think this is what Hanbin-hyeong meant by 'fall in line,'" Robbie breathed out beside my ear.

I groaned and pushed at him. "This isn't the time for your awful puns."

Robbie chuckled and pushed himself onto his elbows, relieving some of the pressure on my chest. "You okay?" he asked. His arms were like a shelter around me, blocking out the rest of the room. I couldn't see anything but his face as it hovered over mine.

"I'm fine," I whispered, even though I couldn't fully fill my lungs. This close, he was still handsome, but I could see that he had the same slight overbite he'd had when we were kids. And his nose was still just a bit too big for his face, rounded at the end in a way that made him look boyish.

"You have the same nose," I found myself saying.

He smiled, and it made his cheeks rise, his eyes tilting into crescents. "Were you worried I'd gotten plastic surgery now that I'm an idol?"

"What? Oh, no!" I rushed to assure him.

He laughed, and I felt it rumble between us. "Don't worry. It's definitely done. I wouldn't blame you for wondering."

Then his smile faded a bit, an oddly serious expression taking its place. I felt something tug at my hair and realized his fingers were tangling in it. "Lani," he said in a voice so low I felt it vibrate in his chest. He lowered a bit, moving closer. What was he doing? What was he thinking?

"Yes?" My eyes dropped to his lips. They were so close I could see his perfect Cupid's bow. My heart was thudding so hard I was sure he'd feel it.

"I think we should get up now," he whispered.

"Huh?" I frowned.

"People are starting to stare." His eyes shifted to the side.

When I looked around, every eye in the room was on us. My stomach dropped, and a tingle of embarrassment swept across the back of my neck.

"Ohmigod," I said, pushing Robbie off. He laughed as he stood, quick and spry. He offered a hand, but I ignored it. Pushing to my feet, I couldn't even meet his eyes.

"I've never heard someone squeal at quite so high a decibel before," Robbie teased with another laugh. I seethed, annoyed that he found this all so amusing while I was absolutely mortified.

"Smart-ass," I murmured.

"Oh, wow, Elena Soo curses now!" Robbie placed a hand over his heart in comic astonishment.

I couldn't help it; I laughed. And Robbie smiled, like that was all he'd wanted. And I suddenly remembered that had been one of his skills when we were younger. Making you feel like you were the center of his focus.

"You two ready to try again?" Hanbin said.

"Again?" I asked, surprised that they hadn't scrapped this horrible idea. My lack of coordination was painfully obvious.

"Hyeong, can you give me a second to practice with Elena alone?" Robbie asked.

Hanbin glanced at his watch. "Sure, but you only have five minutes. We need to get this video recorded soon."

"I don't think I can do this," I told Robbie as Hanbin walked away. "I'm going to ruin it, and all your fans will hate me even more."

"You're being too hard on yourself," Robbie said. Then I thought I heard him mutter, "Like always." But I couldn't be sure.

He took my shoulders and said, "Just think of it like when we did those practice dances when we were nine."

"You mean when I made you do the *High School Musical 2* rooftop performance with me and I almost *killed* you during the lift?" I asked.

Robbie laughed. "Okay, so let's skip the lift this time."

I just couldn't see any result that wouldn't end in my total humiliation. But that feeling warred with my need to keep my promises. "Fine," I said, giving in.

Robbie nodded. "Just try to have fun. And don't hold your hand out like that. You're not supposed to expect me to take it. It has to be natural."

I counted the beat, concentrating on keeping my steps smooth, my arms normal. It was hard, the way it is when you're concentrating too much on doing something that should be instinctive.

"Loosen up," Robbie said, poking me in the ribs. Right in my most sensitive ticklish spot.

"Hey!" I started to say, but before I could slap at his hand, he'd grabbed mine and pulled me into a spin.

His arms came around me, holding me in place. His face was only a few inches from mine, so I watched as the smile spread slowly over it. That dimple crease deepening in his cheek. And for a breathless second, all I could do was stare at him as my pulse echoed like thunder through my head. "See, it's not so hard when you stop thinking about it."

After three more practices, Hanbin declared we were ready. Minseok bounced over, a small vlogging camera in his hand. "This is Elena, our savior! Elena, say hi to the Constellations."

"Um, hi," I stuttered, shrinking back.

"Hyeong!" Robbie said. "Cut it out. Elena's shy."

"Then why did you do that big splashy promposal?" Minseok asked, aiming the camera at Robbie.

I expected him to frown or get annoyed, but instead, he sighed and said, "I just wanted to do something special for my oldest friend in the world."

Minseok nodded in approval, then turned the camera on himself. "I guess I can't blame you for that. It's shocking anyone has stuck by your side this long. Elena, you should get an award or something." He spun the camera back to me, and I let out an awkward laugh. Jun popped over, shoving his face so close to the lens it probably only shot his nose. I used the distraction to slip away as Jun did a goofy, wild-limbed version of their choreography while Jaehyung sang the lyrics in falsetto.

I laughed at their antics. They all seemed to really enjoy each other, and even when Robbie rolled his eyes at his group members, he was smiling. One of his big goofy smiles. He turned a bit, his eyes catching mine, pulling me into the moment. And I grinned back. He shot me a thumbs-up as JD called for them to take their places.

It was like night and day as the playful personas disappeared. The boys' expressions turned serious when they took their positions.

The music began, and they started to move. Gone were the goofy smiles; now they were powerful and charismatic performers who filled the whole space with their presence. When they danced, no one else in the room mattered; all eyes were on them.

I was busy counting the beat in my head, trying not to lose it once I found it. So I almost didn't realize my part was coming up until Hanbin leaned close and whispered, "Ready?"

I nodded and stepped forward.

I was hyperaware of the camera on me but also knew I shouldn't look at it. So I kept my eyes straight ahead. Robbie came over and smiled. I gave him a weak smile back. He was mouthing the words to the rap, and it was so fast I couldn't understand most of it. But he wrinkled his nose at me like he was saying, "Come on, have some fun."

My smile widened. I couldn't help it. When the camera could see him, his expression was fierce, like the Robbie in music videos. But whenever he turned to me, he gave me his goofiest grins and expressions of exaggerated smolder, like he was making this into our own little game. I couldn't help but laugh. He was somehow taking my mind off the performance, making me feel more comfortable in a way that only Robbie could. It felt like we were completely in sync again. Then he took my hand and spun me into his arms. And now all I had to do was smile and walk away.

But Robbie held on to my hand and lifted it to his lips. A spark raced up my arm, zapping my heart like a bolt of lightning. Dazed, I walked out of the frame, barely noticing the congratulatory thumbs-up from Hanbin.

The rest of the song flew by in a blur. I could still feel the touch of Robbie's lips on my hand, like they'd left an imprint. Why had he done that? I pressed my other palm to it, like I could seal the feeling onto my skin.

Wait, what was I doing? I wasn't a swooning fangirl. This was Robbie. My oldest friend. The one I'd watched swallow a pebble once because I'd dared him to. My heart should *not* be racing just because he'd kissed my hand as part of video playacting. Except he hadn't done it with the dancer. It was something he'd done just with me.

The music ended, and everyone froze for the final pose, chests heaving from exertion. And suddenly they went from being mysterious and brooding to happy-go-lucky boys again. I watched Robbie hug Jongdae, still obviously filled with adrenaline. The staff broke out into applause, all laughing and talking at once. I could feel the charge moving through the air. If this was the feeling after a good dance practice, how much more heightened must it be after a performance? Was this why people became performers? To constantly chase this high?

Robbie's eyes latched on to mine, and despite myself, I could feel my pulse take off like galloping horses. He'd always had that little crease in his cheek, but it had been more adorable before; now it was charming. Was that what seven years did to someone? Did it take all their sweetest features and sharpen them just enough to make them dangerous? Because that dimple was a serious weapon.

"You were amazing!" he said, and before I knew what he intended, he'd scooped me into a hug and turned me in a circle. I had to hold on to his shoulders or else fall. I felt his muscles bunch beneath my hands as he spun us. I became dizzy as my hair whipped into my face. And even when we stopped, I had to keep holding on because my knees were suddenly as solid as Jell-O.

"I think I was making weird faces," I said.

"No, you looked great. Like you were trying not to be charmed. It was very sexy."

Sexy? Was my brain melting? Or had Robbie just called me sexy?

"Elena!" Minseok said as Robbie finally let me go. "You were amazing!" He held up a hand, and it took me a second to realize he wanted a high five. When I gave him one, his hand closed around mine, and he brought it to his lips with a wink.

"Ya! Hyeong!" Robbie pulled me away.

"What? I wanted to thank her for helping out. I was just following your lead." Minseok winked at Robbie this time. But Robbie must not have liked it, because he broke out into Korean, his voice low and rushed.

"Don't be rude to your guest," Jongdae said, walking up. He nodded at me. "You did well. We appreciate you stepping in."

"Sure," I said, unable to meet his intense stare. He was the kind of handsome that made you feel flushed when you stared at him too long. And this close and in person, it was a bit too much.

"Come on," Robbie said, touching my elbow and pulling my attention away from Jongdae. "I'll walk you out."

"Oh, yeah, sure." I was actually grateful for the out; I was starting to feel overwhelmed encircled by this group of gorgeous boys.

"Thank you, Elena!" Jun called from the far corner.

"Komawayo!" Jaehyung said.

I nodded and followed Robbie into the hallway.

When I started toward the side door, he took my shoulder, turning me the other way. "We'll go out the back. One of our managers already went to get the car to drive you home."

"Oh, you don't need to do that."

"It's fine. We're mostly done with our schedule for the day, so they have time," he said so casually, like it was normal to ask people to drive you around. And I guess, for him, it was.

I awkwardly cleared my throat. "No, I mean I have my car. It's just in the front lot."

"Ah," Robbie said, and motioned to a staff member. "Can you go get Elena's car and bring it around back?" He leaned closer to me and said, "It'll save you from dealing with the fans out front."

I nodded slowly; did that mean he intended to walk me all the way to my car? I handed my keys to the manager, who turned quickly and jogged toward the front entrance. I hadn't even told him which car was mine or that the driver-side door kind of stuck and you had to jiggle it to open it. But it was too late as he rounded the corner.

"Sorry about Jongdae-hyeong," Robbie said as we started to walk toward the back. "He can be pretty overwhelming to new people."

"You all are."

"Really? You find me overwhelming?" Robbie's lips twitched like he was trying not to smile.

"I mean, it's just that you've changed so much," I tried to explain. "You got so much taller. And you have those arms now. And your dimple crease is distracting." Had I really said that? I wondered if it was possible to just sink into the ground and get buried right here.

"Dimple crease?" Robbie asked, smiling so it flashed.

"Yeah, and you keep smiling at me in a way that feels on purpose. If that makes sense." Except none of this made sense, not even to me. I knew I was rambling nonsense words, and I was getting frustrated. "And then you added that . . . thing you did at the end. And I was thrown off. It's not fair. I always used to tell you I don't like surprises, but you always did them anyway. And if this was just another one of your jokes, it's not funny, Robbie Choi!"

I stopped when Robbie let out a snort. And I realized he was trying not to laugh.

"Don't laugh at me when I'm yelling at you," I said, punching him in the arm.

He winced, but I could tell it was him exaggerating as his shoulders shook with his laughter.

"Robbie," I warned.

"Okay, okay." He held up his hands to ward off another punch. "I'm sorry I laughed. It's just that you make me smile. I can't help it when I'm around you."

Wait, what did that mean? Was he *flirting*?

I lowered my fist as confusion replaced my anger. "So you're not laughing at me?"

"No, I promise, I'm not." But he was still aiming that strange smile at me. It made me want to squirm.

"Okay, fine," I said, realizing I hadn't been angry so much as embarrassed. I felt so unused to this new world of Robbie's, and I couldn't figure out how to keep up. It was wreaking havoc on my desire to anticipate the outcome of things.

I winced at the telltale roar of my muffler-less car as it drove up.

"Oh my god, you have the maroon monster?" Robbie's eyes widened.

I hadn't heard that name in years. It's what Allie had called the car when she drove it. Even back then, it hadn't been in the best shape. I laughed. "I forgot we called it that."

"I can't believe it's still running," Robbie said, sliding his hand over the hood. The car let out a little cough as it idled, like it remembered him.

"I mean, it barely does," I admitted. "But I have faith she'll hold out until the end of high school."

"Maybe I should have one of my manager-hyeongs drive you home." Robbie eyed the car warily. "I'm not sure it's responsible to send you home in this thing."

"Hey! She can hear you," I said, patting the car like it was my best friend.

"Fine." Robbie laughed.

But when I went to open the door, Robbie stopped me with a hand on the shoulder. "Wait."

I froze. Was he going to ask me to stay? He'd said he had the rest of the day off; maybe he wanted to hang out more.

"You said you came here to ask me something."

Oh yeah, that's right, I couldn't believe I'd forgotten my whole mission. "It's actually about the community center," I said, trying to hide my disappointment.

"Did something happen after I left last night?" Robbie asked, worry tightening his face.

"Oh, no, it's fine. I was actually thinking . . ." I paused, trying to figure out how to phrase the question. "I want to use my next wish."

"Your wish?" Robbie's brows lifted.

"Yeah, so, remember how we need to fundraise to keep it open? Well, I was hoping . . ." I trailed off, trying to gauge his reaction, but he was frustratingly expressionless. ". . . could I use my wish to get your help?"

"Of course," he said, and my twisting stomach relaxed. "What can I do?"

"Well, my friend Josie and I were thinking you could maybe do a pop-up benefit concert?" I was speaking quickly now, not wanting to lose my momentum or his interest. "It could spread the word about the community center, and I know that you said you didn't come last night for the PR, but people seemed to really love the idea that you were volunteering. So this couldn't hurt, right? And it would mean so much to the kids. And to me?" I ended that last one like a question, I wasn't sure if it mattered to Robbie if this was important to me, but I was hoping. . . .

Robbie smiled, and some of my anxiety was replaced by a seed of hope. "That sounds great! I think the guys would like it too. I'd just have to run it by Hanbin-hyeong." Then his smile disappeared.

Oh no, would his manager hate this? Did he hate last-minute things? Was this some kind of breach of contract to ask him to do something like this?

"What is it? Do you think your manager won't go for the idea?"

"No, it's not that. They love this kind of stuff. Shows that we're 'still connected to our roots.'" Robbie moved his fingers in air quotes. "But they'll want to film something like this for WDB TV. And post about it on social media. I know you hate being on film, and you just did us a huge favor with the dance practice video. I don't want to force you to do anything else."

Aw, this was kind of sweet. Seeing Robbie worrying about my comfort. "That's really nice of you. But this is for the center. I think the more coverage it gets, the better. Even I can suck it up for that."

"Great, then your wish is granted! I'll message you with more details. Let me get your number." He held out his hand, and I gave him my phone.

"I thought you weren't supposed to have phones," I said.

"Yeah, we all bought ourselves phones on our own in the last year. It's technically a secret," he said. "But everyone on our team knows." He held out my phone to me. "Text me when you get home safe."

"I'm not twelve, and it's not that far."

"Yeah, but I still want to know you're okay, especially since you're driving that thing."

"Fine, *Dad*. I'll text you."

Robbie smiled and it was warm and sweet and I had the weirdest urge to hug him. No, I realized as I stared at his lips; I didn't *just* want to hug him.

Suddenly I felt like I had to get out of there before I did or said something to embarrass myself more. I scrambled into my car and closed the door firmly between us. The engine revved as I drove off, hoping the tinted windows hid my blush.

Oh crap, I thought. *Am I getting a crush on Robbie Choi?*

TWENTY-ONE

When Robbie walked back into the practice room, Jongdae threw an arm around his shoulders.

"Well, well, little cousin," Jongdae said with a grin. "I guess you're not so bad with girls after all."

"Of course I'm not," Robbie said. He was kind of annoyed. He knew Jongdae was the visual of the group. He was used to girls practically throwing themselves at him. But to see Elena look so starstruck by his cousin, it made him jealous.

"Who told you to go for that hand kiss?" Jongdae asked.

"No one." Robbie elbowed his hyeong in the ribs. He wasn't in the mood to joke around. With a grunt, Jongdae tightened his grip until Robbie was in a headlock.

"Ya!" Robbie yelled, trying to pull free, but the more he struggled the more entangled he became.

"Tell me who gave you the idea for the kiss."

"No one!"

"Yeah, right, you're not that smooth." Jongdae tightened his hold.

"Hyeong!" Robbie shouted, and he wasn't sure if he was yelling at Jongdae or asking for one of the other members to come help him.

In his struggle they lost their balance and went tumbling to the floor. Robbie was now half protesting and half laughing. He poked his fingers into the sensitive part of Jongdae's side, the only place where he was ticklish. With a shout of surprise, Jongdae's grip loosened, and Robbie would have wiggled free except Minseok shouted, "Robbie pile!"

"No!" Robbie said, but it was too late. The other members had piled on top of him and Jongdae, creating an unmovable weight that pinned Robbie in place. Only Jaehyung abstained, but he stood beside them laughing and filming with one of the vlogging cameras.

"Do you admit defeat, Robiya?" Jongdae demanded.

Robbie grunted and tried valiantly one last time to push the boys off, then let his arms flop down. "I admit it."

"Undefeated!" Minseok announced, jumping up with his arms raised like he'd just won the heavyweight championship.

"Yeah," Robbie said, accepting Jaehyung's offer of a hand to stand up. "It's not hard to be undefeated when it's three against one!"

"We have to give our maknae a hard time," Minseok said, then turned to the camera Jaehyung still held. "Even our Robiya has to be brought down to earth, right, Constellations?"

"You okay?" Jun asked with a laugh.

"Sure," Robbie said. "I might have a dislocated shoulder, but it'll heal, right?" He laughed to show he was just joking.

"I'm going to get a cider. Want one?" Jun asked.

"No, I'm fine," Robbie said.

"Snack break?" Jaehyung perked up, the way he always did when food was involved. "I'm in!"

"Me too!" Minseok announced. "Jongdae-hyeong, Robiya, you coming?"

"No, I'm going to sit here and nurse my wounds," Robbie said.

"I'll keep you company, cousin," Jongdae said. "Get me chips!" he called after the others.

"What kind?" Minseok asked, even though he was already halfway out the door.

"The good kind!" Jongdae raised his voice, but there was no sign that Minseok had heard. And Robbie and Jongdae were left alone with Hanbin.

"Today went well," Hanbin announced, taking out his notepad and writing something on one of his endless lists.

"I think the video will turn out well," Robbie said.

"And you made progress with Elena," Hanbin said. "That's good too. I was starting to think we'd have to scrap everything."

"Yeah, I'm proud of you." Jongdae slapped Robbie on the back.

Something rose up in Robbie. A flare of heat around his heart. "I guess so," he said cautiously. He didn't really want to talk about this right now.

"You okay?" Jongdae squinted his eyes in concern as he stared at Robbie.

"I'm just tired from practice." Robbie wanted to change the subject quickly. The warm glow he'd felt from seeing Elena, from working things out with her, was slowly fading, replaced by this uncomfortable burning sensation in his chest. Almost like acid reflux, but he hadn't eaten anything yet, so it couldn't be that.

Robbie walked back to his bag. And a text lit up his notifications.

It was from Elena.

> **ELENA:** I'm home, safe and sound. You can tell all emergency crews to stand down.

Robbie smiled at the sarcasm that practically leapt off the screen.

> **ROBBIE:** I'll have to call back the SWAT team, it may take a little time to abort the rescue mission.
> **ELENA:** It takes a while to turn an armored tank around.
> **ELENA:** But seriously, thanks for agreeing to help the community center, Robbie. It means a lot to me.

He smiled, then stole a glance at Jongdae and Hanbin; they were busy talking to each other. So he quickly typed back.

> **ROBBIE:** Of course, anything for you, Elena. <3

WDB (원더별) MEMBER PROFILE
STAGE NAME: JD
NAME: Lee Jongdae (이종대)

GROUP POSITION: main vocal, leader, center

BIRTHDAY: October 29

SIGN: Scorpio

HEIGHT: 185 cm (6'1")

WEIGHT: 67 kg (147 lb)

BLOOD TYPE: A

BIRTHPLACE: Seoul, South Korea

FAMILY: Dad, older sister

HOBBIES: Playing guitar

EDUCATION: Bora High School

LIGHTSTICK COLOR: Green

JD FACTS:
- Debuted when he was 18 (19 Korean age).
- Was a trainee for 6 years.
- Has lived in Seoul his whole life.
- Favorite number, 1.
- Ideal type is SNSD's Yoona.
- Is friends with Sooyeon, Ateez's Wooyoung, Stray Kids' Changbin.
- Sometimes writes songs for fun with his cousin Robbie (cowrote the song "If U Can" for the last mini album).
- His best friend is his band mate, Minseok (Moonster).
- Has been singing since he could talk.
- Was #3 rank in his middle school class.
- Used to sing in front of his mom's real estate office.
- He would sneak out and go busking when he was 13 (14 Korean age) until his father finally agreed to let him become a trainee.

TWENTY-TWO

f school last week was unbearable, then school on Monday was . . . surreal.

True to his word, Robbie announced the pop-up concert on social media. He'd even texted me to say there would be a special surprise guest.

It would happen Saturday. Which meant we had less than a week to prepare. And less than a week for kids at school to come up to me like we were suddenly best friends.

"Wow, everyone's singing a brand-new tune," Josie said with a laugh when we finally broke free of people stopping me in the halls. It was lunch. Time to set up our booth, which I felt much less enthusiastic about now that people were paying so much attention to me. Seriously, I bet 75 percent of these people hadn't known my name before last week.

"Kids these days. Am I right?" Josie quipped.

I laughed and elbowed her in the side. "I checked the fundraiser site. We're getting more donations already."

"I told you this would work," Josie said. "We can probably end the alterna-prom initiative too. And maybe you could reconsider a certain someone's invitation."

She elbowed me back as we entered the cafeteria. I hunched at the implication. I wasn't really ready to talk about me and Robbie. If there even *was* such a thing as me and Robbie. It all felt so confusing and complicated, and the memory of his lopsided grin outside the dance studio wasn't helping.

I decided to focus on helping Max and Josie set up the table. I knew it was probably unnecessary to continue soliciting donations at lunch with all the pre-concert buzz. But we'd committed to two weeks at this booth. It didn't hurt to finish them out.

I was putting out the pamphlets when Caroline stormed up to me.

"I bet you're so happy this happened!" she spat out.

I lifted a hand to wipe the flecks of actual spit that had landed on my cheek. "What are you talking about?"

Knowing my luck, it was another viral video. Maybe someone had caught a photo of that security guard lifting me off my feet at the dance studio. It wouldn't have surprised me at this point.

"The venue flooded, and now prom is ruined!" Caroline sobbed.

"What?" I didn't know what else to say.

"Prom is ruined, and I refuse to stand here and see you rub it in our faces!" Caroline reached out and grabbed a pile of pamphlets, then tore them up.

"Hey!" I tried to grab them from her. "Stop that."

Caroline turned away just as I made another grab, and I accidentally latched on to her purse. The strap broke in my hand.

"You bitch! This is Fendi!" Caroline screeched, and instead of grabbing more pamphlets, she grabbed my hair.

Stars exploded in my vision as she pulled, and I let out a scream that echoed off the high cafeteria ceiling and silenced half the conversations around us.

"Caro, get a grip," Felicity said. I had a brief thought that it was a poor choice of words before pain stabbed through my skull again.

I heard the gleeful chants of "Fight!" as other students started to crowd around us.

Josie jumped onto Caroline's back with a battle cry, trying to pry her fingers free from my hair. It only caused Caroline to screech so loud it almost burst my eardrums.

"What is going on here?" a voice boomed.

Finally my hair was released. I was sure it now sat in a tangle on top of my head, but at least it wasn't torn out of my skull. I stared at the principal, Dr. Agarwal, as she strode over.

"Caroline, Josefina, we do not allow fighting in school. I'm going to need the four of you to come with me."

"But," I started to say, but the principal just gave me a sharp look.

Josie reached out and squeezed my hand before we filed out of the cafeteria. A few kids gave her discreet head nods, and one brave sophomore gave her a low five.

This was so unfair. I hadn't started the fight. And, as pathetic as it made me feel, I really wasn't fighting so much as getting my hair yanked from my head.

We all crowded into the principal's office, the silence so thick you could stab it with a fork.

"There is a zero-tolerance policy when it comes to fighting at this school," Dr. Agarwal finally said, folding her hands on the desk.

"They started it," Caroline said immediately.

"Bullshit!" Josie said. "She came at Elena for no freaking reason."

"Language, Josefina," Dr. Agarwal said.

"Sorry," Josie mumbled, leaning back. Caroline looked smug, like she'd already won.

"What's your side of it, Elena?" Dr. Agarwal asked, and there was something in her eyes, like this was some kind of test. Like if I gave the wrong answer something worse than detention might happen. If I got suspended my mom would kill me.

Normally I'd slump down farther and just mumble, "I dunno." But something came over me. Maybe it was having Josie beside me, ready to back me up. Or maybe I was just so over random internet people calling me names and not being able to do anything about it. But, in this instance, I could defend myself. So I sat up a little straighter. "Caroline was really mad. She told us about the prom venue getting flooded. Then started tearing up our pamphlets."

"You little rat!" Caroline said.

Dr. Agarwal cleared her throat pointedly, which got Caroline to stop her tirade.

"Well, she broke my purse," Caroline said, holding up the snapped strap.

Dr. Agarwal sighed. "And, Felicity? Did you see who started it?"

I wanted to groan. If this was two against two, I wasn't sure who Dr. Agarwal would believe.

Felicity didn't speak for a long time. She was playing with the hem of her skirt, rubbing it anxiously between her fingers. I remember she used to pull at the hem of her shirts in middle school until they'd wear down and fray. Whenever I caught her doing it, I'd let her hold my hand instead. Strange, the things we remember about old friendships.

"Elena didn't do anything," Felicity finally mumbled.

I shared a shocked look with Josie. I couldn't believe Felicity had backed us up. This was unprecedented. I had to write this date down.

"Okay, fine!" Caroline blew up. "I was upset, but I just didn't think it was fair about what happened with the hotel for prom. I was just being emotional. I care *so much* about prom." She stared at Dr. Agarwal with her best puppy-dog impression. I thought I even saw the glint of tears in her eyes.

"Well, Felicity, I really appreciate your honesty. Josie, Caroline, if you two can wait outside. I'll talk to you separately about your detention."

"Detention?" Caroline cried. "Dr. Agarwal, can't you just give me a verbal warning this time?"

"Caroline, please, wait outside."

With a huff, Caroline wrenched open the door. Josie stood to leave.

"I'm sorry," I said, grabbing Josie's hand. "You were just defending me."

"Oh, don't worry about it. I've always wanted to smack Caroline over the head. Any detention is totally worth it."

"Josefina, please wait outside," Dr. Agarwal said, using her "final warning" voice.

Josie squeezed my hand before leaving.

I couldn't imagine what Dr. Agarwal wanted to talk to me and Felicity about. Unless it was to take our witness statements. Was that something they did in school if you got in a fight?

"So, I was actually coming to the cafeteria to talk to you two because of what happened with the prom venue."

I sat up straighter. This was not what I'd been expecting.

"As you know, the venue the prom committee chose is no longer available due to flooding in the kitchen last night."

"Prom isn't for a few weeks. Do you know if it can be cleaned up before then?" Felicity asked. She sounded pretty dejected. I actually felt a little bad for her.

"They said the damage has affected half the floor, including the ballroom and the basement storage room. They'll need to bring in a crew to tear down the drywall and treat it for water damage. It'll take a while and won't be ready by prom time."

"So, is prom canceled?" Felicity asked.

"Well, luckily we got our deposit back. The hotel felt really bad about having to cancel on us, so they returned it in full. But there's no other event venues large enough that are available at such short notice."

"Then what are we going to do?"

"We could have the prom here," Dr. Agarwal suggested.

"In the gym?" Felicity frowned.

"Why not? It's where we had our prom when I went here."

I always forgot that Dr. Agarwal had been a student here almost twenty-five years ago.

"No offense, Dr. Agarwal, but school gym proms stopped being cool after the eighties," Felicity said. I almost rolled my eyes. Who was judging our prom? A national prom council?

"Well," Dr. Agarwal said with a strained smile. I bet she didn't like that '80s dig. Like Felicity was calling her old. "There's another possibility. That's why I brought Elena here, because I thought this might be an opportunity to come together."

"Come together over what?" Felicity asked. "She hates prom."

And we were back to being on opposite sides again. That truce had lasted a whopping three minutes. "I don't *hate* prom," I said, sounding like a broken record. But this time, I realized that I really didn't feel the same annoyance I used to whenever prom came up. Wow, had Caroline shaken something loose in my brain when she attacked me?

"So, there is a venue close by that's large enough to host the prom and fits within our budget. I just called them before coming to find you," Dr. Agarwal said, and her eyes moved to me. "The West Pinebrook Community Center."

"What?" Felicity and I both exclaimed at the same time, but for distinctly different reasons.

Did this mean they were giving the whole venue fee to the community center? That was so much money!

"That place is like an old factory, isn't it?" Felicity pursed her lips.

"They renovated it really nice," I said, getting into the idea now. "The big rec space is huge, with vaulted ceilings, and the old windows are original. Very retro."

Felicity looked intrigued by the word "retro."

"I guess it could work," she mused. "But I'd have to see the space, and we'd have to up the decoration budget."

"I think that can be done," Dr. Agarwal said, then held up her hand before Felicity could make demands. "Within reason. And, Elena, I was thinking perhaps you and the Awareness Club could lend a hand. We have less than a month to find decorations for such a big space."

"We don't need their help," Felicity said. "We can do it on our own."

"I'm sure you could, Felicity. And I'm sure it would look lovely. But I think that we should take this opportunity to find a silver lining. Maybe try to make the new prom more eco-friendly and sustainable," Dr. Agarwal said. "Does that sound like something the Awareness Club could help with, Elena?"

Oh, Josie would love this project. It was right up her alley.

"Yes!" I said enthusiastically. I could see Felicity glaring at me out of the corner of my eye, but I didn't care. This was great news. With this money and whatever we'd raise from the pop-up concert, it had to be enough to cover the center's expenses until the budget vote.

For the first time, I really thought we could do it. I really thought we could save the community center.

TWENTY-THREE

an a life become a literal seesaw of emotions? After talking to Dr. Agarwal, I felt like the stars seemed to be aligning. The center had two new ways to raise funds, and even though I wasn't stoked about the idea of working with Caroline and Felicity to plan prom, it was worth it for the boost to our fundraising efforts.

And then the dance practice video was released.

If kids were weirdly interested in me before, it was bordering on stalking and harassment now. The final straw was when two freshman girls followed me into the bathroom to ask me if I could get them Robbie's autograph. *While* I was peeing!

After that, I tried to hold my bladder while I was at school.

It felt wrong, like attention I hadn't actually earned. I had literally just walked across the screen for ten seconds. It didn't mean anything. But still my pulse danced when I watched the video for the first time. If I didn't remember filming it, I wouldn't have recognized myself. I looked so . . . in control. And when Robbie kissed my hand, I'd felt myself blush even though I'd been alone in my room.

At least the first prom planning meeting had gone better than anticipated. I'd suggested we lean into Felicity's '80s comment and make the new theme John Hughes movies. Surprisingly, everyone went for it. Felicity even begrudgingly said that retro themes were in. But even the universe couldn't make Josie and Caroline Anderson see eye to eye.

"That girl is dreaming if she thinks we're getting ice sculptures. And how am I supposed to find fabric that's made from recycled material, looks like silk, and costs less than five hundred dollars? Who will even be able to tell what the tablecloths look like in the dark?" Josie seethed as we arrived at the community center early Saturday to help set up for the concert.

Someone had placed stanchions in front of the entrance, and I was shocked to see people already waiting outside. There was a big burly security guy who I recognized as the one who'd lifted me off my feet at the dance studio. It seemed he recognized me too, as he gave me a raised brow nod and let me and Josie through.

"And I'm sorry, but why are *we* the errand people for the prom committee all of a sudden?" Josie continued as we approached the temporary stage that had been set up overnight. There was a banner on the back of the stage that read #SaveWPCommunityCenter with the website for the fundraiser.

"Yeah, it's annoying," I murmured. I couldn't stop my eyes from traveling around the large rec space. Robbie said they'd be here by now, but I didn't see them anywhere. I checked my phone again. The last three texts were from me:

Thanks again for doing this today!
We're here, setting up.
Hey, text me if you need anything.

I winced. That last one sounded so desperate. I shouldn't have sent it. At the time, I thought it sounded like something a host would do for a guest. But could there even be a host of a pop-up concert?

"He'll probably be here soon," Josie said.

"What?" I asked, shoving my phone into my back pocket, as if that wasn't super obvious.

"I bet they're still doing their beautiful hair or something."

"Yeah, probably," I said, making my way to the back hallway. If they were here already, I should check on them, right? But when I opened the door, Cora rushed out and wrapped her arms around me.

"Elena, have you seen the fundraiser site? People have been donating all week. It's wild!"

"Yeah, it's been great." I grinned, even as I tried to see past her down the hallway.

"So, we're going to set up the water stations along the side wall," Cora told us. "And that cute Max has been really great setting up all the tables." She pointed to Max, who was struggling with one of the ancient folding tables.

Josie sighed and went to help him. She batted his hand away from the leg and yanked on it herself. It jerked into place. I tried to resist checking my phone again but pulled it out just in case I'd accidentally put it on silent. And felt ridiculous when I saw the ringer was on and there were no new messages.

Tia walked over with Cora's wife, Sofie. They were both wearing T-shirts with the center's logo printed on them. All the volunteers were wearing them.

"This is really great," Sofie said, coming over to give me a hug. She ran a restaurant in the city. Apparently she'd met Cora there when Cora had been on a disaster of a blind date. "I know this means a lot to Cora. You've really come through for the center."

Her words reminded me that I was here for the community center. Not to stress about what Robbie and I were or weren't.

"Thanks, Sofie," I said, and I really meant it. I needed this nudge to get my head on straight.

Tia joined me as I started unpacking a box of water cartons (which Josie insisted on as they were biodegradable). "So, I wasn't able to talk to you on Wednesday," she said.

"Oh yeah, I've just been really busy with this whole concert thing." In reality, I'd been kind of avoiding "the talk" with Tia. I knew she was going to ask me about Robbie, which would inevitably become a conversation about my feelings for Robbie. Except, I had no idea what my feelings were right now.

"Looks like our main act has arrived," Josie said, poking me in the ribs.

The back doors opened, and the guys entered. Individually, they looked great, but when they walked together as a group, it was like watching a music video play out.

My palms immediately started sweating. Why was I nervous? I'd just seen Robbie last weekend. I spent half the day with him. So why was my heart beating so fast like this?

Maybe I had just let Josie's teasing get to me after the dance practice video was posted. Every time someone mentioned it at school, Josie would make exaggerated kissy faces at me.

"Lover boy looks good," Josie whispered.

"Stop it," I said. Who even said "lover boy" anymore? But as I watched Robbie, I had to agree. He looked amazing. He was wearing a simple pair of black jeans and a graphic tee with lines slashing across the middle. But somehow he looked glamorous. Like he could be on his way to a photo shoot for *Elle Korea*.

I could never have dreamed that a boy who'd once put Jell-O in my sneakers would be walking toward me like a slow-motion shot in a drama. All it needed was those epic instrumental soundtracks they used whenever the hot heir-to-a-conglomerate love interest was introduced.

But this was not a K-drama and Robbie was not a love interest. He was Robbie Choi. The boy who thought puns were the height of humor and had reread my Percy Jackson books until their spines fell apart.

But he was also Robbie Choi, K-pop idol and my first kiss. The boy who could make my heart race with his deep dimple smile. How was I supposed to fit all these puzzle pieces together?

"Hey, Elena!" Minseok wrapped me in a hug so fast I didn't have time to react. I was smashed into his chest. He smelled like soap and doughnuts.

When I was released, Robbie was standing next to me. Was he standing closer than normal? Wait, what was a normal distance to stand from another person? I suddenly wasn't sure.

"Hi, Robbie." I clutched my phone with those sad unanswered texts.

"Hey, Elena."

I wanted to ask if he'd been busy this morning, but I felt like it would make me sound like I was upset that he didn't answer my messages.

"How did you sleep?" I asked instead, and then immediately regretted it. *What kind of question is that?*

Robbie grinned good-naturedly. "Fine. You?"

I tried to smile back but my face felt stiff. "Pretty good. Could be better, but I'm a finicky sleeper."

"I remember," Robbie said.

Minseok's eyes widened, and his mouth became a surprised O.

"From sleepovers," I explained quickly. "When we were like eight. And I'm not that bad anymore."

"She was a kicker," Robbie said with a wider smile. Activate dimple crease. Activate Elena's speeding pulse.

"Not anymore," I insisted.

Josie stepped forward and looped her arm through mine.

"Aren't you going to introduce your *best friend*?" she asked through her exaggerated smile, which was aimed directly at Jaehyung, who stood slightly behind Minseok. Max glowered at them from his place behind the table.

"Oh yeah, this is Tia, Josie, and Max," I said, grateful for a change in subject.

"Hi, I'm Moonster," Minseok said, taking Josie's hand and giving it a light kiss like he was a prince instead of a pop star.

Josie let out a giggle, and I gave her a wide-eyed stare. Josie was *not* a giggler. And from the surprised look on her face, she was just as shocked.

Minseok held out his hand to Tia and then Max, who hesitated before manners took over and he reluctantly returned the shake. But when Minseok flexed his fingers after, I had a suspicion Max had squeezed harder than was necessary.

"How are you doing?" Robbie asked, and put his arm around my shoulders. I was surprised. It was one thing being spun into his arms during a choreographed dance, but this wasn't a dance. And it felt like everyone was watching us.

"I'm g-good," I stuttered out, trying not to wince at how awkward I sounded. "How are you?"

"Good. Better now."

What does that mean? I felt like hummingbirds were flapping in my stomach.

I looked over at Josie, who was giving me a not-so-subtle thumbs-up and mouthing, *Get it!*

Before I could tell her to calm down, the back door opened again, and some of WDB's managers came in with JD and Jun. Jun was carrying a camcorder on a selfie stick. JD was laughing at whatever Jun was saying. It took me a minute to realize they weren't alone. There was a girl with them, and I recognized her immediately.

She was taller than me but still somehow looked petite, probably because she was so thin and wispy. She had long black hair that trailed down her back. A pale heart-shaped face, a button nose, and wide eyes. I'd done some more K-pop research after Robbie came back to town. And it was impossible to be into K-pop these days and not know who Sooyeon was. She was the biggest female idol currently topping the charts.

"Sooyeon-noona!" Robbie took off, jogging toward her and wrapping her in a one-armed hug. His hand lingered a bit on her hip. She smiled and hugged him back.

"What's she doing here?" I asked, shocked.

"She's our special guest for the pop-up concert," Minseok said as Sooyeon's laughter echoed across the space. Robbie grinned and hugged her again, and all of a sudden it didn't feel so special that he'd put his arm around me, not when he still held on to Sooyeon's waist. My stomach dropped. Was there a thing between Robbie and Sooyeon? She had the label of "nation's girl next door," cute and pure. She'd never been in a dating scandal, never done anything but top charts and win awards. Her music was the type I'd have loved in middle school. Very sweet and innocent pop.

"Why would she want to come to this? It's just a small concert in a community center," I said.

"I think she was curious where Robbie grew up," Minseok explained.

Why would she want to see where Robbie grew up? My stomach felt like it was weighed down with stones. That's the kind of thing you did with the guy you were dating.

Should I be surprised that Robbie would be with a girl like Sooyeon? Even from afar she was more stunning in person than on TV. And the way she looked up at him, I could tell she really liked him back. I tried to tell myself I was happy for him. As his friend, of course I should be happy for him. But the rocks that filled my stomach told me I was a big fat liar.

WDB (원더별) MEMBER PROFILE
STAGE NAME: Moonster
NAME: Moon Minseok (문민석)
GROUP POSITION: Subvocal, lead rapper
BIRTHDAY: February 18
SIGN: Aquarius
HEIGHT: 176 cm (5'9.5")
WEIGHT: 62 kg (136.5 lb)
BLOOD TYPE: B
BIRTHPLACE: Paris, France
FAMILY: Mom, Dad, older brother (older by 5 years)
HOBBIES: Watching movies
EDUCATION: Seoul School of Performing Arts; Global Cyber University
LIGHTSTICK COLOR: Yellow

MOONSTER FACTS:
• Favorite foods are any type of meat.

• His favorite season is spring.

• His favorite color is green.

• His favorite number is 13.

• Debuted when he was 18 (19 Korean age).

• Is friends with SF9's Chani, Stray Kids' Han, Stray Kids' Felix, The Boyz's Sunwoo, Itzy's Yeji, (G)I-DLE's Shuhua.

• He was born in Paris, but moved to England with his family when he was only three. And then to Shanghai when he was seven. They finally moved to South Korea when he entered middle school (equivalent of seventh grade).

• The story goes that he was scouted on the street while he was busking at the age of 13 (14 Korean age) after school (instead of attending his hagwon).

• Ideal type is Bae Suzy.

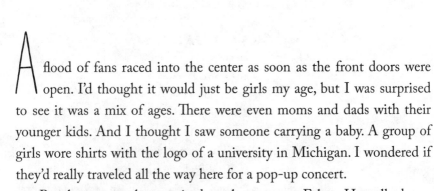

TWENTY-FOUR

A flood of fans raced into the center as soon as the front doors were open. I'd thought it would just be girls my age, but I was surprised to see it was a mix of ages. There were even moms and dads with their younger kids. And I thought I saw someone carrying a baby. A group of girls wore shirts with the logo of a university in Michigan. I wondered if they'd really traveled all the way here for a pop-up concert.

But the person who surprised me the most was Ethan. He walked over and said, "Two waters, please, with a twist."

I frowned at him as I held out two cartons. "What are you doing here?"

"What? I can't support my twin?"

"You can, but are you really?"

"Elena, you have to lighten up sometimes," he said in lieu of actually answering me, and then walked off with his two cartons of water. I watched in shock as he joined Felicity Fitzgerald and handed her the second carton.

"Um, what's going on there?" Josie whispered beside me.

"I have no idea." I scowled, trying to convince myself not to overthink this. Maybe Ethan and Felicity had just randomly run into each other.

I told myself to forget it and turned to the next person to hand them a water carton and a pamphlet for the center.

Ten minutes later, I leaned toward Max at the other table and asked him, "Hey, you have any more water? I'm out."

"Josie went to get more five minutes ago, but she probably got distracted by her new best friends." He pouted.

"Here. If you're going to the back, bring some of these for the boys," Cora said, handing me five ice-cold cartons.

I cradled them in my arms as I wove through the crowd toward the doors to the back of the center. They were locked, but Cora had entrusted me with the spare set of keys. They dangled awkwardly from two fingers as I tried to juggle the key ring and all the water.

I found the boys in the kitchen area, gathered around a large table. Josie was there flirting with Jaehyung. Even though Jaehyung was the worst at speaking English and Josie didn't know a word of Korean other than food names, that didn't stop her from valiantly smiling and regaling him with stories that he just smiled and nodded at. Minseok and Jun were there too. And it seemed like they were getting a kick out of Josie. Minseok even leaned in and whispered something in her ear that made her laugh.

"Josie, you're supposed to be helping at the tables," I reminded her.

"I'm trying to make sure the honored guests are entertained before the show," she said, but she also grabbed two of the water cartons before they spilled out of my arms.

"She's doing a great job of it," Minseok said with a grin, and I watched in shock as Josie blushed. Josie Flores was not a blusher. But I guess in front of these guys she became one.

Jaehyung pried open a container of candied almonds and started eating them by the handful. The whole table was strewn with snacks, some still half-wrapped in colorful wrapping paper. It looked like some of the wrapping paper was handmade with the logo of the band printed or drawn on.

"What is all this?" I asked.

"Jogong," Jaehyung replied.

"What?" Josie asked.

"Gifts from our fans," Minseok clarified. "They gave them to our manager-hyeongs outside."

"The fans brought *all* of this?" The table was completely covered, and I noticed an unopened stack in the corner.

"It's not all of it," Jun replied.

"Yeah, the hyeongs couldn't carry them all." Minseok shrugged, like it was no big deal.

I couldn't believe this many people had brought gifts for the band. And some of them looked expensive. I even spotted a set of steaks in a Styrofoam container over dry ice. Was this really what Robbie's life was like? Being showered with adoration and gifts wherever he went?

"Well, in case you need something to wash all this food down with," I said, handing Minseok a water carton while Josie gave hers to Jaehyung and Jun.

"Where's Robbie?" I asked, looking around.

"I think he was just getting a last-minute hair fix with Sooyeon," he said.

My stomach dropped at the words. I had yet to introduce myself to her. And the longer I didn't, the more awkward I felt.

"Do you want me to help you find them?" Josie asked.

"No, I can do it," I said, and walked down the hall to the individual study rooms. I spotted them in the large playroom that we'd rearranged as their greenroom. There was makeup and hair spray scattered over the folding table, but Robbie and Sooyeon were the only ones in there. Were they standing closer than normal? Was that how close friends stood? Or was Robbie . . . leaning?

Stop it, Elena. It doesn't matter what they are.

Sooyeon smiled up at Robbie. She laid a light hand on his arm. And he didn't seem to mind.

I didn't mean to eavesdrop, but I caught the tail end of what Sooyeon was saying.

". . . so happy that we can hang out. I honestly don't know what I'd do without you." She squeezed his arm, and he put his hand on top of hers.

"Of course, Noona. I was really starting to miss you," Robbie said.

My heart shrank in my chest, and my stomach clenched. There was no mistaking the affection in his voice. Robbie might have changed a lot, but I could still recognize when he cared about someone.

I left quickly before they could notice me. I didn't want them to think I was listening to a private conversation. And I definitely didn't want to see Robbie flirting with a girl I could never compete with.

And why would I want to compete? I asked myself.

Robbie was just someone I knew once who was back in town for a few days. And that was it. That was always what it was going to be.

"Hey," Josie said, jogging to catch up to me. "You okay? You look really pale."

"I'm just feeling a little overheated," I said, not caring if she believed me or not. I felt like I was about to start hyperventilating. So I concentrated on deepening my breaths.

"Did something happen?" Josie asked.

"No. Why?"

"Well, because you kind of crushed those water cartons." She pointed at my hands, and I looked down to see the cartons ready to burst in my tight fists.

"Oh" was all I said, dropping them in a trash can at the edge of my table.

"Hey, did you forget the extra waters?" Max asked.

"Max, if you want more water, why don't you stop being so lazy and get it yourself?" Josie said sharply.

Usually I'd tell her to ease up on him, but I couldn't bring myself to do anything but lean heavily against the table.

"I mean, I will, but you both said you'd get more," Max mumbled as he went to retrieve the water.

Cora came over and put one hand on my shoulder and the other on Josie's. "Isn't this something?" She grinned as she surveyed the packed room. "I'm going to give Robbie a huge hug after this."

My stomach clenched just hearing his name. Then Cora smiled and said, "I really like that boy."

Yeah, so do I, I thought. *That's the problem.*

TWENTY-FIVE

ven in my bad mood, I had to admit the show was amazing.

As soon as the lights dimmed and the music picked up, I could sense the anticipation from the crowd as they waited for the boys to appear. It changed the feel of this space that I was so familiar with. It was no longer an ordinary place where kids played pickup games or where we put on our annual Halloween movie night. It felt like electric currents were traveling through the air. And finally, the lights brightened as the boys walked onto the stage.

The sound of the crowd reached decibel levels that I didn't know were possible. The screams rang in my ears as the first note played and the boys moved into their latest title song.

I'd never been to a K-pop concert, but I'd seen performances on Korean music shows. It felt different from Western pop concerts. The fans were so involved in the performances. As the song started up, so did the fans. The intro music blared out, and cheer sticks waved along to the beat. WDB's cheer sticks were shaped like stars blinking on and off in five different colors. Then the fan chant started: *Lee Jong-dae! Moon Min-seok! Xiao De-jun! Do Jae-hyung! Choi Ji-seok! Sa-rang-hae-yo Won-deo-byul!*

It amped up the adrenaline, made the whole space feel alive. And I found myself joining when the chant repeated despite myself.

WDB's music videos were epic. Their dance practice videos were precise. But still, I wasn't prepared for the spectacle that came with the added lights and bass, and live singing. The power they emitted as they performed was addictive. Like they weren't just singing, but infusing everyone in the crowd with their energy. It was no wonder they'd become global sensations. And a part of me felt proud as I watched Robbie. That he'd become this charismatic performer people couldn't take their eyes off of. That *I* couldn't take my eyes off of.

After the song ended, Robbie and the boys sat on stools to talk to the crowd.

"How's everyone doing today?" Minseok called out, and the crowd erupted into cheers. "We're so happy to be here. Shows like this remind us of our roots. When we first debuted, we'd play wherever people would let us. We were a brand-new group from a brand-new company. I might get in trouble for saying this, but we had no idea what we were doing."

"We still don't," Robbie added with a sheepish smile, and the crowd broke out into laughter.

"Speak for yourself," Minseok said with a sly grin. More laughter.

Wow, they were good.

"We were lucky that music shows eventually gave us a chance. That we were allowed to play our music on radio shows. But when we were debuting, our favorite performances were where we could do guerrilla concerts in Myeongdong or Dongdaemun. We loved those because it helped us get to know our Constellations, who are our hearts!"

More cheering, and even I had to admit it sounded awfully sweet. The idea that these five boys had started from almost nothing, not sure if they would succeed. But now they were the biggest K-pop act in the world. They hadn't had one of the Korean powerhouse entertainment labels to back them up. They truly had risen up through their own hard work.

"We also don't ever want to forget our humble beginnings," Robbie said. "We were always lucky to have a roof over our heads and food to eat, even if it was only ramyun."

"I mean, I still prefer ramyun now," Jun interjected.

"Really, Hyeong? What would you choose between Hanwoo beef and Shin Ramyun?"

"Trick question!" Minseok piped up. "You always choose both!"

Even I laughed at that.

"Well, we want to acknowledge that we have a lot to be grateful for, and we'd like to give back," Robbie said. "Many of you know that I grew up in this area for a few years."

Cheers and whoops erupted from the crowd.

"This place is really important to this community. But now it's lost some of its funding. So you can do two things for us. You can donate to their fundraiser, and if you live here, you can call your local representatives and tell them to vote to give funding to West Pinebrook Community Center! Can you do that for us, Constellations?"

The crowd cheered so loud that it echoed long after the clapping was over. It was more than I could have ever imagined. I hadn't wanted to admit it to anyone, but the anxiety over the thought of failing to save the center had been eating away at me for the last two weeks. I hated to acknowledge that even my careful planning wasn't enough to make a change on its own.

But now I had hope that it was a possible dream. And I knew I owed that renewed hope to Robbie.

"I also want to give a shout-out to someone. She was my best friend when I lived here and she's the one who introduced me to this community center. You might recognize her from a certain video." He gave a comical wince before slicing his hand over his throat like he was being murdered. Laughter and chatter rose up from the crowd, and some of the kids from my high school turned to look at me. I resisted the urge to hide behind Cora. "I want you all to cut her some slack. It was my fault for surprising her. My Elena is not someone who likes too much attention, but I wouldn't have survived many things without her by my side. So, let's all support Elena and the community center!"

More cheers rose up, and I didn't realize my tears had spilled over until Cora held out a tissue to me.

"He's a special guy," Tia said, wrapping her arms around me. "I think he's definitely a keeper."

Tia couldn't know how her words made my stomach lurch. "Yeah, he's a good friend."

"Just a friend?" Tia asked, pulling back to give me a questioning look. I looked up at Robbie as Minseok tried to force him to do aegyo, an exaggerated form of baby talk the fans often demanded that their idols use. Robbie tried to avoid the request but was forced into singing some exaggerated children's song to the cheers of the crowd. He looked so ridiculous, but he also looked like he was having fun. And he glanced over and caught my eye and gave me a pained smile. And I could practically imagine his voice in my head: *Do you see what I have to put up with?*

Why did he have to be so charming and goofy at the same time? It was an unfair combination.

Then Robbie spoke into the mic again.

"Now we have a special surprise for everyone! Let me introduce the amazingly talented and lovely Sooyeon!"

The crowd started screaming in surprised excitement, and my heart dropped into my stomach.

Sooyeon walked onstage, and Robbie wrapped her in a big hug.

No, Robbie was still part of a completely different world. I shouldn't let myself forget that. Because I'd only be more hurt when he left for that world again.

told myself not to be nervous as I walked to the back rooms after the concert. I would just thank Robbie for doing the show. And if Sooyeon was there, I'd be gracious and polite. After all, I was well trained in fake politeness every time my parents had friends over or when my halmeoni dragged me and Ethan to Korean church. It wasn't that hard. Though most of Halmeoni's church friends didn't speak English.

When I entered the temporary greenroom, the boys were cracking up at something Josie must have said, because she was enclosed in their little circle. Max was pouting in the corner, his car keys gripped in his hand.

He looked at me with sorrowful puppy-dog eyes. "I gotta go. My parents have tickets to the philharmonic tonight, and I'm on babysitting duty. I thought maybe you guys might need a ride. . . ." He trailed off as he glanced longingly at Josie again.

"Josie drove us here, so I think we're good."

He sighed, and his shoulders drooped with resignation. The downtrodden look on his face was a good representation of how I was feeling inside as I spotted Robbie sitting on the worn couch with Sooyeon. I gave Max a shoulder pat in solidarity. "See you at school on Monday, Max."

As he pushed out of the room, he almost hit Tia with the door. He muttered an apology before he hurriedly escaped.

"Is Max okay?" Tia asked, joining me.

"Yeah, just a little heartsick." I nodded at Josie, who grabbed Minseok's shoulder as she laughed so hard she snorted.

Tia laughed too. "I don't think he needs to worry. It's the steady and resilient guys who tend to get the girls in the end."

I hoped she was right. Josie had never seemed like someone who got starstruck, but she looked pretty enamored right now.

"El!" Josie called, finally noticing me. "The guys invited us to dinner. Can we go?" She asked me like a kid asking their mom to stay later at a friend's house.

"Oh, I was going to help clean up here more."

"No, you should go have fun with your friends," Tia said. "You've done enough today. We can handle the rest of cleanup."

I tried not to let my eyes trail to Robbie on the couch to gauge his reaction. Would he want me to tag along? Wouldn't he want to spend time alone with his girlfriend?

"Go," Tia said, giving me a little shove in Josie's direction. "We'll be fine."

"Okay," I finally agreed, and Josie lifted her fist in triumph.

"Let's talk next time you're here, okay?" Tia said. She sounded so serious as she said it.

"Is something the matter?"

Tia smiled and shook her head. "No, I just want to catch up. We haven't had time lately."

Even though Josie seemed keen on riding in the idol van with the boys, I insisted that we take her car. That way we could leave the restaurant early if things became awkward or weird.

We pushed out of the community center, and I jumped back as screams filled the air. At first, I thought some kind of accident had happened. Then I blinked at the crowd of at least a dozen fans who rushed forward, stopped only by the staff that moved forward calmly with arms outstretched like a human barrier. They didn't seem surprised at all. And neither did the guys as they moved toward the human barricade. Fans held out albums, magazines, and photo cards. Each guy signed as many as they could reach. One girl got half her body past Hanbin and held out her phone, which JD gracefully took and leaned a bit in to snap a selfie together.

I watched as Robbie laughed with one of his fans as he swiped his autograph across a CD case, a magazine cover, and a girl's arm all without missing a beat. Like this, he seemed so unapproachable. As if there was a barrier surrounding him, keeping him separate from the managers who held the fans at bay.

I'd never felt more distant from Robbie than I did now. Not when he was thousands of miles away. Not when he was on the other side of a television screen. Now, when he was merely a few feet away, smiling for a photo with a crying fan, he seemed more removed from me and my life than ever.

I was silent for the first ten minutes of the drive. Josie either didn't notice or was valiantly trying to fill the silence by talking a mile a minute about all the stories and jokes Minseok and Jaehyung had shared with her. I gave acknowledging grunts at regular intervals, but I wasn't listening. Going to dinner with Robbie and his band was starting to feel like a big mistake. The more time I spent with him, the more I was falling for him. Wouldn't it be smarter to cut this off now before it went any further? I almost told Josie to turn around a dozen times.

It wasn't until we merged onto the highway that I snapped back into focus. "Wait, where are we going?"

Josie shrugged. "Just following the GPS to the address they gave us."

I finally noticed the location of the restaurant. "We're going into the city?"

I don't know why I was imagining a quiet dinner at the local Chili's like we used to do after middle school band concerts. But of course a group like WDB wouldn't go to a suburban chain restaurant.

We didn't end up at a restaurant at all, but at a small, fancy boutique hotel. The lobby had soaring ceilings and columns made of marble. It was as quiet as a museum. The kind of quiet that screamed money. The clientele of this place definitely expected a certain level of service that would never be found at a Holiday Inn.

Our footsteps sounded too echoey and loud as we walked toward the elevator bank.

"Excuse me?" The voice was the kind of snooty that bordered on British without having an actual accent. The man who spoke was dressed in a sleek black suit with a black satin tie. His name tag merely read MANAGER. The check-in desk stood between us, but I still felt like shrinking away from him.

"Us?" I asked, glancing around.

"Yes, are you members?"

"Of the hotel?" I asked.

"Yes, only members or hotel guests can go to the upper floors."

"We're guests of WDB," Josie said, her voice mimicking the snooty tone. "Why don't you call up to room 1603 and let them know Elena and Josie are here?"

"1603?" he asked, obviously surprised. I wondered if that was like the VVIP suite or something.

But before he could pick up the phone, Hanbin walked into the lobby. "Girls, good, you're here. I can take you up."

I gave a last thank-you nod to the manager, who was still watching me like I'd smudge dirty fingerprints everywhere.

Hanbin took us to the top floor. He had to swipe his keycard to access it. Fancy.

The nicest hotel I'd ever stayed at was one that had complimentary continental breakfast. And the muffins had been stale.

We emerged in a rooftop dining area enclosed by floor-to-ceiling windows that showed off the soaring views of the lake to the east and the city to the west. Even though there were two dozen tables, the entire space was empty save the boys and a few of their staff.

"Is the restaurant closed?" I asked.

Hanbin laughed. "Closed to the public."

Josie leaned in and whispered, "Elena, this is a Michelin-star restaurant. The chef is, like, famous. My parents have been dying to eat here. The wait list is two years long!"

My eyes widened as I looked around the space. There must have been at least half a dozen waiters, all lined up along the wall as if ready for a single sign that someone wanted service. The center table was round, large enough to seat ten. But only the band and Sooyeon sat there, the managers and other staff electing to sit at the smaller tables around it, as if they were planets in WDB's orbit.

Aren't we, though? I thought. When you're around people who shine as bright as WDB, you can't help but focus on them.

"Josie! Elena! You made it." Minseok waved us over with a bright smile.

The boys were all clustered to one side of the table with Sooyeon at their center, sandwiched between Robbie and Jongdae. Josie quickly sat beside Minseok, which left me to take the seat farthest away from everyone. Directly across from Robbie and Sooyeon.

"Thanks for inviting us," I said politely, trying not to stare at Robbie.

"Of course! We're always so amped after a show. We have to do something or we'll probably explode," Minseok explained.

"Well, I really appreciate what you did today. It means a lot to everyone at the community center." I didn't know what else to say. I hated being the center of attention; it made me fidgety. I glanced at Josie, who picked up on my silent, awkward signal.

She turned to the table. "So, what do you guys do after a concert?"

"We eat, a lot," Jaehyung replied.

I looked around at the fancy decor of the restaurant. It looked like one of those places with tiny, overpriced portions. How much could they actually eat here?

"Usually we go somewhere that can handle Jaehyung's huge appetite," Minseok explained, as if reading my mind. "But the chef here invited us."

"Invited you?" My brows lifted. No wonder they'd closed the whole place down if they were here at the personal invitation of the chef.

I was sipping my water slowly when the seat next to me was pulled out and Sooyeon sat down. I almost choked on my water in my surprise but managed to gulp it down.

"Hello," Sooyeon said softly. Wow, even her speaking voice was pretty.

"Yes. I mean hello," I said, cringing inwardly at my fumble. She was even more beautiful up close.

"I feel so bad that we haven't had a chance to talk. I didn't mean to be so rude. I just get nervous before shows in new places." Was she really apologizing to me, when I'd been avoiding her all day? I tried to study her face, to see if I could read any deception, but she truly looked sincere. She really did deserve the title of "nation's girl next door."

"Oh, no, it's okay. We were all so busy." I picked up my water again, turning it nervously until I'd rubbed off all the condensation. "Thanks for performing today, by the way."

"Of course. When Robbie told me about it, I thought it was an amazing cause. I'd be happy to post about the community center directly on my SNS accounts too. Just tell Robbie to send me the links to the fundraiser."

Dammit, why was she so nice? Why couldn't she be condescending or arrogant?

"That would be amazing," I said, accepting that I was doomed to like this girl even though she was the one who'd stolen Robbie's heart.

It made sense. Sooyeon not only fit into the bright world that Robbie lived in; she was their reigning princess. Much better suited to be with Robbie than someone who had two left feet, questionable hand-me-down fashion, and couldn't speak in public without turning beet red.

"You did such a good job coordinating," Sooyeon said with a kind smile.

I hunched, uncomfortable with compliments. "We ran out of water too quickly. And we should have had a better system of letting people know where the fundraiser website was."

"You're still such a perfectionist," Robbie said, pulling out the chair beside Sooyeon. "I thought you'd outgrow it."

"It's not being a perfectionist to want to anticipate things."

Robbie laughed. "It is when you want to anticipate every little thing as if you're actually psychic."

I scowled at that. I wasn't in the mood to have my flaws nitpicked in front of Robbie's perfect girlfriend.

"Did you want something?" I asked, glancing pointedly at his vacated chair.

"Wanted to make sure you two weren't talking about me," he said.

I shook my head. "Not everything's about you, Robbie."

"But most things are." He grinned that cocky idol smile and I wanted to be annoyed, but I saw the glint of mischief in his eyes and heard the note of self-deprecation in his voice. It was easier to pick out now that I was used to the cadence of his voice again. Too bad that familiarity also kept tricking me into thinking we were closer than we really were.

I decided it was safest to ignore him and focus on Sooyeon. "So, is this your first time in Chicago?"

"Yeah, I was really excited to see where he grew up in America." Sooyeon sent Robbie a wide grin.

"You know I never grew up," Robbie said with an answering smile.

Sooyeon laughed, and I swear it was like music. "Yeah, I know. Remember when you dunked me during that episode of *Running Man* and Yoo Jae-suk called me Ip-Sooyeon? That nickname stuck for the whole year. Don't think I forgot," Sooyeon said, punching Robbie.

He grabbed his arm like she'd fatally bruised him, and I felt a pang in my chest. I knew Robbie had had a whole life after he left, but I guess I'd thought it was filled with practice rooms and concerts. I'd completely forgotten the fact that he was a cute idol who hung out with other gorgeous celebrities.

"What does that mean?" I asked, feeling like I was on the outside of a joke.

"Oh, ip-soo-hada means 'get in the water.' He was just making a pun." Robbie and Sooyeon laughed, and I knew they were laughing at the joke but it felt weirdly like they were laughing at me.

Just then a line of waiters came out of the kitchen, each carrying a plate. They circled the table before they set the plates in front of us, like a coordinated dance. A man came out, wearing a crisp chef's coat. I was surprised to see that he was Korean. He spoke in a voice with a slightly southern twang and explained his philosophy of mixing the flavors of Korea with other cuisines and said that he hoped we'd enjoy the tasting menu he'd prepared for the night.

The dish in front of me looked like the long rice-dough tubules of tteokbokki, but the sauce was light and creamy instead of the spicy red I was used to. Apparently the chef had mixed the tteok with a cheese-and-truffle sauce. It melted in my mouth as soon as I tasted it, and I closed my eyes; I felt like I'd gone to heaven.

I'd devoured the whole plate and was wondering if it would be rude to lick it, when I noticed Sooyeon hadn't touched hers.

"Is everything okay?" I asked her.

"Oh yeah, I just can't eat carbs or dairy," Sooyeon said.

"*Ever?*" I asked, shocked. Okay, maybe being Sooyeon wasn't that great. I would die without pizza and doughnuts.

"Mostly. But definitely not when I'm promoting." She sighed. "It's okay. I'll just have a seltzer."

"And right before you feel like you're going to faint, eat a cube of cheese," I mumbled.

"*Devil Wears Prada!*" Sooyeon said with a grin.

Wow, now *I* wanted to date Sooyeon.

We were served seven more courses, each more decadent than the last. A fusion take on kalbi jjim—braised short rib. Bibimbap made with poutine instead of rice. Kimchi made with things I'd never have imagined like kale and brussels sprouts; one was even made with apples. Kimbap—seaweed rolls—made with egg instead of rice. (This Sooyeon could eat, though she still picked delicately at them.)

When dinner was over, I leaned back in my chair, wondering if it would be rude to unbutton my pants. I watched in wonder as Jaehyung devoured more dishes. He'd volunteered to eat Sooyeon's uneaten dishes and was happily gorging himself on a second serving of kalbi jjim.

"He's like a black hole," I found myself saying.

"This is nothing. I went to an all-you-can-eat buffet with him once, and I thought the manager was going to have an aneurysm at how much he ate," Sooyeon said with a laugh.

"Well, I'm stuffed," Josie announced, throwing her napkin onto the table. "What's next?"

"I think we should get going," I started to say, but Minseok cut me off.

"Now for the after-after-party at our place!"

My eyes slid to Robbie, who was draining the last of his Diet Coke.

"You don't have to feel obligated to invite us over," I said slowly, waiting to see if he'd say anything. I hadn't felt this unsure around someone since I'd had an irrational crush on Luca Mendoza three years ago. He'd been a senior on the lacrosse team, and his eyes were an odd shade of gray like a werewolf (but less full-moon-murdering). I'd hung around after school to get picked up with Ethan for two weeks just so I could watch Luca run around the lacrosse field. But I don't think he ever even knew my name.

"You shouldn't leave on a full stomach. You have to wait at least thirty minutes," Minseok insisted.

I frowned. "That's swimming."

"That's what they want you to believe." Minseok offered his hand like a gallant suitor at a debutante ball.

I laughed but took his hand. "Fine, we'll stay for thirty minutes."

Minseok pulled back Josie's chair with all the drama of a period actor and offered both of his arms so we had no choice but to take them. He led us down the hall to what looked like a private elevator with a keycard pad. It was decked out in marble and gold so shiny I saw my reflection in it. Only half of us could fit, so Robbie, Sooyeon, and Jongdae had to stay behind. My eyes lingered on Robbie as the doors began to close, but he'd already turned to Sooyeon to murmur something. I heard her laughter as the doors shut.

When the elevator arrived, I was expecting a hallway and gaped when the doors opened directly into a hotel suite. Another sign that this was not the type of place I'd ever find myself staying. It was like stepping into an upscale condo, not a hotel room. There wasn't even a bed in sight. Just a large lounge area with sleek white furniture. A kitchenette with marble counters. And an actual bar, with full-sized liquor bottles and crystal glasses.

Josie flopped down on the couch beside Jaehyung, who'd already picked up a container of nuts and was munching happily on the snack like he hadn't just had two gourmet dinners.

The elevator arrived again, depositing Robbie and the others into the room. I tried not to look like I'd hung back to wait for him and picked up a crystal vase like I was studying it. Turning it over, I noticed it was Swarovski and immediately put it back, ensuring it was steady before carefully letting go.

"Hey! Let's play charades!" Josie called out.

"Why?" I asked.

"Because it doesn't require talking," she said with a wink at Jun and Jaehyung.

"Your friend is funny," Minseok said. "But she talks too fast for the boys to understand."

I laughed, grateful for Josie's antics to distract me from my nerves. "Okay, I'm in."

"Me too," Sooyeon said, linking her arm with mine. "Be on my team, Elena."

I couldn't help but accept that Sooyeon was too nice for me to keep my walls up, so I shrugged. "Sure, why not. But I warn you, I'm really competitive."

★☆★

If you'd have told me two weeks ago that I would be joking and playing with a group of international pop stars, I'd have told you to get your head checked. But lounging in their hotel suite, laughing at each other's antics, they weren't as intimidating.

I mean, they were still gorgeous, but they were also so real. Jaehyung was shy and sweet. I liked how he always tried to give me a reassuring smile. Like two introvert souls who could recognize each other. Jun was really funny. He was always saying offhand things that made the other boys laugh.

Even Jongdae couldn't resist smiling at Josie's attempts to act out movie titles. And he'd gotten up to refresh Sooyeon's drink without a word. I wondered if he was so nice to her because of her relationship with Robbie.

"Okay, what's next?" Minseok asked, clapping his hands. "Another round?"

"No, if I have to watch Jun act out another kiss scene with his own hand, I'm going to poke my own eyes out," Jongdae announced.

"You're such a buzzkill," Minseok said.

Robbie laughed beside me. As we'd all gotten up to take our turns, our seating got rearranged, and I'd ended up next to him on the sofa.

He was holding an acoustic guitar that had been leaning against the back of the couch and was slowly tuning it.

"Play something, Robbie," Josie said.

"Yeah, play that ridiculous love song you used to sing when we were trainees," Minseok teased.

"What love song?" I asked.

"Nothing." Robbie glared at Minseok. "I don't even know what he's talking about."

"You don't remember?" Minseok asked, incredulous. "Oh my god, it's *embedded* in my brain, you played it so much."

"Who's it by?" I asked.

"I don't know," Minseok said. "But it got stuck in my head because

Robbie would play it so often." He hummed a bit, and to my shock, I recognized the melody to the song I'd written with Robbie when we were kids.

"It's our song," I said, turning to Robbie, surprised. "You kept working on it?"

Robbie hunched his shoulders. "No, I just couldn't get it out of my head, so I'd play it sometimes."

I was oddly pleased thinking that even when Robbie was on his way to becoming a big star, he'd kept ahold of something from his time with me.

"Will you play it?"

"Come on." Robbie laughed. "It's just a basic melody. It's not really a song."

My cheeks reddened with embarrassment at his rejection. The pleasure I felt at hearing he remembered the song disappeared.

"Play that ballad you cowrote last spring, Robbie," Sooyeon said.

"Okay." Robbie shrugged.

I tried not to be bitter he was so willing to play her request and not mine.

He started strumming, and a slow and sweet melody came out. And even before he started singing, I knew it was a song about loss. His voice was low and lilting, so different from how he sounded onstage.

"What's it about?" I heard Josie ask.

And Robbie's eyes shifted to her as he changed seamlessly to English lyrics.

He sang about a boy searching for his first love. But she was gone and he couldn't find her again. So he wanders the shores. The salt of the sea mixes with his tears, creating lines on his face that turn into the wrinkles of time and age. And he never forgets her.

"Is the song supposed to be in English?" I asked Minseok.

He chuckled. "No, Robbie's just showing off."

He was translating the lyrics on the spot? How? It was so beautiful.

He shifted back into Korean for the next chorus, and Sooyeon joined in. Their voices mixed well. It was a more melancholy song than she usually sang, but it somehow fit her voice. It highlighted her smoky tone well.

Robbie's eyes shifted to me as he sang the last lines, drawing them out slowly. And even though they were in Korean, I could understand what they meant. *I'll wait for her. She'll never come. But I'll wait for her through the night.*

When the last note faded, everyone applauded.

"What's it from?" I asked.

"It was on a drama OST," Robbie said.

"It was beautiful," Josie said, wiping at her damp cheeks. And I realized that I'd been crying too. Was that why Robbie was watching me so intently? Was I making a fool of myself in front of him again?

"Okay, let's get the mood up. Play something more upbeat!" Minseok demanded.

Robbie thought a moment; then the opening chords to their debut song rang out.

"Oooh!" Minseok said, jumping up with Jaehyung. They started singing together.

My pulse was racing, like I'd just run a marathon. And I was worried my face looked a mess from crying. So I squeezed out of my place on the couch and went looking for a bathroom.

The suite was huge, with three separate bedrooms. Two of them were connected by a Jack-and-Jill bathroom, and I shut myself inside.

I stared at my face in the mirror. It wasn't as bad as I'd thought. Still, I splashed some water on it. I couldn't stop thinking about how Robbie had looked at me as he sang that song. Like he was trying to tell me something. But what? And why was my heart still beating so fast? I pressed my hand over my chest, like I could will my pulse to slow.

This crush I'd been developing on Robbie had to stop. I could predict exactly how this would end, and it would definitely be in disaster. I tried to remind myself of all the bad things he'd done to me since he'd been back.

He embarrassed me in front of the school. *But he apologized for that*, I thought.

The paparazzi in front of the center. *A misunderstanding.*

Making me miss him all over again. There. No easy excuses for that.

When I opened the bathroom door, Sooyeon was standing there, and I jerked back in surprise.

"You okay?" she said with a laugh.

"Just a little jumpy," I admitted.

"Yeah, I'm always on an adrenaline high after a show." She grinned, and it lit up her face. Like this was the reason for everything, this glowing feeling after a performance.

"You were amazing today. I loved your song."

"Thanks," Sooyeon said. "It's a fan favorite for sure."

"It's really happy and fun."

"That's me. Happy and fun Sooyeon." She smiled, but it didn't quite reach her eyes.

I remembered how beautifully haunting her voice had sounded while singing with Robbie. "Would you ever consider doing something different?"

"Maybe," she said. Then she leaned in conspiratorially. "Can I tell you a secret?"

"Oh," I said, caught off guard. "Sure."

"I have an idea for a different direction for my next album. Something that's a mix of soul and folk-pop. I've been dropping hints with my company."

"Oh!" I was surprised she was confiding this to me. But the more I thought about it, the more I could see it fitting her voice. "That's amazing. I think it would work really well for you."

"Really?" She looked so pleased, and I felt a warm glow for being the one who'd made her smile. I saw why Robbie liked her. She was someone who made you feel happy when she was.

"So, how long have you known Robbie?" I asked, deciding I should be a good friend and at least try to be glad for the two of them.

"I was a debut the same year as WDB. So, four years?" Sooyeon said, grinning wistfully. As if they were fond memories for her. Memories of Robbie.

"I can tell you're really close." Did my voice sound tight?

"Yeah," she said with another of those nostalgic smiles, and my stomach suddenly felt like it had been tied in knots.

"I'm going to get a drink," I said, needing a minute to gather myself. "You want one?"

"Sure."

I took my time grabbing myself a Coke and Sooyeon a seltzer. I told myself to get it together. Sooyeon was great. If she wasn't a super-famous celebrity, I'd think we could become close friends. I'd make some small talk for ten more minutes; then I'd grab Josie and make up some excuse so we could leave. I would be fine. Drinks in hand, I walked back to the couches but didn't see Sooyeon. Maybe she'd actually had to use the bathroom. But when I walked back, it was empty too. The cans were starting to make my fingers freeze, so I put them down on the counter when I saw movement in the other room and the murmur of voices beyond.

"Sooyeon?" I said, stepping through the bathroom and pulling on the pocket door.

I stopped short when I saw Sooyeon and Jongdae in an embrace that would definitely not be mistaken for "just friends."

TWENTY-SEVEN

"Elena!" Sooyeon gasped, pushing away from Jongdae.

"I'm sorry," I said, and spun around, escaping back into the other room. Jongdae overtook me, blocking my path as I tried to flee. He looked pissed.

"I'm sorry," I said again.

"You better not tell anyone," he said, his jaw muscles twitching.

"Oppa, stop it." Sooyeon caught up to us and pulled on Jongdae's arm. JD didn't even blink, his eyes still boring into me. It felt like they were burning laser holes through my skull. But with a mighty yank, Sooyeon got him to focus on her. "Let me talk to Elena."

Jongdae looked like he was about to protest, but Sooyeon crossed her arms and said firmly, "Alone, Oppa."

He finally gave in and turned to leave, but not before glaring at me ominously and saying, "If this gets out, I'll know it was you."

There was a small seating area in the room with two armchairs and a low table covered in notebooks and papers. Sooyeon sat in one of the chairs, and not wanting to hover awkwardly, I picked up the papers covering the other so I could sit down too.

"I'm sorry about Jongdae-oppa," she started.

"He was so angry at me."

"No, not at you," Sooyeon assured me. "I think he was kind of angry at himself. We were being reckless. We knew better than to do that in mixed company. I just hadn't seen him for weeks because of their tour."

"So, are you two . . ." I trailed off, not sure if I should even say the word.

"I love him." She said it quietly, a small smile quirking her lips.

"If you love him, then why can't you just announce that you're together? Would it really affect your image that badly?" I knew that fans were really intense about their idols dating sometimes. Especially an idol with the sweet girl-next-door image that Sooyeon had. Flooding message boards. Creating anti hashtags. Sometimes they even hired big billboard trucks to park outside an idol's house or company with a message of disapproval. But was it really worth all the sneaking around?

"It's not just about image. If that's all it was, I'd tell the whole world tomorrow," she said, her voice deep with passion. "But my company isn't as . . . relaxed as Bright Star."

Bright Star was considered relaxed? When the boys had staff tailing them twenty-four seven?

"I was really young when I signed my contract. I wanted to be a singer more than anything in the world, and I didn't want to mess up my chance. So I didn't think anything of all the extra clauses. But my company demands that its singers not date for at least four years after debut," she explained.

"That's actually in the contract?" I asked, shocked. That sounded a bit much. Could a company really control what you did with your personal life just because you were a celebrity?

She nodded. "I didn't really think they'd take it that seriously when I was just a trainee. There were some unnies in the company who had secret boyfriends. But most of them broke it off right before debut. And then, last year, two of my sunbaes were caught secretly dating. The company canceled both of their contracts immediately. No second chances, just done."

"That's awful. I can't believe they'd be so strict."

"It's a competitive industry. Everyone has their own idea of what it takes to make it." She shrugged like there was nothing to be done about the strict totalitarian control the company had over their lives.

I hesitated a moment, then slowly asked, "If they're that strict, then why . . ."

"Why am I taking the risk?" she asked with a self-deprecating laugh. And I felt bad bringing it up. She sounded pretty miserable. "Debut year was harder than I ever anticipated. Four a.m. call times. Never home before midnight. Squeezing in practice when you can. Eating when you can, but having to watch your weight the whole time. It's like being in boot camp. Celebrity boot camp." Sooyeon laughed, but there wasn't any joy in it.

I was surprised at how honest she was being with me. Every time Sooyeon ever gave an interview about her debut, she always claimed it had been a dream. The best year of her life. I'd heard that being a new idol was hard, but I always assumed they never talked about it. Like *Fight Club*.

"The guys debuted the same year as me. We ended up on the same show and event circuit. Always running into each other on *Music Bank* or *Inkigayo*. It was nice, to have friends to share the pain with. In the beginning Jongdae-oppa was just my friend. He was my confidant when I was feeling down and vice versa. But then, last year . . ." Her voice got low, a small line forming between her brows. "My mom got sick. And with my schedule, I couldn't go home to be with her. Jongdae and Robbie both lost parents when they were young. They understood. We all got pretty close. And things between me and Jongdae, they just kind of . . . evolved."

I remembered the stabs of jealousy I'd been feeling all day at how close Sooyeon and Robbie were. And now, hearing their history, I felt like a total jerk for how completely shallow my worries seemed. I had been letting myself spiral and act like a fool all day for no reason. Why hadn't I just asked?

I knew the answer to that. Because I was so sure the answer would be the one that would hurt the most.

"I didn't realize I was falling for him so hard until I already had," Sooyeon confessed. "We tried to deny it. To stay away from each other. But the closer we get to my clause ending, the stronger my love for Jongdae grows. And I just need to be close to him. To reassure myself that everything is the same, that we'll still be together when we're free."

"If he loves you, he'll wait for you," I pointed out.

"He would totally wait for me." Sooyeon smiled, one of those grins that I recognized from whenever Sarah had been totally into a new boyfriend. "It's not his fault that I can't keep my hands off him."

Whoa, definitely not in line with the girl-next-door image.

"I know we can trust you, Elena. Robbie has always been a good judge of character, and he cares so much about you," she said.

For some reason, her words caused a lump to form in my throat. I started fidgeting with the papers still in my hands. Stacking them neatly together.

"I promise I won't tell anyone," I said. Should I pinkie swear? Or was that too juvenile for this situation?

I was saved from having to decide when the door opened and Robbie came in. "Elena, are you okay? Jongdae was saying—"

"It's fine," Sooyeon said, standing up to take his hands in reassurance. "Elena's fine. I'm fine. Jongdae should calm down too."

"Well, maybe you'll have better luck with him. He's in one of his *moods*." Robbie emphasized the word with a meaningful look.

Sooyeon sighed. "Where is he?"

"The other suite," Robbie said. "I figured it was better that he work off his energy somewhere more private."

With a nod, Sooyeon went off to look for him.

"Are you sure you're okay?" Robbie asked me.

"Yeah, I'm good," I started to assure him, but Robbie had frozen in place. His eyes were staring at my hands still tapping the papers on the table.

"Oh, sorry, are these yours?" And for the first time, I really looked at them. It was sheet music with notes and lyrics scribbled over them. Korean in one column and English in the other. And before I could help myself, I'd skimmed the top page.

"I didn't realize I'd left them out," he said, starting to reach out for them. But I leaned away, still reading.

"This is good," I said as I turned to the next page and read more lyrics.

Robbie cleared his throat. "Thanks."

"No, like Robbie, this is really, really good," I said, finally looking up at him.

It wasn't a love song or a dance track like WDB's usual music, but was about the anxiety and depression that could come with being a teenager faced with adults demanding you define yourself. It spoke of the pressure of achieving. And being good enough to be chosen or risk falling into the faceless crowd. And if you do, will your parents regret the hopes and dreams they pinned on you? How can you live up to that?

It was as if Robbie had reached into my soul and ripped out all of my deepest insecurities. The lyrics spoke so honestly about anxiety and stress. I lowered the papers, and Robbie finally took the stack from me. He opened a drawer and tucked them away.

"Robbie, that song . . ." I trailed off, unable to find my words.

"It's just experimental," he said with a dismissive shrug. "Just playing around, nothing serious."

"Nothing serious?" I said, offended on behalf of the song. "Robbie, you are so freaking talented, you know that?" I was practically shouting now, but I couldn't stop myself. "Why would you not share that with the world? Do you know what I'd give to have half the talent and drive you do?"

Robbie looked shocked at my outburst. To be honest, so was I. "Elena, I didn't mean it like that."

"So, you're showing this to your company?" I asked.

Robbie hesitated before answering. "It's complicated. This song might be too different. The company isn't really into us talking about such serious topics in our music."

"That's ridiculous," I scoffed, starting to pace, feeling a wave of frustration that I couldn't express myself half as well as Robbie could in a few stanzas. And he wanted to hide it away in some drawer? "You're a freaking artist, you know that? This song obviously came from somewhere really personal for you. The company would be totally dense not to see that song is amazing." I tried to think of a way to convince him. "Josie knows how to make online petitions. I bet we could start one to get your company to let you write more songs like this."

Robbie laughed and grabbed me by the wrists, and I was forced to stop in the middle of pacing. "You really think it's that good?"

I paused, realizing he was sincerely asking my opinion.

"Yeah." I turned my hands to grip his, hoping he could see the truth in my words. "I mean, I'm not a professional songwriter or anything, but I'm telling you that this one is meaningful. You have to record it."

He linked his fingers with mine, holding tight. "It means a lot to hear that from you."

Robbie's hands were warm, and the longer he held mine, the more aware I was of it. Were my palms starting to sweat? Did he notice it? I thought about letting go, but the image of me trying to shake his hands off as he gawked at my freak-out flew through my mind. And I overcompensated by staying as still as possible.

Trying to pretend I wasn't affected by our prolonged hand-holding, I said, "Well, I did coauthor your first-ever song. So I have a unique perspective on this whole thing."

"You really do." He smiled, and standing like this, our hands linked, it felt somehow intimate.

Should I step away? I wondered. *Had we been holding hands too long? Would this send the wrong message?*

But maybe it was exactly the message I wanted to send. Maybe I should tell him I didn't just think of him only as a friend. Except . . . what if he didn't feel the same way? No, it would be better to just play it safe. I knew that we could work as friends; we'd done it before. That was a road I could navigate much better. "Today was fun," I said awkwardly instead.

Robbie nodded. "I'm glad we got to spend some time together after. I hardly saw you at the center."

Yeah, because I was spiraling about a girl who is actually your cousin's secret girlfriend and avoiding you like a pathetic loser, I thought.

But out loud I said, "Yeah, me too."

"Maybe we could spend more time together while I'm in town?" Robbie asked.

"Maybe," I said, trying not to let my heart flutter too much with anticipation at the suggestion.

"Do you think, maybe, you might want to spend time with me at the prom?" Robbie asked, so hesitantly it would have been cute, except the word "prom" hit me like ice water to the face.

I pulled away now, and Robbie let go, like he'd been expecting this.

A big part of me wanted to say yes. So many of my reasons for not going to prom were gone now. The center fundraising was doing well. I was technically on the prom planning committee now. And Robbie was the one asking me. The thing I'd always wanted. So why was I so reluctant?

"Why does this matter to you so much?" I asked, gripping my own hands together and twisting them nervously. For some reason, it just felt like I was missing something here. A piece of the puzzle that would help me understand the bigger picture.

"It matters." Robbie paused to think. "Because I *need* to go to prom with you," he finished.

I was so surprised at that answer that I let out a short laugh.

"You don't believe me?" Robbie scowled.

"Of course I don't," I said, still laughing on the words.

"It's the truth."

"Then it's a truth that sounds like a lie." I shrugged.

"Fine, but you still have to answer my question. Will you go with me to the prom or not?"

He was watching me intently, waiting for my answer.

I guess we had made a promise. And that promise was the only time I'd been able to laugh that long-ago day. Everything else had been so sad, but that promise had given me hope that we'd be together again. So I could see why he cared about the promise. I'd cared about it too.

"Okay," I said. And a giant, full-of-teeth smile spread across Robbie's face. His real smile. The one that made his eyes squint like we were sharing a secret.

"But as friends, right?" I found myself saying, like I had to be the one to say it first. Because as long as I was the one saying it, then it would hurt less.

"Yeah," Robbie said. Did his smile seem to dim? Had I ruined the mood? Well, it was too late to change it now.

"Of course we're going as friends." Robbie took my hand again and squeezed it. "Good friends who keep their promises."

TWENTY-EIGHT

Robbie sat on his bed, flipping through the sheet music he'd hidden away in his drawer. He kept coming back to the song Elena had read. Her words echoed like a warm memory, and he found himself smiling even as he read the serious lyrics.

"Hey," Jongdae said, standing in the doorway that connected his hotel room to Robbie's. "You okay?"

"Yeah, why?" Robbie asked, tucking the sheet music back into the drawer of the nightstand.

"I'm sorry about how I treated Elena," Jongdae said, flopping onto his back at the foot of Robbie's bed.

"Did Sooyeon tell you to say that?"

"No. I really mean it. I'm sorry."

"You should be saying it to Elena, then."

"Yeah." Jongdae rubbed his hands over his face like he had the weight of the world on him. Sometimes it seemed like he did. Robbie didn't envy Jongdae his position as the leader of WDB or how he had double the schedule commitments as the rest of the boys. He was the face of WDB, and his workload showed it.

"Elena is loyal, Hyeong. She'd never tell anyone about you and Sooyeon."

"I mean, if you trust her, I trust her," Jongdae said, sitting up now. "Did I ruin your chance to ask her to prom again?"

"What makes you think I was going to ask again?" Robbie asked, his stomach rolling, like he'd eaten something that didn't sit quite right with him.

"I heard Hanbin-hyeong telling you that it was the perfect chance after we rocked that show for her community center."

Robbie hated how calculated that made it all sound, and his queasy feeling intensified. The sensation he could now identify as a sign of guilt. "I asked."

Jongdae straightened, his eyes becoming laser sharp. "What did she say this time?"

"Yes."

"She said yes?" Jongdae shouted, a smile spreading on his face. "That's great, Robiya!"

"Yeah," Robbie said, but it didn't feel like it was that great anymore.

"Come on! That means step one is complete. Now that she said yes, we can see how the public reacts to someone in the band dating."

"Yeah, about that," Robbie said slowly.

"What?" Jongdae frowned, confusion clear on his face. "It's a good plan."

"But I'm not really dating Elena. She said we were just going as friends."

"That's fine," Jongdae said, shrugging. "We just need to make it look like you're dating on social media."

"That seems like lying," Robbie said with a grimace.

"It's not. We're not actually claiming you're dating. We'll officially deny everything in a few weeks once we're back in Seoul, when things are back to normal."

Robbie didn't like how dismissive Jondgae sounded. Like he thought Robbie was being overdramatic.

"I just don't want to risk hurting Elena. She's my friend." But for some reason, the word "friend" didn't seem like enough to define his feelings for Elena. Not anymore.

"I know. It's why it's kind of a good parallel, right? The fans already know Sooyeon and I were friends from debut. So Hanbin has a good point that it's the closest comparison. Plus, can you imagine one of the other guys trying to fake-date someone? They'd probably fall in love for real." Jongdae laughed.

"Yeah, that would be ridiculous, right?" Robbie murmured. Now the queasiness had turned into full-on nausea. "It's just that when Hanbin explained everything, he made it sound like an even trade. I help test the WDB-is-dating waters, and he'll push for my solo debut at the next developmental meeting."

"It's your dream, Robiya. And your songs are good. You deserve this," Jongdae said, patting him on the shoulder.

"Then why do I have to jump through hoops to get it?" Robbie asked, frustrated. *Why do I have to potentially hurt someone I care about to get it?*

"I thought you were into the idea," Jongdae said. "*You* were the one who brought up Elena, remember?"

"But that's when I was just asking for one day off to visit her," Robbie said. It all felt like so long ago now. When he saw that the group would be in the Chicago area for a couple weeks before KFest, he thought it was fate. That he could come to Pinebrook and see his old friend again. He'd always wondered what she was up to.

Hanbin had been so against it at first. Bringing up dating scandals and Robbie's image.

Then a paparazzo had taken a grainy photo of Jongdae and Sooyeon coming out of a convenience store together. It was vague enough that Bright Star had shut down any speculation by explaining that Jongdae and Sooyeon were just good friends and had run into each other close to a broadcast station. But it had been a close call.

The next day, Robbie had been called into a meeting with Hanbin and Jongdae. They explained the idea that Robbie could visit Elena to test how fans would react to a member of the band hanging out with a girl. It would be easier to test the waters with a relationship they could eventually deny wholesale. And it would give them a chance to see if they could control the relationship narrative once Sooyeon's dating clause had expired. They needed to think ahead, Hanbin-hyeong had explained. They needed to control the story to protect both WDB and Sooyeon.

It had seemed innocent enough, so Robbie had agreed, thinking it was a case of snapping a quick photo for Instagram.

Then it had all snowballed. Jongdae brought up Robbie's old prom promise. And Hanbin had gotten that look he got when he was scheming. And it had turned into a whole plan to take Elena to prom, to spend significant time with her, to let the press find out. And to gauge if the Constellations were ready to see one of the boys in a potential relationship.

Robbie had said no at first. It was too much. He just wanted to see his old friend. Visit his old neighborhood. Then Hanbin had dangled the solo album in front of him. And not just a solo album, but one where he wrote and produced all of his own songs without micromanagement from the company. Where he could use the music that he'd been secreting away. It wasn't that he didn't like the love songs and dance tracks that WDB was known for. And he got why the company chose those types of songs. It fit the success formula that Bright Star felt it had to follow since it hadn't had any other clout in the industry when WDB debuted.

But sometimes Robbie wanted to say something more with his music. Talk about the realities of being a teen while he still was one.

Plus, mental health was still often thought of as a taboo subject in Korea, but Robbie had had the advantage of living abroad and seeing that it didn't always have to be like that. He wanted his music to help open the door to it, especially after he'd dealt with depression after his dad died. At the time, music had been one of the only ways he could express that. And it had taken him a while to want to share that with the world. But he'd been ready for a while now. If only the company would give him the chance.

"Don't you think things have all gotten too complicated?" Robbie asked. "It sounded simpler when Hanbin-hyeong explained it."

"We're doing it for the band. And Sooyeon," Jongdae said. "It won't hurt Elena the same way. She doesn't have a career to think about."

"But she's still a person with feelings," Robbie said, slouching down into his pillows, wondering if maybe he could just bury himself in them to stop this conversation.

Jongdae shrugged. "She never has to find out about any of this. Anyway, she knows you're not here to stay."

"Yeah . . ." Robbie trailed off. Why did it upset him so much when Jongdae pointed that out?

"If you're uncomfortable with things, you don't have to do this." But Jongdae already looked disappointed.

"I know," Robbie said. And he did. Jongdae had always had Robbie's back. He was the one who'd told Hanbin that if they wanted Robbie to agree to this plan, then he had to get something in return. Robbie wouldn't even have the hope of having his songs presented to the company if not for Jongdae. He'd been so grateful that he'd have agreed to shave off his eyebrows if Jongdae asked. But he wasn't in a conference room in Seoul now. He was in Pinebrook, and he could still feel the warmth of Elena's hand in his.

But Elena wouldn't be in his life in a few weeks, he reminded himself. Jongdae and Sooyeon would. They were his family. And he wanted to protect them if he could. He knew how easy it was for the public to turn against them just for trying to live normal lives. Idols weren't allowed to be normal. They had to be better, shinier, cleaner. Sexy but still pure. The perfect balance of attractive and approachable. And no one was better at it than Jongdae, until he'd fallen in love. And now he would do anything to protect Sooyeon. Including ask his cousin to let the fans believe he was dating someone he wasn't.

"We're lucky Bright Star is willing to support us. But they'll only do it if we prove that the fans will stay with us after we announce my relationship," Jongdae said.

"Can't you go to your father?" Robbie asked, even though he already knew the answer.

"He'll be even harder on us because he doesn't want us getting preferential treatment, Robiya. You know that."

"I know." Robbie sighed.

"Do you want to stop?" Jongdae asked. "I can tell Hanbin we're not going to do it."

Jongdae was watching Robbie with careful eyes. And Robbie knew that if the situations were reversed, Jongdae would help him without blinking.

Robbie glanced down at his sheet music, which had become crumpled in his tightened fists. He carefully smoothed it out and sighed. "I'm not going to tell Elena anything that's an outright lie."

"I'd never expect you to," Jongdae said, relief already clear in his voice as he quickly agreed.

"And we'll do whatever we can to protect her if the netizens turn against her," Robbie said.

"That was always the plan."

Robbie sighed. "Okay, let's keep going."

"Thanks, Robiya." Jongdae leaned forward and laid a loud wet kiss on Robbie's forehead.

"Gross!" Robbie complained, pushing Jongdae off the bed.

His cousin laughed and popped up. "I'm going to call Sooyeon," he said, and strode into his room, closing the door.

And Robbie was left with nothing but his conflicting thoughts and the certainty that no matter how Jongdae and Hanbin assured him Elena would be fine, he knew better. Elena liked to be in control of situations, to anticipate every move. But with Robbie hiding the truth from her, there was no way she could prepare for the possibility that things would go south. Which meant Robbie had to be prepared for the both of them. He owed that to his friend.

He remembered the night his father had told him they were moving. Robbie had yelled at his parents for maybe the first time in his whole life. His mother had been shocked, his father stoically disappointed. But Robbie had been so upset because he'd been spending a week writing the perfect lyrics to the song he'd written with Elena. The song he planned to use to confess his feelings for her. But it had all been ruined.

Still, that night, he'd mustered his courage and kissed her. It was all he thought he'd ever get, and it was what had given him the bravery to do it.

He'd thought of that kiss on and off for the last seven years. And what could have happened between them if he stayed.

And now he was able to live out that what-if. Except it was all a lie.

A facade created for social media reactions. Just like everything else in his life these days.

It's a truth that sounds like a lie, she'd said.

Robbie hadn't anticipated what it would feel like being back here and being forced to keep things from Elena.

His phone lit up with a new text, and his heart shook when he saw it was from Elena. Half of him felt elated that she'd messaged him so quickly after seeing him. But the other half felt his guilt rise so high it threatened to suffocate him.

Still, he couldn't help but torture himself by reading the message: *So, does this mean I'm required to get you that Lego boutonniere?*

Robbie's fingers hovered over the screen. A dozen different replies raced through his mind. Some of them jokes, some of them flirty, some of them caught somewhere in between. But the real text he wanted to send—the one confessing the truth—was the only one he couldn't type. So he pressed DO NOT DISTURB on his phone and put it facedown on his nightstand.

Robbie had never kept anything from Elena when they were kids. She was the one who knew everything about him. Even things his parents hadn't known. Like how he hated living in America for the first year. The year he'd been in Pinebrook before he'd met Elena.

After Elena had moved in next door, he'd been able to imagine a future in America. And he'd always wanted it to be with Elena by his side. His best friend. His favorite person.

And now he was lying to her. And if she ever found out, she'd never forgive him.

TWENTY-NINE

never thought that it would take throwing a concert for my mom to acknowledge how important the community center was. But when she dragged us to another family brunch at Halmeoni and Harabeoji's house, she kept bragging about all the charitable work I did there like it had been her idea for me to volunteer.

"Our Elena has such a giving soul," Mom said as she spooned the kalbi jjim into a serving dish. The braised ribs were stewed to perfection and made my mouth water. I watched as a soft chestnut splattered into the sauce. I wondered if I could sneak a taste before it was served.

"Wow, Elena, I can't believe you actually got WDB to perform," Como said.

Mom straightened with what I could only call pride and said, "Elena is so nice to use her connections for such a good cause."

"Taught her well," Halmeoni said in a gruff voice.

I smiled despite myself. I knew it was mostly that they were impressed by my connection to Robbie, but I hardly ever got such positive attention during a family gathering. It was usually why don't I have a boyfriend, why don't I play sports like Ethan, and nagging me to follow in my successful sisters' footsteps. This time, I was finally being acknowledged for something that was *mine* completely. Even if the thing that was mine—my relationship with Robbie—was fleeting.

"You really should come spend the summer with me in Seoul," Como said. "You haven't been since you were a little girl."

"Yeah," I said slowly, my eyes sliding over to my mom. I didn't want to press it, but the idea of going to Korea for the summer, not having to say goodbye to Robbie for good after prom, was enticing for sure. I could see it all clearly, spend the time really getting to know each other again. Maybe let our feelings develop naturally. Maybe Robbie would open the door to something more so I could be sure that he felt the same way before I had to risk embarrassing myself with unwanted confessions.

But Mom shook her head firmly. "I don't see why Elena can't wait to go when her sisters did."

I sighed and made eye contact with Como, who gave a good-natured shrug. At least she'd tried.

"Don't be so strict, Hyunjoo-ya," Halmeoni chastised.

For the first time all day, Mom's face fell. No, I couldn't let her mood drop. This was the nicest Mom had been to me in a long time. I didn't want to lose the temporary glow of mom approval, so before I could stop myself, I blurted out, "Mom, can I get an appointment at your hair salon?"

"Really?" She looked at me in surprise. "Why?"

"Well . . ." I hesitated, wondering if I was making a mistake, but there was no going back now, as Mom, Como, and Halmeoni were all staring at me. "I'm going to prom. With Robbie."

"What?" Mom practically screeched. "Why didn't you tell me this before?"

Her eyes widened with glee, like she'd won the lottery. And I guess she did feel like she'd won the Korean mom lottery.

Esther used to say that Mom and Dad had grown up in a different generation and culture. In Korean culture, it's frowned upon if you brag about yourself. So parents compensate by bragging about their kids any chance they get. It would be nice, if they didn't constantly pressure us to come up with more and more accomplishments.

"Did you hear that, Unnie? She's going to prom with Robbie Choi," Mom said, beaming.

"Yes, I heard, Hyunjoo. That's great, Elena. What kind of dress are you going to wear?"

"Oh, she'll get something great. Maybe we'll go shopping this afternoon. I'll just have to move some things around."

I let my mom ramble on. She seemed so happy, and for the first time in a long time, it was because of something I'd done. Even if all I'd done was say yes to going to prom.

If this was the only time that I could be the source of my mom's pride, I might as well take it. After all, once Robbie went back to Korea, I'd lose the one thing that made me interesting, even to my own parents.

I helped carry the food out to the table and was surprised when Mom told Ethan to trade spots with me. She wasn't making me sit on the trash stool?

Ethan frowned as he took the wobbly seat while I sat next to Mom, who passed me the kalbi jjim first. *Yeah, I'm definitely taking advantage of being the golden kid for the day,* I thought as I took a giant serving of meat.

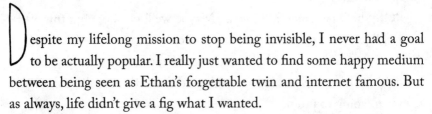

THIRTY

Despite my lifelong mission to stop being invisible, I never had a goal to be actually popular. I really just wanted to find some happy medium between being seen as Ethan's forgettable twin and internet famous. But as always, life didn't give a fig what I wanted.

Of course, the rumor that I was going to prom with Robbie had spread through my class like wildfire. I was now being presented with high fives and congratulatory slaps on the back everywhere I went.

"Great concert, Elena," Diana Walker said as I walked past her to my desk.

"Oh yeah, thanks," I stammered out.

"Well, well, well, look how the turns have tabled!" Josie declared, taking her seat, and Diana's head lowered at being called out for the one-eighty in her attitude.

All the attention felt so weird. I wasn't used to it, and I kept waiting for the other shoe to drop. For the whole junior class to dump the punch line in an epic *Carrie*-pig-blood-level way.

I tried to tell myself I was being ridiculous. This wasn't out of the blue. People appreciated the concert I'd helped organize. I should just accept the praise and stop overthinking everything. Except even then, a little voice in me kept saying the attention was only because of Robbie. Without him, I'd be a nobody still. No one cared about who the real Elena was.

I'd thought about texting Robbie a dozen times the last couple days. But he still hadn't responded to my joke about his Lego boutonniere. I'd been going for a cavalier, things-are-still-fun-and-free-between-us attitude. But I guess he didn't reciprocate it. And now it took all of my will to keep myself from overanalyzing and spiraling.

By Wednesday, he still hadn't texted back, and I was starting to think that something could be wrong. I told myself he was probably busy. That he had a lot to do to prepare for KFest, or was giving interviews, or whatever it was that idols did.

But even going to the community center didn't brighten my mood.

Even when Jackson squealed with delight and ran up to me.

"We won!" he said, reaching for me. "We won! We won!"

"Won what?" I asked, picking him up.

"Elena!" Tia said, running over in a funny parallel to Jackson. "We did it!"

She wrapped her arms around both of us, jumping up and down. Jackson let out a giggle and raised his arms in delight.

"What did we do? What did we win?" I asked.

"I can't tell you. Cora wants to be the one," Tia said, letting me go. "Cora, she's here!"

Cora came striding down the hallway, a giant smile on her face. "You amazing, wonderful girl." She wrapped us all in a hug, and my confusion slowly shifted into a hopeful thought.

"Did we do it?" I asked, looking from Cora to Tia. "Did we raise enough money?"

"Not only that," Cora said. "But I've been on the phone all day. It looks like people have been flooding the phone lines of our representatives demanding they approve our funding. I pretty much have a verbal promise that our budget will be approved in June!"

"Oh my god." Now I was the one jumping in excitement.

And as we danced around, celebrating, the only thing I could think was that I wanted to tell Robbie.

That's how I found myself outside his hotel.

This is a bad idea, I told myself for the hundredth time. I couldn't quite get my feet to move. I was stuck in place under the ornate covered driveway beside the valet stand.

"Elena?"

I spun around, relieved when I saw Robbie and Jaehyung climbing out of a dark van. I started to smile, but Robbie didn't seem happy to see me. In fact, he looked a little annoyed. It made me want to turn right back around and escape. But I knew that would be the coward's way out.

So I turned to Jaehyung as the van drove off to park. He held an armful of snacks. Seriously, this guy was a bottomless pit. Every time I saw him he was snacking or talking about snacking.

"You go on a food run for the band?"

"What?" Jaehyung looked confused for a moment before a smile of understanding bloomed. "Oh, no. These are mine."

I laughed. "I can't believe you never gain weight."

He nodded. "I have good . . ." He trailed off, then asked Robbie something in whispered Korean.

"Metabolism," Robbie said, filling in the blank.

"Oh," I said, trying to smile at Robbie, who still refused to look at me.

The heady anticipation I'd been feeling at the prospect of seeing him fled.

I found myself staring at my hands, picking at the cuticles until they became red. Was he starting to regret asking me to prom? Was he realizing that he didn't want to go after all? Maybe he was trying to figure out how to let me down gently and me being here was ruining it.

My anxiety quickly shifted to anger. If he didn't want to go to prom with me, then he should tell me directly. *He* was the one who wanted to go. *He* was the one who kept nagging me about it. I didn't even like prom. If he didn't want to go, then I didn't care.

"Wellll." Jaehyung drew out the word as his eyes shifted between me and Robbie. "I am going upstairs." He bowed to me, almost dropping a bag of chips. He clutched it to his chest and gave me a kind smile before heading inside.

I half expected Robbie to escape with him, but he didn't.

"What are you doing here?" he asked quietly.

"I just wanted to let you know that the community center raised enough money to stay open." I held out hope that the news would clear his mood.

But he just nodded. "Great."

An awkward silence fell between us. I wondered if I should just leave. Just say that I really only came here to tell him about the center and had something else to do. Any of the excitement I'd felt about sharing the good news faded away.

I was trying to think of how to gracefully exit when he blurted out, "You want to go somewhere?"

"What?" I couldn't quite pin down his mood; it seemed almost frantic now. Like he couldn't stand still.

"You have your car, right?" he asked quickly, turning to lead the way to the parking lot.

"Well, yeah," I said, following him.

"Let's go. I'll drive." He held out his hand with such authority that I held out my keys without even thinking.

I started to ask if he could even legally drive here when he grabbed my arm and ducked behind a large SUV.

"What are—"

Robbie cut me off by cupping his hand over my mouth. I narrowed my eyes at him and considered licking his palm in protest. But I decided against the childish gesture. For now.

Robbie obviously wanted to hide from someone. So, when he released me, I peeked cautiously around and watched Hanbin and another manager walk toward the hotel.

"Are we on the lam?" I whispered.

Robbie frowned. "What lamb?"

"Are you sneaking out?" I clarified.

He shook his head. "I'm just not going directly up to my room."

I decided against getting into an argument of semantics as we reached my car.

I hurriedly buckled my seat belt. I wasn't quite confident that Robbie was a good driver. After all, he spent most of his time being chauffeured around by his managers.

"Do you always have to do this when you want to go out?" I asked, keeping my tone light as possible.

"Do what?" Robbie asked without even looking at me.

"Sneak out."

Robbie shifted in his seat and gave a little cough. "Yeah, I guess so."

"That's awful," I said, thinking about how frustrating it would be if I was never allowed to go out on my own.

Robbie shrugged, his eyes still glued to the road. "It wasn't always like this. When we first started out, we were nobody. So we could all go out and no one even recognized us. But a couple weeks after we were on the VMAs, Jongdae got chased down by a mob of fans. He got all scratched up and sprained his wrist. So now the company worries so much about our safety when we're in public that we can't go anywhere alone."

"Not even to the grocery store?"

"Yeah, I guess." Robbie still wouldn't look at me.

"When do you have to be back?" I asked, glancing at my watch. "Will your managers be mad if you're out too long?"

"Not everything needs to be planned to the minute, Elena. It's possible to just do something without trying to guess how everyone will react to it."

He sounded so annoyed, and I pushed myself back into my seat, stung at his sharp tone. Did he think I was too controlling? I was letting him drive me off to some mystery location, wasn't I?

I tapped my foot anxiously, suddenly feeling like the car was too small and claustrophobic with all the tension buzzing around. My newly solidifying crush on Robbie wasn't making matters any easier. I could feel myself stewing over his words. Did this mean he didn't like spending time with me? Because he thought I was too controlling? I hated that his opinion obviously mattered to me way more than mine did to him.

I shouldn't have acted like everything was rainbows and roses between us just because we were going to prom together. Just because we were keeping an old childhood promise didn't mean we were back to the way we were before. I'd made way too many assumptions, and now I felt the sting of rejection even before it happened. I should prepare myself for that inevitability. It's not like I hadn't done it before.

"I'm sorry that I just surprised you by showing up at your hotel," I started, trying to stave off the worst of the embarrassment by admitting I'd jumped the gun first. "I should have called."

"No, I'm sorry I'm in such a weird mood," Robbie said. "I'm glad you came. I wanted to talk to you all week."

"Really?" I asked. I couldn't help myself.

"Yeah, I just . . . I didn't want to come on too strong," he said, still never taking his eyes off the road. "I know how intense everything was on Saturday with the show and Jongdae. I was worried you'd need time to process it."

"I'm okay," I reassured him, grateful that the friction in the air was easing up. "I can handle it. I'm a big girl."

"I know." He smiled. "Trust me, I know you've grown up." And I noticed that the tips of his ears were red. Was he blushing?

Suddenly I felt a hundred butterflies in my stomach. A strange new tension descended between us. The kind that made my skin feel itchy. "So, what did you want to tell me?"

"What?" he asked, his voice a sharp crack.

"Um, you said you wanted to talk to me," I said, confused about his strange mood swings. "About what?"

"Oh." He shrugged, relaxing again. "Nothing, just wanted to hear your voice."

I started to blush and turned back to the window to hide it. Robbie had driven us out of the city, I realized as we entered the nature preserve. I'd driven by it before but never actually gone in. People liked to come here to see the wildlife and take hikes. Both things that didn't really appeal to me.

"What are we doing here?" I asked.

"I want to take you somewhere," he said, parking the car.

"Okay," I said, glancing down at my Keds. They weren't really hiking shoes. "But if you try to murder me and throw my body into the lake, I'm going to be really mad at you."

Robbie laughed. "Darn, there goes my whole plan. Now I'm going to have to think of something else to do."

I smiled, glad that he was relaxing enough to start joking. I finally let myself relax too as I followed him.

"So, *where* are we going?" I asked, glaring at the tall trees around us as I slapped at my arm where I thought I felt a bug.

"We're almost there," Robbie said with a mischievous smile. It reminded me of when he was about to pull a prank when we were kids. So I was wary as he led me farther down the tree-lined path. I heard the sound of water and wondered if he was taking me to a lake so he could push me in.

It wasn't a lake. It was a creek running under a rudimentary covered bridge built out of branches and sticks, the kind of structure that was definitely haunted. And I wondered if it was even stable, but with Robbie's warm hand wrapped around mine, I felt more willing to get pulled onto a rickety bridge.

After a few steps, I was a little more confident it would hold our weight, and followed Robbie to the middle of the bridge. He leaned against the railing, watching the water flow beneath us.

"When it's the wet season, the creek becomes more like a river," Robbie explained. "My appa brought me out here a few times."

"Does it hurt?" I asked quietly, watching him instead of the water. "Being back here where there are memories of him?"

"A little." His shrug was a jerky, defensive gesture. I wanted to wrap my arms around him, but he still held my hand tightly in his.

"I wonder if he'd be proud of me. Of what I'm doing now with my life."

"I'm sure he would," I said reassuringly, even though I'd never really gotten to know Robbie's dad that well. He was like mine, always away at work.

"He used to say that he just wanted me to go to a good college. I don't think he'd have let me enter Bright Star as a trainee so young." Robbie sighed and finally let go of my hand. It throbbed a little from blood deprivation, so I shook it lightly.

"Our parents want us to go to a good college because it'll help us get good jobs later. But you're already successful. Your dad would want that for you."

"I guess we'll never know," Robbie murmured, like he was talking to himself more than to me.

I wanted to comfort him, but wasn't sure how. "You're the reason the community center is going to be saved. You accomplished something in one day that I couldn't do in a month."

He frowned. "Why do you do that? Keep comparing yourself to me? Do you do that with everyone?"

"What?" I was taken aback. He sounded like he was angry at me. "No, I'm just saying that you're a good person. Your dad would be proud."

His eyes flared and for some reason he seemed even more angry. What had I said this time?

"You're a much better person than I am," he said.

"Who's comparing themselves now?" I asked with a hesitant smile.

He smiled back but his eyes still seemed troubled and distant. "Fair."

He was quiet a moment, watching the water flow below us. I was trying to think of what to say, or if I should say anything at all, when he asked, "Would you sacrifice anything if it meant achieving your dream?"

He said it so seriously that I tried to think of a good answer. But the problem was, I didn't know what it was like to have a dream. "I'm not sure," I admitted. "Depends on what I'd have to sacrifice."

I waited for him to continue. To clarify what he was talking about. And when he didn't, I asked, "Is this about your music?"

He frowned down at the water. "I lied to you."

I stiffened, scared of what he was about to confess.

"When I said I was just playing around with that music you found. It's something I've been working on for years. Some of it before we even debuted."

"Why haven't you shown it to your company?" I asked.

"Because I know what they'll say," he said. "They like promoting the *idea* of me being a singer-songwriter, but they want to control the kind of music. The type of music I want to write doesn't fall in line with the image they built for me. But if they'd just give me a chance, I know I can do it. They just have to believe in me enough to let me. This all has to be worth it."

"I'm sure it will be." And even though my fingers still throbbed, I reached out and squeezed his hand.

"I've waited so long already and I have so many ideas in my head and I want to make them real. I need to make them real."

The passion in his voice was so thick. I don't know if I'd ever talked to anyone who was so certain of what they wanted out of life as Robbie was right now. It made me sad that I didn't feel even a fraction of this passion for anything. "You've been given a gift," I murmured. "To love something as much as you love your music."

"It's only a gift if I can make it happen. Writing my own album in my own style has always been a dream of mine." Robbie's voice became a tense whisper, like he was confessing a deep dark secret. "Something I can make without worrying if it'll top charts or fit an image. Something honest, from just me."

"It's great that you know what your dream is. A lot of us don't."

He released my hand almost violently. Like he was throwing it away. "It's not that simple. Nothing is simple in this industry. It's always 'You're too young,' 'You're too rookie,' 'The sound is too different from what your fans expect.' Everything is controlled so tightly to make the perfect package. Until you realize nothing is your own anymore."

I stepped toward him. "Don't be so hard on yourself, Robbie. You'll get your chance. I just know it."

Then I let out a gasp as, without warning, he turned and wrapped his arms around me. He held me so tight, I could barely suck in another breath.

"You have to understand, it's my dream," he said into my hair.

"I do," I said, bringing my hands up to pat him awkwardly on the back.

He let his cheek rest against mine and my heart clenched. His skin was so soft and smooth. His hands gripped the back of my shirt. So I gave him a squeeze to assure him I wasn't going anywhere.

And then he whispered, "No matter what happens, I need you to know how much I care about you."

He sounded so sad, like he was about to cry. I tried to pull back to look at his face, but he was holding on to me too tight. So I just whispered, "I know."

"I've never stopped caring about you," he said, and I felt my cheeks burn. Now I was grateful he couldn't see me; I'm sure I looked like a fire truck. "I really did miss you, Lani."

"I missed you too, Robbie," I let myself say. And I knew I'd done the thing I promised I wouldn't. I'd completely fallen for Robbie Choi.

WDB (원더별) MEMBER PROFILE

STAGE NAME: Jaehyung
NAME: Do Jaehyung (도재형)
GROUP POSITION: lead vocal
BIRTHDAY: January 12
SIGN: Capricorn
HEIGHT: 174 cm (5'8.5")
WEIGHT: 59 kg (130 lb)
BLOOD TYPE: AB
BIRTHPLACE: Daegu, South Korea
FAMILY: Mom, Dad
HOBBIES: Taking photos, taking long walks
EDUCATION: Cheongdam High School
LIGHTSTICK COLOR: Blue

JAEHYUNG FACTS:

- Called him mong-do because he always looks confused.
- Debuted when he was 15 (16 Korean age).
- Trained for 3 years.
- His favorite color is white.
- His favorite number is 3.
- Jaehyung is ISFP.
- Is friends with Treasure's Doyoung, Itzy's Yuna.
- His favorite foods are jelly, chocolate, peaches, strawberry milk, honey butter chips, Oreo Pepero, tteokbokki, fried chicken, ramen, shrimp chips, and Flamin' Hot Cheetos.
- Can play violin and piano.
- He won a singing contest when he was only five years old.
- He used to sing in his church choir.
- Jaehyung loves taking photos.
- Ideal type is a girl who eats well.

THIRTY-ONE

On Friday, my phone started buzzing like wild in the middle of Precalc, to the point that Mrs. Hewitt (arguably the most relaxed teacher when it came to phones in class) started giving me sharp looks. I tried to express my deep and sincere penitence with my eyes before jabbing the power button to turn it off.

I was hoping that maybe a flock of telemarketers had somehow gotten ahold of my number and it wasn't another netizen-related situation.

I truly should have known better.

When I turned my phone back on at lunch, my Instagram notifications exploded on my screen.

I checked my DMs. There were a bunch of random accounts sending message requests. I didn't open those. But there were a few from kids at school. All of them linked me to the same post.

It was on Robbie's account, a photo from the day of the concert.

Robbie and I were sitting next to each other on the couch in the hotel suite. He had the guitar in his lap. The caption read *after-concert performance*. You could see Minseok and Jaehyung in the background, but Robbie and I were the focus of the photo. My body was turned toward his, so you couldn't see my expression, but I remembered the moment. I'd been enamored of Robbie's guitar playing. I'd loved watching his fingers move over the strings.

Why would he post this? The fans had only just moved on from the promposal disaster. Robbie had been so moody and strange the other day. And now he was posting photos of us for his millions of followers to see and judge? What was Robbie's deal? Why was he being so hot and cold? I texted him.

ELENA: Hey, what's up with that pic on Instagram?
ROBBIE: Sorry, my manager does my social media.
Do you not like it? I thought you looked pretty.

He thought I was pretty? No, I couldn't let him distract me. Then the bubbles danced again for a few seconds, like he was typing for a while: *I can ask them to take it down if you want . . .*

Now I suddenly felt like the bad guy. Was I being high maintenance asking him to take down the post? I remembered his comments the other day about me being too controlling. I told myself I could let this go. Even though some snarky comments said I didn't deserve Robbie. Most of them were actually kind of nice. Some even said we were friendship goals. One of them said that Robbie looked so relaxed after spending time with his childhood bestie.

Did he really look more relaxed? I guess he did look pretty comfortable as he strummed the guitar. No, I would not be swayed. I should take him up on his offer to take down the photo, but then . . . so many people had already seen it. Would they read into things if he took it down?

This was so complicated. If this was how *I* felt just being friends with Robbie, I had no idea what it would be like for him on a daily basis. Debating if he could post a picture or not. How the fans would receive it. How they would judge it or him.

I decided not to make things harder for him.

> **ELENA:** No, it's fine. But next time post my good side.
> **ROBBIE:** So the back of your head?
> **ELENA:** Hey! I take it back! You get NO photo posting privileges.
> **ROBBIE:** ;) <3

Josie sat down next to me, a giant slice of gooey pizza in her hand. "So, you see your photo shoot?"

"Don't even get me started. Give me a bite." I grabbed the pizza and took a giant bite.

"Hey!" Josie protested, but I didn't care. I deserved melted cheese and carbs.

THIRTY-TWO

was still feeling kind of weird about the photo, especially when I noticed the odd looks from other kids at school. I heard someone say, "I don't get it. She's not that special" as I passed. And when I glanced over, they were staring at me. They didn't even have the decency to look away or act embarrassed for getting caught gossiping. I tried to tell myself I was being paranoid. But I had a feeling that some of the kids were getting tired of my new fame-by-association. And if I was honest, so was I. As I passed Ethan and his friends in the courtyard, Tim said loudly, "Hey, Ethan, how does it feel to be related to an Insta influencer?"

I hunched my shoulders against his mocking tone and hurried past, not wanting to hear any more of their teasing.

I decided to throw myself into prom planning. The decorations for the prom had been delivered to the community center, and we had to organize them all and start the DIY projects. So far, Josie and Caroline had only gotten into one fight. So I counted it as a good day. Although, maybe worrying about them fighting would help distract me.

Great, now I was hoping for a fight just so I wouldn't have to stress about what random comments might be flooding in on that photo.

My phone lit up. I'd put it on silent but had forgotten to turn off notifications for texts. I was about to shove it into my bag when I saw Robbie's name on the screen.

ROBBIE: go outside

ELENA: outside where?

ROBBIE: just open the door.

I was curious enough to open the door and poke my head out.

"Hey!"

I almost screamed and jumped back. The door would have slammed in my face if Robbie hadn't grabbed it.

"What the hell!" I punched his arm. "Don't scare me like that."

"I told you I was outside."

"You told me to 'go outside' all cryptic. How was I to know what was out there?"

Robbie laughed, but I wasn't in the mood for his jokes, not when I was still all mixed up in my head about the whole photo post.

"Elena, are you slacking off already?" Caroline called, storming over. Then her face did this weird thing where it just froze. Her mouth hung open, her eyes wide and almost buglike.

"Oh yeah, I guess you've never met," I said awkwardly. "Robbie, this is—"

"Caroline Anderson. I'm a huge fan!" she screeched, racing over to grab Robbie's hand. "Did you come alone?" Her eyes shifted over Robbie's shoulder, where Hanbin hung in the doorway. I hadn't noticed him at first. But I guess wherever the talent went, so did he.

"Caroline, let the boy breathe," Josie said, shaking her head. "I'm sorry, some people just can't be normal around celebrities."

I almost laughed at the ridiculousness of the current situation.

"Hi, Robbie," Felicity said with a small smile.

Robbie squinted his eyes at Caroline and Felicity, and with a jolt I realized he probably remembered them from that mortifying encounter at the mall.

He reached out and gripped my hand. "I was just hoping to steal Elena for a bit." His eyes were as dark and hard as Jongdae's as he stared down the other girls.

Caroline was staring at our joined hands with a mix of horror and envy.

"Sure," Josie said brightly. "I know you probably want as much time with Elena as possible to plan your prom date."

Caroline puffed out her cheeks at the not-so-subtle confirmation that the prom rumors about us were true. And despite the fact that I should've been reveling in her discomfort, the attention just made me uncomfortable, and I pulled on Robbie's hand. "Come on, we can talk over here," I said, taking him to a hallway that led to a set of restrooms.

"You didn't have to be so mean to them," I said to Robbie.

"I wasn't mean. But I don't have to be polite to people who bully my friends," he said.

I almost winced at the word "friends." Which was ridiculous. That's what we were. Even if a part of me wished it were more.

"So, what are you doing here?" I asked, trying to change the subject.

"I wanted to apologize," he said, shoving his hands into his pockets.

"For what?"

"I should have asked you before posting the photo," he said. "I wasn't thinking. I was just remembering that night and how much fun we had. And how I'm glad you're back in my life."

Back in my life. The way he said it, like it was a more permanent thing. *No, Elena, you can't think that way. This is temporary*, I reminded myself.

"Well," I said, trying to come up with a response when I'd already insisted I was fine with the photo. "I have to admit I'm not used to caring about social media likes. But I understand that it's part of your job."

Robbie frowned. Crap, was that the wrong thing to say?

"Well," he said, "I feel like I keep having to say sorry, so I wanted to also make it up to you. And this won't count as a wish. It's a free bonus event."

I laughed at his excited expression. Like he used to look whenever he gave me a present.

"I got special permission from Hanbin-hyeong to take the night off. I thought maybe we could go to all our old favorite places. I already had Hanbin-hyeong call the old Pinebrook Crossing Cinema about renting a theater for us."

"A whole theater?"

"Yeah." Robbie rubbed the back of his neck sheepishly. "It's the only way we can go to the movies without getting mobbed."

"Oh," I said, overwhelmed at the idea of renting a whole theater just to hang out. And then my stomach dropped. "Oh no, I can't tonight."

"Why not?" he asked, and I could feel his disappointment wafting off him in waves.

"I have to stick around here," I said.

"Can't you reschedule?"

I frowned at his assumption that it would be so easy for me to drop everything just because he wanted to hang out. "Can *you* reschedule?"

"Of course not. You know how busy I am."

"Well, I might not be a fancy celebrity who can rent out whole movie theaters," I said, feeling defensive. "But I do have commitments and I can't just disappear on them."

"That's not what I meant," he said contritely. "I guess I'm just disappointed."

I sighed. Maybe I was overreacting. Being around Robbie was like being on a constant emotional roller coaster. "It's fine. I just have to help with prom decorations. Felicity and Caroline are insistent we make this look like not-a-gym, and we're already tight on time."

"Oh." Robbie nodded, the disappointment still clear in his voice.

"I gotta go," I said, itching to escape. "Caroline might dock me prom points or something." I started back to the others.

"Do you need help?" Robbie asked, falling in step with me.

"Nah, I can handle Caroline."

"No, I meant with the decorations."

I stopped short. "*You* want to make prom decorations?"

"Sure, it'll be fun."

"But what about your private movie screening?"

Robbie laughed. "I took tonight off to be with you, not to watch a random movie I could see anytime."

Dammit, why did he have to be so charming? I could feel myself being pulled in.

I worked on making my voice calm and casual. "We're just, like, cutting out cardboard stars and painting them gold."

"Sounds good to me!" he said, taking my hand. My heart started performing a tap dance against my ribs as he pulled me toward the others.

Josie was busy cutting out the stars before putting them in a pile in front of Felicity to paint. Caroline stood over them, a clipboard in her pristine, manicured hands.

"Robbie's helping." I plopped onto the ground next to Josie and grabbed a pair of scissors, refusing to look at the others.

Robbie sat next to me. "Can I paint?" he asked, like someone asking to lick the frosting off the spoon.

"Sure," Josie said with a laugh, handing him a brush.

I could tell Caroline hadn't moved an inch since Robbie had come over. She was frozen in place, hovering over us.

"Caroline, if you keep breathing down my back, I'm going to mess up," Felicity said without even looking up.

In a huff, Caroline snapped out of her daze and moved to the far boxes to sort the silver tassels. I never thought I'd be grateful for Felicity's sharp tongue.

Robbie picked up a bottle of gold paint, twisted off the cap, and began pouring it in the middle of his star.

"Robbie, don't—" I started to warn him, but it was too late. The paint squirted out of the bottle, splattering all over his pants.

I tried to hold in my laugh. "You shouldn't just squeeze it so hard like that. And you don't just squirt it on the star or it'll clump. We pour it on scrap pieces of cardboard and spread it with a brush." I pointed to Felicity, who was doing just that.

"Oh," Robbie said, blushing.

It was actually pretty adorable how clueless he was about something that seemed so basic to me. It reminded me of celebrities in K-dramas trying to learn how to cook and clean for the first time. "Wow, Hanbin must regret he didn't call the paparazzi to get a shot of that. Robbie Choi trying to be a real boy. That would be a publicity story." I laughed. And at first I didn't realize Robbie wasn't laughing with me. In fact, he looked annoyed.

"Not everything I do is for publicity," Robbie said.

"I didn't mean that," I said.

But Robbie stood up, brushing at the paint on his jeans. "I'm going to go try to rinse this off."

"I think you hurt his feelings, El," Josie whispered to me.

"I didn't mean to." I was just making a joke. Did I really go too far?

"Yeah, well, even if you don't mean something, it can still hurt people," Felicity said.

"What's that supposed to mean?" I asked. Why was she even getting involved?

"It's like when you stopped being friends with me."

"What?" I practically shouted. "*You* were the one who stopped being friends with me."

"Yeah, *after* you made it clear you thought I wasn't smart enough for you."

My mouth was open so wide I could catch flies with it. Was Felicity living in some alternate reality where everything was backward?

"I never thought you weren't smart enough. You became a popular cheerleader and dumped me. You told me I couldn't even sit at your lunch table anymore in front of half the freshman class."

Felicity gave an imperious huff. "Fine, I did do that, but I was just really pissed off. That whole week during tryouts you made it clear that you thought cheerleading was for popularity-chasing airheads."

"That's not fair. *You* were the one who told me that all the coolest kids did cheerleading," I said.

"That's because I was trying to convince you to do it too," Felicity said, sounding frustrated. "I thought it was a good way to make friends."

"I didn't want new friends. I already had *you*." I crossed my arms.

"You just don't get it, Elena. You wanted us to be the exact same people we'd always been in middle school. But I didn't. High school was a chance to be a new person. And cheer was how my mom made friends at Pinebrook. I always wanted to be a Vikings cheerleader like her."

Oh yeah, that was true, I remembered. Felicity idolized her mom.

"When I made the squad, you said I was selling out for popularity, and I guess I lost it. I told you to stop sitting with us that day. But I thought you'd come back, and you never did." Felicity shrugged. "I really didn't think you'd be so stubborn."

I was shocked. I remembered saying all those things, but it had been like a horrible defense mechanism. I was afraid that if Felicity fit in with the cool kids, then I'd get phased out. I knew that once she was in that world, there was no way I'd be able to hold on to her friendship. That I'd lose her just like I'd lost Robbie. And then it had come true. Never once had I stopped to think that I'd forced it to come true.

"Look, I'm not telling you this because I want us to hug and make up. I'm telling you because you're doing the same thing with Robbie. It's like the moment he does something that doesn't fit into your idea of 'Elena's Life Plan' you start to poke at him. But not everyone wants the same things as you, Elena." Felicity finished her speech with a shrug and went back to painting her star.

I looked over at Josie, who looked as shocked as I felt. I wanted to ask her if she agreed with Felicity, but I was too scared of what the answer might be.

I'd spent so much of my life feeling like I was invisible that I never stopped to consider that my words could hurt someone else. Especially not someone who'd always been as confident at Felicity.

"I'm going to go find Robbie," I said, standing up.

"Go get 'im," Josie said, raising her fist in solidarity.

Even Felicity gave me a nod of encouragement.

The world had really turned on its head if Felicity Fitzgerald was the one giving me relationship advice.

THIRTY-THREE

waited outside the bathroom for Robbie and caught him right as he came out.

"I'm sorry," I blurted out before he could say anything.

He crossed his arms, and I realized he was waiting for me to continue.

"I didn't think before I said those things about the paparazzi and publicity. I don't know why I said them."

Robbie lifted a brow.

Felicity's words rang through my head, like a nagging reminder that I wasn't telling the whole truth.

"Fine, I know why," I admitted. "I'm . . . scared."

"Why?" Robbie finally spoke.

Relieved that he was at least talking to me, I replied, "Because things are so different between us now. And it's so hard to figure out the right thing to do in your shiny new world. I'm constantly afraid I'll mess up and embarrass you in front of all of your fans and famous friends."

Robbie shook his head. "I don't care what the fans think of you and me, Elena. I only care what we think."

My heart contracted. *You and me.*

"I just wish that I didn't have to always wonder if what I'm doing is going to be caught on camera or a photo to be scrutinized by a bunch of faceless people hiding behind their keyboards."

"Trust me, I know exactly how you feel," Robbie said with a wry laugh. "Just because I'm an idol doesn't mean I only post on social media for likes or fan opinions. Or . . . at least, I don't want to." He sounded so frustrated that I wanted to hug him. "Sometimes I wish I could go somewhere far above the rest of the world where no one can have an opinion about what I do."

"Really?" I asked. "You want to go now?"

"Wait, what?" Robbie looked worried, the way he did whenever I got a harebrained idea when we were kids.

And this time I took his hand. "Come on."

"Where are we going?"

"You'll see. I hope you're not still afraid of heights."

★☆★

"Are we allowed up here?" Robbie asked as I stepped onto the roof of the community center. He looked nervously toward the edge.

"Well, no one's stopping us." I shrugged.

"And that means you should definitely do it," Robbie said, and I noticed he wasn't leaving the doorway.

"Robbie Choi, you *are* still afraid of heights," I said with a laugh.

"Yeah, of course I am. Because gravity still works the same way it did when we were ten, and I don't want my obituary to read, *Robbie Choi could have avoided dying, but he was too stupid to have any sense of self-preservation.*"

I laughed and stepped toward the edge, glancing over my shoulder and smiling as I saw Robbie's wide-eyed stare.

"Elena, stop it," he said, his voice shaking a little.

It only made me want to inch farther out. "Sometimes I come up here at night. It's really beautiful then."

There was a low lip, maybe two feet high. It was definitely not tall enough to protect someone from pitching over the side. So I was careful as I craned my neck to see the ground below.

I let out a whistle. "I don't know if it's a death height. But definitely a maiming height," I mused.

"Elena, I'm serious. Come back," Robbie called. He'd stepped fully onto the roof, but he stood solidly in the middle.

"Come on. You can't even see anything from over there," I called to him.

He shook his head, and his stubborn expression made me laugh. I kind of wanted to lean farther out to see how he'd react. But even as I had the thought, the wind picked up a bit behind me, and I involuntarily tipped forward. I let out a gasp, my arms wheeling for balance.

"Be careful," Robbie said, and to my surprise, his voice was right next to me. He pulled me back, his arm wrapping around me securely.

I laughed. "My hero." But when I looked up, my smile faded. Because we were so close our noses were practically touching. He stared back at me. His expression seemed purposely blank. And I had a moment to wonder which of us would blink first.

"You're right. It is a good view," Robbie whispered, but his eyes were still on me. It reminded me of those tropey moments in dramas where a boy pretends he's calling a view beautiful, but he really means the girl. But this wasn't a drama. This was Robbie and Elena.

Except everything in my life felt ten times more dramatic ever since Robbie had come back. Everything felt ten times heightened. Like my pulse. Like my feelings for Robbie. Like this weird urge to move foreward and just kiss him. And before I could overthink it or dwell on every possible outcome, I lifted onto my toes, my eyes glued to his lips.

Robbie pulled away, turning his face and releasing me. I stumbled back, the wind whipping at my hair.

I felt my cheeks heating in mortification as my heart did a deep dive into my stomach. Oh my god. This was so embarrassing. The one moment I let myself jump in without overthinking, and I'd been rejected. I spun toward the exit when Robbie caught me by the hand.

"I'm sorry," he said.

"No, I'm sorry," I said, unable to look at him right now. "I shouldn't have assumed. I mean, I didn't think . . ." I trailed off, afraid that if I said any more I'd make even more of a fool of myself.

"I care about you. So much."

I closed my eyes. I could hear the silent "but" at the end of his sentence. *I care about you* but *only as a friend.*

Stop wishing for more, Elena, I thought. *Or you're going to get hurt even more.*

THIRTY-FOUR

Robbie was silent most of the ride to the hotel.

He kept replaying the same moment over and over in his head. Elena had been in his arms. Her hair had smelled like lavender. She'd looked at him like he was the only person in her whole world. And then she'd lifted toward him. All he'd wanted was to meet her in the middle and kiss her. But he couldn't, not with his lie hanging over them.

And when he'd turned away and she'd looked so hurt, he knew that he couldn't do this anymore.

"You can't keep taking so much time off," Hanbin warned him from the front seat. "I've given you special passes because of what you're doing for Jongdae. But next week we start full rehearsals for KFest."

"I know," Robbie said, slouching in his seat. He didn't want to talk about Elena with Hanbin. Every time he did, it felt like the warm feelings he got from being with her leached out of him until he couldn't feel her anymore.

"The reaction to the Instagram post was mainly positive. It's a good sign," Hanbin said. Robbie almost expected him to take out his list and check it off. But Hanbin wouldn't write this down. If it was found by anyone, they'd be exposed, and there would be no coming back from this lie.

And Robbie wasn't sure who he was more afraid of finding out, the fans or Elena.

"It would be good if we could post another photo with her, maybe a selfie this time?" Hanbin said.

"No," Robbie heard himself say.

"What?" Hanbin frowned into the rearview mirror.

"No more posting," Robbie said, more forcefully this time. "No more testing the waters. No more lying. She's a real person with real feelings."

"I thought we talked about this. We're not lying. We're just letting the fans believe what they want and seeing how it plays out."

"I don't want to be your testing ground anymore. I should never have agreed to this in the first place," Robbie said. "I just want to be able to spend time with my friend before I have to leave her again."

"And if I tell you that pulling out of this deal means I won't present your music to the company?"

Robbie's heart dropped at that. He'd waited years for the chance to have his music heard. But getting his dream at Elena's expense would forever mar it.

"Then I'll accept that."

THIRTY-FIVE

didn't talk to Robbie all weekend. I didn't even know WDB had left Chicago until I saw their performance in Times Square on *Good Morning America.*

Maybe this was for the best, I told myself. We should go back to living our separate lives now so it wouldn't be such a shock when he went back to Seoul. It was a smart plan. So why was I disappointed whenever another day passed without a message from him?

With prom less than two weeks away, we were spending a lot of time at the community center to prepare the space. Tuesday, Caroline claimed she couldn't come due to "personal business." No one protested. And, to be honest, I preferred it when it was just me and Josie and Felicity. Strangely, things between me and Felicity had really evened out. Like once we'd had our little confrontation, the animosity between us had sifted away. Turned to dust that neither of us cared enough to hold on to anymore.

The nice thing about no Caroline was that Felicity and Josie didn't care if the kids from the center helped paint a few stars. And if they smudged it everywhere, that's what the drop cloth was for.

"Good thing the paint is child safe," Josie said as she watched Jackson smear it all over himself.

I laughed and decided he'd had enough fun with the paints for the day. If we let it continue, Tia would come back to a completely silver child. I plucked him up and ignored his protests as I carried him into the bathroom to wash off.

When I stepped back out, I stopped short at seeing Robbie sitting with Josie and Felicity, untangling fairy lights.

Immediately my fists clenched by my sides. What was he doing here? I figured he'd want space after the disaster moment on the rooftop. But now he was just here with no warning.

"Hey! We recruited two new volunteers," Josie said, pointing to Robbie and his perplexed manager (not Hanbin today), who'd been put on silver-garland-hanging duty.

I forced my hands open to rub my sweaty palms against my jeans. I tried to say something, but my mouth felt too dry to make a sound.

Robbie solved the problem by walking over. He stopped a yard away, like he sensed I needed space. And he was right. I felt like one giant exposed nerve. I was afraid the slightest touch would set me off.

"Hey," he said.

"Oh yeah, hi," I said, still not able to lift my eyes to his. I wished we didn't have an audience for whatever this was. Especially if he was here to officially call off our prom date.

"Sorry I've been so busy the last few days."

I finally looked up and saw him bite his bottom lip. Was he nervous too? And seeing that he was, I relaxed a bit.

"It's okay. But you don't really have to help with the decorations," I said.

"It's worth it if I get to spend time with you," Robbie said with a tentative smile that gave a slight glimpse of dimples.

I couldn't fight the pull of a smile at the corner of my own lips. Now that I was finally studying him, something felt different about Robbie. He seemed looser, more relaxed. Like a giant unknown weight had been lifted from him. I wondered if his trip to New York had somehow helped.

"So, why'd you come?" I asked.

Robbie's grin became mischievous. "What? You don't believe I had a sudden and deep urge to paint cardboard stars?"

I couldn't stop my answering laugh. "I mean, sure, that's the coolest thing to do these days. But I figured it was polite to ask if there was anything else."

"I wanted to invite you somewhere."

"Today?" I asked, looking at the mess of arts and crafts currently spread out beside us. "I don't think I can leave right now."

"Oh, no, I would never pull you away from your . . . art," Robbie said with a good-natured laugh. "But this weekend, are you busy?"

"Um, aren't *you* busy?" I said. "Isn't that KFest?"

"Yeah, and I want you to come. If you're free."

I didn't know what to say. I knew tickets had been sold out for months, within hours of going on sale. Kids at my school were dying to get tickets. I'd even heard Karla saying she'd begged her parents to give her $500 to buy resold tickets online.

"Really? You want me to be there?" I said, a little uncertain. "I wouldn't be in the way."

"In the way? You're our unofficial good-luck charm now. That dance practice video is our most watched. Minseok says that we'll fail miserably if you don't come."

I laughed. "Well, I can't let Minseok down."

"Come on, less talking, more painting! I don't pay you to waste business hours with gossip," Josie cut in, pretending to tap an invisible watch.

"Yeah, about that," I said, sitting down next to her. "What do you think about a raise now that we've brought in contractors?"

"What are your demands?" Josie narrowed her eyes as Robbie sat beside me.

"How about three times our current rate?" Robbie asked.

"Well, three times zero is zero. So, agreed. Now get to work," Josie said, holding out a paintbrush.

As I strung metallic flowers into garlands to make a photo background, my eyes kept sliding over toward Robbie. There was definitely something different about him. He seemed . . . brighter. It was hard for me to stop stealing glances. Right now he was focusing intently as he painted cardboard stars metallic gold. As he tried to get the brush in the small edge crevices, his concentration was so deep that he was doing that thing where he lightly bit his tongue in the corner of his mouth. When we were kids, I used to warn him that if someone surprised him, he might bite the tip of his tongue off, but he said he couldn't help it and I guess he'd never lost the habit.

I reached out and poked his cheek, and he jerked his head up, blinking.

"What was that for?"

"You were making that goofy tongue face. I didn't want you to accidentally bite it." I laughed.

His brow furrowed. "Thanks, Hanbin-hyeong hates when I make that face too."

"I don't hate it. It's actually kind of cute."

He lifted a brow at me. "Really? You used to give me a hard time about it."

"Yeah, well. You know what they say about how little kids flirt," I said.

"Flirt?" Robbie asked.

Why did I say that? I'd just been so at ease that it had slipped out.

"Yeah, I mean. You know. Like you do silly things when you're younger," I said, just stringing together nonsense answers hoping he'd let me off the hook. I lowered my head, deciding I needed to concentrate really hard on threading string through metallic flowers.

"When did you ever flirt with me when we were little?" Robbie asked, leaning closer so I couldn't avoid his stare.

I gave up and put down my garland. "Come on, you had to know that I had a crush on you."

"What?" he said. "When?"

"For a hot second in third grade I thought you were kind of cute." I kept my tone light, careful to make sure I kept everything in the past tense.

"Stop joking around. That's not true." Robbie shook his head.

"I'm telling you it is." I laughed. "But I gave up because you were oblivious and I hate waiting."

"You should've just told me then," he mumbled, going back to swirling his brush in the drying paint.

"Well, I guess we'll never know now what would have come of our great third-grade love." I shrugged.

Robbie frowned and picked up the paint bottle to squirt more into his pan. But after shaking it for a full minute, he looked up. "It's out."

"I'll get more," I volunteered. I needed to stretch my legs anyway. They were starting to fall asleep, and I hit my fists against them as I walked to the storage closet. It was filled with all of the center's sports equipment, but Cora had given us a high shelf to put the paint supplies we needed for the prom decorations.

I heard the door open and half expected it to be Josie coming to gossip about Robbie, but it was Robbie himself.

"I said I'd get the paint," I said, stepping back as he crowded into the closet.

"I know," he said as the door closed behind him. The closet was only lit by a dim lightbulb, which threw everything into shadows. It made it impossible for me to read his expression.

"Sooo." I drew out the word nervously. A hundred hummingbirds had taken flight in my stomach. "You can go back out with the others."

"Did you really have a crush on me before?" he asked, his dark eyes pinning me in place.

"I mean, it was forever ago." My voice sounded weak as the air suddenly felt too thick.

"Not that long ago if you're still bringing it up." He lifted a brow.

"Whatever." I laughed but it sounded tense and forced. "What's gotten into you? You're acting so weird today."

"Nothing. I'm just being myself," he murmured, leaning closer. "More myself than I think I've been in a while."

"That's ... good," I stuttered, feeling like the space was actually way too small for two people.

"You know, I had a crush on you too." He stepped even closer. I tried to retreat, but the shelf dug into my back.

"When?" I whispered.

He leaned in until our eyes were lined up.

"When did you like me?" I asked again, and I could hear my blood rushing so loud it could rival Niagara Falls.

"Guess."

I wanted to say "Now" because I wanted it to be true so badly, but I just shrugged, too scared to answer. I'd learned my lesson last week on the rooftop.

Robbie shifted closer, and I squeezed my eyes closed, waiting for what would come next. But he just lifted on his toes and reached behind me to pull down a bottle of gold paint.

"Is this what you came in here for?"

"Huh?" I said as he placed the bottle in my hands, folding them closed with his. We stood like that, hands cupped, for a breathless ten seconds. Then he stepped back and opened the door. I swayed forward, like my body was magnetically attracted to his.

"See you out there," he said with a grin.

The door closed behind him, and I hugged the paint to my still-racing heart. What had just happened? I was so confused. But I knew one thing: I'd need to stay in here another second to pull myself together before going outside again.

THIRTY-SIX

'm not the kind of person who cares too much about what I'm wearing. I just pull on whatever is clean and comfortable (and "clean" is negotiable). But as I stood in front of every piece of clothing I owned in this world, I realized that, for the first time in my life, I was having outfit issues.

It wasn't prom that worried me. I had that covered. I'd gotten a really cool secondhand dress from the thrift store on Main Street. It was electric blue with a retro A-line silhouette and had sleeves that puffed just a bit, but not so much that it looked ridiculous. I'd even had it hemmed to just above my knees to modernize it. The look was perfect for the '80s theme, and it had cost me less than thirty-five dollars total.

It was KFest that had me in my predicament. There were whole vlogs of YouTubers who went all out picking their outfits for the event. And this was going to be the huge kickoff concert. I couldn't look like a frump.

Plus, Robbie had told me he'd gotten me a VIP pass so I could come backstage. Which meant I would be mingling with dozens of idols. And I kept remembering some of the mean comments on the promposal video. The ones that said I looked like a soccer mom.

I held up another shirt and considered it. It was the only thing I owned that had any kind of sparkle. Though the sequins seemed more sad early '00s than fashionable in any way. I tried to remember if this had been a hand-me-down from Sarah.

I took a photo and texted it to Josie. Then, before I could change my mind, I sent it to Sooyeon too. She'd given me her number and said I could text if I ever needed anything. And I definitely needed help from someone who actually knew what fashion was in at these things.

When Josie and Sooyeon both texted back, I got confirmation that the shirt was fine for school but not a big concert.

"Hey, Elena?" Ethan knocked on my open door and then froze in the doorway. I looked around; I guess it did look like a bomb had gone off in my closet.

"Ethan, I'm in trouble," I said, flopping onto the pile of clothes. At least they made a nice cushion. But that was honestly all they were good for.

"What are you doing?" he asked, laughter beneath his question. I narrowed my eyes at him, and he wisely clamped his lips shut.

"I'm trying to find an outfit for this weekend, but I honestly have nothing that doesn't look like it's . . . used."

"That's what happens when you don't buy anything new for three years." Ethan shrugged, stepping in and picking up a pair of leggings. He rolled them in his hands in a half-assed attempt at folding them.

"Being friends with Josie makes me too aware of the fast-fashion environmental crisis. Do you *know* how many pounds of clothing we throw out each year?"

Ethan laughed. "I honestly don't, and I don't think I want to know. Actually, I wanted to talk to you about prom."

"Oh, please lord, no, not another prom issue. What is it now? Is there a petition for more balloon archways or something?"

"There's going to be a balloon archway?" Ethan asked. "Why?"

I shook my head. I could already feel a tension headache coming on. "I don't even know at this point."

Ethan sighed, twisting the leggings tighter. I wanted to tell him if he kept doing that he'd stretch them, but before I could, he said, "So, the thing is, I thought maybe I should tell you who I'm taking to prom."

Was *Ethan* telling me about his love life? Had the sun started to set in the east?

"I'm taking Felicity."

I sat up now. "Felicity? Fitzgerald?"

"Yeah," Ethan said slowly, watching me the way a person might watch a feral cat.

A dozen reactions raced through me. But the strongest were confusion and annoyance. Of course Ethan would ask Felicity to prom. No thought at all given to the fact that Felicity had been regularly tormenting me publicly for the last three years.

But weren't you just thinking you were getting along with her more now? a voice said in my head. A voice that sounded suspiciously like my mom.

It would be easier to just let this go. It was what was expected of me. But I kept thinking of all the times Ethan's friends had mercilessly teased me the last few weeks and he hadn't stood up for me. I didn't want to just let it go this time. This was part of a larger pattern where Prince Ethan did whatever he wanted without caring about how I would feel.

"I don't know why you're telling me this when I know nothing I say will change anything."

Ethan scowled. "I'm not telling you to get an opinion. I'm just giving you a heads-up 'cause I know you'd freak if I didn't."

I seethed at his wording. "It's not freaking out. It's being annoyed that you don't care enough about my feelings to not take the only person I could reasonably call my archnemesis."

"You're being so overdramatic." Ethan raised his eyes to the ceiling, and it just made me even angrier.

"Fine, do whatever you want. You never even care what's going on in my life. So why should I care what's going on in yours?"

Ethan looked pissed now. "That's so unfair when it's the way *you* want it!"

"What?" He wasn't making any sense.

"*You're* the one who wants us to stay out of each other's lives." Ethan twisted the leggings so hard that they started to strain, turning see-through at the seams.

I tried to grab them from him, but he pulled back.

"You're stretching them!" I said. But he lifted his arms over his head. "Ethan, stop it!" I jumped but still couldn't reach the leggings.

"What is happening up there?" Mom's voice snapped from downstairs. "Elena, don't yell at your brother!"

My jaw clenched in silent frustration.

Ethan's arm finally lowered, and I snatched the leggings back.

"Just leave me alone," I whispered so Mom couldn't catch it with her super hearing.

"Fine. I shouldn't have even bothered talking to you about this." He stormed into his room, slamming the door behind him.

"Elena!" Mom shouted.

I held in a scream and shut my own door, throwing my leggings on the floor in frustration. They were definitely stretched out.

THIRTY-SEVEN

didn't have the energy to look for an outfit anymore after my fight with Ethan.

I almost texted Josie to complain about the whole thing, but I felt like it wasn't something to share. To be honest, Ethan never got mad at me like that. I'd always assumed it was because he never cared enough about anything I did to get mad.

I started to pick up clothes, thinking I better clean before Mom came upstairs and had an aneurysm.

My phone buzzed, and I almost ignored it but knew if it was Josie she'd just keep texting. I sat up in surprise when I saw Robbie's name:

ROBBIE: Answer the door.

And then the doorbell rang.

A thrill raced through me, my previous exhaustion forgotten, and I jogged down the stairs. I had a fleeting moment of thinking this was what it must feel like to have a boyfriend. To be so excited to see him, you can't get to the door fast enough.

I flung it open and then just stood there. Letting the electricity of the moment sizzle between us. Ever since his strange behavior in the closet, I'd felt like there was a rubber band pulled tight between us and the first one to move would snap it.

"You okay?" he asked, a hesitant smile brightening his features.

"Oh yeah, I'm good," I said, snapping out of my reverie. "Wait. *How* are you here? I thought you were booked with rehearsals until KFest!"

"I snuck away." He grinned and held up a duffel bag.

"What is that?" Was he going on a trip?

"It's a surprise."

"Oh, well. It's a . . . nice bag," I said, even though it was pretty standard. And used.

Robbie laughed. "The bag isn't your surprise." He stepped in and pulled off his shoes. "Open it."

I eyed the hallway that led to the kitchen, wondering if my mom would stick her head out. "Okay, but let's go upstairs first."

When we stepped into my room, I remembered the state it was in a second too late. I started to spin around to block Robbie's view. But he stepped in and let out a low whistle.

"Lani, I hate to tell you this, but . . . I think you've been robbed," he said.

"Don't make fun. I've been having a wardrobe meltdown."

"Well, that's what your present is for."

"Really?" I asked, confused. "Is it clothing organizers or something?"

Robbie laughed as he unzipped the duffel. He pulled out a red sequined dress. It was a one-shoulder situation with an asymmetrical hem. I did not know fashion stuff, but I knew this dress was gorgeous.

Oh my god, was I having a *Pretty Woman* makeover situation? Was Robbie my Richard Gere?

"How did you know?" I asked, walking over to the duffel bag and pulling out outfits, each more beautiful than the last.

"It's from Sooyeon. From her tour wardrobe. She doesn't need any of these outfits for her set at KFest. So she said you can pick whatever you want to wear this Saturday."

It wasn't a *Pretty Woman* situation. It was a *Cinderella* situation. And Sooyeon was my fairy godmother.

"Do you want to try on stuff?" he asked.

"No," I said, carefully picking up the precious duffel and placing it delicately on my desk chair. "I want you to be surprised."

Robbie smiled. "But you sent me a selfie of you in your prom dress?"

"That's just prom." I shrugged.

"You're an odd one, Elena Soo."

"It's why you adore me," I said with a playful wink. I was feeling giddy from the gift.

"Sure," Robbie said, moving to my dresser and picking up an old jewelry box.

"What are you doing?" I asked, suddenly self-conscious at how he was inspecting the space.

"I haven't been in here for seven years. It hasn't changed too much."

"Yes, it has," I said.

He gave me a skeptical look.

"I have new . . ." I looked around. "Sheets."

Robbie laughed as he pulled a notebook off the shelf.

"From my poetry phase," I said, plucking it out of his hand. I didn't want him looking at my bad poems when he was such a talented lyricist.

He slid out a crumpled sketchbook.

"My art phase." I took that from his hand too.

He laughed and pulled out three more notebooks and held them up.

"Creative writing. Journalism. Bullet journaling." I grabbed each of them as I listed the abandoned hobbies, now holding a stack of my failures in my arms.

"It's nice," he said as I shoved the notebooks back onto the shelf.

"That I suck at everything I try?" I scoffed.

"That you keep trying," he said. "We're not supposed to know who we are at this age, Lani."

"You do," I pointed out.

Robbie looked at me oddly then, his head tilting. "Why is it so important to you?"

"Huh?" I said, unsure what he was actually asking.

"Why does it matter if you know what you're passionate about right now?"

"Because . . ." I trailed off. "I'm like an empty book. No one is interested in reading a blank page."

Robbie frowned and put his hands on my shoulders. "Elena, careers and hobbies and dreams can be discovered whenever. What makes you interesting isn't any one thing. You're so many small beautiful things put together. You know that, right?"

I had to blink hard because suddenly my eyes were burning. It was the first time anyone had told me I was good enough the way I was since . . . well, Robbie. "Well, tell that to the college counselors at my school."

He shook his head and let his hands fall from my arms to turn and pick up random things from my cluttered dresser. He picked up a well-worn edition of *To All the Boys I've Loved Before* and revealed a brand-new copy of the latest WDB album. I tried to grab it, but he was too fast.

"Oh, well, well, well. Are you a secret Constellation, Elena?"

"No," I said, snatching the album out of his hand. "I'm just being supportive of my friend. Every sale counts, you know."

"You're right. I shouldn't tease. We appreciate your support," he said with a low bow.

I laughed as I shoved the album onto my crowded bookshelf between Simon and Starr.

"You know," I mused, "I *was* kind of into WDB when the company released your pre-debut teasers."

"What? No, you weren't," Robbie said, eyeing me suspiciously.

"I was," I insisted, smiling at his doubtful look. "I knew all the bio facts about JD and Minseok."

Robbie frowned.

"What?" I asked, enjoying his obvious annoyance.

"Why them?"

"Well, Minseok is hilarious. Anyone could see that even back then. And JD." I just sighed. And held back a laugh when Robbie's frown deepened so much he looked like Jackson when he pouted.

"Did you . . . ?" He trailed off.

"What?" I prodded him, folding my lips to hide my smile. It was almost too easy to tease him now that I knew where to poke.

"Did you ever have a crush on him?"

"Maybe," I admitted. "He was just so cool."

"Do you *still* like him?" It was hard to keep a straight face at the sight of his serious expression.

"Of course not." I finally laughed. "Oh, come on, don't pout. I *told* you I had a crush on you in third grade. So it's all equal."

"No, it's not. Things are never equal between you and me." Robbie was looking at me so funny. It made my insides twist and my heart feel too tight.

"Of course they are," I said quietly, trying to ignore my speeding pulse. "Why wouldn't they be?"

"Do you really not know?" he asked. "That I would've done anything for you?"

"Really? Will you steal a new car for me?" I asked, trying desperately to joke my way out of this. Because I had no experience with being looked at the way Robbie was looking at me. I couldn't think. If he just blinked or stepped back, then maybe I could catch my breath.

"I'm being serious," he said. "You were my first love, Lani."

I tried to smile, but it felt wobbly on my face. "Come on, 'first loves' are just things from movies and dramas."

"Why?" Robbie tilted his head. "You were my first crush. My first kiss. The first person I wanted to say 'I love you' to outside my family."

"When did you want to say it?" Why did I sound so breathless? Could Robbie hear it in my voice?

"That night that I told you we were moving," he said without hesitating. "I had planned a whole thing where I'd play our song and confess that I loved you."

"That's ridiculous." I forced a laugh, but it came out as a nervous sound. I told myself that he was talking about the past. That it didn't mean he felt the same now. Except he was staring at me so intently that it was jumbling my brain. "Why would you go through all of that effort?"

"Because you're worth it." I tried to search for a smile, for the joke. But he looked so serious.

"But you're not here to stay," I pointed out. "You're going to go back to Seoul soon, and you'll be half a world away again." Why was I arguing with everything he was saying? Why did I feel like I had to reject him before he could reject me?

"You're right," Robbie said, and my shoulders dropped at his easy agreement.

Then he stepped toward me.

"My appa used to say that to start making a change, you just need to take a single step."

I held my breath, waiting for what he'd say next.

"So, do you think you could give it a try? Just one step."

I couldn't seem to say anything, but I did step forward. And he smiled, framing my face with his hands, his palms warm against my cheeks. "You don't talk like any high school boy I know," I finally said when I found my voice. "Makes sense you write songs."

Robbie laughed, a low sound that was half hum. "It's all the dramas I watch," he said. And he lowered his head slightly, his eyes latched on to mine. His brows lifted, and I realized he was asking me a question. *Are you in?*

In answer, I lifted onto my toes and closed the space between us. It was the second time I'd kissed Robbie Choi. And it blew the first time out of the water.

WDB (원더별) MEMBER PROFILE
STAGE NAME: Jun
NAME: Xiao Dejun (소데준)
GROUP POSITION: subvocal, main dancer
BIRTHDAY: December 5
SIGN: Sagittarius
HEIGHT: 182 cm (5'11.5")
WEIGHT: 65 kg (143 lb)
BLOOD TYPE: A
BIRTHPLACE: Haidian District, Beijing, China
FAMILY: Mom, Dad, 2 sisters (younger)
HOBBIES: Soccer
EDUCATION: He graduated from Beijing Shida Middle School
and attended boarding school.
LIGHTSTICK COLOR: Red

JUN FACTS:

• Before joining the group he was a soccer player. He still loves to play soccer.

• Auditioned for a big entertainment agency when he was 14
and came over to Seoul to train.

• Ended up leaving that agency and joining Bright Star when he was 15.

• Debuted when he was 16 (17 Korean age).

• His favorite foods are anything with or on bread (pizza, sandwiches, etc.).

• He likes the number 7.

• His favorite color is black.

• Can play guitar.

• Is friends with NCT's Sungchan, NCT's Chenle, Wanna One's Kuanlin.

• His favorite comedian is Yoo Jae-suk.

• The best cook in the group. Always cooks for the group when they're home.

• Ideal type is Kim Tae-hee.

THIRTY-EIGHT

The Thursday before KFest, I was back at the community center to volunteer, but mostly I was waiting for Tia to arrive. I needed to talk about what was happening between me and Robbie. I had so many thoughts whirling dangerously around in my head. What were we? What did this mean now that we'd kissed? Was this just until prom? And what would I do when he had to leave?

I heard Jackson's shout of joy behind me and turned to catch him mid-leap.

"Elena-lena-lena!" he sang, practically vibrating in my arms.

"What's up, Jack-Jack?"

"We're getting a new house!" Jackson shouted, throwing his arms in the air just as Tia raced in.

"What?" I gave Tia a surprised smile. "How?"

I was confused. Tia hated her apartment, which had wiring problems and a leaky faucet, but every time I suggested she move, she said it was the only place she could afford.

"Jackson, go find Miss Cora," Tia said, taking him from my arms. He took off immediately, calling for Cora and shouting about his new house.

"Did you get the promotion?" I asked, my grin widening.

"Yeah, but—"

I grabbed Tia in a hug. "This is great! I'm so happy for you."

"Really?" Tia asked. "That's so good because I've been wanting to talk to you about this for a while."

I laughed. "You didn't have to make it a whole thing. You could have just told me." Why was Tia giving me this weird, cautious look? This was good news.

"Yeah, it's not because of the promotion. It's because of where the promotion is."

"What? Is it not at your same store?" Her hesitant tone was making dread settle in my stomach.

"No," Tia said. "But the promotion isn't just floor manager. It's assistant manager. In Ann Arbor."

"Ann Arbor?" I frowned, still not fully processing what she was talking about. "Michigan?"

No, that couldn't be right. Tia and Jackson lived in Illinois. This was where he went to school. She was an integral part of the center. Of my life. She couldn't be leaving.

"That's why I wanted to talk to you. I wanted to make sure you were . . . okay," she said slowly, watching me carefully.

"But why can't they just keep you at your same store? What about the floor manager job?"

"It's a good job, but, Elena, with the raise I'd get as assistant manager,

I could afford a new car. And pay for after-school programs for Jackson."

"He has after-school stuff here," I insisted, and almost winced at my bitchy tone. I could feel the spiral start. Tia was leaving me. Like Esther and Allie and Sarah. She was moving on with her life, and it no longer included me. She would leave and promise to keep in touch, but soon she'd be "so busy" that the calls would slow and then stop completely. And she'd just move on. And I'd be forgotten.

"Fine, you're right. This is a good opportunity. I'm happy for you," I said, my voice tight. I didn't want to risk saying anything more. I knew this was a big opportunity for Tia. That she deserved it. I knew that if I let the tears burning at my eyes fall, I'd look like a total brat.

"Elena, I don't want you to be upset."

"What?" I tried to laugh it off, but it came out a hiccupping sob. "I'm not upset. I'm just really busy. I have to clean in here, and I have homework I've been putting off. So, congratulations again." I turned back to the box of toys I'd been sorting, squeezing my eyes shut to fight off the tears.

I heard Tia shuffle her feet behind me. Like she was debating between continuing the conversation or not. Then she said, "I'll call you later." And she left.

I finally let the fat tears fall, pushing at them with my sleeve futilely. I'd heard those words so many times before. But they never called.

THIRTY-NINE

The day of KFest, I knew I needed a distraction. Ethan was avoiding me at all costs at home. And now the center didn't feel like a place I could escape to just in case I saw Tia or Jackson and burst into tears.

So the idea of going into the city felt like a great change of pace. When I was younger, I assumed that every day in Chicago was just like *Ferris Bueller's Day Off,* because it was Esther's favorite movie and she'd watched it over and over. But after I turned thirteen, I realized no one was as lucky or bold as Ferris in real life. And if they were, I was too scared to hang out with them.

Then again, I was doing a lot of things I'd have been too scared to do four years ago. Like dressing in the outfit I was wearing. I'd chosen something with shorts, thinking it was more modest, even though they were two inches shorter than ones I'd usually pick. There were long boots made out of suede that came up over my knees. At first I thought I'd put them on wrong, but when I texted with Sooyeon, she assured me that was the style. My top was slightly cropped but low enough that it didn't show my whole stomach (unlike some of the other options). It was baby pink and elastic, which I needed because Sooyeon was a size smaller than me. Frilly flounces decorated the sides and sleeves, giving a little more skin coverage. Unfortunately, my shoulders were left bare.

I'd even broken out my measly collection of makeup and used the mascara and lipstick. It was mostly stuff Josie had forced on me, but I had to admit it looked pretty good. When I was done, I sent a photo of myself to Josie, and she'd written back with a bunch of heart-eye emojis.

In this outfit, I felt almost like a different person. I finally understood now why some girls said that they used their makeup and fashion like battle armor. Dressed like this I felt like I could be braver. I could be bolder. Like maybe . . . maybe I could tell Robbie that I wanted to see if we could give being together after prom a try. The thought of having to say goodbye to him hurt too much now. There had to be another way, right? And maybe my mistake the last time Robbie left was that I'd given up. Maybe if I fought for us, he'd want to fight too.

I had it all planned out. I'd tell him we should keep in touch for the rest of the semester. And in the meantime, I'd convince Mom to let me stay with Como for the summer.

I'd even started dropping hints and asking Mom about random things she remembered from growing up in Seoul. After every story, I'd say, "Wow, I wish I could go there myself soon." It wasn't that subtle, but I figured I needed to at least try.

If I had the summer with Robbie, I knew we could make it work. And having a plan made it easier for me to build up the courage to admit that I didn't want this to just be a temporary thing. My heart felt like it was going to explode just thinking about it. But a good kind of explosion. Or . . . You know what I mean.

My Nissan coughed as I pulled into the parking lot of Soldier Field, where KFest was being held. It had been making seriously pathetic sounds on the highway, and I'd prayed to every god that it wouldn't break down. It had been bumper-to-bumper the whole way and reminded me of Dad complaining about "traffic on the Kennedy" every time we drove into the city.

Robbie said he'd left a special pass at Will Call. Hoping to avoid the crowd, I'd shown up early. It didn't do me any good. There were long lines waiting for the doors to open.

The stadium had huge banners hung on the outside with each member featured. And the biggest banner of them all was a giant group photo. Robbie and his bandmates looked down on me as I joined the crowds. Whenever anyone glanced over, I lowered my face, hoping no one recognized me.

At the window, I muttered my name to the woman running the booth.

"Don't have you down," she said in a thick South Side accent.

"What?" I asked, pulling out my phone to text Robbie. "He said it would be here. Maybe it's under Robbie Choi?"

"Robbie?" the girl behind me in line said. "Did you say Robbie Choi left you tickets?"

"What? No, I . . ." I trailed off as I watched recognition dawn in her eyes.

"Oh my god. It's Robbie's prom girl!"

Heads turned at the girl's squeal and I tried to back away, but the crowd converged.

I shook my head, thinking maybe I could still deny it. But someone else shouted, "Totally. I recognize her from the dance practice video!"

Hands reached out to squeeze my shoulder, and phones were shoved in my face. People were shouting a dozen unintelligible things at me. Some-one even held out a WDB plushie of Robbie and asked if I would sign it.

"I'm not—I don't—I'm sorry, but . . ." I stuttered out, unable to respond to the clashing shouts.

A strong hand pulled me back, and I let out a little scream, almost losing my balance. If I fell, would I get trampled? Or worse, become another internet meme?

But I turned to face Hanbin, and I let out a half sob of relief.

"Come on," he said, pulling me after him until we were jogging away from the mob of fans. Hanbin hurried me past a security barrier, and the guards closed ranks to block anyone from following.

As we pushed into the stadium, I finally took a full breath.

"Sorry," Hanbin said, still guiding me through winding hallways that reminded me of those behind-the-scenes shots from films about rock bands. People were carrying cords and microphone stands. Staff were scurrying past with their arms filled with sequined costumes. And everyone looked like they had ten places to be.

"There was a mix-up and they couldn't hold your backstage pass at the booth. With everything happening, Robbie didn't get a chance to text you. The boys always have really full schedules on show days." He held out a pass, and I looped the lanyard around my neck.

"Oh, that's fine," I said, craning my neck. Was that Exo? I used to love them when I was in middle school.

"Here you go," Hanbin said, opening a door that was labeled *WDB* with a paper sign.

The waiting room was a quiet oasis compared to the bustling hallway. The counters were covered in hairstyling supplies and makeup. And there was a staff member checking off items on a list as they looked through a rack filled with outfits.

Minseok sat in the corner having his makeup done. Jun was next to him, earphones in. It looked like he was sleeping as the hairdresser pulled a comb through his hair.

Jaehyung stood up from a small couch.

"Elena," he said, giving me a one-armed hug. He had some kind of paper towel situation protecting his collar, so I figured I shouldn't hug too tight. I didn't want to mess up his makeup.

"This place is wild," I said.

Minseok grinned. "Yeah, it's always like this before a concert, but you'll get used to it."

He talked like I would be at more of these. Did he truly think that or was he just being polite?

I looked around the room. "Where's Jongdae and Robbie?"

"Jongdae disappeared as soon as we got here. I think Robbie got pulled somewhere for an interview."

"Oh," I said. I was a little disappointed he wasn't here to greet me. But I knew the boys weren't here for fun; they were working.

"They never give us enough Flamin' Hot Cheetos," Jaehyung said with a sigh, riffling through a basket of chips. "Do you think they have any at the snack counter?"

Minseok laughed. "Yeah, good luck going out there and not getting mobbed. You know the manager hyeongs will kill you if the fans rip your shirt . . . again."

"I'll get it," I volunteered.

"You don't have to do that," Jaehyung said, but he looked adorably hopeful.

"I don't mind," I said. "I wanted to grab a snack for myself anyway." And I wanted to find Robbie. I felt awkward here without him.

I had to ask two different techs which way the food stands were. And after getting lost for a third time, I was about to give up when I saw a familiar face.

"Sooyeon!" I lifted my hand in a wave.

She was still in sweats but already in full stage makeup, and she sparkled every time she moved her head.

"Elena! You look amazing. I knew that outfit would look good on you."

"Thanks. I feel a little like I'm cosplaying right now." I laughed, and Sooyeon cracked a smile but looked distracted. "Is everything okay?"

"Yeah, of course," she said, and smiled again, but this time I could tell it was forced.

"Are you sure?" I asked. "If you need to talk . . ."

"Remember how I told you I was trying to get my company to let me choose my next album concept?" she said. "They rejected it. They said that fans would be upset if I tried to go in a more mature direction."

"They didn't even pretend to consider it?" I asked, annoyed on her behalf. "You're one of the top idols in Korea right now!"

"That's the thing. When you're at the top, you can always fall. My company is just looking out for me." She shrugged, but she didn't sound convinced.

"You should try to talk to them again. Didn't you say you had a manager unnie you were close to?"

Sooyeon shook her head. "It's not worth it. I don't want them to think I'm being difficult. I'll just go with what they think is best. They're the experts at this, right?"

"I guess so," I replied. I couldn't help but remember Robbie's face on the bridge. How he'd wanted his company to take his new music seriously. I'd told him I was sure it would happen, but maybe I'd been wrong. If Sooyeon could fail at convincing her company, could Robbie fail too? I started to feel anxious. Had I made a mistake in encouraging him?

"Sooyeon for sound check!"

"I gotta go. I'll see you later," she said.

"Sure." I watched her jog toward the technician, who checked her mic pack.

I thought about asking another staff member for directions to the snack bar when I heard someone call my name. "Elena!"

I turned to see Robbie jogging down the hall, and it was another of those slow-motion K-drama moments that kept happening to me these days. He looked amazing. He was wearing jeans and a loose T-shirt, but they'd done something to his hair to sweep it back. And instead of pink, they'd toned the roots to look darker while making the ends an electric blue. I smiled, remembering Jackson demanding that blue be Robbie's next color.

A giant grin spread on Robbie's face, his dimple crease flashing as his eyes moved up and down. "Wow, you look . . . wow."

I couldn't help smiling wider, preening under his appreciative look. "You think so? I don't look like a little kid playing dress-up?"

"No," he said, taking my hands and spreading my arms like he wanted to get a better look. "You look perfect. But there's a problem." His face and tone became so somber that anxiety wove through me. Oh no, was I wearing part of my outfit wrong? The weird frilly straps across the bodice had been so confusing. But Sooyeon hadn't said anything.

"I don't know how I'm going to be able to concentrate on my performance knowing you're watching me looking like this."

I laughed and shoved him. He smiled and took my hand before I could pull back again. "You're going to have the best seats in the whole stadium, right off the stage."

I let my fingers intertwine with his. "So, will you be able to see me while you're performing?"

"Yeah," he said. "And every song I sing will be for you."

"Cornball." I laughed. "Isn't one of your songs about lighting stuff on fire?"

"It's about *burning up* for love." He wiggled his eyebrows playfully.

"Sunbae!" A group of glamorous girls in matching sparkling mini-dresses shuffled over and I pulled my hand from his quickly. Each of them was at least five eight if not taller. I vaguely recognized the name of their group, and they all bowed low to Robbie.

We couldn't walk ten steps without running into someone else Robbie knew. And they were all so gorgeous and done up that even in my new outfit I'd have felt invisible. Except each time, Robbie made a point of pulling me closer and introducing me. He'd mostly speak in English, but I'd been practicing my Korean since Robbie had come back and I could follow along with the conversations even if my pronunciation was still off. Still, I realized that whenever Robbie spoke Korean, he did it slowly to make it easier for me to follow along. It felt good to realize that he was doing that for me. That he cared enough that I didn't feel left out. It was nice to realize that Robbie knew what I needed without asking me. And I couldn't wait for the show to be over so I could take him aside and tell him how much he meant to me.

"Robiya!" someone called, and I almost fainted. It was D.E.T., one of the biggest Korean rap stars of the last decade. I'd *loved* him in middle school. I actually used to have a poster of him from his five-year anniversary tour. And now he was standing in front of me.

"When are you going to share those songs with me?" D.E.T. asked. doing that casual, cool handshake-pull-into-a-hug thing.

Robbie laughed. "When they're done."

"Man, nothing is ever done. You just have to let it go. There's this unannounced project I'm working on, and I'd love to talk about bringing you on board to write and produce some music. We should set up a time to meet."

"Produce? Really?" Robbie asked, his voice high with surprise. His hand squeezed mine so tight my fingers throbbed. I don't think he even realized he was doing it. "I'd have to ask my CEO. I'm not sure if he'd sign off on it."

"Don't worry about that. I'll take care of it." D.E.T. waved off Robbie's concern.

"That would be so cool," I said. "You're going to at least listen to the pitch, right?"

"Yeah, listen to your girl," D.E.T. said, smiling at me, and I almost evaporated into mist. "Sorry for being so rude. I'm—"

"You're the All-Kill king of the last decade, the dance machine of BT Entertainment, the leader of M-Battle," I blurted out, and felt like I was twelve all over again.

"Oh, a fan," D.E.T. said with a grin. "You have good taste in girls, Robiya."

"I didn't know you were a fan, Elena," Robbie said, finally letting go of my now-throbbing hand.

"I told you I followed K-pop when you debuted, Robbie. And M-Battle was my favorite," I said, not able to meet D.E.T.'s eyes.

D.E.T. laughed. "Well, you should stop by my dressing room. I'll give you a signed album and introduce you to the rest of the guys."

"Wow, really?" I breathed.

D.E.T. gave me a wink. "I've gotta get back, but, Robbie, think about what I said."

When he left, I turned to Robbie, who looked lost in thought. I gave him a poke in the ribs that made him jump a bit. "You're going to do it, right? Take the meeting?"

"I'd have to ask my company first. . . ." He trailed off, a small frown line forming between his brows.

"Okay, but don't write it off before that. Your music is good!" This was promising and helped erase the bit of unease I'd felt after talking to Sooyeon. If someone as huge as D.E.T. wanted Robbie to write music with him, it had to be a good sign.

"I guess it doesn't hurt to hear what he has to say."

I could see him finally starting to smile. "Your company would be fools not to let you work with D.E.T. He's one of the top idols of the decade."

Robbie's eyes narrowed. "I can't believe you're a fan of him and not me."

"I *am* a fan of you," I said, holding back my grin. "But you were just a baby debut when I was into K-pop. M-Battle is a legendary group. They've been around forever."

Robbie scowled, and I finally let out a laugh I was holding in, poking him in the ribs. "You're not really jealous, are you?" I smiled. Knowing that Robbie cared so much about whether I was his fan pleased me. It showed he cared about my opinion, just like I cared about his.

"I'm not jealous," he said, but his voice was low and pouty.

I wrapped my arms around his waist. He lifted his chin, refusing to look at me.

"Oh, come on. You know that if I had a choice between the coolest performers here today and you, I'd pick you every time."

"No," Robbie said, sniffing haughtily. "I do not know that."

"What can I do to make it up to you?" I asked, batting my lashes at him.

He glanced down his nose at me. "Well, there's one thing."

"What?" I asked. "I'll do anything."

"Anything?" he asked, a sly grin spreading over his face, and he leaned down so our eyes were in line.

My heart jumped. And I glanced around; though the hallway was empty now, anyone could walk by. I started to let go of him, but his arms came around me, holding me close.

"Nuh-uh, you promised," he said, leaning closer.

"Fine," I said, giving up on trying to wiggle free. "What do you want?"

Then he leaned closer and whispered, "This," before pressing his lips to mine.

I had a fleeting moment to wonder if anyone was looking. And then I couldn't think about anything. Because Robbie's lips moved on mine and they felt so soft. They made every thought fly out of my brain as I lifted my arms again to hold on to him.

I could kiss Robbie Choi all day. I could kiss him all year. If I didn't have to breathe, I'd just want to kiss him forever.

He pulled away too soon. And I sighed with disappointment.

"Your debt is officially paid," he said.

"I think you're onto something new with this kind of currency," I murmured. Robbie laughed and offered his hand again. And, taking it, I let him lead me.

FORTY

Robbie was right—my spot during the show was the best in the house, right off the stage.

When it was WDB's turn to perform, the big screen on the stage flickered through the darkness. The introduction video began. It highlighted each boy in a special setting. The crowd cheered for each member, and call me biased, but it definitely sounded like they screamed the loudest for Robbie. Then all the boys came together, walking through a flat and empty desert. The video flashed, and they were in some kind of industrial compound. Then again and they were in the mountains. And finally they were just silhouettes, and the real boys were lifted onto the stage from below. And the crowd really went wild.

They opened with their big hit from last year. The one that had rocketed them to global stardom. It was a mix of EDM and traditional Korean instruments. I remembered hearing JD talk about it in an interview. How they wanted to pay homage to their Korean heritage in their music. The lights of the stage expanded to show a dozen Korean drummers dressed in black-and-white hanboks, their movements coordinated as they struck the hourglass drums. Then the other side of the stage lit up half a dozen yanggeum players. The yanggeums sat like low tables before them, flat slabs of wood strung with dozens of strings that they hit with thin bamboo sticks in such precise movements that it looked like a dance. And I noticed for the first time that the dance moves that WDB used were mirrors of the motions used to play each instrument.

I'd never thought much about my Korean heritage. I guess I was lucky for that, never having to overthink it or stress about it. But I also never thought I'd watch a performance of a song rooted so deeply in Korean culture at the largest concert venue in Chicago. This must be the pride the Korean salon ladies felt whenever a Korean performer made it big.

When WDB finished the song, they immediately moved into their debut single.

I couldn't keep my eyes off Robbie. He broke apart from the group to do the rap bridge. Then his gaze shifted, and he looked at me. And it was like, for just a second, he was singing just to me. A thrill raced through me so quickly I almost shivered.

This bright and shining idol that thousands—no, millions—adored was my person. He'd been my person since before fans chanted his name in a packed stadium.

He was the Robbie I remembered, with the slow smiles and the goofy jokes. The one who insisted I always sit next to him on the bus so he didn't have to sit alone. But he'd also changed, grown into someone new that I also cared about. A boy who was passionate about writing music. A boy who was super loyal to his bandmates. And a boy who'd put himself out there to come back and keep a promise he'd made seven years ago. Was it any wonder I'd fallen for him? All the parts of him.

The music ended, and the boys froze in their final poses, breathing heavily enough that we could hear their labored breaths after the crowd finished cheering.

They stepped to the front of the stage.

"How are you doing, Chicago?" Minseok shouted, and a cheer rose. "We're so excited to be here for the first-ever KFest Chicago!"

"Now, our next song is our most recent single," Robbie said, and the crowd went wild. "It's a song that we really enjoy performing."

"Well, I think Robbie enjoyed filming the dance practice video a bit more," Minseok joked.

The crowd cheered, and I felt some of the eyes around me turn my way. I tried to ignore them, focusing all my attention on Robbie.

"Hyeong," Robbie said indignantly.

"What?" Minseok said. "It's true, right, Jun-ie?"

"I think it's the only single we have where the dance practice video has as many views as the MV," Jun teased. Traitor.

"Did you all like that video?" Minseok asked, and it was as if the whole stadium yelled back "Yeah!" together.

"You know, I feel like we owe the crowd something special," Minseok said.

"No, Hyeong," Robbie said, laughing. "Stop joking around."

"What? I'm just trying to make things interesting," Minseok said. "Do you want to see Robbie re-create that video?"

The crowd cheered.

"Look, I'll just pick someone from the audience today," Minseok said. Robbie sighed. "Fine."

But Minseok didn't move to the edge of the stage; instead he moved to the side. Right toward *me*. And I felt all the blood drain out of my face.

"What do you say, Elena?" Minseok asked, holding out his hand. "Give the people what they want?"

I started to shake my head, but I felt my hand come up and take his. What was I doing? I felt him pull me onto the stage. The lights were more blinding out here. I couldn't even see the crowd, just bright balls of lights and flashes from cameras.

"Looks like we've got a special guest," Minseok said into his mic as he pulled me to the center of the stage. It felt like it took an eternity to get there, the stage was so huge. Jaehyung and Jun gave me encouraging smiles. Even Jongdae was laughing and shaking his head. Only Robbie looked serious. He came over, lowering his mic so it wouldn't pick up his voice. "Elena, you don't need to do this if you don't want to."

"Why not?" I said, my voice shaking only slightly. "Give the people what they want, right?"

"That's a girl," Minseok said, slapping my back, then said into his mic, "We've got the very lovely Elena here to re-create her role in the video. Everyone give her a round of applause!"

I almost stumbled back from the cheering that rang out. It echoed uproariously, enhanced by the acoustics of the stage.

"Can we get Robbie's section cued up?" Minseok called out.

Robbie stepped closer to me and lowered his voice. "Okay, just like in the dance practice video, except on a stage."

"And with thousands of people watching to see if I fall on my ass," I said.

Robbie smiled and squeezed my hand. "I'll be here with you the whole time."

"Good, because if I fall, I'm taking you with me," I warned.

"Music cue!" Minseok said.

The song began, playing the bridge right before Robbie's rap. JD and Jaehyung harmonized together, standing off to the side as Robbie gave me a final nod and lifted his mic for his rap. And I took a deep breath and started across the stage.

Robbie danced beside me, and I don't know if it was the lights, or the outfit, or just the adrenaline of being on this giant stage, but I just let go. I added a little attitude to my steps. I rolled my eyes as Robbie rapped the line "If she'd just give me a chance, I'd prove the choice is me." And then I added a little hair flip that made the crowd cheer loudly. Robbie smiled, giving me an approving nod as we got to the part where he grabbed my hand. And I let him spin me into him. He was a little sweaty from dancing, but I didn't care as I wrapped my arms around his neck. And then, instead of releasing me, he lowered me in a dip and placed a kiss on my nose. He pulled me back up to my feet to thunderous cheers and applause.

My heart was pounding loud enough to drown out the audience, and I couldn't stop the smile that split my face. I took Robbie's hand, and he lifted it in the air before we both folded into an exaggerated bow.

"My good friend Elena!" Robbie said into his mic, gesturing to me to bow again. I did and then jogged back to Hanbin, who was clapping in the wings.

"You ever consider being a performer?" he asked.

"I think that was the first and last performance of my short career," I said with a laugh.

"Well, you and Robbie looked good together," he said.

"You think so?" I asked, still giddy as the boys now moved into the full song with their dancers.

"Yeah, he's different with you. He's more assertive, asks for what he wants. It's good. He needs that if he's going to have staying power in this industry."

"What do you mean?" I asked.

Hanbin was still watching the boys on the stage, his eyes sharp like he was monitoring for any mistakes. "It's a hard place to be. We have to push them because we need more and more from them. And for Robbie and WDB, it's ten times worse. All of Korea is watching because they represent the country all over the globe now. Robbie has always been the softest of the boys, and I worried about him. Maybe I tried to push him harder because of it. I've asked him to do things that I'm not proud of—" Hanbin broke off with a sigh, kneading his neck with his hand, like he was stressed.

"Like what?" I asked, worried all of a sudden.

"It's nothing. It's over. I'm just glad you make him happy."

I wanted to ask more, but the music ended and the boys jogged off the stage. Robbie came right for me and scooped me into a hug.

"Ew! You're so sweaty!" I protested, but I didn't try that hard to push him off.

"You were amazing!" he said, and swung me in a tight circle until my head spun.

FORTY-ONE

During intermission, I was standing in the hallway of the venue, talking to Jun and a folk music duo from one of the bigger labels.

"I saw a few episodes of that competition show you were on," I told them. "If they'd had international voting, I'd totally have voted for you two."

"Thanks," the girl said with a sweet smile that made her cheeks round. "I saw you onstage. You were a natural."

I blushed, feeling surreal receiving a compliment from someone who'd hit the top ten with her songs every time she released one.

"Lani." Robbie came over and took my hand. "You want to get something to drink?"

I didn't have a chance to agree before he pulled me away.

I laughed as he quickened his pace.

"What's your rush?" I asked as he led me into a side hallway that was filled with discarded wooden pallets. It was completely empty, and he spun me until my back was to the wall and he'd caged me in with his hands.

"I just wanted to get you away from all your new admirers," he said.

I laughed and shook my head at his claim.

"Hanbin is going to be annoyed if he can't find you," I said. "And he's going to blame me."

"If that happens, then I'll defend you," he said, leaning closer. I could feel myself blushing and couldn't do anything to hide it. He was too close, and my hands were trapped between us.

"Come on, Robbie. You have another performance after the intermission. You probably need to do a costume change or something."

"There's time for that," he murmured, leaning even closer. Now his lips were a breath away from mine.

"What's gotten into you?" I mused.

"You have," he said. "You've gotten into me, Elena Soo. And I don't think I can get you out again. I don't think I want to."

I felt a thrill race through me. I started to lift onto my toes, to close the space between us, when a crash sounded backstage. People raced by, some of them shouting. And I heard Sooyeon's voice scream, "Jongdae!"

Robbie's head whipped up at that, and he took off down the hall. I was right behind him, and we stopped when we saw what had caused the commotion. Where I'd been standing to watch the performance earlier, Jongdae now lay on the ground, blood pooling beside him, his leg trapped under the metal rod that had been holding the lights.

Sooyeon stood on the walkway above the stage, crying as she gripped the railing. Her manager scrambled up the narrow stairs, rushing to her side.

"Hyeong!" Robbie shouted, running to his cousin.

The crowd around Jongdae was thick with managers, stagehands, and other idols. So I went to the base of the stairs to wait for Sooyeon as she descended, thinking she'd need a friend right now. When she saw me, she collapsed into my arms. I rubbed her back as she buried her face in my shoulder.

"What happened?" I asked Sooyeon.

"We wanted to find somewhere private to talk, and Jondgae suggested we go up there." She hiccupped as another sob racked her body. "I shouldn't have looked down, but I did and I got scared. He was trying to make sure I didn't fall and must have overbalanced. Oh god, what if he's really hurt?"

"He'll be okay," I said as paramedics pushed through the gathering crowd. "They'll take him to the hospital, and he'll be okay."

But as I watched Robbie crouch beside his cousin, I wasn't sure if I was right.

★☆★

Robbie and Hanbin went with Jongdae in the ambulance. I could read the anxiety in the tension of his jaw and reassured him I'd be fine when he hesitated beside me before rushing after Jongdae.

I went to check on Sooyeon, worrying no one would be thinking about her in all of this since her relationship with Jongdae was a secret. She was alone in her dressing room, changed back into her sweats. Her hair was a tangled mess, and her makeup was running when she looked up as I opened the door.

"Elena." She jumped up, rushing to me and grabbing my hand, crushing used tissues between our palms. "Have you heard anything about Jongdae?"

"They took him to the hospital, but I don't know anything else."

She sighed, tears welling in her beautiful eyes. "I don't know what to do. I hate just sitting here while he's hurt like that, and it's all my fault!"

"No," I said, wrapping my arms around her. "It was just an accident."

"But I should be with him. He got hurt because of me, and I should be by his side."

"Well, it's not too late," I said, looking around and finding a napkin to wipe at the streaks of mascara running down her cheeks.

She shook her head. "My manager would never let me. She's been begging me to break things off for months. There's no way she'd let me go to the hospital."

"Then don't ask her," I said. I knew that there were parts of this world that I didn't really understand, but there were also parts I didn't want to understand. And the one that said you weren't allowed to love who you wanted was the part I hated the most. If Sooyeon wanted to be with Jongdae, she should be allowed.

"How do I even get there?" she asked.

"I'll take you."

"Really?" she asked, sniffling into her fistful of crumpled tissues. She looked so lost and confused, it made me want to protect her.

"Of course," I said. "Who's to say you're not just a worried friend checking on a friend?"

Sooyeon's face settled into a resolute expression. "You're right. I should be allowed to visit a friend. Let's go!"

We didn't even consider telling anyone, worried they'd stop Sooyeon from leaving. We just booked it to my car. Halfway there, we spotted a crowd of fans waiting outside to see their favorite artist with signs and presents clutched in their arms. I grabbed Sooyeon's hand and ran in the opposite direction, weaving through cars and rushing through the parking lot at a sharp diagonal to race past rows to avoid anyone tracking us. It took twice the time to get to my car, but we made it without being recognized. And we were both out of breath when we got into my car.

"You should be a manager," Sooyeon said with wonder as we climbed in.

"You know, you're the second person to imply I fit in around here. It's weird."

"Why?" Sooyeon asked as I pulled out of the parking lot, my car revving unnaturally on the turn onto the road.

"Because . . . look at me."

"I am. And I think you fit in really well. Especially with Robbie." I lowered my head to hide the smile that spread over my face at her words.

When we got to the hospital, people were staring at us, and I realized we looked like we'd just come from a party. Sooyeon was still in stage makeup. And my boots clicked against the linoleum with every step I took.

Rushing to the large information desk at the front, we gave them Jongdae's name, and I hoped to god that the receptionist wasn't a K-pop fan. I figured she wasn't when she replied in a bored tone, "He's in pre-op bed twelve."

"Pre-op?" Sooyeon choked out. "Elena." She gripped my hand.

"It's okay. Let's go find out what's happening."

I followed the signs to the pre-op staging area, but there was a giant *Staff Only* sign on the large metal doors and a swipe pad with a glaring red light.

"What now?" Sooyeon's voice sounded weak and resigned as she glanced around, pulling her hoodie lower over her face.

"Hold on," I said, determined that we wouldn't be stopped by a sign.

I tried to channel my inner Josie and lifted my chin with purpose as I walked up to a nurse who was reading a tablet as she approached the doors.

"Excuse me." My voice wavered a bit, and I took a deep breath to steady it. "Our, um, friend is in the pre-op room, and we were hoping to see him."

"Sorry, sweetie, staff and family only past this point."

"The thing is that he's visiting from Korea." I spoke quickly. "He hardly understands English, and his parents are still in Seoul. But my friend can translate for him." I pulled on Sooyeon's arm so she stepped closer. I could see the nurse considering us, her eyes moving over my sparkling outfit. "Please.

He must be so scared, not understanding anything the doctors are saying."

I held my breath as the nurse considered this. Then she sighed. "Fine, but stay where I put you," she said to Sooyeon, who nodded emphatically. Sooyeon mouthed *Thank you* to me as she was led back, relieved, I leaned against the wall. I'd barely even had an anxiety attack while talking to the nurse. Josie would be proud.

I pulled out my phone to text Robbie and saw that he'd already messaged me. He said he was stuck at the hospital, apologizing profusely for abandoning me.

I texted back that I'd *told* him to go with his cousin. And to stop worrying. I was already at the hospital too.

I had a moment to wonder if he was in the pre-op area with Jongdae, but since I'd used all my courage begging for a pass for Sooyeon, I figured I could check the waiting rooms to see if Robbie was there. I didn't see him but spotted fans wearing WDB shirts occupying half the couches. They must have come here to check on Jongdae. If they were WDB fans who'd just been at the concert, would they recognize me? I decided it was best not to tempt fate and made my way back to the door outside the pre-op area.

The nurse who'd let Sooyeon in saw me and waved me over. "Today is slow, so if you want, you can go back to see your friend too, but be quick."

"Thank you!" I said, thinking Robbie was probably back there if he wasn't in the waiting area.

There were beds along both walls, each separated by a curtain. Most of them were empty, which made it easy for me to spot Sooyeon's shoes beneath the curtain around the final bed. I was about to call out, when I heard her say my name.

"Elena choahhae, kibuni nappa."

I felt pleased hearing she liked me, but I was confused about the second part.

Why would Sooyeon feel bad? I wondered.

Jongdae replied in a voice so low, I didn't catch it all, but I heard the words "Robbie" and "prom."

"I don't love this plan," Sooyeon replied in Korean.

Plan? What kind of plan that involved Robbie and prom?

My heart slowed with dread. My breath caught in my lungs.

I heard footsteps approaching and quickly ducked into the empty bed cubicle next to Jongdae's. My fingers shook as I held the curtain closed. One of WDB's managers walked by to station himself in front of Jongdae's bed, his arms crossed like a bodyguard's.

Jongdae and Sooyeon shifted to English, probably not wanting the manager to listen in on their conversation.

"Hanbin set it all up to protect us," Jongdae said softly. "Once your dating clause has expired, we can go public. And now we know how the fans will react to someone in WDB dating."

"But Robbie and Elena are so cute together," Sooyeon said. "I hope Elena doesn't get hurt."

Jongdae scoffed. "She'll be fine. After this, Robbie will go back home to his real life. He's just letting the fans *think* he's dating her. It's not like any of it was real."

"I think you're wrong," Sooyeon said softly. "I think there *are* real feelings there."

It's not like any of it was real. Jongdae's words echoed in my head. It was all a lie. Robbie coming back. Asking me to prom. Pretending like he liked me. Making me think we could be together.

All a lie.

FORTY-TWO

My thoughts reeling, I raced out of the pre-op area, almost knocking into the kind nurse from before.

"Honey, are you okay? You look pale."

"I'm fine," I said. "I just need to get out of here. I need air." She started to lift her hand to my forehead, and I jerked back before taking off down the hallway. Needing to escape. I would have kept going if I hadn't barreled right into Minseok.

"Elena! Robbie is looking everywhere for you," he said. "They gave us a private conference room to wait in."

"Robbie?" I said. Robbie had lied to me. It was all fake. He'd done this as some kind of experiment.

Oh god, I had to get out of here.

"Elena?" Jaehyung said, stepping forward. I hadn't even seen him there.

"I just need some air," I repeated, and raced away toward the elevators.

"Elena!" I heard Robbie's voice. He was jogging down the hall toward me.

No, no. I couldn't talk to him right now. I spun around and pulled on a door. It was locked, so I raced to the next one and pulled on it. I entered an unoccupied office. One that apparently belonged to a Dr. Mitchell. I hoped she didn't mind that I borrowed it to have a mental breakdown.

I tried to shove the door closed, but Robbie was too fast and pushed it open.

"Elena, what's wrong?" he asked, letting the door close behind him.

I retreated from him. "Don't touch me."

"Okay," he said slowly, holding up his hands as if to show he wasn't dangerous. And it only angered me more. I wasn't a jumpy house cat. I was a person he'd lied to for weeks!

I tried to move around him, to get out of this room, but he shifted to block me.

"Talk to me, Elena. Tell me what's wrong."

"Fine," I said, my anger spilling over. "So, you asked me to prom as some kind of plan with Jongdae? Why?" I wish I didn't need to know his reasons, but I did. Even as my heart was already breaking.

Robbie looked dumbstruck, his mouth hanging open.

"What? No perfect lie to explain this away?" I bit out.

"Elena, no, it's not like that." He reached out, and I stepped away.

He closed his eyes and lifted his hands to his temples like he couldn't think. Probably trying to come up with an excuse for all of this. But I wouldn't believe it. I knew better now.

Of course someone like Robbie Choi, who had everything, wouldn't need to reconnect with a nobody from the suburbs if there wasn't an ulterior motive. And I'd let him come back and convince me that I was somehow special to him. *That all he wanted was to keep a promise. And*, I realized, I'd let him make *me* feel bad for not keeping the promise.

"Please, I'll explain. Just tell me who told you this."

"Why?" I spat out. "So you can figure out how much I know? So you can avoid exposing more lies?" I paced to the far side of the room, needing more space.

"No, so I can figure out why they told you and hurt you like this."

"You're the only one who's hurting me," I whispered, and I hated how choked my voice still sounded. I stared at the bookshelf full of medical guides instead of at Robbie. I didn't want to see his face right now.

"I'm sorry. God, I wish it hadn't happened like this."

Of course he wished it hadn't happened like this. He wished I'd found out when he was already back in Korea so he wouldn't have to deal with the fallout.

"You know about Jongdae and Sooyeon. They want to be together, and Jongdae is my family. I'd do anything for him. Hanbin wanted to see how the fans would react to one of us dating." Robbie spoke quickly, racing through his explanation. It didn't matter. I didn't care why he did it. Just that he'd done it and hadn't cared about how it would make me feel. Just like Ethan didn't care. Just like my mom didn't care. No one gave a shit about invisible, forgettable Elena.

"Jongdae remembered the stories I used to tell him about you," Robbie continued, barely pausing to take a breath. "Because I would talk about you all the time when I first became a trainee. Remember how Minseok said I played our song all the time? It's because I kept trying to write the perfect lyrics for it. For you."

I spun around. Robbie had moved closer, but he took a cautious step back now. "You think that fixes everything? Some pretty story about how eleven-year-old Robbie harbored an old crush on me? Eleven-year-old

Robbie isn't the one who lied to me. He isn't the one who made me look like a complete—" My anger choked off my words. I took a deep breath to collect myself. "Why would you think it was okay to do this?"

"Hanbin said if I helped ensure the stability of the band, then I could have my—" He broke off, biting his lip. It was a move I'd been starting to find so endearing, and now it just stabbed at my heart. "He said I could produce my own music. Full creative control."

"Your songs," I whispered. "The ones you were desperate for the company to accept."

"I called it all off, though," he said. "I told him that I wouldn't lie to you anymore."

"Before or after I agreed to go to prom with you?"

Robbie pursed his lips and I knew the answer, but I still wanted to hear it. "When did you call off the plan, Robbie?"

"After you agreed to go to prom."

I crossed my arms tight to stop them from shaking. "I knew better than to let myself trust you, but I still did it. What else was I supposed to expect when you've lived the past four years only thinking about how to make WDB and Robbie Choi look good?"

He opened his mouth and then snapped it shut again, sucking in his cheeks like he had tasted something sour. "I wasn't trying to lie to you."

"Then what were you trying to do?"

Robbie hesitated. One second. Three. Ten. Too long. And I knew he didn't have a good answer. At least not one that wouldn't expose him for the liar he actually was.

"That's what I thought." I pushed past him into the hallway, but Robbie caught up and held out his arms to block me.

"Please, there's more to this. Let me explain it all better."

"You know what the worst thing is about all of this? If I'd met Sooyeon first and you'd all asked me to do this for her, I might have said yes. Because I like her and I agree she shouldn't have to hide her relationship with Jongdae. But you couldn't trust me." My voice cracked on the last word.

Tears welled up in my eyes. And I turned away from Robbie. These tears weren't for *him*. They were for me. Because I'd agonized over the fact that I was falling for him and the whole time it had been a game. A lie to get what he wanted. Because that's who people like Robbie were; they were selfish liars.

Except he helped you save the community center.

I told my inner self to shut up and swiped at the tears. And then I blinked because standing in front of me were half a dozen girls, their phones held up, their eyes wide.

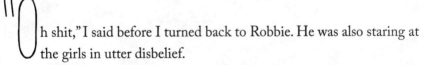

FORTY-THREE

"Oh shit," I said before I turned back to Robbie. He was also staring at the girls in utter disbelief.

"Is JD-oppa really dating Sooyeon?" one of the girls wailed. It seemed to unfreeze all of us as they rushed forward. I started to lift my hand in defense. But Robbie grabbed my arm and pulled me down the hall.

We burst into the elevator bank just as one was letting out a group of people, and Robbie pushed through them to scattered protests, pulling me inside the car and jabbing the CLOSE DOOR button. They did just as the fans spotted us inside.

"Robbie-oppa!" they called, but their voices were cut off as the doors shut.

"I didn't mean to say it in front of them," I mumbled, guilt crowding into my gut along with its siblings, anger and embarrassment.

Robbie pulled out his phone. "Shit, I have to call Hanbin."

He glanced up at me, hesitating a moment.

"Go ahead. Call Hanbin." I waved my hand at him. "Tell him I messed up the plan, and now you have to go fix it so you can maintain your precious reputations. I know the drill."

"You don't know it all, I promise. And I'll explain it later. I just have to find Hanbin right now."

"Don't bother trying to explain any more. I understand enough."

"Dammit, Elena. This isn't easy!" Robbie exploded.

"I don't care!" I yelled back, angry tears welling again, and this time I didn't try to hide them.

Robbie rubbed his hands over his face and into his hair, mussing it. "You don't understand what it's like to be told who you're supposed to be. To not be allowed to breathe wrong for fear it will be in an article for everyone to read and judge. I'm told how to act, how to speak, how to *think* by a company. And I have to toe the line or else I'll lose everything."

The elevator doors opened, and I was frozen in place. My anger telling me to leave. But my heart wanting to stay. Because I could hear the hurt in his voice. But the hurt he'd just caused me was too big.

"Well, you should go back and salvage what you can so you don't lose it. Because you've already lost me." I forced my feet to move, to carry me forward just as the warning ding signaled the closing doors.

Robbie slapped a hand against them to hold the elevator open.

"Elena, please." His eyes bored into mine. They pleaded with me to believe in him. And a part of me still wanted to. I wanted to stay here and let him convince me I'd misunderstood. That he still cared about me. But I knew that wouldn't work out. Nothing ever would have worked out between me and Robbie.

The elevator doors buzzed in warning as Robbie held them open.

"You know," I said quietly, "I always thought being invisible was the worst thing in the world. But what you did was worse than making me feel invisible. You make me feel like even though you could see me, I still didn't matter. I was just a tool to be used in your celebrity games." As more tears fell, I couldn't bring myself to be embarrassed or mad anymore. I was just exhausted.

"Elena," Robbie said, but his phone buzzed and I could see Hanbin's name flash across the screen. He hesitated, his finger hovering over the button to answer.

"I know what I want my last wish to be," I said. "I wish that you'd stay the hell away from me." I walked away, not sure where I was heading. Not even sure what floor I was on.

And despite myself, I listened for the sound of his footsteps. Because, no matter how much I knew I shouldn't, I still hoped he'd come after me. But I heard the ding of the elevator doors closing, and when I turned back, he was gone.

FORTY-FOUR

My tears threatened to blind me as I drove home, so I pulled onto the shoulder of the road and let myself sob into my arms until my ribs ached.

After, I pulled down the visor, trying to see the damage. The brush of mascara and eyeliner I'd used was running down my face. I wiped at it with a tissue, but there was nothing I could do for my puffy red eyes.

When I turned the key in the ignition, the engine gave a pathetic sputter that turned into broken clicks.

"No, come on! Not now," I said, turning the key again, this time with angry force. The engine coughed in protest, the clicking turning into loud knocking as if in warning. And all I wanted to do was punch or kick something. But with my luck, I'd just end up hurting myself.

I pulled out my phone and dialed Josie. When I got her voicemail,

I hung up and stared at my contacts. I could call my mom, but she'd take one look at my puffy face and hound me with questions about what happened at KFest. Maybe Ethan? Yeah, right, he'd probably laugh at me and hang up.

Finally, reluctantly, I clicked on the number for Tia.

She came without question, which somehow just added to my awful mood. Tia took charge, calling AAA, which I should have thought to do, but my brain was just too jumbled to think straight. Finally, I was sitting in her car as she drove back to Pinebrook. Before she could turn into my neighborhood, I said, "Can we not go to my house right now?"

Without a word, she merged back into traffic and kept driving.

Tia's understanding silence started to weigh on me. Why was she being so nice when the last time I saw her I was such a total brat? Was I really that pathetic-looking right now? Or maybe she just didn't give a crap that I had been mad. Maybe she just thought I was a kid throwing a tantrum, and it didn't matter to her one way or the other. Just like lying to me hadn't mattered to Robbie. And I didn't even know I'd started to cry until tears splashed against my fists, which were clenched so tightly in my lap that my knuckles were white.

Tia parked the car and leaned over, unbuckling my seat belt to pull me into a hug. The center console dug into my hip, but I didn't care. I just pressed my face into her shirt and let myself sob until my lungs burned and my eyes were too puffy to open.

When I was all cried out, Tia finally opened the glove compartment to pull out tissues. I used them to wipe at the raw skin under my eyes. It stung, but I didn't care.

"Do you want to tell me what happened?" Tia asked.

I shook my head.

"Do you want to drive around more?"

I shook my head again. I knew that I wasn't making sense. But in reality, I didn't know what the hell I wanted right now.

And then, on a hiccupping whisper, I finally said, "Why is it so easy for people to just throw me away without a second thought?"

"Oh, sweetie, is that what you think?" Tia started to reach for me again, but I shrank away, pushing my body against the passenger door.

"Well, all of the people I've cared about have left and I'm the only common denominator."

Tia sighed and leaned back again. "You can't think of it as people leaving you. I didn't realize that's how it felt for you. I guess I get it, though. Even though I was the one doing the leaving, it did feel like my family abandoned me after I had Jackson. It's really hard to feel abandoned. I'm so sorry I have to leave."

I took in a long, shuddering breath, trying to use all my willpower to calm my heart. It felt so delicate right now, like it was just one squeeze away from bursting. "I know going to Michigan is what's best for you and Jackson," I finally said. "I just . . . I hate losing people."

"You're not losing us, Elena. You're like family to me and Jackson. And anyone who can't see how special you are isn't worth your time to begin with," Tia said, reaching out to push back a strand of hair that had gotten stuck on my tear-dampened cheek.

I nodded. Tia was right. Anyone who couldn't appreciate me wasn't worth my time. And number one on my list of people to let go of was Robbie Choi.

FORTY-FIVE

spent all of Sunday avoiding human contact.

I must have given off some really pathetic vibes, because even Mom didn't yell at me to get out of bed all day.

Robbie called a dozen times before I turned my phone off. Then I heard the home phone ring downstairs. A second later, Mom was knocking on my door.

"Elena, it's Robbie," she said.

"Tell him I'm busy," I said, pulling my covers over my head. "Or that I died."

I heard her murmuring on the phone, and I waited for her to check on me. Willed it. But of course she didn't. I told myself I didn't care. And I fell asleep repeating that lie.

★☆★

School the next day would have been torture if not for Josie. Seeing her so angry somehow helped me feel calmer myself.

"I'm going to slash his tires," she said as she helped me string up more fairy lights in the community center.

"He doesn't have a car," I pointed out, grunting as I stretched my arm to press a command hook into the wall.

"Then I'm going to set his luggage on fire," she said.

"Just be careful of arson charges. I hear they're pretty strict in the state of Illinois," I said, climbing down.

There was definitely something weird about being on the committee for a dance that you had no intention of attending.

Every gold star I hung reminded me of joking around with Robbie as we painted them. Every silver garland I put up reminded me of Robbie holding my hand and telling me that he needed to go to prom with me. Yeah, he did. Just not for the reasons I'd assumed.

There were already posts on fan sites. Next to articles about Jongdae's outed relationship with Sooyeon, there were speculation posts about rumors of a fight between Robbie and his childhood love. Wondering whether we'd go to prom after all. Karla had asked if the rumors were true during Chemistry and I'd just shrugged, which was my way of confirming them without confirming them. She'd looked kind of sad and told me she was sorry.

I didn't want anyone to feel sorry for me. I didn't want anyone to think *anything* about me. I just wanted to sink back into obscurity and not have to be connected to WDB or Robbie Choi ever again.

The one good thing that came from this: I no longer cared if anyone knew who I was. I'd had enough attention and notoriety to last me a lifetime.

"Hey, guys." Max walked over carrying another box of fairy lights, then stepped back at the look on Josie's face. "Whatever it is, I'm sorry."

"Tell me something, Max. Why are all males complete and absolute asses?"

Max blinked. "Are you mad because I asked if my mom could drive us to prom?"

Josie made a throat-slashing motion with her hand, but it was too late.

I paused in the act of grabbing another string of lights. "Wait, you're going to prom? Together?" I glanced between them.

Josie sighed and shrugged. "We don't have to talk about that in front of you. We're here to be the brand-new Anti-Robbie Club. It'll be the new mission statement of the Awareness Club. Making people *aware* of how much of a jerk Robbie Choi is."

"You don't have to keep secrets just because you think it'll hurt my feelings," I said. "I'm really over secrets right now."

Josie nodded. "Yeah, I get that."

"So," I said, forcing a smile. "How did it happen?"

"Well, I got tired of waiting for Max to get off his butt and do something about his crush. So I asked him to prom last Friday."

I had to laugh. It was a classic Josie move. "I'm happy for you guys," I said, separating the string of lights from the others. "Let me know how prom is."

"We don't have to go anymore," Josie said. "We can just all hang out at my place and watch horror movies like we originally planned."

I saw Max's disappointed frown, but he nodded along with Josie in solidarity.

"No, I want you to go and have fun." I took her hand. "You've worked hard on this. You deserve to enjoy it."

"Okay, but Sunday we're having a total girls' day. Korean face masks and everything."

"It's a deal."

FORTY-SIX

was finally getting around to cleaning up my clothes that had sat in a sad pile in the corner of my room and realized I still needed to return the duffel of Sooyeon's clothes. I sent her a message, telling her she could send a manager to pick it up. She replied that she'd send someone to my house Thursday afternoon.

But when I opened the door after school, I was left speechless at the sight of Sooyeon herself standing on my doorstep. She was wearing an old set of frayed sweats, the hood pulled over her head, a large pair of sunglasses over her bare face. Somehow she still looked more glamorous than I could in full makeup.

"Oh, I didn't realize you'd come yourself," I stuttered out.

"I was hoping we could talk?" She took off the sunglasses, revealing bags under her dark eyes.

"Sure." I led the way into the living room, where the duffel sat on the couch. I sat beside it so she could sit in my dad's armchair. It was the nicest piece of furniture in the room, though it looked dull and faded with Sooyeon sitting in it.

"Um, do you want something to drink?" I asked, unsure what to say.

"No, I'm fine," she said, then cleared her throat, her eyes moving around the room.

"Did you know?" I asked. "About what Robbie and Jongdae planned?"

Sooyeon frowned. "Yes. But not until after the promposal."

I nodded. It helped somehow, knowing she hadn't been a co-mastermind of the deception.

"I didn't mean to expose your relationship," I said. "I wish the press would just let you live your life."

"It's how the game is played," Sooyeon said with a shrug. "To be honest, it could be worse. I think people are sympathetic because of Jongdae's accident."

"Oh," I said, not sure how to react. "I guess that's good?"

"I suppose so, now that we know he's going to recover," Sooyeon said. "When the news sites dropped the scoop that we were dating, most of the fans thought it was callous and inappropriate to do while Jongdae was recovering from surgery. They said I was loyal because I stayed by his side in the hospital."

"I'm glad they're being kind," I said.

"Yeah." Sooyeon nodded. "And I owe that to you. I'd never have had the courage to go to the hospital in the first place if it weren't for you."

I smiled in true relief until I saw Sooyeon's sad expression. "It's not all good news, is it?"

"My company decided to terminate my contract."

"I'm so sorry, Sooyeon!" I said. "I should have been more careful."

Sooyeon shook her head. "It's not your fault. The truth is, I've felt my company pulling back from me ever since I started hinting I wanted to try a new sound with my next album. It's like they were looking for an excuse to cut me loose as soon as they thought I was being too difficult. So, this isn't about the dating clause. Not really," she said. "And I know you didn't expose us on purpose. Even if you did, I wouldn't have blamed you. Not after what we all did to you."

A part of me, the part that hated confrontation, wanted to claim it was okay. That I was over it. But I wasn't, and I figured Sooyeon could see that in my face.

"Robbie feels really bad about how it all went down," she said.

"Yeah, I'm sure he's really upset that he got found out before he could dump me himself. Probably had a whole plan to do it in a way that paid me back for the promposal fiasco." Even as I said the words, I knew they weren't true. Even if I thought Robbie was a selfish liar, I knew he wasn't intentionally cruel.

"You gave me advice for Jongdae, and it really helped me. Can I pay you back for that?"

I shrugged. I wasn't sure if I wanted advice when it came to Robbie and me. I wasn't sure if there still *was* a Robbie and me.

"Robbie might be seventeen, but he's emotionally still . . . how do you say 'choding' in English?"

I frowned. "Like choding hakyo? Elementary school?"

"Yes, he's still like an elementary student emotionally," Sooyeon said. "Lots of us only know the practice rooms once we enter agencies as trainees. Robbie was so young, he just never got a chance to figure out some things. But he has a good heart, and if you give him a chance, I think he can learn with the right teacher."

"What if I don't know what I'm doing either?" I admitted.

"Then isn't it less lonely to learn together?"

I sighed. "I just don't know if the Robbie I care about is real or not. I used to be able to anticipate him, but now he feels like a stranger."

Sooyeon narrowed her eyes thoughtfully. "Do you really think that everything new you've learned about Robbie is a lie? Or maybe you're just convincing yourself it is because then it's easier to dismiss how you still feel about him."

I scowled. When Sooyeon put it that way, it made me sound like a coward. Then I sighed, realizing that's exactly what I was being.

"It's like losing my contract," Sooyeon continued. "I used to think it would be the worst thing that could happen to me. But now that it has, I'm not as scared of the uncertainty as I used to be. I'm kind of excited about not knowing what comes next."

I nodded even though the idea of not knowing what to do next gave me secondhand anxiety. But I sensed a calm about Sooyeon. I envied it.

"Well, whatever you do, I'll always be a fan."

"Thank you," Sooyeon said, leaning forward to wrap her arms around me. "I'm not telling you that you have to forgive Robbie. But I personally think you both deserve a chance to see what you can be together."

I wanted to be as brave as Sooyeon. To stop being so scared of the unknown. But I was just too afraid of how much power Robbie had over my heart. Forgiving him would mean trusting him not to hurt me again, and I wasn't sure if I could do that.

FORTY-SEVEN

After Sooyeon left, I felt restless. Like there were too many thoughts in my head churning around and making me jittery. So I went out to my mom's garden and found myself on the old swing bench. I leaned over the back and found a spot where Robbie and I had once carved our initials. I traced my finger around the letters, worn away a bit with time.

I heard a car pulling into the drive and watched as Ethan came home from lacrosse practice. He started inside but stopped when he saw me. And, after a moment of hesitation, he walked over and sat with me on the bench. In silence, Ethan pushed his foot against the ground, making it swing back gently.

"You okay?" he finally said.

"Aren't you mad at me?"

"Aren't you mad at me?" he asked right back.

"I'm too tired to be mad at you anymore."

"Same. It's no fun to fight with you. You're my only ally against Mom and Dad."

I laughed. "Like you need help with them. Prince Ethan."

He frowned, kicking at the ground again, making the bench swing so wildly that I had to hold on to the chain or fall off. "You think it's so easy for me, but it's not," he said.

"You can't deny that Mom totally gives you preferential treatment."

He shrugged. "Maybe, but that's not my fault."

"It's not your fault, but it's made you think that everything is no big deal. To some of us it is. Not everyone can afford to be as easygoing as you are."

Ethan didn't look impressed by my speech. "That's the thing, Elena. If you were more easygoing, then maybe you wouldn't get your feelings hurt so easily."

"If you know I get my feelings easily hurt, then why don't you ever seem to care about them?" I shot back.

That made Ethan frown. "I guess because I'm tired of being rejected by you." He dragged his feet in the dirt to slow the swing.

"What?" I stared at him, wondering if he was messing with me. But he looked serious, almost embarrassed. "I don't reject you."

"Yes, you do," he said with a humorless laugh. "It's why I hated hanging out with you and Robbie when you were kids. You never let me in on your games or jokes."

"That is not fair. We let you play with us, but you always said our games were boring."

"Yeah, because you made up those ridiculous wizard-monster games with a thousand rules that lasted for days. And I could never keep up. And you two would use, like, code words and inside jokes and I was always left out. So I just said that I thought your games were boring."

I was shocked. "I didn't know that."

Ethan hunched his shoulders. "Yeah, well, I guess I never wanted you to know how much it hurt whenever you chose him over me."

I'd always assumed that Ethan thought he was too cool for Robbie and me. It had never occurred to me that we'd made him feel left out.

"Even this time around, you brought him to the center and you never even asked me to go with you."

I remembered him saying this to me at Halmeoni's house and then brushing it off. I didn't realize he'd been trying to tell me I'd hurt his feelings. "I was worried you'd make fun of it," I admitted. "Like you and your friends did to my pamphlets."

"If you were upset about the pamphlets, you should have said something."

"Like how you said something to defend me every time Tim made fun of me at school?" I asked pointedly.

He grimaced, then nodded. "Fine, I should've told him to cut it out. But that's not why you have this aversion to me. You had it even when we were younger. You hated when people called you my twin. You always corrected them that you weren't 'Ethan's sister,' you were 'Elena Soo,' like you were ashamed to be connected to me."

"That's not why," I said. "I just . . . felt invisible next to you, Ethan."

"Why?"

"Because I was always just 'Ethan's twin' when you were around. When I wasn't Sarah or Allie's sister. It made me feel like who I really was without you didn't matter." I shrugged. *And when you don't matter, people don't care enough to stick around.* But I was still too embarrassed to say that last part.

Ethan frowned. "But people did that to me too."

"No, they didn't. Mom always puts you first."

"Yeah, *Mom* does. But teachers would call me 'Elena's twin.' And sometimes they even called me 'the boy Soo.'" Ethan shrugged. "It annoyed me sometimes, but I just figured it was because there were so many of us."

For the first time, I wondered if maybe I'd been seeing things wrong this whole time. What I saw as self-preservation, Ethan saw as rejection. What I saw as being forgettable, Ethan saw as coming from a large family.

"Maybe you're right," I said. "But you're still more popular and better at making friends. You've never needed me, so I didn't want to need you either."

"You do that a lot," Ethan murmured. "Quit things before they get hard. You do it with your hobbies too. The moment it stops going the way you thought it would, you quit. Sarah once said it's like you never give yourself a chance to mess it up."

Sarah said that about me? To Ethan? "That's not true," I muttered. "I don't quit people, they quit me."

"Elena." Ethan laughed. "You just admitted you pushed me away before I could do it to you. And didn't you kind of give up your friendship with Felicity in ninth grade the moment it got hard?"

"Did she tell you that?" I scowled, unsettled that she'd told Ethan something so private.

"Do you admit it's true?" he pushed, not letting me deflect.

"Maybe." I shrugged.

"Is that why you're pushing Robbie away? Because he's going back to Korea soon?"

"No, Robbie lied to me. I should have just listened to my instincts and never have gotten involved with him again."

"Okay," Ethan said like he didn't believe me.

"You think I should give him a chance when he's been lying to me since the moment he arrived?"

"I mean, I have no idea what he actually did. But even I can tell you're not getting over this," Ethan said. "Maybe you should talk to the guy. Otherwise, you'll always wonder what if, right?"

I looked at Ethan in surprise. "Since when did you get so smart?"

"I have my moments. Not a total nerd like you, though." He bumped my shoulder with his playfully. And I couldn't help smiling back. I couldn't believe that this whole time I'd thought Ethan never noticed anything about me when it seemed like he knew parts of me better than I did myself.

"You know," I began slowly, "I don't really understand what's so interesting about guys playing football with sticks, but if you want me to come to one of your lacrosse games, I will."

Ethan laughed. "Football with sticks? Where does that come from?"

"That's what it looks like to me. All those pads and helmets and stuff. You'll have to explain the rules to me so I don't accidentally root for the other team."

"Sure, after you tell me which whales we're petitioning to save, 'cause I hear killer whales are kind of assholes."

✶☆✶

Later, I lay in bed thinking about my conversations with Sooyeon and Ethan.

I guess I *was* guilty of pushing people away before they could leave me first. Like Ethan. Like Felicity. And now was I doing it to Robbie? No, it was different with him. He'd really hurt me. But, still, I didn't like the idea of letting him leave without talking first.

And Sooyeon was right; I owed it to myself to figure out how I felt about him.

I must have written ten different versions of the same text before I finally told myself to just send one. Or I knew I never would. So I just typed: *If you still want to talk, let's talk.*

FORTY-EIGHT

"Remind me again why you're getting ready for prom at my house?" I asked as Josie carefully applied mascara in my floor-length mirror.

I was already in my pajamas, lying on my stomach on my bed watching her get ready.

"Because I don't think you should be alone tonight. So, I see this all working out one of two ways. You see me getting ready and get an intense case of FOMO and decide that you *must* throw on that amazing dress you repurposed and come with me and Max. *Or*, and this is my preferred option, Robbie shows up in a huge romantic gesture and whisks you off your feet and we all go to prom and dance our butts off."

"Aw, you are both sweet and delusional," I said.

"Hey!" Josie threw an eyeliner pencil at me.

I dodged it, laughing. "I am not going to change my mind about prom.

And Robbie is *not* going to show up here. But that's fine. I reached out. I wanted closure, and the way I see it, even if he doesn't call me back, then I've got it because I know I did the mature thing." I shrugged to show how zen I was being about everything.

"You're such a bad liar, El," Josie said.

"I know," I said, turning onto my back to stare up at my ceiling.

"Can I say something?" Josie asked.

"Of course," I said, staring at a crack in the corner of the ceiling and tracing it with my eyes.

"I don't think it would be the worst thing in the world if you forgave him," Josie said quickly.

"What?" I asked, turning back around to stare at her. "How can you say that? Darrel Pratt stood you up for a date last year and you somehow got him barred from his favorite diner."

"Darrel Pratt was a health hazard. He wore flip-flops! That breaks the no-shirt, no-shoes policy."

"I'm pretty sure flip-flops qualify as shoes," I said.

"Not after I made my argument."

"I can't believe you think I should forgive Robbie. What he did was way worse than standing me up for a date," I said.

"I didn't say you *should*. But I think you want to," Josie said. "And the difference between Darrel Pratt and Robbie is that you have history with Robbie. And there are things about his life that neither of us could understand."

Sighing, I sat up. "Yeah, maybe you're right," I admitted. "And maybe I do want to forgive him. I just don't know if it'll work out. You see how much of a ball of sadness and anxiety I am after not-actually-dating him. How much more will it hurt if we really *try* and it doesn't work out?"

Josie nodded. "I mean, yeah, I guess there's always the chance you'll break up when you date someone. Are you going to become a nun because of that?"

I let out a laugh and shook my head. Josie had a knack for making my anxiety spirals seem so ridiculous that I was shocked out of them.

"El, you know I love how much you think ahead. It really helps when we're planning rallies and stuff, but you can't always predict how things are going to play out," Josie said. "And besides, life would be so boring if we always knew what was going to happen."

I frowned, not sure if Josie was calling me boring or not, but I didn't have a chance to be indignant because the doorbell rang and we both froze.

Josie smiled and wiggled her brows suggestively.

"Stop it," I said, throwing a pillow at her. "It's not him."

"You don't know!" Josie sang out. "And the unknown is exciting." She got up and danced around, and I laughed at her ridiculous energy.

"Elena!" my mom called upstairs. "It's for you!"

I didn't want to hope, but my heart hadn't gotten the memo, as it was currently copying Josie's dance. I tried to walk as slowly as possible down the stairs instead of leaping down them like I wanted.

And when I got to the foyer, I let out a disappointed sigh. "Oh, hi, Max."

"Gee, thanks. I guess it was really worth it to shell out for the tuxedo upgrade," he said.

"No, sorry, I didn't mean that," I said. "You look really nice. Josie is going to be totally impressed."

"You think?" he asked, nervously fidgeting with the corsage.

"Of course," I said, straightening his bow tie.

I was right. Josie couldn't stop grinning at Max as he put her corsage on her wrist. And she made an exaggerated show out of pinning his boutonniere on his lapel without accidentally stabbing him. I offered to take photos of them, and even though Josie rolled her eyes, she was wearing a big toothy grin in all the pictures.

"You sure you don't want to change really quick and come with us?" Josie asked one last time.

"I'm sure," I said with a forced laugh to show her I was fine. "Go, have fun. Send me pics of the place with all the lighting and stars and stuff."

"Okay," Josie said, wrapping me in a tight hug. "He could still come," she whispered.

"I'm not holding my breath," I said.

And when Josie and Max were gone, I went back up to my room. It felt weirdly empty now. I'd meant it when I said I didn't want to go to prom with Josie and Max. Because, I admitted to myself now that I was alone, I still wanted to go to prom with Robbie. But he wasn't here.

FORTY-NINE

The next afternoon, I was sitting on the stairs, waiting for Josie to pick me up. My car was still in the shop, and we had to go help clean up the center after prom.

Mom walked into the foyer, a dust rag in her hand. I started to shift over to let her pass, but instead she sat next to me. I stared at her, confused. Mom never just sat with me like this.

"Mom?"

"I talked to Ethan," she said.

"Okaaay," I replied, not sure where this was leading but tensed in case I was in trouble.

"He was saying he thinks you two should go to Seoul this summer," she said.

"Ethan said that?" I asked, my voice high with surprise.

"I guess, if you're together, then I'd be less worried."

Wow, I thought. *I can't believe Ethan did this for me.* "So, you're saying we can go?" I asked hesitantly.

"Do you still want to?" she asked, eyeing me like she was trying to see through my skull to all my deepest thoughts.

I hesitated, thinking about it a second and then I nodded. "Yeah, I do." And I really did. Even without Robbie, I wanted to go. I hadn't been to Korea since I was little, and I liked the idea of helping kids at Como's hagwon. Like how I did at the community center.

"Then I'll call Como."

I was left to muse at how Ethan really did have Mom wrapped around his finger. But now that he was using his powers to help me, this opened the doors to a lot more possibilities in the future. I laughed and pulled out my phone to text Ethan just as Josie honked from the street.

When I climbed into her car, she asked, "Ready for intense manual labor?"

I sighed. "Sure, it'll be my exercise for the day."

When we arrived at the community center, I pulled on the door and found it locked. That was weird; the doors were never locked in the middle of the day.

I knocked on it with the side of my fist. "Hello? Cora? Anyone?"

When no one answered, I tried calling Cora and heard her phone ringing on the other side of the door just as she opened it a crack.

"Hey, Elena!" she said, a little louder than normal.

"Hey, Cora. What's up? Why is the door locked?"

"We were just doing a thing," she said.

"Are the others here already? Are they starting the cleanup?"

"Um, not yet." She glanced behind her again. She was acting so weird. I asked. "Well, can you let me in?"

"Yes, sure, but you have to close your eyes."

I narrowed them instead. "Why?"

She laughed and said, "Just trust me!"

"Fine." I figured if she was trying to cheer me up, I might as well let her. It was actually kind of sweet. Cora really didn't have to do this just because I'd been in a grouchy mood the last week.

I closed my eyes and let her lead me forward.

"'Lena!"

"Jackson?" I said, starting to open my eyes.

"You can't peek!"

I chuckled at his worried voice and shut my eyes tight again. "I won't," I assured him.

"Hold out your hand."

I obeyed and felt something wrap around it. Like a hair tie but with weight.

"What is this?"

"No looking," Cora said, leading me forward again.

I could see lights moving over my closed lids and was about to impatiently ask what was happening again when a very familiar voice said, "Open your eyes."

Jackson, Tia, Josie, and Cora stood off to the side of the still-decorated gym. Not a thing had been moved or taken down. The stars and moons hung from the rafters, twirling lightly. The main lights were off, and the two disco balls we'd strung up were casting patterns over the walls and floor, which was strewn with loose silver and gold balloons. The fairy lights twinkled overhead like little stars. And in the middle of it all stood Robbie, holding an acoustic guitar.

I looked down at my hand, and my heart stumbled at the sight of a corsage decorated with silk butterflies. I looked up at Tia and

Cora, tears starting to pool in my eyes as they gave me mile-wide grins.

"Elena," Robbie said, pulling my attention back to him. "I wanted to give you something that I should have given you a long time ago."

Then he began playing the song we'd written together as children, and he started to sing.

> *Shouldn't be surprised that you opened this locked door*
> *Thought I'd shut my heart away so tightly*
> *But seeing you is like remembering how to laugh again*

I let out an involuntary surprised cry-laugh myself. The words were somehow perfect for the tune, which he'd slowed down to a ballad. Nine-year-old Robbie had been right—it was a love song.

> *I hate to be the one to make you cry*
> *I regret the moments that I lost my faith because it made*
> *You lose faith in me*

I tried to hold back my tears. Why was it that Robbie always knew the exact words to say (or sing) to make me cry? How could he know that this was exactly the right way to apologize?

> *You were always the one who knew how to reach my heart*
> *But I forgot that actions counted more than intentions*
>
> *Please believe that to me you are the one*
> *Who has always seen the best of me*
> *Who will always understand the worst of me*

Please believe
Please believe
In me again

My vision became a blur of shapes as tears filled my eyes. I blinked hard, and fat drops fell down my cheeks.

Robbie stepped forward and took my hands in his. "I wanted to tell you I'm sorry, Elena. That I messed up big-time. But I *do* see you. I know that you're loyal. You'll do anything to defend a friend. That you hate talking in public. You like making plans, and you love your spreadsheets."

I let out a tear-filled laugh.

Robbie smiled now. "You're stubborn, smart, and you hate puns, but you let me make them anyway. You don't want anyone else to define you, but you're still figuring out who the real Elena Soo is. But I can tell you that to me, the real Elena Soo is someone who always challenges me to be better. And I know that this place means everything to you, so I wanted to apologize to you here. In a place you love. Because I love you."

"I don't know what to say." I didn't want to admit that his words made my stomach twist and my chest tight.

He nodded, like he'd been expecting this. "Can we talk?"

I looked at where the others had been standing and realized they'd left us alone. "Sure," I finally said.

"When this all started, I thought of it as doing a favor for my hyeong," he said. "I watched him struggle to give up the girl he loves. But I always knew he couldn't do it. I didn't get why it was so hard until I was back here and I was asked to let you go."

My breath hitched at that, but I kept quiet, letting him finish.

"You were right when you said I've only thought about how things would make me look. For the last few years, I convinced myself that I had to learn how to play the game if I wanted to get anything that was truly mine."

I watched his fists clench and fought the urge to reach out and thread my fingers through his. "But I don't want to play the game anymore," he said. "Not if it hurts people I love."

Now I did reach out and take his hand. "I could never understand what it would be like to be thrown into that world like you were. I mean, I could barely commit to staying on the school soccer team when I was fourteen, let alone debut in a K-pop group. I admire you for doing it and for being so good at it. I really do. But, I have to be honest, the world you live in scares me because it's a place that can make a good person do bad things to get ahead."

Robbie nodded. "I understand. And I would understand if you never wanted to see me again. But just know that I didn't go along with the plan just for Jongdae-hyeong, or for a stupid album. I did it because I wanted to see you again so badly. And this felt like my in. Not only were they going to let me see you, but they'd let me spend time with you. And maybe I was using it to stop myself from chickening out."

"Chickening out?" I asked. "From what?"

He shrugged, his eyes lowering. "I told you, I'm not good at talking to girls."

"Yeah, I'd believe that if I hadn't seen a dozen videos of you at fan meets, making all those girls blush."

"That's work." He laughed, a small, embarrassed chuckle that made his dimple half flash. "Elena, the last time I was around a girl I liked, I was ten. And I feel like I'm no better at talking about my feelings now. It's kind of embarrassing to realize that I can sing in front of crowds of thousands, but that there are thirteen-year-olds out there who are probably better at talking to girls."

I laughed at that. Robbie was seriously underselling his skills, because this girl was swooning despite her better judgment. I tried to tell myself that this would be a doomed relationship from the start. That we had too much between us. Soon there would be whole countries between us. But my heart wanted Robbie, and standing here in front of him, I couldn't ignore that.

"I could apologize a thousand times for the next thousand days and still never deserve your forgiveness," Robbie said. "But do you think it would be possible for you to take into account that I'm an emotionally stunted, overly sheltered K-pop idol who has been in love with you for the last seven years, and maybe cut me some slack?"

And even though it terrified me to think of all the what-ifs, Josie had been right: Trying to predict everything was a losing battle. Even though I had no way of assuring myself that Robbie wouldn't leave me again someday, I couldn't give him up. I had a need for him that had been growing every day for the last month. Maybe the last seven years.

Live in the moment, Elena. I was going to work hard on making that my new mantra. The future would be what it would be. But fear of the unknown wouldn't stop me from living my life.

"Yeah, I guess I could cut you some slack," I said. "But only because it was seven whole years. If it had only been six and a half, you'd be out of luck."

Robbie let out a relieved breath; then he ran his hand down my arm until he laced his fingers with mine.

"It can be a fresh start," he said.

"No." I shook my head, and his face fell. "There's too much between us to be just starting out. But we can see how we fit together now, after all of our history, the good and the bad. A K-pop idol and a regular girl."

Robbie smiled and leaned forward until our noses touched. "A boy and the girl he's always loved."

"You're so lucky you're an artist, or you'd have no good excuse for sounding so corny." I laughed.

Robbie chuckled and then pulled out his phone. He clicked through it, and the original version of "Gobaek Hamnida" started.

"May I have this non-prom dance?" Robbie held his hand out.

I couldn't stop the goofy grin that slid onto my face. I took his hand and then laughed when he gave an exaggerated bow like we were in a period film. I curtsied and then let him pull me into his arms.

It was my first non-prom, but I gotta say, it was a pretty good one.

"You know, you owe me two wishes now," I said.

The twinkle lights made sparkle patterns on his cheeks as he leaned back with a surprised frown.

"Because you failed to grant the last one. It's your penalty."

Robbie smiled as we swayed together to the song. "It's a penalty I'm willing to accept, because nothing in this world will keep me away from you for long."

I smiled back and kissed him. Robbie Choi. My childhood best friend. International K-pop star. My first kiss. And my first love.

EPILOGUE

Two weeks into my summer trip to Seoul and I still felt like I was living someone else's life.

It was one thing having the kids at my school ask me if I was really dating Robbie now. But Korea was a whole other level. WDB weren't just celebrities here, they were icons, bringing the Hallyu wave around the world. And a lot of the fans seemed to really embrace us, claiming our story was like a teen rom-com or K-drama.

Still, the thing that surprised me the most had nothing to do with Robbie or K-pop. It was teaching at Como's hagwon. At first, it had been terrifying. Como had assigned me the youngest class, but they were still in middle school and they didn't feel that much younger than me. Thank goodness for Korean age hierarchy, or else I'm sure the kids would have taken advantage of my awkwardness more the first week. But I guess I owed another thing to Robbie, because all the girls in the class thought it was so cool that I was rumored to be dating him.

And I'd found out that, after getting over my initial nerves, I was actually pretty good at teaching. Even today, I'd helped my quietest student work through his issues with prepositions. I could still remember the look in his eyes, his bright smile as he said, "Thank you, Sunsaengnim."

The strangeness of being called "teacher" was tempered by the glow of actually helping someone.

I couldn't wait to tell Robbie over FaceTime tonight. He'd been locked away in the studio on a mystery project the past week, hinting that it would be big. I'd tried to pry it out of him. Claim girlfriend privileges, but he wouldn't budge.

I still felt weird saying that aloud. "Girlfriend." But Robbie had started calling me that, so I'd just followed his lead.

I was about to push through the exit to the street when someone tapped me on the shoulder. Before I could turn, they'd grabbed my hand and pulled me into the empty side stairwell.

I let out a squeak, lifting my fists to protect my face. There were still some Constellations who weren't that happy I'd taken Robbie off the market.

"Are you going to threaten me with your kickboxing skills again?"

I lowered my hands and gasped out, "Robbie?"

"Lani." He grinned, and it made butterfly wings flap against my heart.

I wanted to throw my arms around him, but I was still so confused. "What are you doing here?" I asked. "I thought you had work."

"I finished. Secret project officially done."

"And?" I asked.

He took my hand in his, letting his fingers lace through mine. "And I wanted to celebrate with my girlfriend."

My heart swelled at the word, just like it always did. "And will you tell your girlfriend what the project is?"

He thought about it and said, "It'll cost you one of your wishes?"

I gaped in exaggerated indignation. "You expect me to spend a whole wish on this?"

He leaned closer so our eyes lined up and my pulse jumped. "It's a really good secret."

I knew exactly what game he was playing here, but I still walked willingly into the trap. "Fine, tell me the secret as one of my wishes."

"D.E.T.'s opening his own agency. And he needs a new song for the first artist he's signed . . . Sooyeon."

I grabbed his shoulders in my excitement. "Are you serious? This is amazing! Oh, wow!" Now I did wrap my arms around him, and his hands came around my waist.

He bent down close enough to nuzzle my nose with his. "I don't know if I'd have had the courage to do this without you."

I laughed despite my throat going suddenly dry and punched at his shoulder. But he didn't move back, just tightened his grip on my waist. "You'd have gotten here. You're so talented, Robbie."

"It's easier to take chances when you know someone believes in you. You're really special, Lani, you know that?"

The awkwardness of accepting a compliment warred with the swell of warmth spreading through my whole body. And I went with the warmth and lifted onto my toes to kiss him. Leave it to Robbie Choi to make a girl feel like the center of the universe when he was the one with millions of fans all around the world.

"Robbie!" Hanbin burst through the door.

Robbie sighed but didn't let go of me as he turned to his manager. "Hyeong, you said I had five minutes. It's only been three."

"Too bad, someone posted about you being here. We gotta go."

Hanbin ushered us out the door quickly, but it was too late. The moment we stepped into the sweltering summer sun, half a dozen paparazzi raced forward, snapping photos of us. Robbie's hand tightened around mine, pulling me closer to his side, like he could hide me.

"Robbie! Is this your girlfriend?" someone called out in Korean.

"Hey! Robbie's girlfriend, how about a smile?"

Robbie started to turn, to block me, but I squeezed his hand and turned to the paparazzo that had asked the question.

"Actually, my name isn't 'Robbie's Girlfriend.' It's Elena." And then I quickly flashed a V with my fingers and let them snap a photo before climbing into the idol van.

As Hanbin pulled away from the snapping cameras, Robbie turned to me. "Well, how does it feel to be fully in my world now?" He lifted a brow as he waited for my answer.

I thought about it a moment: The constant chance of having our photo taken. The conjecture by netizens. The sometimes-rude internet comments nitpicking about everything from my hair color to my outfits.

And then I thought of Robbie sharing his dreams with me. How he liked to rest his cheek on my head whenever we hugged. How he liked to lace our fingers together, like he was doing now. How he could make my heart race by just saying my name. And I smiled and said, "It's definitely unpredictable. But that's the fun of it, right?"

ACKNOWLEDGMENTS

If you had told fifteen-year-old Kat she'd get to write a K-pop romcom one day, she'd probably have fainted from happiness. This book has truly fulfilled a huge childhood writing and fandom dream of mine!

First, I'd like to thank SG Wannabe for getting me addicted to melodramatic K-pop music videos when I was younger. "살다가 살다가 살다가 너 힘들 때!"

Thank you to my awesome agent, Beth Phelan. You've provided me with such amazing support and counsel that has made me the person and author I am today, and for that, I am forever grateful.

Thank you to my amazing editor, Rebecca Kuss! A wise person once told me that I should just identify the one person I knew would completely get what I'm trying to accomplish with *K-Prom* and ask them to read. And, immediately, I knew that person was you. So, I feel extremely lucky that I got to officially work with you on this book!

Thank you to the team at Hyperion who helped me bring this story to life. Thank you to Kieran and Rachel for believing in my writing. Thank you to the design, publicity, and marketing teams who worked on bringing this book to readers! Thank you to Velinxi for the gorgeous cover art!

To my sister, Jennifer Magiera, thank you for introducing me to H.O.T. when I was in middle school. And I love you very much!

To my cousin and favorite author, Axie Oh, thank you for introducing me to GD and Fin.K.L/Lee Hyori. Thank you for trying to memorize the lyrics of BtoB's "Thriller" with me even though it was a losing battle. Also, thank you for singing really bad "Spring Day" karaoke with me every time we went to a noraebang in Seoul! 사랑해!

Thank you to my publishing friends who are working hard to make positive change in the industry and inspire me every day: Deeba Zargarpur, Emily Berge, and Alexa Wejko.

Thank you to the authors who have always supported me during my publishing journey! Rena Barron, Ronni Davis, Samira Ahmed, Gloria Chao, David Slayton, Karuna Riazi, Nafiza Azad, and Swati Teerdhala!

To my writer group: Janella Angeles, Alexis Castellanos, Maddy Colis, Mara Fitzgerald, Amanda Foody, Amanda Haas, Christine Lynn Herman, Katy Rose Pool, Tara Sim, and Melody Simpson. Thank you for your constant support. Akshaya Raman, thank you for helping me work through my brain issues and be more productive! Ashley Burdin, thank you for listening to my random musings about my characters as I drafted. Meg Kohlmann, thanks for talking with me all the time about BTS and Taemin.

To Claribel Ortega, knowing how much you love RM and his dimples confirms that I was right to slide into your DMs six years ago. Thanks for being my friend, podcast cohost, and fellow chicken nugget lover!

Thank you to my family: Halmeoni Oh, Emo Helen, Uncle Doosang, Emo Sara, Uncle Warren, Uncle John, Aunt Heejong, Emo Mary, Uncle Barry, Adam, Alex, Saqi, Jim, Sara Kyoung, Wyatt, Jason, Christine, Kevin, Bryan, Josh, Scott, and Camille. I love you!

Lucy, thanks for being my K-pop dance buddy! Nora, can't wait for you to join in on our dance parties!

Mom and Dad, I love you. 보고싶어요.

And finally, thank you to all the readers who've supported my books and have followed my writing journey so far! I couldn't do this without you!